PRO... ...WYER DEAD;

BIOLOGIST HELD

According to sources close to the investigation, Mr. Abramowitz was squeezed in a python-like grip, then beaten viciously. He had bruises on his face, presumably from a fight with Darryl Paxton, a 33-year-old researcher at Johns Hopkins medical school, who visited the victim at his office just after 10 P.M., according to a security guard's log. The body was discovered by a custodian . . .

There was nothing new beyond that, only boilerplate on Abramowitz and his career. Certainly nothing was new to Tess. The style and reporting were as familiar to her as a lover's kiss. All the trademarks were there—unnamed sources, a memorable description of the death at hand, over-the-top prose, a damning detail. Still, she felt genuine admiration at the guard's log; she bet no one else in town had that.

"But I know more," she said out loud.

Books by
Laura Lippman

NO GOOD DEEDS
TO THE POWER OF THREE
BY A SPIDER'S THREAD
EVERY SECRET THING
THE LAST PLACE
IN A STRANGE CITY
THE SUGAR HOUSE
IN BIG TROUBLE
BUTCHERS HILL
CHARM CITY
BALTIMORE BLUES

LAURA
LIPPMAN

BALTIMORE
BLUES

AVON BOOKS

An Imprint of HarperCollinsPublishers

AVON BOOKS
An Imprint of HarperCollins*Publishers*
10 East 53rd Street
New York, New York 10022-5299

For my parents

I am indebted to a special trio—Michele B. Slung; my agent, Vicky Bijur; and my editor, Carrie Feron. Generous colleagues at *The Sun* taught me things I should have already known: Joan Jacobson, Jay Apperson, Arthur Hirsch, Michael James, Jacques Kelly, Joe Mathews, Patrick A. McGuire, Jon Morgan, Michael Ollove, Scott Shane, Melody Simmons. Thanks also to Melinda Henneberger, Jim MacAlister, and Susan Seegar. Finally, thanks to my husband, John Roll, for calling my bluff.

Of all escape mechanisms, death is the most efficient.

—H.L. Mencken, *A Book of Burlesques*

[W]hile I love the dear old City of Baltimore much, and many of her people more, past experience has taught that, in their collective or municipal capacity, they are the most silly, unreflective, procrastinating, impracticable and perverse congregation of bipeds to be found any where under the sun. Wise in their own conceits they are impatient of advice, no matter how thoughtful and well matured, from any one, preferring always their own crude extemporaneous conjectures to the suggestions of sound common sense, which can only be elicited by the patient exercise of judgment, observation and reflection.

—Dr. Thomas Hepburn Buckler of Baltimore, in a letter home from his self-imposed exile in Paris, published in "Baltimore: Its Interests—Past, Present, and Future," 1873

And down in lovely muck I've lain,
Happy till I woke again.
Then I saw the morning sky:
Heighho, the tale was all a lie;
The world, it was the old world yet,
I was I, my things were wet,
And nothing now remained to do
But begin the game anew.

—A.E. Housman
"Terence, This is Stupid Stuff"

Chapter 1

On the last night of August, Tess Monaghan went to the drugstore and bought a composition book—one with a black-and-white marble cover. She had done this every fall since she was six and saw no reason to change, despite the differences wrought by twenty-three years. Never mind that she had a computer with a memory capable of keeping anything she might want to record. Never mind that she had to go to Rite Aid because Weinstein's Drugs had long ago been run into the ground by her grandfather. Never mind that she was no longer a student, no longer had a job, and summer's end held little relevance for her. Tess believed in routines and rituals. So she bought a composition book for $1.69, took it home, and opened it to the first page, where she wrote:

Goals for Autumn:

1. Bench press 120 pounds.
2. Run a 7-minute mile.
3. Read *Don Quixote*.
4. Find a job, etc.

She sat at her desk and looked at what she had written. The first two items were within reach, although it would take work: She could do up to ten reps at a hundred pounds and run four miles in thirty minutes. *Don Quixote* had defeated her before, but she felt ready for it this fall.

Number 4 was more problematic. For one thing it would require figuring out what kind of job she wanted, a dilemma that had been perplexing her for two years, ever since Baltimore's penultimate newspaper, the *Star*, had folded, and its ultimate paper, the *Beacon-Light*, had not hired her.

Tess slapped the notebook closed, filed it on a shelf with twenty-two others—all blank except for the first page—set her alarm, and was asleep in five minutes. It was the eve of the first day of school, time for the city to throw off its August doldrums and move briskly toward fall. Maybe it could carry Tess with it.

The alarm went off seven hours later, at 5:15 A.M. She dressed quickly and ran to her car, sniffing the breeze to see if fall might be early this year. The air was depressingly thick and syrupy, indifferent to Tess's expectations. Her eleven-year-old Toyota, the most dependable thing in her life, turned over instantly. "Thank you, precious," she said, patting the dashboard, then heading off through downtown's deserted streets.

On the other side of the harbor, the boat house was dark. It often was at 5:30, for the attendant did not find minimum wage incentive enough to leave his bed and arrive in Cherry Hill before first light. The neighborhood, a grim place at any time of day, had long ago been stripped of its fruit trees. And though its gentle slopes offered a sweeping view of Baltimore's harbor and skyline, no one came to Cherry Hill for the views.

Fortunately Tess had her own boat house key, as did most of the diehard rowers. She let herself in, stashed her key ring in a locker in the ladies' dressing room, then ran downstairs and grabbed her oars, anxious to be on the water before the college students arrived. She didn't like being lumped in with what she thought of as the J. Crew crews, callow youths with hoarse chatter of tests they had aced and kegs they had tapped. But she also felt out of place among the Baltimore Rowing Club's efficient grown-ups, professionals who rushed from morning practice to jobs, real ones, at hospitals and research labs, law firms and brokerage houses.

"Watch my line, girlie," a crabber called out, his voice thick in the humid morning air.

"I see it," she said, balancing an Alden Ocean Shell above her head as she threaded her way down the dock and the crabbers' gauntlet of string, chicken necks, and bushel baskets. The crabbers, Cherry Hill residents supplementing their government checks with the Patapsco's bounty, were having a good morning, even if much of their catch was illegal— pregnant females, crabs less than five inches across. Tess wouldn't tell. She didn't care. She didn't eat anything from the local waters.

At least the city-owned Alden was easy to launch. The sun was still lurking just beyond the Francis Scott Key Bridge when Tess pushed off in the choppy water and started for Fort McHenry. Almost reflexively, she hummed "The Star-Spangled Banner." *Oh say can you see?* She would catch herself, stop, then unconsciously start again; after all, she was rowing toward the anthem's birthplace. *And the rockets' red glare, the bombs bursting in air . . .*

The water was rough this morning, making Tess nervous. It was difficult to tip an Alden, but not impossible, and she didn't want to be immersed in the Patapsco's murky middle branch under any circumstances. Once she had gotten a little of the river in a cut on her hand, and the cut hadn't healed for three months. Better to take it easy, warm up, let her morning-tight muscles relax and expand. On the way back she would push herself, rowing as if in a race.

This was Tess's routine, her only routine since the *Star* had been shuttered. Six days a week she rowed in the morning and ran in the evening. Three times a week she lifted weights in an old-fashioned boxing gym in East Baltimore. On the seventh day, she rested, soaking her long frame in a hot tub and fantasizing about a man who could rub her feet and neck simultaneously.

In college Tess had been a mediocre sweep rower, recruited by a mediocre team because she was strong, with muscular legs and a swimmer's broad shoulders. Switching to two oars had not enhanced her style. Tess knew, or imagined she knew, how ugly she looked moving across the water. *Like a beetle caught in the toilet bowl, all twitches and spasms.* Even on the easy trip out, she scowled and chewed her tongue, so fierce was her concentration. No, there was nothing natural about Tess's rowing. She didn't do it well. She didn't do it in order to compete. Yet she seldom missed a day. Her friends often said Tess had never met a rut she didn't like. She took no offense. It was true. And her fondness for routine had helped her weather the jobless months.

But this morning, as she tried to feather her oars in air thick as particleboard, everything suddenly seemed futile. The first day of September should be cool, she thought, or at least cooler. She should be good at this by now, or at least better. Abruptly, she pulling her oars out of the water and let the boat drift. She scanned the skies for rain, hoping for an excuse to quit. A thick haze hung over the skyline, but no clouds. From this vantage point Baltimore simply looked dirty and discouraged.

"Welcome to Charm City," she said to a seagull that was diving for dead fish. "Welcome to Baltimore, hon."

Neither Tess nor her hometown were having a good year. She was out of work and out of unemployment benefits. Baltimore was on pace to set an unprecedented murder rate, breaking the once-thought-unbreakable record of 1993, which had broken some previously impossible record. Every day there was a little death, the kind of murder that rated no more than four paragraphs deep inside the *Beacon-Light*. Yet no one seemed to notice or care—except those playing the homicide tally in the Pick 3. the mayor still called it the City That Reads, but others had long ago twisted that civic motto.

"The city that bleeds, hon," Tess called out to the unimpressed seagull. The city that breeds. the city that grieves, the city that seethes. *The city one leaves.* Only Tess never could, any more than she could have swum from the bottom of Chesapeake Bay with an anchor around her neck.

As she stared off into the distance, another sculler emerged from the shadows under the Hanover Street Bridge, moving easily and swiftly toward her as if the water were greased glass. His technique was perfect, his back broad, his white T-shirt already gray with sweat. His image seemed to pop out, the way things did at a 3-D movie. In seconds he was almost on top of Tess, coming right at her.

"Behind you," she called, confident such an assured rower would have no problem changing course. Her voice carried across the silent morning, but the rower paid no heed.

"*Behind you*!" Tess called again more insistently, as the boat kept coming right at her. A collision seemed inevitable. She had never watched anyone row from this angle, never realized how fast a boat seemed to move when one was in its path. Flustered, she began making fruitless, tiny movements with her oars, trying to turn the Alden and get out of the oncoming boat's path. Her only thought was to minimize the damage to the other boat, which looked fragile and, consequently, expensive.

The Alden, an amiable shell designed for beginners, moved beneath Tess with all the alacrity and finesse of a large cow. In her haste, trying to steer the boat through the rough water with rushed, incompetent strokes, she didn't seem to move at all. Frantic, Tess slid forward in the seat and pulled as hard as she could, using her legs' full power. Her boat shot across the water, leaving the oncoming boat's path clear. The other rower then braced his oars against his body, executing a perfect panic stop inches from where she had been.

He had known she was there all along.

"That's what you get," a familiar voice called out, "for dogging it."

"Thanks, Rock," Tess yelled back. "Thanks for scaring the shit out of me. I thought you were some kamikaze rower, trying to sink me."

"Nope. Just your personal rowing coach, trying to make sure you give one hundred percent every day. What's the point of coming out here if you don't push yourself?"

"What's the point of coming out here at all? That's what I was asking myself before you sent me into adrenaline overload."

But Rock considered rowing his true vocation. On weekdays, from eight to five, Rock was Darryl Paxton, a researcher bent over one of the 20,000 microscopes at Johns Hopkins medical school. Tess wasn't sure what he was looking for, as Rock was one of those rare people who never talked about his work. Rock worked to row, putting aside as much money as he could to underwrite his singular passion. He also ate to row, slept to row, worked out to row. Until he got engaged last spring, Tess had suspected he performed no nonessential tasks. It would be interesting to see how his fiancée responded to the fall schedule of head races, which kept Rock on the water twice a day through Thanksgiving. If the engagement survived the season, Tess thought, she'd be happy to dance at their wedding next March. Maybe she'd even dance *with* the bride. After all, she was going to be the best man.

Funny to think she had been scared of Rock once. He had what Tess thought of as a serial killer's physique: short and broad, his skin crammed with more muscles than it could safely contain. Every now and then one got loose and twitched in some unlikely spot. The veins along his arms were thick and blue, like Bic ballpoints under the skin; his short, stocky calves were so overdeveloped it looked as if softballs had been surgically implanted below the backs of his knees. A premed on the Hopkins crew once theorized Rock could not feel pain, claiming it had something to do with his mitochondria. Tess knew he felt things all too deeply. It was evident in his face, a child's face—clear, guileless, with the round, brown eyes of a cartoon character.

"You look like Dondi!" she had blurted out one morning, five years ago, as he pulled alongside the dock at the end of a hard workout, his blue black hair plastered to his head with sweat. She had known him only by sight, one of a handful of scullers at a boat house dominated by crews of fours and eights.

To her surprise the ferocious face had smiled. "Now *that* was a good comic strip. How come the *Beacon* dropped it? And Mr. Tweedy. I still can't believe Mr. Tweedy is gone."

"Mr. Tweedy? You poor, deprived *Beacon* readers, living for such paltry things. The *Star* has all the good comics."

So they had gone out to breakfast, sharing the comics pages of Baltimore's three newspapers. That had been five years and two newspapers ago. Tess, like Mr. Tweedy, had disappeared from the local newspapers. The *Beacon*, which had subsumed the *Light* and killed the *Star*, now had excellent comics pages, three in all, the usual spoils of a newspaper war. But Rock was still her friend, their relationship cemented in one of Tess's beloved routines—rowing, then breakfast at a diner in her neighborhood. Other rowers skipped practice, overslept, made excuses about the weather. Rock, nationally ranked, and Tess, chronically underemployed, were faithful to the boat house and to each other.

She studied her friend, who had been on vacation the past two weeks, rowing. He looked gray beneath his summer tan and the circles under his eyes had only deepened.

"Didn't you get any rest in New York? I thought that was the point of a vacation."

Rock shook his head. "All those crickets. And the more I worked out, the less I slept. But I feel pretty good."

"I feel pretty good myself." It was only a half lie. She was in great shape physically.

"Well, if you're in such good shape, wanna race back, all the way to the glass factory? Loser buys breakfast."

"Don't be ridiculous. I'd need a huge head start to make it competitive. Race the cars along Hanover Street Bridge if you want a challenge."

"I'll give you a five-hundred-meter head start."

"Not enough at this length. You'll pass me midway."

"One thousand, then."

"For breakfast? You always buy me breakfast, anyway."

"Well, I won't buy you breakfast today if you don't at least try."

"Oh." Poverty ennobled some people. Tess was not one

of them. She existed on an intricate system of favors and freeloading, which had made her cheap and a little spoiled. "I guess you've got a race, then."

"Start as if it were a head race. I won't come on until I see you disappear under the bridge."

Tess positioned her boat and slid forward in her seat. She never raced anymore, except against herself, but the routines were second nature.

"Start rowing," Rock called. "Build up to a full stroke in ten."

The water had smoothed out, allowing Tess to find her groove quickly. She rowed as she would have in her old women's eight, following the calls of an imaginary coxswain. Full power for ten, using everything she had, then ten strokes with legs only. She passed under the shadow of the Hanover Street Bridge and into the light again, feeling confident and loose.

Then she saw Rock coming toward her. She had thought he might lie back a bit, give her a slight edge, but Rock was incapable of giving anything but his best. A peculiar liability, one from which she had never suffered. He crossed the water with amazing speed, his technique so perfect Tess was tempted to stop and watch. But she had to try. She wanted breakfast. Blueberry pancakes, perhaps even a western omelet, were at stake.

They were even with the boat house when Rock shot past her. In head races, one boat passes another boat a seat at a time, the coxswain hurling insults at the rowers left behind. But Rock seemed to flash past Tess in a single stroke. She caught a glimpse of his face, grim and almost cruel looking, sweat pouring from his forehead.

Doggedly she kept going. Behind her she could hear the roar of the glass factory, a malevolent-looking place that blew gusts of hot air across the river. There always seemed to be a dozen fires going, no matter what time of day one rowed, yet no human forms were ever seen. Tess rowed toward this wall of heat, full power for the last thirty strokes. Her arms stung from the lactic acid built up in the muscles, and she felt as if each stroke might be her last. Rock had won, of course, but she had to finish. She surged past his waiting boat just as she began to think she could not force another stroke.

When she looked up, Rock was bent forward, his shoulders heaving. He often pushed himself to the point where he vomited, and Tess was used to seeing her friend with a bit of saliva trailing from his mouth. She felt a little nauseated herself. When she could move again she paddled forward, pleased with herself for pushing him so hard.

But Rock wasn't throwing up; he was crying. Hunched forward, his face resting on his huge thighs, his whole body shook from the force of silent sobs. From behind he had looked to Tess like any rower after a tough workout. For some odd reason, it made her think of Moses and the burning bush. It was fascinating and bizarre. She reached across the water and tried to give him a there-there pat. Her hand glanced off his tricep as if she were trying to stroke a tree or, well, a rock.

"Sorry," he said.

Tess checked her oarlocks, feeling embarrassed and inept.

"Ava," he said succinctly.

Ava. His fiancée. Tess had met her at last spring's races. Rock never seemed to do as well when she was there. Perhaps it wasn't Ava's fault, but she still was not the woman Tess would have chosen for him. Not the woman his mother would have chosen either, or his coworkers, or anyone with a remote interest in his happiness, Tess was sure. Ava was a lawyer, beautiful, accomplished—and an absolute bitch in a way only other women could fathom. Despite three meetings she never remembered Tess's name.

But all Tess said was: "Ava?"

"I think she's—" He groped for a word. "In trouble."

"What kind?"

"Some kind she can't talk about. She's not at home when I call her late at night, but she's not at the office, either. She was supposed to come up to the Adirondacks for the second week, but she called at the last minute, said some emergency had come up at work. That boss of hers, Abramowitz, works her to death on these asbestos cases.''

Tess remembered how proud he had been when Ava had gotten the job at O'Neal, O'Connor and O'Neill, how proud he was that the flamboyant new partner Michael Abramowitz wanted her for his assistant.

''That's plausible, isn't it? The Triple O is a pretty high-powered law firm, and those asbestos cases just keep coming.''

''Yeah, especially when one of your biggest clients is Sims-Kever, which would rather pay one hundred million dollars in fees than pay one dollar in damages to a single old guy who can't breathe.'' Rock picked at one of his calluses. ''Except Ava wasn't at work last week. I called and the secretary told me she was on vacation. I'm sure there's a logical explanation, though.''

''Then why don't you ask her?''

''Ava's funny that way. If I asked her she'd get so offended that—'' He shook his head, as if Tess couldn't imagine what Ava was like when offended, how absolutely frightening and adorable. ''She's very sensitive.''

They drifted on the light current. Here, in a cove near the marina, the water was still and smooth. Tess tried to think of the right thing to say, the thing to end this conversation and bring her closer to some blueberry pancakes. Ava's behavior suggested all sorts of theories to her, all unsavory.

''I'm sure there's a good reason,'' she said finally.

''But there's only one way to *know*.''

''Ask her? You said you couldn't talk to her about this.''

''No, *follow* her.''

''Wouldn't she notice if you followed her?''

''Of course,'' Rock said. ''But I've been thinking she wouldn't notice if you did.''

''How could I follow her? I mean, how could I afford the time to do it? I know I have flexible hours, but I don't just sit around my apartment all day, watching television.'' This was a sore point with Tess. A lot of people seemed to think being unemployed was a lark. She had to work two jobs just to stay afloat.

"Because I would pay you. Thirty dollars an hour, what private detectives get. You find someone to take your place at the bookstore for a few days."

"I'm not a private detective," she reminded him.

"No, but you used to be a reporter. Didn't you tell me something about following some city official? And you write reports for your uncle. This could be like a report." He pretended to dictate. " 'At seven-thirty P.M. I saw Ava going into the Hemispheris Clinic at Hopkins. Did not come out for three hours. Receptionist confirmed she is donating platelets for a young cancer victim.' See?"

Jesus, she thought, *he really can't come up with a good story*. It was more plausible that Ava was going to Hopkins's sex change clinic and didn't want to see Rock until she had her new equipment.

Still, thirty dollars an hour, for even five or six hours, was a frighteningly attractive prospect. Easy money. If Ava was doing nothing, Tess would make a friend happy. If Ava was up to no good, Tess would be paid to save her friend from a disastrous mistake.

"A computer upgrade," Rock wheedled. "Car repairs. A nest egg for your own racing shell, so you don't have to use the shit ones here."

Tess was compiling another list: A pair of earrings that didn't come from a Third World country. Leather boots, including the soles. Student loans. But she turned her mind away from those things, determined to find the flaw in the plan.

"Why not a real private eye, if you're willing to pay private eye prices?"

Rock looked across the river, suddenly fascinated by three young children wading on the northern bank.

"A real private eye would be sleazy," he said slowly, as if he was working the answer out for himself. "This is just a favor between friends. I'm offering to pay you because I know your time is valuable. And because I know you're always strapped for money.''

As a freelancer Tess billed her time at twenty dollars an hour and often settled for less. As a contractual state employee she made ten dollars an hour. Her aunt gave her kitchen privileges, health insurance, and six dollars an hour for working in the bookstore. Her time had never been considered worth thirty dollars an hour.

''Where does Ava work?'' she asked.

He smiled. He really did look like Dondi, although not so vacant around the eyes.

''I'll fill you in at Jimmy's.''

Chapter 2

Tess did not have blueberry pancakes after all. She wanted them, but as soon as she walked into Jimmy's in Fells Point, the cook threw two bagels to toast on the griddle and poured fresh orange juice into a red plastic tumbler. Her usual: two plain bagels, toasted, one with cream cheese, one without. She had been eating the same breakfast at Jimmy's for two years, at least five days a week.

She had always wanted to walk into a place and have someone ask, "The usual?" Of course, in her original fantasy the place had a long mahogany bar, men wore suits and women wore hats, and she would order a martini, straight up. No olive.

Rock, after a quick look at the place mat menu, ordered the carbohydrate special, a meal of his own creation: toast, pancakes, orange juice, fruit cup, and cereal with skim milk.

"No syrup or butter," he told the waitress. "Just lots of extra jelly."

"That all?"

"Do you have any rice? Or some pinto beans?"

The waitress stalked off, unamused. Rock was an ardent believer in the idea that diet could boost athletic performance, although the parameters of that diet kept changing. Currently he shunned fat and most meat. Given his workout regime, however, he had to eat enormous amounts and drink protein supplements to maintain his weight. He never ate for pleasure and he never drank alcohol. His one vice was caffeine, which he claimed enhanced his performance. The kitchen in his little apartment in Charles Village was a shrine to coffee. Rock didn't own a VCR, a CD player, or a microwave, but he had a French press, a cappuccino and espresso maker, and a freezer filled with nothing but ice trays and bags of coffee beans, all labeled and dated. His chronic insomnia surprised only him.

Breakfast arrived within minutes, and both ate intently, swiftly, as if racing again. For Tess, meals were the high point of her day, which only made her more ravenous. Rock simply wanted to stoke the vast machinery of his body and get it over with. Tess was still working on her second bagel when he wiped the last bit of jelly from his plate with his last pancake.

"Now," he began, rummaging in his wallet. He slid an envelope across the table to Tess, who took it happily. A check, she thought. A retainer. But inside she found only a small photograph of Ava and two sheets of paper with phone numbers and addresses. Rock also had included a basic outline of Ava's day—when she went to work, when she got home—and the places she frequented. That was his word, written on the list. She *frequented* a gym in Federal Hill, a bar near her office, and an Italian restaurant known primarily for its breathtaking views and inedible food.

"Funny," Tess said, examining the envelope's contents.

"What?"

"You had this with you, all ready. Did you assume I'd say yes?"

Rock blushed. "I know you can always use some extra cash."

"Well, it's not as if I would do *anything* for money, you know. I have turned down PR jobs." Being broke had become something of a shtick for Tess.

He didn't smile.

They said good-bye on the cobblestone street in front of Jimmy's, suddenly awkward with each other. Tess had worked for a lot of relatives, but never a friend. Rock seemed equally uncomfortable with the new relationship. He kept punching her on the shoulder, light taps for him, which left tiny black-and-blue marks. Finally he took his ten-speed out of Tess's trunk and headed up Broadway, the long gradual hill to Johns Hopkins Hospital and his life as Darryl Paxton.

Tess crossed the wide plaza on Broadway, cutting over to pretty little Shakespeare Street, where she sneaked glances into unshuttered windows. It was only 8 A.M. and other people, normal people as Tess thought of them, were still gathered at breakfast tables, or venturing out in bathrobes to grab the *Beacon-Light*. It was the kind of existence she had once imagined for herself, to the extent she had imagined such mundane details at all. A husband, a baby, a dining room table. Sometimes her aunt and her aunt's latest boyfriend set a place for Tess at their breakfast table, but their attempt at homeyness only exacerbated Tess's feeling of strangeness. It was odd, sitting down to Cheerios and blueberries with her aunt and her aunt's man of the month, both usually in bathrobes and flushed.

Shakespeare ended at Bond, the street on which Tess lived. She stopped and looked at the building she called home, a hulking warehouse of garnet brick with white trim, all buffed up with her aunt's love. The windows gleamed in the early morning light and the books inside—mellow shades of red, green, and amber—glowed like jewels in a box. Above the door the scarlet letters were so bright and bold they seemed three-dimensional: WOMEN AND CHILDREN FIRST. And, in smaller letters, for the occasional oaf who thought it was a lifeboat store: A SPECIALTY BOOKS EMPORIUM.

Not everyone would have seen the potential in a store that sold only women's and children's books. Tess's aunt, Katherine "Kitty" Monaghan, was not like everyone. She was not like anyone. A librarian with the city schools for almost twenty years, she had taken early retirement after a parent complained fairy tales were godless, encouraging belief in Satan and the occult.

That was the official version. The longer version included the Super Fresh, a cabbage, and a rutabaga. Kitty was fired after she decked a mother who stopped her in the produce section and complained about *Jack and the Beanstalk*. It encouraged antisocial behavior, the mother complained. It glorified robbery. Kitty blackened her eye. The administration dismissed her: Apparently there was a policy against assaulting parents. She sued for wrongful dismissal. Kitty pointed out that the woman had accosted her in the Super Fresh, where she was clearly going about her business as a private citizen, and hurled a cabbage at her head when Kitty disagreed with her. That was the part Kitty found galling—not the cabbage at her head, but someone daring to talk to her about school while she was at the grocery store, a place she found quite trying under the best of circumstances. She threw a rutabaga back. Her aim was better.

"It was self-defense, pure and simple," she liked to say. Luckily the union arbitrator agreed. The Baltimore school system settled for a substantial sum, and Aunt Kitty bought this old drugstore from Tess's mother's family, the Weinsteins, after they declared bankruptcy.

She converted the three-story building into a store and a home, adding an apartment on the top floor for a little extra income. More out of laziness than any sense of design, she left the old soda fountain, which divided the primary business, children's books, from the secondary one—feminist tracts, erotica, anything written by women and, in some cases, anything about women. It was possible, for example, to buy books by Philip Roth and John Updike at Women and Children First.

WACF was a cozy place, with armchairs, two working fireplaces, well worn rugs, and the original tin-pressed ceilings. People came to buy, stayed to browse, ended up buying more. The profit margin was slim, yet far more than Kitty had ever dreamed. Entranced by capitalism, she talked constantly of expanding. Perhaps she would serve espresso from the old soda fountain, or afternoon tea. Buy the building next door and open a bed-and-breakfast. Perhaps a bookstore just for men? Like a novice at the track, she was dangerously intoxicated with beginner's luck. Tess wouldn't be surprised if she lost all her money as quickly as she had made it.

"Dead White Males, how's that for a name, Tesser?" Kitty asked as Tess came through the front door. Kitty was sitting on the old soda fountain, wearing a silky kimono covered with cherry blossoms and sipping a cup of coffee. "We could sell—well, I guess we could sell *everything*, all the classics. That would be the gimmick. It would be just an ordinary bookstore, but people would think it was special. And between the two stores I'd have most of the territory covered. Eventually everyone dies. Even Norman Mailer."

"I like it," Tess said. "Then again, knowing the local immunity to irony, I see a men's group and the NAACP picketing out front, claiming you're glamorizing gendercide and discriminating against people of color. And those Mothers Objecting to Violence and Everything Related—you know, the MOVERS—would interpret it as a pro-violence thing."

"MOVERS! There's no such group, not even in Baltimore."

"Don't you read the paper? They've set up a permanent picket outside the multiplex in Towson. It's convenient to shopping. They march up and down for an hour, take a break, and go shop at Nordstrom."

Kitty laughed, a startlingly loud and wonderful sound. Most of the Monaghans were a little dour, even Tess. Kitty, however, was a changeling. She was the happiest person Tess knew, with an endless capacity for delight. She asked only that life be tangible, full of things to touch and hold, smell and devour. Soft fabrics, new books, full-bodied wines, well-made dresses, defined calves. Twelve years older than Tess and nine inches shorter, she had flame red curls and the only green eyes in three generations. Her latest beau was one of the city's new bicycle cops, lured into the shop after Kitty saw his legs flashing by. Thaddeus Freudenberg. He was twenty-four, as big and cuddly as a Labrador, and only a few IQ points dumber. Tess figured he was on the bike patrol because he couldn't pass the test for a driver's license.

Thaddeus was not in evidence this morning. Tess leaned

against the fountain. "I've had an interesting offer," she began, filling Kitty in on Rock's proposal. She thought her aunt would be impressed, especially given the fact Tess often had trouble coming up with the rent.

But Kitty was dubious. "It sounds like meddling for a fee. Don't the ethics bother you?"

"I can't afford ethics. Summer was slow, and I need some cash on hand."

"I suppose." She stared Tess down, a feat she could manage only because she was seated on the old fountain and Tess was slumped over it. "But you don't really like this woman. So how can you be objective? If you see something ambiguous you might draw false conclusions because you want to catch her. You might not even realize what you're doing."

"What do you mean?"

"Well, you might see her kissing someone on the street, for example, and assume it's her lover. But it could be her brother, or a friend."

"I think I'd know the difference between a lover and a brother."

"I don't know, Tesser. It's been awhile since I've heard any feet but yours climbing up to the third floor." Kitty smiled and tugged the slippery silk kimono back over her left shoulder.

"Don't be smug just because you have Officer Friendly to tuck you in at night. Some people do sleep alone, you know."

"Maybe Jonathan will turn up again soon. It's been awhile, hasn't it?"

"I gave up Jonathan for Lent."

"And you'll forgive him for Yom Kippur. You always managed to get the full mileage out of your dual religions, Tesser, even when you were a little girl."

With that, Kitty swung off the counter and padded to her living quarters behind the store, leaving Tess to think about Jonathan Ross. It hadn't occurred to her to miss him until Kitty mentioned him. Yom Kippur, the day of atonement, was next month. And Jonathan had more to atone for than she did, much more.

Her thoughts scattered when Crow, one of the clerks, rapped on the front door.

"Only two hours early today," Tess said as she let him in, feeling mean. Crow, infatuated with Kitty, often showed up as early as 7 A.M. for his morning shift and stayed late into the night, trying to computerize the inventory system.

"Yeah, well, I thought I could eat my breakfast here." He held up a greasy sack of doughnuts and a bottle of orange juice. A battered guitar case was strung across his back. "I like the light here in the morning. It's very . . . inspiring."

Tess almost felt sorry for Crow, simply the latest in a string of workers to fall in love with Kitty. Maryland Institute of Art students seemed particularly vulnerable. But her pity was tempered by a vague grumpiness. He never looked at *her* that way, with his moist brown eyes and pretty mouth.

Crow hoisted himself up on the counter, as if drawn to the spot where Kitty's kimono had slithered just minutes before. Ignoring his breakfast, he took out the guitar and began playing. An original tune, Tess judged, or a particularly bad version of a well-known one.

"I'm writing a song," he told her.

"You won't be the first. Just remember, though—you're going to be limited to pretty, pity, and shitty for rhymes."

"Not necessarily." He strummed a few bars and began to sing. His voice, while thin, was charming and true. " 'The first time I saw Kitty/She made me feel like Walter Mitty/My heart did that tapocketa ditty/And I wanted to rescue her from this grim, dank city/Tapocketa. Tapocketa. Tapocketa/I'm almost a hero now.' "

"Find a rhyme for Monaghan and I'll really be impressed."

"If I did I could write a song for you, too," Crow said, grinning at her. "Tess rhymes with so many things."

"Less," she told him. "Primarily it rhymes with less."

Tess left Crow to his doughnuts and his daydreams, climbing the back stairs to her apartment. It was a steep climb,

given the high ceilings on the first two floors, more like a
fifth story walk-up. When Kitty renovated the building she
had intended to rent the third floor to help carry her mortgage. Tess, its first and only tenant, paid much less than Kitty
could have commanded on the open market.

It was small, essentially a large room divided by book-
cases. The living area was big enough for only a desk, an
easy chair, and a small mission table, which she used for
meals. The kitchen was an alcove with a miniature refrigerator and a two-burner stove. One had to pass through it to
get to the bedroom, the largest space. This, too, was plain,
large enough for only a lumpy double bed, a small table, and
a bureau.

But the apartment did have one outstanding feature: a terrace off the bedroom, with a ladder leading to the rooftop.
On this morning Tess went straight to the roof, hoping the
view would help her mind expand and clear so she could
concentrate on her latest odd job.

She preferred the view to the east, the smokestacks and
the neon red Domino Sugar sign, turning her back to downtown and the city's celebrated waterfront. Tess had little use
for that part of Baltimore, which had been reinvented as a
tourist haven. To her way of thinking it wasn't much different from the old strip bars, which let people in for free, then
jacked up the prices for everything else. She had nightmares
in which she was trapped in a papier-mâché head, forced to
greet people. *"How you doin', hon? How you doin', hon?"*

Tess reviewed the addresses Rock had given her. Ava's
life was neatly contained. She lived in a condominium at one
end of the harbor. She worked at the other end at the white-
shoe firm of O'Neal, O'Connor and O'Neill. She could walk
to work in less than fifteen minutes—assuming Ava walked
anywhere.

The photograph was crudely cropped into an oval shape,
a man's clumsy handiwork. It had probably been in a frame
at Rock's bedside, or on his desk. A picture from a spring
regatta, with Ava standing next to Rock. He wore a red T-
shirt and black Lycra rowing shorts. She had on a crisp, navy

striped T-shirt that looked as if it cost more than Tess's best dress. Her right hand could not even span Rock's wrist, yet she seemed to have a firm grasp on him. Her hair was a dark cloud around her face, a face so perfect it was easy to understand why her parents had dared to give her a sex goddess's name. Ava lived up to it.

Tess knew all about beautiful women. She had been surrounded by them all her life—her aunt, her college roommate, Whitney, even her mother. Some were generous, allowing you to bask in their glow. Others shut you out, made you feel fat and clumsy. Ava fell into the latter group.

At twenty-nine Tess had made peace with her face and body. She wasn't beautiful, but her looks served her well. She kept things simple: long brown hair in a single plait down her back, no makeup on her pale face or hazel eyes, clothes designed for comfort and speed. One thing was certain, she had the wardrobe to be a spy—drawers full of old, baggy things in dark colors. She knew how to be invisible.

Chapter 3

Ava lived in Eden, in Eden's Landing, a mid-rise condominium of pink marble and glass bricks near the National Aquarium. Ahistorical and asymmetrical, it was modeled after the Pyramid of the Sun in Tenochtitlán and would have looked perfect anywhere between San Diego and Malibu. On the Baltimore waterfront the building seemed to shrink away from its neighbors, folding its terraces into itself. Eden's Landing gave the impression it was horrified to find itself in Baltimore. On Tess's part, the horror was mutual.

She had stationed herself at a bus stop on Pratt Street, figuring she would see Ava's Mazda Miata pull out of the garage. According to Rock's tip sheet, she left for work at 7:15. At precisely 7:20 Ava appeared on foot. The first surprise of the day, Tess thought. It actually made it easier for Tess, as she had parked her Toyota in a lot across President Street, planning to follow by bicycle, which was far more practical in downtown. She stowed the bike in her trunk and hurried back to Pratt Street.

Luckily Ava was moving slowly, sauntering along Pratt. The street was congested, but it was still early for many people to be walking. Tess stopped and started her way along Pratt, trying to measure her stride against Ava's more leisurely progress. Her hair still damp from a quick shower at the boat house, she felt particularly conspicuous on the almost empty sidewalk.

Ava wasn't the type to wear running shoes and white socks beneath her trim little suit. She glided along on suede pumps with three-inch heels and ankle straps, looking straight ahead, oblivious to the bright morning, the breathtaking view of the harbor to her left, the dark hulk of the USS *Constellation*. Tess could have trailed her on a tricycle, ringing a metal bell, and Ava would not have noticed. She spared glances only for expensive cars and well-dressed men. Her head would turn, just barely, when she saw one with the other, giving Tess a glimpse of a familiar profile. Half the women in Baltimore had the same profile, thanks to a certain surgeon.

Despite her perfect nose Ava did not look like a real lawyer to Tess, but like a fashion magazine's idea of a lawyer, an important distinction. Her glossy black hair was curly and loose, unbound by a headband or tortoiseshell clips. Her pearl gray skirt was short and snug, her crimson blouse silk and low cut. Her pumps, which matched the blouse, would have been at home just four blocks north along the strip of nude bars and porno stores known as the Block. And Ava's briefcase, shiny black leather that looked softer than Tess's pillow, swung too loosely in her hand, as if it held nothing more than a mascara wand and lipstick.

Doubtful, Tess reminded herself. As a young associate at O'Neal, O'Connor and O'Neill, Ava would be loaded down with work, paper-intensive, nonglamorous work. But who needed glamour when you started at $80,000 a year? *Nice work if you can get it,* Tess hummed as Ava disappeared into the Lambrecht Building, the mirrored skyscraper that housed the Triple O. Its reflective surface made entering the building look like a magic trick: Now you see her, now you don't. Tess waited a few seconds, then circled the block, noting the building's rear exit along the alley. It also had a coffee shop with a separate entrance. There was no spot from which she could clearly see all the doors. And if Ava left in someone's car from the underground garage on the east side of the building, Tess would be clueless.

How could she be otherwise? Tess had never followed

anyone in her life. She had not been that kind of reporter. As a general assignments writer she had written about people more likely to stalk her, so desperate were they for publicity. She had written about street corner evangelists, precocious premed students, even LBJ's podiatrist, now retired to Arbutus. ("Hard-working feet, but more delicate looking than you might think," the podiatrist had told her.)

She walked back to the front of the building and found a bench affording an unobstructed view of the front door and the intersection of Pratt and Howard. A homeless woman eyed her suspiciously.

"Do you know the power of the mind?" the toothless woman asked Tess.

"Yes," Tess replied, pulling a well-worn copy of *Love's Lonely Counterfeit* out of her battered leather knapsack, then rummaging for her Walkman.

The woman scooted a little closer to her. It was almost eighty degrees and, although the morning haze was beginning to burn off, Tess could tell it was going to be another sticky day. Yet the woman wore a gray wool cardigan over a gingham-checked housedress, thick crew socks, and heavy hiking shoes. She smelled of cigarettes, sweat, and cheap wine. Beneath it all Tess picked up a fainter, familiar scent. Lily of the valley perfume. Her grandmother, Momma Weinstein, wore it.

"Do I scare you?" the old woman asked hopefully.

"No. No, not at all."

"Could I have a quarter, then?" Tess fished in her pocket and handed her a crumpled dollar bill. She had little sentiment for panhandlers and none for her grandmother, considered a harridan by those closest to her. But a dollar should buy her a morning of silence.

The woman tucked the bill into the voluminous folds of her dress and rocked happily, singing to herself. Tess sighed and turned on her Walkman. Ella Fitzgerald, *The Johnny Mercer Songbook*.

She and her new friend sat on the bench for four hours without exchanging another word. Johnny Mercer gave way to Jerome Kern. "All the Things You Are." "You Couldn't Be Cuter." "I'll Be Hard to Handle." Good theme song for Ava. Tess finished her book and started over again. Obviously too short for surveillance work.

She was about to start the book for a third time when Ava appeared a few minutes past noon. She walked briskly east, briefcase in hand, looking every inch the important lawyer on her way to an important trial. A lawyer, Tess thought, who felt coolly confident because she had used the right deodorant that morning. Catty, she chided herself. *I'm just jealous because her suit costs more than I make in a week.* It fit perfectly, too, Tess noted. She had never been so polished. Tess considered herself well dressed if her hose didn't run and her blouse didn't pull out of her waistband.

Today, of course, Tess had dressed to disappear. Jeans, a white T-shirt hanging loose, basketball sneakers. She didn't worry about Ava remembering her face, but she had tucked her braid under a black wig, one of the Gabor sisters' creations. The wig belonged to Kitty, who wore it one memorable Halloween, playing a fortyish Cleopatra to a twenty-one-year-old Julius Caesar, an anachronism she said Shakespeare would have loved. Tess liked her raven tresses, but she wasn't sure she had achieved the low-key look she wanted. She had a feeling the ropy black strands made her look more like a would-be Rastafarian, or Crow, with his green and black dreadlocks.

She had assumed Ava would walk east, then head north on St. Paul toward the courthouse. But Ava kept going, bearing down on the Gallery like a homing pigeon. The Gallery was a four-story mall topped by the Renaissance Harborplace Hotel and filled with the same stores found in every mall in America. Tess would have thought it a little common for Ava, but Ava almost cooed with pleasure as she walked through its glass doors, throwing out her arms as if to embrace all the potential purchases waiting there.

Sweating profusely beneath her wig, Tess ducked and bobbed through the crowded mall, trying to keep a comfortable distance between them. Luckily Ava had eyes only for the shop windows. She lingered to check out her own perfect reflection, then moved on, sometimes glancing at her watch. There seemed to be an itinerary to her browsing, some kind of agenda, but Tess couldn't figure it out.

Amaryllis, a small jewelry store, lured Ava in. Tess watched from outside as Ava asked a clerk to show her an odd, flamboyant necklace, a silver chain loaded with charms and lockets. It would have looked hideous on most people, but against Ava's white throat and crimson blouse, it was just the right touch. Ava handed it back with a pretty shake of regret. *It's just not as perfect as I am*, she seemed to be saying.

She returned to her window-shopping, venturing into stores only to sneer at the merchandise. Again and again Tess watched her hold something in front of her—a bag, a dress, a scarf, a belt—then put it back with that same charming shake of her head. Nothing suited her. The more expensive it was, the sadder she seemed.

In Victoria's Secret, Tess got as close to Ava as she dared, hiding behind a rack of Miracle Bras. Ava trailed her hand along a table of underwear, then recoiled as if the polyester fabric had shocked her skin. Yet she reached out again, running her hand more lightly still over the pile of burgundy panties. This time two pairs fell into her open briefcase.

Tess blinked in shock. Her aunt's cautionary words echoed in her mind. The underwear must have fallen on the floor. Or Ava was using her briefcase as a shopping basket and planned to pay for everything when she was finished.

She couldn't be a thief.

Ava walked to a table full of camisoles and repeated the same trick. Touch, recoil, brush—into the briefcase! By Tess's count Ava now had two pairs of panties, burgundy, and three emerald green camisoles. A salesclerk approached her as she fingered the lace on a nightgown, and Ava threw her right hand up, a friendly but stern warning. "Just looking," she pantomimed and quickly left the store. No one stopped her.

Ava the shoplifter. She might be having a breakdown, Tess

thought. *Ava the kleptomaniac.* It could explain her strange behavior toward Rock. But was shoplifting the problem or the symptom? And if it was the problem, how did it account for the late hours and the canceled vacation? Was she part of some odd ring, or a bored lawyer, boosting to make her lunch hour fun?

Rock wouldn't care. He would be content with this bit of information, almost desperate for it. Tess wasn't. Instinctively she knew it was one piece of a puzzle, a key to a door she hadn't found yet. A single fact was like an unripe avocado, something whose time could not be rushed. You rolled it in flour and you waited.

Lost in this thought, Tess didn't notice that Ava had moved on. By the time she spotted her, she was a floor below, getting off the escalator. Tess tried to follow quickly, but the escalator was stacked with carefree tourists, the kind of people who don't stand to one side because they assume everyone is on vacation. Unless she wanted to send bodies flying, she had to wait her turn to travel the ten feet of ribbed rubber Ava had already crossed.

By the time Tess reached the first floor, Ava had disappeared. Tess thought she saw her toward the rear of the building, where the shops ended and the hotel lobby began. But there was no flash of crimson or pearly gray, no briefcase overflowing with green camisoles and burgundy panties, no dark hair.

Ava was gone.

Tess ran outside, thinking she might still catch her. Perhaps she was heading back to the office to stick death certificates in the files of asbestos victims or turn away another grieving relative. Or maybe she had stopped by the small amphitheater across the street, where jugglers and fire-eaters performed in the warm-weather months. But when Tess worked her way through the semicircle of gawking tourists, there was no performer at all, just an old man sleeping on the hot sidewalk.

"Do you think he's dead?" a woman asked no one in particular.

Disgusted, Tess yanked the Gabor wig from her head, exposing her own matted, sweat-flattened hair. Three Scandinavian students mistook this for the opening flourish of a street performer's act and threw a dollar bill at her, applauding wildly.

"What do you think this is, some G-rated version of the Block?" Tess asked. "Or my performance-art tribute to Blaze Starr?"

The students clapped and shouted something that appeared to be "More, more, more" in their native tongue.

Tess dangled the wig in her hand and looked at the dollar bill on the pavement. The trio of blondes, their faces red with sunburn, stared at her hopefully. She started to throw the bill back, then thought better of it. She had given her last dollar to the old woman on the bench. This, with the change in her pocket, would buy a cup of Thrasher's fries. Twirling the wig, Tess pocketed the money, blew her Scandinavian admirers a kiss, and ran to the food stands. Surveillance could wait.

It was lunchtime.

Chapter 4

For eighteen years Tess's Uncle Donald had been a moving target in the state government, jumping from do-nothing job to do-nothing job just ahead of the legislators who tried to sack him in a fit of fiscal responsibility. His latest resting place was a small office high up, literally at least, in the Department of Licensing and Regulation. His official title: director of the Office for Fraud and Waste. His unofficial deputy: Tess.

"You know, it sounds as if you commit fraud and waste," Tess said, entering her uncle's office. It was small, but it had a window on St. Paul Place, with a nice view of a long, narrow median, overgrown and choked with weeds.

"Maybe I should," he said amiably. "I wouldn't mind. It would fill up the day."

A short man with a round belly and thinning brown hair, Donald Weinstein had been handsome as a young man, but his looks had faded along with his power, leaving only a full, pouting mouth and lustrous brown eyes, incongruous in his pale, lined face. He handed his niece a slim folder, which represented a week's work for him. Tess sat in the brown plastic chair opposite his desk and sifted through notes and memos from other agencies.

"Very impressive," she said. "I see the Department of Health and Mental Hygiene has cut its water bill by repairing a leaky faucet. The Department of Human Resources has found a cheaper doughnut shop for its monthly staff meetings. And the Department of the Environment has dropped its 800 line for tidal wetlands information, which no one ever used except employees who patched in and made long-distance calls. What will Maryland do with all this extra money?''

In Tess's hands, at her computer, these items would be transformed into press releases. *Department of Health and Mental Hygiene slashes bills and does the environmentally correct thing!* Or, in the case of the doughnuts: *Enterprising DHR employee Linda Fair found out switching catering contracts could result in significant savings.* She would type two copies—one for distribution within the state system, the other intended as a press release. She would leave the Department of the Environment off the second sheet, as it was stamped *NFMU (not for media use).* No reason to alert the media about those long-distance calls. For all this work Donald paid her a hundred dollars, which came out to fifty dollars an hour, although it was billed as ten dollars per on the state time sheet she filled out each week. It wasn't a bad way to make a living. She could have used seven more jobs just like it.

''You eat?''

''Yeah, down at the harbor.''

''Too bad. I thought we could go up the hill to Tio's.''

''I haven't been to Tio Pepe's for years.'' Not since Jonathan Ross had treated her, flush with the success of landing a new newspaper job while he had yet to cash his severance check from the old one.

''We could drink sangria. See and be seen. Make them bring us the dessert cart and then not order anything. Well, maybe one slice of pine nut cake. I don't care what anybody says, it's still the best restaurant in Baltimore.''

''It's still expensive, too. You got an expense account now? Or did you bet some real money at the track?''

''I guess you'd call it a discretionary fund.'' He winked. ''Same one I pay you out of.''

''So you *do* commit fraud and waste.''

Donald laughed. "If it hadn't been for the economy, Tess, I could have found a full-time job for you. Then you'd get six hundred dollars a week and benefits for the same job you do now for a hundred dollars. And I'd have some company."

"Thanks, Uncle D., but I don't think I would have made a very good state employee. I have a hard enough time getting the jargon down in these news releases. You know— 'accessing,' instead of just 'getting' something. Or a 'comprehensive service delivery' plan. I'd never be the kind of bright young thing to track down cheaper doughnuts."

She gave him a quick kiss on the cheek. He smelled like an old lady's living room. Hair oil and musty upholstery, tinged with peppermint candies. Her mother's siblings were old, much older than Judith Weinstein, an afterthought born almost twelve years after Mickey, the youngest of the four boys. Donald was in his early sixties, Tess calculated.

At the door she turned back to look at him. He had been an important man once. A bagman, sure, but an up-and-coming one. If his boss hadn't been convicted of mail fraud, Uncle Donald might be in the state house today, whispering in the governor's ear instead of killing time in this barren room. Uncle Donald had been transferred so often he no longer brought anything personal to the office with him, except the *Daily Racing Form* and a legal pad. Ponies on paper, Uncle Donald called his habit.

"You ahead?" Tess asked.

"For the year. Bad week, though. I don't like these California horses. I can't get a feel for 'em."

"You're not betting any real money?"

"I bet my real money in the market. It's more exciting. Hey—you sure you don't want me to ask around, see if something's available with the state? I bet I could find you a nice little $30,000-a-year job, with good medical."

Tess looked at the bare office, with its one window and the racing form on the desk. She blew her uncle a kiss, then ran down eleven flights as if something were chasing her. Once on the street she slowed to a brisk walk, but she kept going until she was back at her apartment.

*   *   *

Seven hours later, her work for Uncle Donald already done, her evening run behind her, Tess again took up her post outside the garage at Eden's Landing. This time, however, she was in her Toyota, waiting to see if Ava was going to leave her apartment. She knew she was there, because Rock had gotten off the phone with her minutes earlier, then called Tess.

"She told me she didn't feel up to dinner out," he said. "Said she was just going to stay in all evening." He had not asked Tess to go watch, and she had not told him she would. He was paying Tess to think those unsavory thoughts for him.

Twenty minutes later she felt almost smug as Ava zipped out of the garage at Eden's Landing in her silver Miata. Tess followed her about a mile, through downtown and into Federal Hill, to the Sweat Shop, a cavernous building where three women had died in a small fire at the turn of the century.

"Why lie about working out?" Tess asked Ava from inside her car. "That's one thing Rock always approves of, even if the gym's name isn't exactly PC."

When the Sweat Shop opened it had been deemed officially insensitive by the editorial writers at the *Beacon-Light*. Men and women claiming to be descendants of the dead women picketed. Television reporters swooped down on the place, but the handsome gym photographed so well that people clamored to join. Eventually someone remembered the victims had been teenagers, childless and unmarried, and the pickets disappeared. The Sweat Shop was an unqualified success.

Even when she had a job, Tess had never been able to afford such a glossy gym, but she knew how to gain entrance to one.

"I'd like some membership information," she told the anorexic-looking blonde at the front desk. The blonde sighed and depressed a button behind the desk. A mechanized roar, the sound a crowd makes when someone hits a three-pointer at the buzzer, echoed through the club. *Great*, Tess thought. *Just alert everyone that I'm here.*

Dale, as he was identified on his name tag, hurried forward. Short and muscle-bound, he wore a knit polo shirt so tight Tess could see each hair in the cleavage of his well-defined chest. There were seven in all. His white trousers were only a shade looser. Even his slicked-back ponytail, less than an inch in length, looked tight and flexed, curled like a bicep.

"I'm Dale, your fitness ambassador," he said, pumping Tess's hand enthusiastically. "Are you interested in our platinum or gold plan?"

"Probably the zirconium."

He looked at her blankly.

"A joke," Tess explained. "I'm sure I'll want the top-of-the-line membership. But I need a tour of the place before we start talking about fees."

"Of course." He put a proprietary hand on the small of her back, like a rudder. Tess removed the hand.

"I thought I could walk around by myself first. Check out the locker rooms, you know. I assume you do have them for men and women?"

Dale, sensing his commission slipping away, nevertheless kept his broad, peppy smile. "No problem! But I will need you to sign a liability waiver. So we have your name and phone number on file."

Tess took the clipboard he proffered. There was no waiver on it, only a blank piece of paper with a space for one's name and phone number. She had a sudden vision of nightly calls and entreaties from Dale, begging her to try the Sweat Shop for three months, two months, one month.

Tess Duberville, she wrote carefully, adding the phone number for the local weather service. Let Thomas Hardy and the forecasters deal with the sales pitch.

Free to take her own "tour" of the old factory, Tess walked through the gym, inspecting each machine while glancing around for Ava. She didn't have to fake her admiration for the sleek German equipment. The Sweat Shop was a well-kept place, filled with the thoughtful touches people expect when they pay upward of $2,000 a year for membership. Fluffy white towels, piles of current magazines by the stationary bikes, mounted color television sets. You could even rent headsets tuned to the TVs, making it easier to hear above the clanking weights and the whirring sounds of dozens of machines, all going nowhere. For someone like Tess, who spent up to three hours a day streaked with sweat, it was a tempting place. She would have preferred looking at the machines—and, in some cases, the men on them—to looking for Ava.

As it turned out she could do both. The aerobics room sat in the center of the gym, encased in glass, a bigger-than-life ant farm. There, front and center in a step class, Ava high kicked her way through the routine as if it were a competitive sport. Frail and sexy in her street clothes, she didn't look so helpless in white lace bicycle pants and a matching sports bra. Her leg muscles were long and defined, like a dancer's. Her biceps and abdomen were strongly cut, the current style for women's bodies. As for her breasts—impossibly large for such a tiny woman and indifferent to gravity—those appeared to have been fashioned somewhere outside the gym.

As the class moved into the cool-down phase, Ava rushed from the room, mopping at her sweaty face with one of the club's white towels. Only minutes later, glancing at her watch, she popped out of the locker room. She had not showered, although her makeup was fresh and her hair neatly combed. She still wore the tiny shorts and bra, with a filmy linen shirt thrown over them. The see-through shirt only emphasized all the bare skin beneath it.

No longer in a rush, Ava sauntered toward the lobby and stopped at the water fountain. Although she pressed her mouth against the arc of water, she didn't seem to swallow, Tess noticed, and her eyes were busy darting from side to side. When a Waspy white-haired man with a squash racket walked by her, she straightened up like a jack-in-the-box, greeting him in a sweet, clear voice.

"What a surprise! I didn't expect to see *you* here."

Across the lobby Tess pretended a sudden interest in a poster showing the cardiovascular system, but she could hear only snatches of their conversation. The two seemed to know each other, if not terribly well. Ava was unusually deferential, possibly because of the man's age, her eyes fastened on his face as if everything he said was fascinating.

"—come here for the massages as much as anything else," the patrician-looking man was saying. Tess was straining to hear Ava's reply, when she was knocked breathless by a huge hand smacking her between the shoulder blades.

"You want those membership detes now?" Dale, fitness ambassador, had sneaked up behind her, an ominously thick three-ring binder in hand.

"Detes?"

"Details."

"Oh, of course. Just let me go out to the Beamer and grab my checkbook."

Checkbook, the magic word. "Beamer" didn't hurt either. Dale beamed, smacking Tess one more time. As she ran to her car, she wondered if he treated all the female clients like this, or only those at least a foot taller.

She waited in her car for Ava to leave, watching her through the club's glass front. She seemed in no hurry now as she talked to the man with the squash racket. Animated, almost flirtatious, she leaned toward him and touched him frequently, innocently. Feather-light touches to his shoulder, his wrist, his hand. It reminded Tess of her shoplifting technique.

When the man finally walked away, Ava's face seemed to shut down. She wouldn't frown like that, Tess thought, if she knew how her face settled in deep lines along her mouth and forehead. Ava ran toward her car and shot out of the parking lot so quickly, Tess almost lost her on Federal Hill's narrow streets. She caught up on Light Street and trailed her back to Eden's Landing. The Toyota, usually so well behaved, sputtered and backfired, begging for attention. Tess kept it in second and hoped Ava remained oblivious.

Once inside her apartment, Ava refused to answer the

phone. Tess knew this because she called at regular intervals from the pay phone at Vaccaro's, a gelato place in Little Italy, a block away. Not even a machine picked up. How could someone ignore ten, fifteen rings? Ava didn't strike Tess as a particularly tolerant person, or one who could walk away easily from a ringing phone. Perhaps she was on the other line, so involved in another conversation that she refused to heed the click of call-waiting. Or she had unplugged the phone so no one could call her. So Rock couldn't call her.

Tess ate a *pistache* gelato and thought about what she had learned so far. Ava shoplifted. Ava worked out. Ava, in all likelihood, had breast implants. And more muscle than one might imagine. It didn't seem like much. It also seemed pretty damn boring. She totaled up her hours in her head—7:30 A.M. to 12:30 P.M., then another two hours tonight. It came out to $210. Boring, but profitable. In fact she wouldn't mind several such boring days, although she knew she should quit before her billable hours reached $1,000. She didn't want to put too big a dent in Rock's nest egg.

Chapter 5

After the easy rewards of her first day, Tess discovered why surveillance work pays well. On her second day, the Friday before the Labor Day weekend, Tess waited outside the Lambrecht Building until 2 P.M., but Ava did not leave until Rock came to pick her up for an Eastern Shore weekend. Tess watched Rock carry Ava's bags to his car—two, she noted, for a three-day weekend. Suddenly he reached out and caught Ava by the wrist, as if afraid she might dart off. He gathered her to him and hugged her hard. It made Tess's ribs ache just to see it. But Ava only arched her back, submitting her body to the embrace while craning her neck away from Rock, staring above his head at something Tess could not see. They headed for the expressway in Rock's seldom-used Honda, his shell strapped to the roof of the car.

Why are you two engaged? Tess wondered as the car disappeared. She had seen Rock in the grocery store, absent-minded and indifferent about everything except his coffee beans. "The biggest one is always the best buy, right? If this kind of rice costs more, it must be better, right?" He was a few years older than she, and the life he glimpsed through his microscope, as Tess understood it, encouraged one to reproduce, to squiggle on.

And there was Ava, beautiful, accomplished, and willing. He would never question why she wanted to marry him. He would see it as a sign of extraordinary good fortune, proof that the expensive rice is always the best.

Tess spent the weekend at the bookstore, trying to make up the hours she owed Kitty. Too soon it was Tuesday, time to take up her now-familiar post outside Eden's Landing. Then Wednesday, Thursday. The days passed uneventfully. Ava walked to work, she ventured out for lunch, she went back inside, she went home. On Wednesday she met Rock for dinner, and Tess took the night off. Later, when she checked in with Rock by telephone, he said Ava still seemed edgy and evasive, ending the evening early with complaints of work and a splitting headache. Tess, hearing the ache in his voice, wondered if she should tell him about the shoplifting. But then it would be over and Tess, much to her surprise, wasn't ready to quit.

On Friday morning she sat on her bench outside Ava's office and watched the cops rousting panhandlers. Beggars were not new in downtown Baltimore—Tess remembered a legless man at Lexington Market who had chased her down the street on his little wheeled cart when she was eight—but now war had been declared. The city had enlisted "safety guides" who patrolled the streets, making them safer and friendlier for those who asked only for directions. The street people called these guides the Purple People, a reference to their snazzy caps. Maybe city officials thought they would lose their new football team if the NFL found out Baltimore had panhandlers. Then again, it would have been a great name for the team: the Baltimore Beggars. No—the Baltimore Hollow Men. If only T. S. Eliot had died in Charm City instead of Poe, it could have been the Hollow Men instead of the Ravens.

Most of the panhandlers went peaceably, including Tess's seatmate, who had been prying a dollar a day from her with the same routine. But she didn't ask the cops or the Purple People if she scared them, she just kept moving. "I know how not to get arrested," she muttered to Tess as she hurried off, surprisingly lucid. "I'll be up at McDonald's." Stunned, Tess watched her go. *She thinks I'm one of them.*

A few feet away a gentleman in a shiny blue suit refused to yield his ground. Tall and skinny, he held himself with perfect posture, repeating: ''I drove my car over here from the Eastern Shore, but the battery died. Now I just need four dollars for the bus ride back.''

Tess knew the line well; it was a local favorite. Most people tried it and moved on. But this man would not give up, no matter how the cops cajoled or threatened. She was so entranced by this tableau that she almost missed Ava heading out the front door. She was heading toward the Gallery, briefcase in hand. But instead of one of her perfect suits—Tess so far had seen her in gray, black, red, and a stunning shade of olive green—she wore a plum-colored dress, a curious garment with a high neck and long sleeves. Curious, because it should have been demure and conservative, given its length and shape. Yet the dress exuded sex. What did Kitty call the style? A breakaway dress, made to be torn from the body with one deft movement.

In the Gallery Ava started her stealing workout with a quick warm-up. Tess watched her admire the same silver necklace at Amaryllis, caress a cashmere sweater at Ann Taylor, then smirk and shudder at goods she would never deign to pay for, although she might consider stealing them. She loved to touch things. The tactile contact seem to bring more pleasure than the actual moment of capture, when another small, bright item dropped into her ravenous briefcase. Tess found herself eager to see what she would steal today, but after a quick trip inside Coach, where she stroked the forest green twin to her own lustrous black briefcase, Ava checked her watch and abruptly left the store, making a bee-line for the lobby of the Renaissance Harborplace Hotel, just as she had on the first day.

Over the past week Tess had become quite adept at trailing Ava. She hung back at least twenty feet, her eyes focused on some spot two or three feet in front of her, her clothes dark and unmemorable. She no longer worried about her hair, although she wore dark glasses as an extra precaution. Pri-

marily she counted on Ava to walk slowly and never notice
people who were of no use to her.

Today, however, Ava moved more quickly than usual, getting too far ahead. As Tess tried to close the distance without
attracting attention, she smacked into someone, quite hard,
and found herself staring into a man's familiar face. Down
into it, actually, for the man was short, not even up to her
collarbone. Irritated and embarrassed, Tess looked at a face
to which she could not put a name, despite a panicky can-
vassing of her past. College? Newspaper days? A bad date?

Although short, the man had a huge head perched on a
scrawny neck. His head was so big, and his neck so thin,
that his head seemed to bob like a toy dog in the back of
someone's car. Tess gave him her warmest smile and heart-
iest ''Hello!'', hoping his reply would provide a hint to his
identity, or at least the time needed to fish for his name. But
Big Head stared at her as if they had never met.

They hadn't. As he turned away Tess realized she had
been gazing into one of Baltimore's most ubiquitous faces,
a visage seen so frequently everyone believed they knew its
owner: Michael Abramowitz. His close-set eyes had stared
out of newspaper pages and television screens for close to
fifteen years. His ignominy began as a public defender, a
loudmouth who bugged people by having far too much success with the accused killers and rapists he represented.
Abramowitz liked to win, and although he had grown up as
a poor relation—a distant cousin to a local fortune based on
plastic slipcovers—he always insisted the wretched salary
didn't bother him.

Yet when he quit a few years ago, he had gone after
money with the same single-mindedness that had carried him
through the public defender's office. He became the drunk
driver's friend, the king of the slip and fall, the star of won-
derfully campy commercials who noted, in front of a roaring
fireplace, ''Two wrongs don't make a right. You may have
done something wrong, but you can get the right lawyer.''

Over the years the commercials grew increasingly bizarre,
adding to his fame. He appeared with a Dalmatian and, for

a brief time, a fake family. When a newspaper article revealed he had never married or fathered children, he switched to playing the banjo, a line of chorus girls behind him, all singing to the tune of "Sweet Sue." "Ev'ry star above/ Knows when push comes to shove/You'll sue/Yes, you/Stars up in the sky/Tell you he's your guy/Michael who?/Will sue." His lumpy face and thick Baltimore accent made him a celebrity of sorts. The business made him if not rich, then obscenely comfortable.

Yet just when people began to speculate Abramowitz could parlay his visibility into a successful run for office, he again confounded public expectations by joining O'Neal, O'Connor and O'Neill, that sedate stable of blue bloods who shunned publicity, except for the occasional "grip and grin" photo at a symphony party or a pre-Preakness event. Abramowitz had told reporters, affecting a Garboesque accent and the true wording of her *Grand Hotel* speech: "I just want to be left alone."

Perhaps he told the truth. Today he scuttled away quickly enough when Tess feigned recognition. She shrugged and pushed on into the hotel lobby, looking for Ava.

No luck. She checked the board of events to see if there was some conference she might be attending. It seemed doubtful, unless Ava had suddenly become a forensic pathologist, the only meeting listed. She called the front desk from a house phone, asking for Ava Hill's room. No one by that name was registered, a man's prissy voice told her firmly. She turned abruptly away from the house phone and collided a second time with Mr. Big Head, Michael Abramowitz.

Again Tess had to stop herself from smiling as if he were an old friend. Frightening, the intimacy television created with strangers. This time Abramowitz gave her a long, hard look. Tess wondered if he thought she was a chronic litigant, hurling herself into well-dressed people in hopes of a lucrative settlement. He said nothing, however, just turned and walked toward the elevator. He was an absurdly small man, except for that giant head, and Tess thought he must get tired carrying it around. Not even Rock's body could support such a gargantuan head.

The thought of Rock set off a series of small explosions in her brain. Abramowitz, Ava's boss. Ava. Hotel lobby. Abramowitz and Ava. Not in the lobby, but upstairs somewhere.

"But he's so ugly," she said out loud, drawing a harsh look from a young woman sitting nearby, a baby in her lap. The baby, a little boy in a white lace gown and cap, was not, in fact, particularly good-looking. Tess turned away quickly so the woman could not see her face, red with mortification and laughter. When she had contained herself she walked back to the bank of phones near the entrance.

She considered what she had seen. Ava and Abramowitz. It was tempting to jump to the conclusion that they were here together on some illicit business, but what proof did she really have? For all she knew they were meeting a client in one of the suites upstairs, some Sims-Kever executive who still traveled in style, even as he cried poverty to his victims.

Pulling out the crumpled sheets Rock had given her a week ago, Tess dialed Ava's office and asked for her secretary. A woman with an English accent came on the line. Interesting touch for a firm founded by three micks, Tess thought.

"Miss Hill, please."

"She's not available. May I take a message?"

Tess began stammering, which was only partly an act.

"Oh, wow, shit—I mean, sorry, but do you happen to know where she is? This is going to sound really spacey, but I'm this old friend of hers from, like, grade school, and we made these lunch plans and—would you believe—I forgot where I'm supposed to meet her. Could you check her calendar and see if there's anything that might give me a clue?"

The secretary sniffed disapprovingly, then shunted Tess into the vacuum of "hold." She came back on the line a few seconds later.

"Are you sure it was today? Her lunches are blocked out all month, from noon to two."

"I must have *really* screwed up. Does she have anything tomorrow? Does she have anything about meeting . . . Becky for lunch?"

"No, nothing written down. Shall I have her call you?"

"What? What? I can't hear you. I must be in a bad cell." Tess hung up the pay phone and picked up the house phone next to it.

"Front desk."

"Hi, it's me in the kitchen." She figured the front desk attendant wouldn't want to admit he didn't recognize the voice of a fellow employee. "Hey, what room is Mr. Abramowitz in this week? I can't read it on the room service slip and you know how he is if his food is cold. He always threatens to sue!"

"He's in 410. And you better get it up there fast. *You* know he expects the food to arrive no later than twelve-thirty. He doesn't like to be interrupted."

Not enough, Tess thought. Not enough information with which to ruin your friend's life. She took a deep breath and said: "So he can have dessert by one, right?" She barely recognized the coy, snide laugh she produced on cue.

The front desk clerk snorted, then recovered. "Just get the food up to the room. They're both here."

Chapter 6

That night, Tess ran her hardest route.

She ran along Boston Street and into Canton. Past the expensive condos thrown up along the waterfront when Canton had been touted as the next hot neighborhood. It had never quite happened, so only a few high rises squatted among the row houses, Gullivers in Lilliput. It would be sweet, Tess thought, if the residents awakened one day to find their expensive homes staked to the ground, swarming with those who now lived in their shadows.

She increased her speed. Although the sun had gone down, it was still humid, and sweat poured off her. She had hoped a hard run would be cool and cleansing, but she felt sleazy and dirty, haunted by junk food and junk memories. The pizza slices and hot dogs of the past week oozed out of her pores, while her head was filled with unsettling images. She saw Ava pushing lingerie into her briefcase, saw the big head of Michael Abramowitz, floating on top of his tiny body like some unwieldy helium balloon, bouncing across the Renaissance lobby toward his assignation with Ava.

She had been right in her instinctive dislike for Ava, but she found little pleasure in being right. How had she failed to anticipate this moment? For Kitty had seen it all too clearly. From the first Tess had hoped Ava was up to no good and relished the chance to prove it, thinking it would be a good and lucrative deed to break up Rock's engagement.

She had imagined what it would be like to trail Ava, and she'd come to enjoy doing it. She had killed long hours thinking about what she would do with the money Rock was paying her. But she had never imagined what it would be like to report back to Rock.

The thought of Rock's face made her run faster still.

She couldn't do it, not for any sum of money. But she didn't want to give up the money. And she wanted Rock to know what she had discovered, just not the responsibility of telling him.

There was only one way. Ava must confess, and Tess would have to trick her into it.

Back in her apartment, showered and dusted with talcum powder, Tess dialed Ava's number. A machine picked up. She started to hang up, then had a quick inspiration. She knew what could get Ava to pick up a telephone, assuming she was there and screening her messages.

"Miss Hill?" she asked in the high, almost too-clear tones of a young college girl, the type of voice that goes higher still at every sentence's end.

"This is Denise at Nordstrom? I waited on you the last time you were in? Well, I wanted you to know we are having a very special sale on Donna Karan, a two-day preview sale for very special customers, and I just wanted to give you the details? We're taking up to seventy-five percent off some of the fall suits?"

Ava picked up. "Yes, I'm here. Do you have many things left in a size four?"

Stunned by the success of her plan, Tess realized she hadn't figured out what to say next. She fell back on the truth.

"I'm not a Nordstrom sales girl. I'm a private investigator—a kind of one, anyway, and I've been following you. I think it would be in your best interest to meet with me."

Ava hung up. Tess called back and got the machine again, but she knew Ava was standing there, listening.

"I have some information, Miss Hill," she said, hoping her voice sounded cool and experienced. "Information about your . . . lunchtime activities. Information I plan to provide to my client if you don't meet with me.''

She could feel Ava waiting, considering, only blocks away. After a week of following her, Tess felt strangely close to her prey. She still didn't like her, but she sensed something sad and fucked-up in her, which made her harder to hate. She wanted to hear Ava's side of the story, even as she doubted she would believe it. But she did not tell her any of this, did not say anything more as she hurtled toward the beep and another disconnection.

Ava picked up just before the tape on the machine ran out. ''Sunday,'' she said. ''Eight P.M. I can't meet until then.''

''Fine. Meet me at The Point.''

''The Point?''

''It's a bar, also known as Spike's Place, out on Franklin-town Road, near where I-70 dead-ends.''

''I'm sure I can find it. I look forward to meeting you. I've never met a female *dick* before.'' And she slammed the phone down again.

Let her have this round, Tess decided. *The next one is mine.* She sat down at her computer and wrote two short plays, both for two characters. Tess and Rock, Tess and Ava. The only trick would be getting them to follow scripts they didn't know existed.

The next morning, an overcast Saturday, she grabbed Rock's hand as they left Jimmy's.

''Take a walk with me,'' she said. They had not talked about Ava at breakfast. They had been *not* talking about Ava for ten days now, which meant they had practically stopped talking. It was the only subject in the world.

''Do you know something?'' he asked.

''Yes, but it's hard to tell.''

He swallowed hard, pale beneath his tan. Tess led him down the pier to a small bench overlooking the harbor.

''I've been watching Ava off and on for almost a week now. I think I know what's bugging her.''

Rock's eyes held hers, but he was incapable of saying

anything. He reminded Tess of an old dog, trusting a beloved master not to put him to sleep—unless the master absolutely had to.

"She shoplifts. Little things, things she can't possibly need. I saw her take underwear and camisoles, stuff that wasn't even her size."

As she had expected Rock considered this good news. He sighed, the air escaping from his massive lungs as if he had been holding his breath for several days. It was bad, but it wasn't as bad as he had feared. He could fix this. He could help her. He straightened up, ready to take action.

"I bet there's someone up at Phipps who knows about kleptomania," he said, referring to Johns Hopkins's psychiatric wing. Tess turned her face away so he wouldn't see her smile. He was so predictable. Of course he had immediately jumped to the conclusion that Ava's thefts were a sickness, and therefore curable. She had planned on such a reaction.

"I've already done that. Dr. Hauer is the leading expert on this kind of disorder." The lie stung a little, delivered so smoothly to a trusted friend, but the name was correct, taken from one of the media guides Johns Hopkins distributed to the newspaper every year.

"I've heard of him. He has a great rep."

"Yes, he does. His advice may be difficult for you to follow, though. He says it's important *not* to confront her about this. I told him what I had observed, and he said it's his opinion she's reaching a crisis point. If you're patient, she'll confide in you soon enough."

"But what if she gets arrested? It could ruin her career. She'd never be admitted to the bar."

Tess had anticipated this question, too. "I don't think she will. Get caught, I mean. I saw her because I was already observing her, Rock. Clerks don't watch her. She dresses well; she looks like a nice young professional woman. They're too busy chasing around the kids playing hooky to watch someone like Ava. But if she is arrested Dr. Hauer said he'd be able to get the charges dropped. He does it all the time."

A preposterous claim. No psychiatrist, no matter how highly regarded, could get charges dropped down at the police station. But Tess counted on Rock's lack of experience with police officers or bail hearings.

Still, he was uncomfortable. She knew Rock would have trouble doing nothing. This was the riskiest part of her plan—trying to keep Rock from confronting Ava until tomorrow night.

She took his left hand in both of hers. The palm thick with calluses. A rower's hand. It was like holding a huge Brillo pad.

"Trust me," she said, knowing she no longer deserved his trust. "Give it a week. If she hasn't come to you by then and told you everything, we'll go to Plan B."

"Plan B?"

"An intervention, like they do for addicts. But give it a week. Promise?"

"Well, if Dr. Hauer thinks this is the right thing. . . . I won't say anything to her, not for a week. You have my word."

And his word, Tess knew, was actually worth something. It was as good as the check he pressed in her hand, made out for $1,080. Her first one-act play had gone off without a hitch. Now all she had to do was mount and produce the second one. Sequels were always tricky.

Tess hadn't been to The Point for months, a fact Spike lost no time reminding her of.

"Hey, Tesser, you finally come to see your old Uncle Spike? You still like mozzarella sticks? I tell you what. For you I'll have Tommy change the oil. And a Rolling Rock, right? In a bottle, no glass. See, I remember, even if you don't come see me so often."

"You've got a great memory, Uncle Spike. Who do you get that from?"

"I got nothing from nobody, Tesser. You know that." He turned up the sound on the Orioles game, then disappeared into the kitchen to personally supervise her mozzarella sticks.

Spike was a relative, but no one was sure whose, for neither side of the family would claim him. Tess's father always insisted he was a cousin from some weak branch of the Weinstein family tree. Her mother maintained she had never met him until marrying into the Monaghan clan. Spike himself was closemouthed about the connection, though his looks favored Momma Weinstein's springer spaniels. Pale, with an astonishing array of liver spots, Spike was notable primarily for his bald head, which came to a point. Hence the name of his tavern, decorated throughout with silhouettes of his bald head, cut from black construction paper by the dishwasher.

Tess adored him and his bar. When she was fifteen he had given her an open invitation to The Point, telling her it was important to learn to drink among people one could trust.

"You miscalculate here, the worst that happens maybe you wake up on my sofa, some crumbs on you," Spike said. "You drink too much out there—" He pointed with his chin to the world beyond Franklintown Road and didn't bother to explain what could happen to a drunk teenager out there. Accidents, vehicular and sexual.

Spike's plan, while unorthodox, worked well. By the time Tess went off to Washington College, she knew exactly how much she could drink. It was a prodigious amount. Her dates were far more likely to pass out than she. On occasion a few did. A lady, she never took advantage of them.

Tonight she had chosen Spike's Place because she hoped it would throw Ava off balance. She was ready for a second Rolling Rock before Ava arrived, ten minutes late and unapologetically so. She stalked in, wearing a white unitard, a turquoise thong, suede boots, and a leather jacket. Her black hair was pinned up on top of her head in a geyserlike ponytail. It was quite unlike anything ever seen at The Point. One of the older men fell off his bar stool as Ava walked by.

"Don't get too full of yourself," Tess told her, looking at George on the floor. "He does that all the time."

"I *know* you," Ava said, but her look told Tess she

couldn't place her. They had met only a few times. Rock's life was neatly compartmentalized, and Ava had shown little interest in rowing, which only happened to be his reason for existence.

"Maybe you think you know me because I've been watching you for so long. You've probably seen me several times, yet it never registered until now. I've noticed you don't really pay much attention to the world around you."

Ava slid into the booth, arranging herself so only a tiny strip of her tiny behind made contact with the smeared and cracked vinyl. She glanced at a menu, shuddered slightly, then put it aside. Tess had planned to recommend the veal chop, eager to watch her try to cut the rubbery meat. She also hoped she would order a Chardonnay. The white wine at The Point tasted like vinegar, bad vinegar at that.

But Ava had an innate sense for the right thing, even in the wrong place. She ordered—never had the word seemed quite so apt to Tess—a Black Label draft, helped herself to one of the mozzarella sticks on Tess's plate, then sat back and raised an eyebrow. *Your move,* the eyebrow said.

Fine, Tess thought, *I don't have time for this either.*

"I have information you're having an affair with Michael Abramowitz."

Ava looked puzzled, but only for a second. Then she gave Tess one of her full-force smiles. "Information? Possibly. But do you have proof?"

"Of course."

"Really? I'd love to see it, or hear it. I hope I came out nicely in the photographs." She took a dainty sip of beer.

"My proof is for my client. I am interested, however, in any explanation you might want to offer."

Ava ate another mozzarella stick, very slowly. She appeared to be considering something, and she didn't speak again until she had swallowed the last bite of fried cheese, then patted her lips dry with a paper napkin.

"You know, I thought I knew who you were working for when you called, but the person I was thinking of would have hired someone good, someone who knew how to do things—assuming there was anything to do. So who are you working for?''

"Whom. Whom am I working for.''

"Whatever. *Whom*ever.''

"Why don't you tell me who you thought my client was, and I'll tell you if you're right.''

"I'm not convinced you work for anyone. You're probably just a grubby little blackmailer, out for yourself.''

"I work for Darryl Paxton. Your fiancé, I believe. Or thinks he is.''

"Well, I like that,'' Ava said. "I thought engaged people were supposed to trust each other.'' She seemed offended but also a little relieved. Who was her original suspect? Tess wondered. Abramowitz, famous for his monastic devotion to his career, had been single all his life. He had no wife to check on him.

"Does a woman deserve her fiancé's trust if she's having an affair?''

"Do I deserve to endure this conversation when you don't have any proof?''

"I said I did. I've been following you. I saw you in the Renaissance Harborplace with him. I saw you at the Gallery. Do you steal the underwear to wear for your boss? Or is that an unrelated hobby?''

This was more unnerving, Tess could tell. Cheating on your fiancé was one thing, but it didn't keep one from being admitted to the bar. When Ava looked up, her eyes were filled with tears and her lips trembled. *Save it for your next speeding ticket,* Tess thought.

"Are you going to tell Darryl?'' Her voice actually quavered.

"That's my job. He hired me to find out why you were acting so weird. I think I have an answer.''

"But Michael has nothing to—'' she started, then stopped abruptly, her face shifting back into its normal, haughty expression. The tone of her voice also changed, suddenly amused and airy.

"Of course you have to tell him,'' she agreed. "But I need

to talk to him first.'' Tess smiled, a playwright watching happily as the curtain line approached. But she had never anticipated the actress might ad-lib.

''Yes, I'll call him and tell him how my boss has been making me sleep with him so I can keep my job. I'll tell him it's Anita Hill all over again and it freaked me out, which is why I started to shoplift. Darryl will believe me and Darryl will forgive me. It won't matter what you tell him.''

''You're a lawyer. I assume if you were a victim of sexual harassment, you'd know how to handle it a little better than that.''

''Did you hear about that case in Philadelphia? A woman lawyer sued this big-shot partner, and the jury found in her favor, then gave her nothing in damages. What good is that? A victim deserves compensation, don't you think?''

''Are you a victim?''

''At this point it's a matter of opinion, and I think I am,'' Ava said. She stood up, pulling her purse close to her body, making no move to put money down for her beer. ''A court may not agree with me, but I'm sure Darryl will. That's the only jury I need to persuade.''

Tess was flustered, incapable of a response. She had assumed Ava would rush to tell Rock her version, burying herself by revealing too much. She had counted on Ava being more concerned about her affair than her tendency to steal underwear. But in her version the sex, unwanted, was making her shoplift. What if Rock believed her? What if she was telling the truth?

George fell off his bar stool again as Ava walked by, knocking her down with him. The tangle of arms gave Tess some pleasure, but Ava, even trapped beneath the 300-pound frame of a sometimes incontinent alcoholic, kept her Princess Grace cool. As she stood up, brushing off her now not-so-white unitard, she looked smug, untouchable.

''On your mark, get set, go,'' she called back. By the time Tess figured out what she meant, and ran to the door of the tavern, Ava was already in her silver Miata, dialing her car phone as she made an illegal left turn out of the parking lot.

Chapter 7

Tess dawdled the next morning, reluctant to show up at the boat house. When she finally arrived Rock apparently was already on the water, as she had hoped. She rowed her usual route. *If he wants to find me,* she told herself, *he will. If he doesn't he'll stay out of sight, hiding on that little branch that heads south.* It was a tricky route—shallow in spots, with bridges forcing one to duck, pull in oars, and skim beneath them—but Rock preferred it when he felt sulky. Tess rowed to Fort McHenry and back, then out to the fort again. She saw eights and fours and two-man crews, but no other single.

It was a glorious morning, a day to savor. Brilliant blue sky, light wind, crisp air. Indian autumn, Tess called it—a fake fall to be replaced by another wave of muggy weather any day now. Tess felt she could row the length of the Chesapeake, find her way to the Atlantic, and make England by lunchtime. She settled for a power piece back to the dock. Bursting with endorphins, she waited in the practice room, pretending to stretch until 8 A.M., when she finally gave up on Rock. He was off licking his wounds somewhere. He'd come around eventually.

She skipped Jimmy's and ate breakfast at her aunt's kitchen table, feasting on leftover cornbread that Officer Friendly had prepared the night before, and reading the papers her aunt had left behind in a tidy pile. Tess worked from back to front, a childhood habit reinforced by her days as a reporter. When she had worked at a paper, she already knew the local news, so she saved it for last, reading features and sports, then the *Washington Post* and *The New York Times*. She read the *Beacon-Light* last—or the *Blight,* as most readers called it—so it was 9:30 A.M. before she saw the story below the fold: *Prominent Lawyer Dead; Biologist Held.*

Michael Abramowitz, a lawyer whose amateurish but unforgettable advertisements made him an unlikely local celebrity, was strangled last night in his Inner Harbor office at the staid law firm of O'Neal, O'Connor and O'Neill, according to police.

A suspect was arrested within an hour of the slaying, which police described as unusually brutal. Darryl Paxton, a thirty-three-year-old researcher at Johns Hopkins medical school, was to be held overnight in the central district lockup, then taken before a commissioner for bail review this morning.

According to sources close to the investigation, Mr. Abramowitz was beaten and squeezed in a pythonlike grip, then beaten viciously. He also had bruises on his face, presumably from a fight with Mr. Paxton, who visited him at the office just after 10 P.M., according to a security guard's log. The body was discovered by a custodian . . .

Shirley Temple. Tess felt her stomach clutch and saw the child movie star's dimpled face swimming before her, a ghostly apparition in pale blue. When she was a child—well, fourteen—she had broken her mother's Shirley Temple cereal bowl and blamed it on a neighbor's child. No one had ever discovered her lie. Twenty years later, guilt always evoked the same reaction—Shirley's face, followed by nausea and fear. She had never been good, but she had always been good at not being caught.

She picked up the paper again. There was nothing new

beyond that third paragraph, only boilerplate on Abramowitz and his career. Certainly, nothing was new to Tess. Even the style and the reporting were as familiar to Tess as a lover's kiss. In a sense, it was her lover's kiss. The article was the handiwork of Jonathan Ross, her sometime bedmate and a consistent star in the *Blight*'s galaxy. In her shock at the headline, she had skipped over the byline. All his trademarks were there—unnamed sources, a memorable description of the death at hand, over-the-top prose, a damning detail. "The staid law firm." Was there another kind? Still, she felt genuine admiration at the guard's log; she bet no one else in town had that.

"But I know more," she said out loud. What Jonathan wouldn't give to know what she knew—the woman at the center of this triangle, the trysts at the Renaissance Harborplace, Rock's suspicions. She was the one person who could put it all together. With that thought she threw the paper down and called for Kitty, her voice thin and shrill.

"Tesser?" Kitty came on a run, dressed in an Edwardian frock of white lawn, a white ribbon in her curls and white canvas Jack Purcells on her size five feet. The effect was a little bit flapper, a little 1920s Wimbledon, a little 1970s Baltimore, when anyone who wore shoes other than Jacks was ridiculed for appearing in "fish heads."

Tess thrust the paper at her: "Remember my detective job? It was quite a success. I caught Rock's fiancée with her boss. Now the boss is dead and Rock's in jail."

Kitty skimmed the article.

"Did you tell Rock what you found out?"

"No, I goaded Ava into telling him last night. She says it was sexual harassment. She had to sleep with Abramowitz to keep her job. The last time I saw her, she was on her car phone, telling Rock her story."

Kitty was a quick study. "You need to disappear for a while," she announced decisively. "Take a little trip and don't tell me where. Given my relationship with Thaddeus, I'd prefer not to know too much so I won't have to lie if anyone comes looking for you."

"I'll have to talk to them eventually."

"Yes, you will," Kitty agreed. "But it wouldn't hurt to be unavailable for a few days while you figure out how you want to handle this. Take any money you need out of the cash register and leave me a check. I won't cash it unless I have to. Find a cheap motel or a friend's house, then call me collect from pay phones. In a few days we'll know where this is headed, and you can come home."

Tess took the stairs to her apartment two at a time and began throwing clothes into a battered leather knapsack. Her friend Whitney's family had a house on the shore near Oxford, with a small guest house on the property's edge. She and Whitney had used it during college when they had wanted to get away. Rich friends had their charms. She would have to assume she was still welcome there, as calling Whitney would only further complicate things. Whitney worked for the *Beacon-Light*, too, and although she would be under no legal requirement to talk, Tess didn't want to find out what would happen if Whitney had to choose between her friend and some tantalizing details in what promised to be a big story. Asking Whitney not to act out of self-interest was akin to asking a cat not to chase a bird. Better not to test her.

The telephone rang as Tess was gathering her toothbrush and shampoo from the bathroom. She let the machine pick it up. A hoarse, familiar voice filled her small apartment with such force that the glass doors in her kitchen cabinets rattled: Tyner Gray, a rowing coach whose years of working with young novices had turned his voice into a perpetual shout.

"Tess, it's Tyner; call me at my law office as soon as you get a chance.

"It's not about rowing," he added, as if he knew she was standing there and could read her mind as well. "It is about a rower we both know well."

The volume of his voice dropped to a husky whisper, still impossibly loud and piercing. "He asked me to call you, Tess. For some reason he thinks you can help him. Although, from what I know, it would appear you've done quite enough.'' His voice roared back to its usual volume, as if he were shouting a drill to her across an expanse of water. ''Call my office, Tess. ASAP.''

Tess sat on the floor, a pair of underwear still balled up in her hand. If Rock needed her she couldn't run away. She wondered whether Rock was the best judge of what he needed. Or whom he needed. First he hired a fellow sculler to be his private detective. *And see how that had turned out.* Now he had a rowing coach as his lawyer. What did he think he was going to get for his jury—a men's eight and a women's four?

At sixty-four, Tyner Gray still had the lean, sinewy upper body of a lightweight rower. On warm days, when he was on the dock and took off his T-shirt, the college girls stole looks at his chest and arms. No one ever glanced at his legs, withered and lifeless in his sweatpants, almost flat. As far as Tess knew, no one had seen them since his accident almost forty years ago, a year after his Olympic victory. He had been hit by a drunk driver outside Memorial Stadium.

''Did you get a workout in this morning?'' Rock asked when Tess was shown into Tyner's office by his secretary, Alison, a ravishing blonde whose pearls were as big and round as the blue eyes she fastened adoringly on Tyner. ''I hated missing practice.''

Arrested and charged at eleven, bailed out nine hours later, Rock looked good. Jail, or the lack of caffeine, had helped him get some rest for the first time in weeks. In fact he seemed almost serene to Tess. Whatever had happened, he still had Ava.

Tyner sighed. ''Rock, I know your perspective on this is you're an innocent man and some horrible mistake has been made. It doesn't work that way. I'm not sure you'll be allowed to leave the state for the Head of the Ohio, much less the Head of the Charles. You were lucky you had enough cash on hand to pay a bail bondsman.''

Rock looked stunned. Miss the Head of the Charles? Tyner now had his full attention.

"Our biggest problem is that the police are satisfied they have the right suspect," Tyner said. "This is the kind of high-profile case they're pressured to solve quickly, and they're already congratulating themselves on what a no-brainer it was—and that's *before* talking to Ava. We can only hope their investigation will founder on a lack of evidence, or that someone else might be implicated. In the meantime we can begin gathering information to help us get the charges dropped or, if it comes to that, dissuade a jury. This is where Tess comes in."

"Back up. I thought we all agreed I *caused* this mess. Why involve me?"

"Because you now work for me. You're going to turn over your notes from your 'investigation' and, if anyone asks to see them, I'm going to argue they're privileged. Same thing if the police try to talk to you, or the state's attorney. I will show them our employment contract, dated September first—the day you contracted with Rock."

"Am I really working for you, or is this just a scam?"

"You're going to work your ass off," Tyner promised, grinning. "You are going to do things I hate to do. You are going to photocopy and fetch my lunch. You are going to take my jackets to the tailor if I tell you to. And you are going to conduct preliminary interviews with key witnesses, gathering the information I need to play what I call 'tick-tock'—a little game designed to open windows for other murderers while narrowing Rock's opportunity."

Tick-tock, Tyner explained, was Salvador Dalí's timepiece, liquid and flexible. Did Rock really go upstairs at 10 P.M., as the guard told police? Could it have been 10:05? Or 9:45? If the guard was lax about procedures such as calling up, might he have been similarly lax about timekeeping? Who else went in and out? Tess's job was to interview the security guard, the custodian, and anyone else, and—politely, sweetly, deferentially—create as much confusion in their minds as possible.

"Tick-tock," Tyner said. "Open windows, find new doors and exits. 'Did you happen to check your watch? A digital watch? Did you notice exactly what time it was? Of course you didn't, I guess; no one notices the exact time. Ten o'clock is an estimate, right, your best guess?'

" 'Does everyone sign in, sir? Everyone? Does anyone ever sneak in? Never? Did you go to the door to smoke a cigarette or breathe the night air? Are you sure?' That's how you play. And our first player is Rock. Except I want him to be specific and very clear about what he did, and when. Tess, you used to be a reporter. Take notes.'' He threw a legal pad and a pen at her.

Rock looked at Tyner's worn rug as he spoke. The beginning of his story was familiar, at least to Tess. Ava had called him about 8:30 P.M. That could be established with a log of calls from Ava's car phone; even Tess knew that. Ava hadn't told Rock anything on the phone, only asked him to wait at his apartment until she arrived.

"Take your phone off the hook, sweetie," she had urged him. "Don't talk to anyone until I get there." *Nice block,* Tess thought. *She kept me from getting to him first.*

She had arrived by 9:00. Ava told Rock how Abramowitz had forced her to sleep with him, claiming she would never find another lawyer's job in Baltimore if she refused. She figured anyone who had defended rapists and murderers could defend himself against something as ephemeral as sexual harassment, so she gave in. In return he promised her a brilliant future. Although the arrangement had put her on the verge of a nervous collapse, she had been handling everything just fine, until "this woman" had tried to blackmail her.

"Totally untrue," Tess protested.

"I didn't believe that part," Rock assured her. "I figured Ava didn't understand what our arrangement was and misinterpreted your conversation." Still giving Ava the benefit of the doubt, Tess noted. It had not yet occurred to Rock that Ava might be an accomplished liar.

"I stroked her hair until she fell asleep," he continued. "I would look down and see my hand on her hair, and I would think that Abramowitz had touched her, too. It made me sick. And after awhile it made sense to get my bike and go down there, to the firm.''

"How did you know he would be there?" Tyner asked.

"I didn't. Ava had told me he was always there, always working. I figured last night wouldn't be any different. And he was there, but he was watching the O's game. His office is like his own private sky box—it looks right into Camden Yards. If you turn on WBAL it's better than being there. He even had a beer and a hot dog. I think that made me even angrier, the idea that he was sitting up in his office, watching a ball game, while Ava was practically hysterical. So I told him—I told him what I thought of him, and how we could go to the EEOC and the state bar, maybe even the newspapers. He just laughed.''

"He laughed at you?" Tess asked. "He thought it was funny?"

Rock thought for a moment. "It was a nervous laugh, like he was trying to think of what to say next. Then all these lies began tumbling out, about how he was trying to help Ava pass the bar, and she said she'd sleep with him if he could make sure she stayed on staff. She'd failed it twice and she had to pass the third time or she was out. That part is true, actually—she has failed twice. But she didn't offer to sleep with Abramowitz in order to keep her job. She would never have done that.''

She might have, Tess thought.

"Did he say anything else?" Tyner asked.

"He said, he said—" Rock closed his eyes, imagining the scene in his head. "He said, 'I'm sorry.' And then he said, 'But she really is beautiful.' That's when I hit him.''

The blow knocked Abramowitz backward on his Oriental rug and broke his glasses. The metal bridge cut his nose, and his head caught a corner of the desk, a superficial wound that bled copiously. Head wounds do that, Tess knew. They can look much worse than they are.

"I stood over him and I put my hands on his throat," Rock said. "I thought I could kill him. I wanted him to know that, too, wanted to terrorize him the way he had terrorized

Ava. I wanted him to feel as desperate and trapped as she must have. I held his throat in my hands and I looked him in the eyes. I even hoped he might piss himself.''

"Did he?" Tess asked. Tyner gave her a look of disgust. She had never broken her habit of asking any question that occurred to her.

"No. He didn't even seem scared. Maybe because he once defended real killers, he could tell I wasn't one. He smiled at me and nodded his head, as if encouraging me. I pushed him back and his head caught the desk again, harder this time. I remember the sound—it was louder, less hollow than I would have thought, as if his head was very dense. He went down. But he was still breathing when I left. I swear he was still breathing.''

"Did you notice the time?"

"Ten minutes past ten by the Bromo Seltzer tower, when I got back to the street," he said, referring to one of the city's more unusual landmarks, a ghostly clock tower with the letters of the antacid in place of numerals. "Definitely ten-ten.''

"And the log says you signed in at ten, but the security guard may have rounded it off," Tyner said. "So, ten minutes, maybe less, for a somewhat detailed conversation and a brief fight. You could have killed him in that period of time, but you would have had to have been very efficient. And there is still twenty minutes before the custodian finds Abramowitz, time enough for another person to finish your work.''

"But who?" Tess asked. "A disgruntled former client? A robber? One of his law partners? And isn't it awfully coincidental they happened to come along right after Rock had bloodied him?''

"You're thinking like a reporter," Tyner admonished. "Or a state's attorney. It's not your job to solve this case or poke holes in my theories. All you have to do is help me gather enough information so I can go into a courtroom in four or five months and create a reasonable doubt about Rock's opportunity. Unfortunately, thanks to you, his motive is all too strong, so we're going to have to downplay that part of it. I want you to interview the security guard and the custodian as soon as possible. The security guard first—he's more important, as he's the one who puts Rock there at ten o'clock. I'll tell you later if there's anyone else worth checking out. By the way, it would help if you looked like a grown-up. Why don't you cut off that horse's tail hanging out of the back of your head?''

"No!" It was Rock, not Tess, who yelled. Tess wore her hair long because it required less work. She had no sentiment about it. Rock obviously did.

"Then put it up. Wear a suit," Tyner said. "Usually a criminal lawyer has to make his client over, not his assistant."

"Your assistant? Excuse me, Tyner, but am I actually getting paid for this? I haven't heard anyone mention money."

"Yes. You get to keep the money Rock paid you for your initial 'investigation.' But I think your fees are a bit high, so you're starting with a debit of twenty hours. After you put in those twenty, I'll pay you twenty dollars per hour and twenty-five cents a mile."

Shit, Tess thought. She'd have to work ten hours just to buy a suit.

"As for you," Tyner said, turning to Rock. "No interviews. Stay away from Ava, at least for now. And, since you've already taken the day off from work, I think you should go straight to the boat house for a long workout. Do some drills, then go to the fort and back, with some pyramids thrown in for good measure. The Charles will come up before your trial, and I'm going to make sure you're there."

A lawyer cum rowing coach. Maybe Rock had hired the right guy. Not many other attorneys in town knew the fall rowing schedule, or how to train for a head race. If only Tyner felt so kindly toward *her*.

Chapter 8

The security guard, Joey Dumbarton, lived in a part of Baltimore sometimes called Little Appalachia, a valley catching the overflow from the already marginal neighborhoods to either side. Rickety row houses spilled down the slope on the eastern edge of Jones Falls, then went halfway back up Television Hill before petering out. It was one of Baltimore's rare all-white enclaves, and the residents were determined to keep it that way.

Joey greeted Tess at the door of his Formstone row house in a pair of cutoff sweatpants drooping over black bicycle shorts, topped off by an old robe that appeared to have started its life as bright red terry cloth. Now it was dull, the color of dried blood, and the material was flat and matted, like a dog that needed a bath. Since Tess had called in advance, she assumed this was how Joey dressed to meet all his guests.

He did seem delighted to have a visitor, offering her soda and beer, then leading her by the hand up two flights of stairs to his bedroom on the third floor.

"This place is going to be be-you-tiful," Joey told her as they climbed. "We have big plans for this house."

Plans appeared to be all they had. On the first two floors studs waited for drywall, wires hung loose, and plaster dust caked every surface. There was no kitchen as far as Tess could see, and a glimpse of the doorless bathroom convinced her to control her bladder by whatever means necessary.

Once in his bedroom, Joey sat on a bare mattress, too big for the fitted sheet someone had tried to stretch across it. It appeared to be the only piece of furniture in the room, but Tess couldn't be sure. A chair, a sofa, even a breakfront could have been hidden beneath the mounds of dirty clothes scattered across every square foot of floor space. She was ankle deep in underwear.

"Siddown," said Joey the affable host, patting a spot of mattress next to him. He was a pale, colorless man. Only a hint of yellow touched his hair, lashes, and skin; his eyes were flat gray. Tess preferred to stand, but mindful of Tyner's admonition to ingratiate herself, she perched on the corner of the bed, tensing her leg muscles so she didn't make contact with the bare mattress. The gray skirt of her new suit, a consignment find that didn't quite fit, slid halfway up her thighs.

"As I told you on the phone last night, I need to ask a few questions about Michael Abramowitz's murder," she began. "This is just an interview, sort of a predeposition if you will. No big deal."

"You know, murder is really a legal term," Joey said. "You should say homicide. Or slaying, maybe. That's a word the newspaper really likes—slaying."

Great, Joey the security guard was going to instruct her in legal nuance. "Are you studying to be a lawyer?"

"Naw, but I was an extra on 'Homicide' last season. And I watch those real cop shows. You know, those shows where they arrest people on camera? They're very educational."

"Yeah, they're really good." Tess had never seen the kind of show he described, but she had an idea of how they worked. She leaned toward him, trying to yank down her skirt as she did. "If you were on one of those shows, what would they want to know from Joey Dumbarton, perhaps the key witness in the murder—the *slaying*—of Michael Abramowitz?"

"OK, right, I know this," Joey said, as if surprised by a

pop quiz. He liked the idea of himself as the star witness. Tess thought he might.

"I would say"—he looked past her left shoulder, as if staring into a camera, as if he had been waiting much of his young life to look into a camera—"I would say, 'I'll never forget that night. The O's were whompin' on the A's. I had my little radio on, listening to the game, and I could hear the fans yelling over at Camden Yards. Then, at ten o'clock—and I know it was ten 'cause I marked it on my sheet—a white male, about thirty years old, six feet tall, and maybe two hundred pounds, came in, looking anxious and dis-drawed.' "

"Disdrawed?"

"Dis-strawed. You know, all upset. The white male was known to me as one Darryl Paxton, the boyfriend of one Ava Hill, also known to me, as she works in my building, often stays late, and is very good-looking. I let him upstairs without calling up, as he frequently came by for Miss Hill. About ten-fifteen, he ran out. I noticed 'cause I had to mark it on the sheet. I started to yell after him, but I figured he had a fight with his girlfriend, so I just wrote it in for him." He dropped his television face and voice. "How's that?"

"Great," Tess said, giving him her warmest smile. "I just want to go over a few things."

"Have at me."

"You were very specific about the time. Do you wear a watch? Or is there a clock you can see from the desk?"

"I wear four watches, two on each wrist. Eastern, central, mountain, and western."

"Pacific."

"No, ma'am. Just the four. I don't have Tokyo time. I like things nice and even, you know, two on each wrist."

She let that pass. "So you checked eastern time, and it was ten exactly when Rock arrived. Did you check your watch the second he left, or did you get distracted? Maybe the game got exciting and you didn't write it down for a few minutes."

"Uh-huh. I'm very attentive. I take my job seriously. A

lot of guys, they become security guards 'cause they can't find no other kind of work. I'm proud to be one of Miltie's Minutemen.'' Tess gave him a blank look. ''That's who staffs the Lambrecht Building. Miltie's Minutemen. Best security force in town. No felons on our staff.''

Tess was tempted to ask if this was Miltie's motto, but she didn't want Joey tearing off on another tangent. ''So you're sure of the time. What about after Rock—Mr. Paxton—left? Did anyone else come in?''

''There's no one on the sheet.''

''Does that mean no one else came in?''

''There's no one on the sheet,'' he repeated. Tess had a feeling one of Uncle Miltie's knights had a little chink in his armor. She stared into his colorless eyes, trying to muster the authority of a video camera.

''What about someone who worked there? Or someone who didn't follow the rules, who just ran by you?''

''People who work there can come in the back way with a key, go straight to the elevators. I don't even *see* them. But there's no one else—''

''On the sheet. I know. Look, Joey, I'm sure you're a good Minuteman. I don't want to get you in trouble with Miltie. But if someone ran by you—didn't listen to you, sneaked by when you were listening to the game—I need to know. Maybe that's the person who killed Michael Abramowitz.''

He shook his head. ''I do my job right.''

''Could someone get by you?'' she pressed. ''Maybe if you walked away from the desk to see what was going on in the street? Don't you stretch out or sneak a bathroom break without anyone there to spell you?''

''I told'ja. No one got in. Everyone signs the sheet.''

She sighed and gave him one of the business cards Tyner had gotten for her, a rush job from a printer who owed him a favor. The card simply said: *Tess Monaghan* and listed her number at the bookstore and her home number. Plain and stark, the cards had a certain dignity. They made Tess feel downright legitimate.

''Which of these is a home number?'' Joey asked with

great interest. Wonderful—the only thing Tess was going to get out of this was unwanted calls from a horny security guard.

"Both are business numbers. Call if you mean business." She left Joey on his unmade bed, his red robe the only color in the dim room. She hoped one of those reality shows came calling one day. He was a natural.

It was about eight miles from Joey's rundown row house to the West Baltimore home of Frank Miles, the custodian who had discovered Abramowitz's body. Statistically it was a more dangerous place—a once-middle-class neighborhood, undone by white flight, further undone by black flight. But Tess felt comfortable here. She had grown up not far away, a straight shot down Edmondson Avenue. If a place had been safe in her lifetime, she had trouble thinking of it as dangerous.

By the look of things Frank Miles was the only nonrenter left on his block. His house had metal awnings and freshly painted trim. The tiny lawn was a thick green mat, bordered with pink and white impatiens, showing surprising staying power for September. A pedestal with a shiny green gazing globe sat in the exact center of the emerald lawn. It reminded Tess of the glass globe the witch consulted in *The Wizard of Oz,* but all she could see in it was her own distorted face.

When she rang the bell Mr. Miles yanked the door open as if wild with impatience to see her, grabbed her arm, and hustled her past the storm door and heavy wooden door, putting the chain on behind her.

"Not a good idea to linger in open doors on this block," he said. "You don't want to be a mushroom. Would you like a glass of lemonade?"

A little dazed, she accepted it gratefully, sure she need not fear the bathroom here. The house, like the yard, was neat and orderly, although it bore the traces of a man on his own. The screen on the old television was streaky, and a fine coating of dust settled over everything, the kind of dust most men can't see. The framed photographs on the wall had been hung meticulously but were smeary with fingerprints. Mr.

Miles and a woman on their wedding day, lots of children, a girl in a graduation gown. Widower, she guessed. And probably the most eligible man in his church, judging by his casserole-laden girth.

"I like my cookies," he said, and Tess jumped, wondering if he had caught her staring at his waistline. Then she realized he was carrying a tray with a pitcher of lemonade and a plate of Hydroxes. Her favorite. There were mint leaves swirling in the lemonade pitcher and she knew from the taste of it—tart, perfect—that he had made it himself, probably just for her.

"I don't get much company," he said. "It's nice to fuss over someone."

"What about those fine-looking young people in those pictures? Don't your grandkids come visit?"

"No grandkids," he said with a regretful sigh. "No *kids*. Most of those on the wall are from a school where I worked before I retired. I got a niece, but she's just an ol' crackhead. Yeah, she'd love to come around, but she'd have this place turned into a shooting gallery in about two minutes. No, thank you."

"I know that feeling," said Tess, who didn't. She was wondering how to steer this aimless conversation into a detailed discussion about finding a corpse. Mr. Miles seemed to be having such a good time. For every Hydrox she ate, he ate four.

"But you want to know about the other night," he said, again seeming to follow her unvoiced thoughts. "About Mr. Abramowitz."

"Yes. I know you talked to the police, but I want to go over a few details. The security guard called 911 at ten thirty-five after he got your call from the office phone. Did you call him the second you found the body?"

"I doubt if more than twenty seconds passed. I couldn't help looking, you know. There's something about a body that stops you cold. And I tried to find a pulse before I called anybody."

"Do you usually clean Mr. Abramowitz's office? Did you know him very well?"

"I steered clear of him. When he stayed late it was usually for ball games. He didn't want anyone coming in to empty the trash. He told me to stay out of his office."

"So why did you go in that night?"

"The door was open. And I could see something—maybe his leg, I don't know. Something wasn't right."

"And that was what time?"

"I don't have a watch." He flashed a bare wrist at her. "You say the call to 911 was at ten something. I guess I found him no more than a few minutes before then. And I stayed until someone came."

"At ten forty-seven. That's what the EMS log says."

He shrugged. "If that's what the records say. I'll tell you, it seemed longer. It's not much fun, keeping vigil over a dead man."

"How long had you been on the eighteenth floor? Did you see anyone else around?"

"I start at the top and work down. I probably got to their floor about ten-twenty, and I'm pretty sure I had the place to myself. Their office takes up everything, so there's no other place to go."

Shit. The last thing they wanted was to narrow the window of opportunity, making it less likely someone other than Rock had killed Abramowitz. If Miles was right another killer, the *real* killer, had less than ten minutes to get in and out.

"How can you be so sure?" Tess asked, sliding into a harsh tone despite Tyner's warnings. "You said you don't wear a watch."

"I can't." He smiled sweetly. He probably thought this hilarious, Tess realized. On average there had been a murder a day in the city over the past year, many of them within a five-mile radius of where they sat. Drug dealers may have shot innocent people on this very block. They called them mushrooms, because they seemed to sprout from the pavement. The dealers laughed about it. You can bet people didn't get arrested in those murders in less than an hour's time.

"Want to know something funny?" he asked suddenly. "When I saw him the first thing I thought was, 'Well, how am I supposed to get all that blood out of my carpet?' It sounds awful now, but at the time it was the most natural thing in the world. All I could do was think about that carpet. Do you think that makes me a bad person?"

He seemed to really care. She thought back to the dead bodies she had seen as a reporter. There had not been many. The first ones had been the two-dimensional bodies of three teenage girls who had tried to beat a train across an unmarked crossing out in the county. The body of a twenty-three-year-old at the morgue, blue as a raspberry-flavored Icee. He had dropped dead of a heart attack during a job interview, a medical examiner told Tess. Yes, she had seen dead bodies, but her job had been to organize their lives into neat, familiar formulas. Age, a pithy description—"popular cheerleader" had summed up the life of one of the train-flattened girls—school affiliations. Hobbies. Mr. Miles's preoccupation seemed healthier. But Tess didn't know how to tell him that.

"And you felt for his pulse, right? At the wrist, or the neck?"

"At his wrist. His neck was so . . . floppy. I tried to touch it, but it seemed like it might just fall off. I guess that boy must have hated him, to do him like that."

Tess couldn't let that pass. "We're not so sure he did, Mr. Miles. Kill him, I mean. He very well may have hated him, but I don't think Rock—Mr. Paxton—killed him."

He smiled. "That's *right*, Miss Monaghan. Innocent before proven guilty, that's what they say. I tell you, though, I wouldn't begrudge him a bit. I heard on the news at noon that Mr. Abramowitz may have been bugging that boy's girlfriend. A jury hears that, I wouldn't be surprised if he walked. That's not right, what that man did. He was a bad man."

Great. Television had the Ava angle, if not her name. The

police must have leaked a few details this morning, feeling expansive after making a quick arrest. And if TV had that much, the newspaper would want more. Tess knew by the time the morning newspaper came out, Baltimore could know how many silver fillings Ava had in her mouth, and if they tingled when she ate frozen yogurt.

The Hydrox cookies were gone, and even the affable Mr. Miles seemed ready for the visit to end. Tess drove home, thinking about what a wonderful witness he would make for the prosecution and listening to an intriguing noise in her engine. It sounded like a $200 noise. If she was lucky she might break even after all this.

Home. She took the back stairs, ducking Kitty. She'd want a complete rehash of the day. Tess just wanted to transcribe her tapes and written notes for Tyner, then sit on the floor of the shower and let the hot water beat on her.

But she had company—the kind of company who lets himself in with his own key, strips down to his underwear, and crawls beneath the covers. Jonathan Ross had come to call.

Chapter 9

Jonathan Ross had seemed shockingly original to Tess once, but she soon learned every newspaper had a Jonathan Ross. Someone who covers cops, and wants to be a cop, too, dressing like the television version of an undercover vice detective—longish hair, a leather thong at the neck with a charm dangling from it, a diamond stud in one ear. Someone who lards his stories with unnamed officials and "sources close to the investigation." Someone who speaks in the latest street slang, and almost pulls it off. Some of these guys were heroes, some jokes. In his time Jonathan had managed to be a little of both, but his star was rising and fewer people were laughing. Tess still laughed, one reason he kept coming around. She knew him when. They had started out together on the *Star*—her first job, his first big-city gig.

Back then, all of four years ago, they had something called a relationship, complete with dreary late-night arguments that were always about the same thing: What was the point of being together if you knew one day you were going to be apart? They had broken up when the paper folded, a time when a lot of people seemed to be leaving Tess behind, as if her joblessness might be contagious. Then, about a year ago, his latest relationship heading into deeper waters, Jonathan popped up again. Tess became his shield against the new woman. He came, he went, he never called. Tess told herself she didn't care. She preferred it this way, she told others. Jonathan was just another piece of fitness equipment, her home gym. She tried not to think about his girlfriend, and if she did she shrugged and thought: *Well, I was there first.*

From her bed, Jonathan asked, as he always did: "Still got that body?"

Tess replied, as tradition required: "I don't know. Let me take my clothes off and check." She did.

"That body." Her shape had not changed since she was fifteen, when her mother declared it obscene and began the struggle to keep it from public view. Tess, naturally modest, immediately became an exhibitionist, running around in the tiniest two-piece bathing suits she could find. To her surprise this was a much better way to get boyfriends than hitting home runs over their heads and skimming hard red rubber balls off their backs in dodgeball. She had been a popular teenager.

"What are you working on?" Tess asked not much later, grabbing beers from her refrigerator and carrying them back to bed. "I don't recall seeing your name in the paper for a while." She always pretended to have missed his byline, no matter how prominent.

Jonathan didn't bother to remind her he had been splashed across page one just yesterday, with the story on Abramowitz's death. Disdainful of any story reported and written in less than six weeks, he pitched in on dailies only when his sources gave him something too juicy to waste. Productivity cheapened a man, Jonathan liked to say.

"I've been following some guys on Death Row. Ever since Thanos was put to death, they've started feeling like they might really go. You know, some of them have been there forever, long enough to forget they're supposed to be executed. They don't feel so complacent anymore."

"I can't see how his case affects these guys, if they're not begging to die. The law hasn't changed."

"But the appeals have to run out eventually," Jonathan insisted. "Thanos will open—"

"The floodgates? Let me guess—your nut graph is already

written. Your *whole* story is already written.'' She spoke into her beer bottle as if it were a microphone, putting on the officious voice of a newscaster. "We begin with three moving paragraphs on one inmate—'John Smith sits in his cell on Maryland's Death Row, counting down the two hundred forty days left in his appeal'—a little background on Thanos, woven seamlessly in, and then, whammo! The obligatory fourth graph nut, which reads: 'Inmates on Death Row believe Thanos's execution opened the floodgates for a rash of executions in Maryland, where a complicated appeals process once made Death Row a misnomer.' ''

"Bitch," Jonathan said, but there was no edge to it. As an excommunicated journalist, Tess could get away with mocking him. "Not bad, though. Maybe I'll steal it.''

His beeper went off and Jonathan lunged for the phone. The city desk. "No. No. Hey, I'm *trying*. No.'' He winked at Tess. "I'm working on that right *now*.'' Then he put down the phone, pulled her on top of him and started over, taking his time. Better, Tess thought, much better.

Later, the room dark, six empty bottles of Molson on the bedside table, Jonathan hooked his fingers in Tess's unbraided hair and said: "So you know this Darryl Paxton guy, don't you? One of your rowing buddies?''

Tess freed her hair and slid across the bed, trying to put as much distance between them as she could find on the full-size mattress. "You still working that story?''

"Not officially.'' He was cool, not at all embarrassed. That was one thing about Jonathan. His unabashed ambition, his sheer candor about his motives, made his manipulation and callousness almost charming.

"But you could be, if you got some wonderful stuff, I suppose.'' Tess was determined to be as cool as he was, a poker face. "Sorry. I don't have any wonderful stuff.''

"You know something, though,'' he wheedled. "Maybe a little bit more about the motive? Everyone knows it was over a woman, but we don't have any specifics. Did Abramowitz make a pass at her? Was he doing her?''

"Can't help you, Jonathan.''

"A name."

"No."

"A great detail—one fabulous detail no one else has. Something about Paxton. Does he have a ferocious temper? Maybe a history of punching people who piss him off? Where's he from originally? I could work sources, see if he had a history as a juvie."

Tess sat still. She wouldn't even shake her head yes or no.

"We could go with the angle on Paxton hiring an ex–Olympic rower to defend him, and getting a rowing buddy to help investigate the case." He smiled, not very pleasantly. "Oh yeah. I called Joey Dumbarton today to see what else he knew. He's a good guy, gave me the tip about the sign-in sheet. But he had already talked to someone today and was tired of being bugged. He called you a babe, by the way."

"Well, that's the only reason I'm doing this, to meet eligible men."

"The rowing angle could make your friend look stupid. Irrational."

Tess shrugged. It was good for a paragraph. Not even Jonathan could build it into an entire story.

He got up, pulling on his clothes. "I would have come by anyway. I missed you. Missed that body. No hard feelings?"

"Jonathan, if I was going to have hard feelings over any rude, insensitive behavior I suffered at your hands, I'd have turned into a pillar of salt a long time ago."

"That's not why Lot's wife turned into a pillar of salt. She turned back to look at Sodom. As a Catholic-Jew, you should at least know the Old Testament."

"I'm not a Catholic-Jew. I'm nothing, not even an atheist. Just nothing."

"Have it your way." He kissed her neck. "See you later, nothing."

"Whenever. You better get home. Isn't it almost time for bed check?"

She knew almost nothing about his girlfriend, not even her name. Some girl he had gone to high school with down in the Washington suburbs. Probably rich, if she even existed. Sometimes Tess wasn't sure. If she did exist she might as well get used to Jonathan cheating on her. For a good story Jonathan Ross would crawl in with anybody.

Tess's Toyota ended up behind Rock's bicycle on Light Street the next morning. She chased him along Hanover Street and down Waterview to the boat house. The attendant was missing in action again, so Rock unlocked the door with his key.

"Catch you on the flip side," he said to Tess. To get to the exercise room and the stairs beyond, one had to pass through the men's or ladies' locker rooms. Tess threw her keys in an empty locker, stopping to examine her face in the long mirror. Gray, a little puffy under the eyes, as she always was at 6 A.M. Jonathan's visit hadn't left any unusual marks. She pushed through the swinging door into the small anteroom, crammed with weights and Concept II ergometers. Rowing machines to laymen. Torture devices to Tess.

Rock was staring out the window to the west.

"Downpour in fifteen minutes," he said authoritatively, like some movie Indian predicting a herd's movement by pressing his ear to the ground. Tess thought the clouds were the kind that burned off with the rising sun, but she didn't care enough to argue.

"Good," she said. "It's God's way of telling me to go back to bed."

"How about a challenge on the erg? A five-thousand-meter piece?"

"Terms?"

"Breakfast for the one who comes closest to his personal best."

"Above or below?"

"Right. If I come in ten seconds over my best time, and you're nine over, you win."

"Assuming I'd take this bet, what's your personal best for five thousand? Mine is . . . twenty-two minutes."

"You're such a liar. I was here the day you did sub-twenty-one and threw up on your shoes."

"OK, twenty-one minutes and thirty seconds for my mark. But don't forget I've seen you do five thousand in eighteen."

"You're on."

Tess set the distance on the erg and strapped her feet into the blocks. Despite her height she had to stretch to reach the wooden pull bar, worn smooth by rowers' rough hands. The bar was attached to a chain, the chain connected to a large flywheel. She slid the bicycle-like seat to the top of the metal shaft, knees bent, her right arm between her legs, her left arm outside, head down. At Rock's signal she pulled the bar into her rib cage, sliding back, then up, and the meters started clicking by on the odometer. But as fast as the meters went by, the seconds flew faster.

The erg, unlike most exercise machines, measured how hard one worked, precisely the reason Tess loathed it. Unlike a stair-climber, on which she could lock her arms and spare her legs, or a stationary bike on which she could ease up for a few miles, the erg knew if she was trying. Pull hard and efficiently, and the meters mounted up. A fast stroke rate—the number of pulls per minute—wouldn't fool the machine, not if there was no power behind the strokes.

The digital readout said her stroke rate was twenty-five per minute, her five hundred-meter time just over 2:10. Tess closed her eyes and settled in this groove, simulating a head race, powering on and off, barely aware of Rock at her side, locked in his own fantasy race. She was on the Chester River now, eyes fixed on the bony spine and white neck of the team's stroke, Whitney Talbot.

Tess opened her eyes. The first 2,500 meters had clocked in at 9:35, but she knew she could never keep up a sub-twenty-minute pace. She backed off, cruising on the strength of her legs. All she had to do was try. Rock was going to buy her breakfast no matter what. She would shock him, shock everyone in Jimmy's by ordering something completely different. Fried eggs. Scrapple.

Thinking about food actually increased her speed. If she

could pull the last 500 in under two minutes, it would be a personal best for her. Rock was partially right, her previous best was 21:02; only it had been *his* shoes she had vomited on. Only a good friend could forget that salient detail. Pulling at full power for fifty strokes, she began to feel the dizzying nausea of a race. Nothing was like this—not a hard run, not benching 100 pounds, not even throwing one's self at a heavy bag, something she did when the seedy little boxing gym in her neighborhood was empty. Her calves ached, her stomach hovered dangerously near her throat, her forearms burned, her skin felt as if it might fly off. She had nothing left, yet she had to find more. With one final, wrenching pull, she traveled her last ten meters: 20:55, seven seconds off her best time. She let go of the bar and put her head between her knees, gasping and heaving.

"You win," Rock said.

Tess shook her head, unable to speak. Rock had finished aeons ago. Even when he tried to handicap a race for her sake, his competitive nature took over and he won. She lifted her head to read the figures on his clock: 18:30. Possibly a personal worst for Rock, at least thirty seconds off his best.

"I guess I'm a little distracted," he apologized. "But I'm proud of you, Tess. You really pushed today."

She smiled weakly and struggled to her feet. Her legs buckled and she had to lean over, hands propped above her knees, to keep from falling down. Her breath came in ragged, panting gasps. Her brain was forming words, but her mouth refused to say them. It wanted only to gulp down air.

Rock held a plastic wastebasket up to her chin and placed his hand on the back of her neck. "Don't hold it down. It feels better to let it go." Her stomach was empty, so all she produced was a thin, clear drool, like a dog that had been eating grass. Rock wiped her face with the tail of his sweat-drenched T-shirt, then helped her to the room's one chair, massaging her calves after she sat down.

It was strange to have a man move his hands along her body and feel nothing, no sexual tingle. It had always been this way with Rock. They were too large, she thought, almost freakish together, to even think about being a couple. Apparently he thought so, too: His occasional girlfriends had all been tiny, although none so tiny as Ava. So there was no subtext, no tension as he rubbed Tess's legs. How different things might be if there had been. No Ava. No dead Abramowitz. *Not free to choose*, Tess thought wryly, *but free to fall*. And, oh, had they fallen.

"You're good to me, Rock."

"Well, you're good to me, too."

"No. I—I screwed things up. I got in over my head, and I dragged you in with me."

"It was my idea, remember? Don't listen to Tyner, Tess. God knows, I don't."

Now was the time to confess, to tell him how she had manipulated him, tried to manipulate Ava, tried to arrange things so she could take his check without breaking his heart. She said nothing.

Suddenly the rain Rock had predicted began in earnest, a heavy, lashing downpour, with flashes of lightning. If he hadn't warned her she would have been on the water by now, far enough out to be in real danger. In a storm like this it was risky to ride it out, equally risky to try to make it back to the boat house.

"Let's go watch from the front," Rock said. "I like thunderstorms."

They left through their respective dressing rooms, meeting in the large hall that ran the length of the building's north side. Although this room was decorated with plaques, photographs, and etchings of rowers and their shells, real rowers seldom ventured into it. The city rented it out every weekend for wedding receptions, bar mitzvahs, and banquets. A plain room, it was in demand only because of its sweeping view of the Patapsco and the city beyond—Camden Yards, the three large gas tanks that rose and fell depending on the city's natural gas supply, downtown's ragged skyline. The view was better at night, all white lights and silhouettes.

"Maybe lightning will strike the IBM building," Tess

said, referring to a white skyscraper usually listed among the city's top ten architectural offenses.

"Or the Maryland National Bank tower," Rock said. "Excuse me, the NationsBank tower. I still can't get used to that, this North Carolina company owning Maryland's biggest bank."

"Hey, I haven't gotten used to Friendship Airport becoming Baltimore-Washington International, and that must have happened over twenty-five years ago."

"Sometimes I think Baltimore is a city that defines itself by what's gone, what used to be."

"Well, the *Star* is a parking lot across from Harborplace."

"The Colts—the Ravens can't make up for losing Johnny Unitas's team."

"Hutzler's department store is the Department of Human Resources."

"McCormick moved to the suburbs, so there's no more cinnamon smell drifting over the harbor."

"And the flea market at the old Edmondson Drive-In is a Home Depot now.

This was how they spoke: They built lists together, stacks of loosely related facts. Tess did not know if this was a generally masculine way of speaking, or a style specific to Rock. At any rate, she liked it.

He looked over the water, watching the lightning strike. Tess looked at him, remembering Jonathan's questions. *Where was he from? Does he have a history of assaulting people?* She knew only that he wasn't born here, although he had been in Baltimore long enough to consider it home. Their friendship was built on the present, and they seldom spoke of the past. Tess had assumed this was how men became friends—through activities, innocuous riffing and banter, sports scores. *How 'bout them O's?* She liked it. Besides, Baltimore was filled with people who knew her life story. It had been a relief to find a friend who wanted to talk about nothing more than current events, or whether antioxidants boosted performance.

The storm was moving east. Tess could have taken a

crayon and drawn a line straight up the floor-to-ceiling windows. To the right of the line the sky would be black, shot through with lightning; the left was washed-out and clear. An eerie sight, this black and white Baltimore. She slipped her hand into Rock's. Nothing about Tess was dainty, but her hands were especially large, with ragged nails and a rower's calluses. Rock's hand was larger and rougher still. She liked him for that, too. Folding her hand inside his, he squeezed gently. He did know his strength, how to be gentle, how to curb his power. But he had to think about it, Tess realized. He had to try.

Chapter 10

Whitney—former college roommate, sometime best friend, sometime toughest competitor—called at nine that morning, when Tess had finally started to transcribe her tapes and notes. She was grateful for the distraction. She could have written a news story or a press release about her meetings with Dumbarton and Miles, but a report was a foreign form to her. Did one include everything, or edit judiciously? Could she record her own impressions, or did objectivity rule here, too? Hopelessly blocked, she lunged for the phone.

"Word is, you had another Jonathan encounter," Whitney said by way of greeting.

Tess sighed. "I bet he came into work this morning and sent an electronic message to everyone on the *Beacon-Light* computer system: 'Tess Monaghan will sleep with you, but she won't tell you anything.' "

"No, but he did stage one of his special scenes for my benefit, pacing madly around his desk when I walked by, complaining loudly to the city editor about how 'she' wouldn't leak. Lovely imagery."

"I don't leak. It's one of my best qualities."

"Why don't you meet me for lunch at the Tate—on the paper, of course. I can always claim I was wooing a recalcitrant source. But I'm leaving if you start to leak. Or even ooze. I've had enough dates like that recently. It's like a science fiction novel. All they leave behind are little puddles.''

''Talk about lovely imagery. Noon?''

''Twelve-fifteen. If I'm late order me a crab cake and coleslaw. The patty, not the sandwich. Broiled, not fried.'' Whitney never meant to sound imperious, but certain tones came naturally to a Talbot.

The last name was pronounced not like the chain of preppy clothing stores but like the Eastern Shore county where Whitney's family summered. ''Tall, but.'' Tess had been struck by Whitney's drawling rendition of her name when they met freshman year in college. ''Whitney Tall-but,'' she said, squeezing Tess's hand quite hard, as if to measure her strength. Tess squeezed back, staring skeptically at this fabulous creature—straight blond hair, narrow green eyes, long bones, and a jaw so sharp she could have cut cheese with it. *I can like this woman or hate her,* Tess told herself, *but I'll never be indifferent to her.* She decided to like her. It was a decision she seldom regretted.

Still, they could never stop competing. Whitney was the best rower, Tess the strongest. Whitney was rich and thin, Tess wild and impulsive. In the classroom they fought for top honors and dreamed of the Sophie Kerr prize, a no-strings endowment granted to the school's best writer. Whitney took herself out of the running, transferring to Yale to major in Japanese. Tess lost the Kerr prize to a quiet, long-haired young man she had never noticed.

Maybe I chose wrong that day, Tess thought as she waited for Whitney in the Tate's fusty dining room. *Maybe I should hate her after all.*

''If I ever pay for lunch, can we go someplace decent?'' Tess asked when Whitney finally arrived. ''You Wasps have the worst taste buds in the world.''

''This is the perfect comfort food. Iceberg lettuce with bottled thousand island dressing. Macaroni and cheese. Go up the street''—Whitney pointed with her cameo-perfect chin to the nearby Tuscany Grille, currently Baltimore's trendiest restaurant—''and it's food miscegenation. Pistachios and mint jelly. Fajitas with leeks. Goat cheese and peanut butter. Give me a break."

"Miscegenation," Tess mused. "That's not a word you hear much these days."

"Keep reading the *Beacon-Light*. I think they're going to ask me to write an editorial against it next week." She took a sip of iced tea—presweetened, and overly so—and sighed as if it were pure nectar. The old women in the dining room gazed approvingly at the young woman with her blond hair twisted into a soft chignon, her elegant frame encased in a sea green knit dress from Jones & Jones. Whitney's taste was everywhere but in her mouth, Tess marveled, although she did have a nose for fine whiskey. Even in college she had preferred good Scotch, and she had been almost tiresome in her quest for the Eastern Shore's best martini.

Without a trace of self-consciousness, Whitney rapped a spoon against the glass, as if calling a meeting to order. After all, she came from a long line of garden club presidents. The North Side Chapter of the Washington College Alumnae Fund was now convened. Any old business? No. Any new business? Yes, ruthless prying.

"So, what's up with your new career, whatever it is. Private investigator? Paralegal? And working on one of the hottest cases in town. Tell all."

This was Whitney's style, straight up the middle, but Tess had eleven years of experience deflecting Whitney's frontal assaults. "Are you asking me as a friend or as a *Beacon-Light* employee? Either way I can't tell you much. I'm working for his lawyer. Everything I know is confidential."

"Fair enough. What about the rumor that you caused it all, telling your friend Rock that his girlfriend was cheating on him?"

Her casually inaccurate version of events stung. Obviously Whitney had done more than just eavesdrop on Jonathan's conversation with an editor.

"You know, this is the second time in two days a *Beacon-Light* employee has tried to chat me up on this. Don't you have any other ways of getting information?"

" 'Chat you up.' That's an interesting term for Jonathan's method of information gathering. Did you do a lot of 'chatting' last night?"

Working on the editorial page had sharpened Whitney's mind and coarsened her feelings, so she treated every subject as theoretical and abstract. Devil's advocate? Whitney could have been the devil's *mentor*.

"Stop *milking* me," Tess said. "I told you I can't talk about the case, and I can't."

"Oh, Tesser—" Whitney was truly contrite. "I didn't come here to milk you. In fact I'm going to feed you. I just thought I could have some fun first. When did you get so damn prickly?"

She took a manila folder out of her briefcase and dropped it on the table with a heavy plop. Photocopies and clippings about Michael Abramowitz spilled out. Computer printouts of recent news stories, photographs, a résumé, biographical information. Only the *Beacon-Light*'s library, off-limits to civilians such as Tess, could have provided this treasure trove.

"I glanced at the stuff after one of the librarians pulled all the material for me," Whitney said. "Nothing jumped out, although he was quite the controversial little public defender before he went into business for himself. Recently he's been in chin-and-grin mode, trotting around town in a rented tux."

Tess extracted a glossy black-and-white of Abramowitz from last year's Black-Eyed Susan Ball. He stared dutifully at the camera, drink in hand, his narrow shoulders lost inside his tuxedo. She didn't need Whitney's eye to see it was a rental, and a particularly ill fitting one at that. Thin women in ugly dresses, the kind that cost more than pretty ones, stood on either side of him, faces forward but bodies angled away, as if embarrassed to be seen with the once notorious lawyer.

"Interesting—but I'm not sure what to do with all this. Tyner has defined my role in the case pretty narrowly."

"Balls." Whitney's voice was only a shade below a

hoarse cry. Luckily most of the women who lunched at the Tate were too vain to wear hearing aids, so they continued to steal fond looks at the elegant young woman. *Why can't our granddaughters be so ladylike?* they asked one another. "OK, I confess: Jonathan told me you were working for Tyner. Interviewing security guards and custodians—*too* boring. You need to start tracking down anyone who's ever held a grudge against Abramowitz. It shouldn't be hard. He was a world-class shit who defended scum. Then he was a world-class shit who helped scum sue scum. He ended up defending an asbestos company, scum par excellence. There should be no shortage of people who loathed him."

"Yes, but Tyner said—"

"*Tyner said.* Since when do you give a fuck what anyone tells you to do? When did you become this cautious little mouse, waiting for permission all the time, terrified to take the initiative on something?"

Direct hit.

"I became a cautious little mouse, to use your perfect phrase, at precisely the same moment I realized my last fling with initiative may have inspired one of my dearest friends to kill someone. You see, the grapevine has it more or less right, Whitney. I got Rock's fiancée to confess to him she was sleeping with her boss. I thought he would break up with her, not break the guy's neck."

"Do you think he did it?"

"He says he didn't, and he's not a liar. But if he had been angry enough . . ." Tess didn't want to finish her own thought.

"I remember him from some of the races." Whitney hadn't kept up with her own rowing, but she still attended the big events. "He struck me as one of those guys so immense and strong he has to be gentle, or else he'd destroy everything in his path."

"Like Lennie in *Of Mice and Men.*"

"Exactly."

"There's only one problem with that comparison, Whitney. Lennie had a bad habit of breaking people's necks by accident.''

Back home, Tess changed into a T-shirt and shorts and turned on her stereo. Although she had a CD player, she owned almost no compact discs—she had signed on to the technology revolution about a month before the *Star* folded. By financial necessity she listened primarily to the albums and tapes of her college days. Alternative stations kept her current with new music, but she found herself more interested in old music: Cole Porter, Johnny Mercer, Rodgers and Hart. All the standards, except Irving Berlin. She had been forced to play the Statue of Liberty in eighth grade and never quite gotten over ''Give me your tired . . .'' And one of the immigrants had pinched her ass.

The Abramowitz file was a mix of old and new technologies. Photocopies of old clips, printouts from microfiche, the computerized printouts of a Nexis search, which scanned a national data base of newspapers. The *Beacon-Light* librarian had even found a fawning profile of him in the city magazine, a deservedly defunct rag called *B-more*.

Her desk was too small to hold these riches. She spread the contents of the folder across the floor, separating the clips and photos into three piles representing the distinct phases of his career. Public defender. Plaintiff's attorney. Corporate.

The first phase of his career seemed the most promising, given that many of the people he defended had already either killed or raped someone. Tess knew a disgruntled defendant was much more likely to track down his own lawyer than a prosecutor or a judge. After all, the prosecution is supposed to put you away, and the judge is just following a rule book, but your lawyer is paid to put up a good fight. Even if it's not your nickel, as in the case of Abramowitz's early clients, one expects to get his money's worth. As a reporter Tess once saw a nineteen-year-old react to a guilty verdict for manslaughter by grabbing his P.D. by the back of the neck and methodically pounding her head against the table until the bailiff intervened.

But Abramowitz's clients, at least the ones who made the papers, seemed to adore him. The stories about him as a public defender stressed his heroics. He had won three out of the seven death penalty cases he tried, which made his early reputation, but that accomplishment had faded with time. In fact, the state's attorney's office seldom went for the death penalty in Baltimore any more.

Cop Killer Goes Free on Technicality. Tess remembered that case. The ''technicality'' had been an illegal search and seizure, that pesky fourth amendment thing. Abramowitz had been vilified for his unapologetic defense of Donald Bates, who in all probability *was* a cop killer, but the state failed to prove it when the judge excluded key evidence from the trial. Bates ended up dying two years later, shot to death by a cop answering a call for a domestic dispute. Interestingly there had been no record of the 911 call summoning the cop to the scene, but no one had pressed the issue. Bates would have lived longer, much longer, on Death Row.

Tess jotted down the name of the cop who had killed Bates, and the names of the relatives of the cop who had been killed. It had been twelve years ago, but time passed differently for some people. Again, Tess wrote down the names of the victims' relatives.

Abramowitz's losses were more interesting, but men on Death Row seldom had the funds or mobility to pursue vendettas. And, again, none of Abramowitz's convicted clients seemed to bear him ill will. A photo of one showed him bear hugging the lawyer, while Abramowitz stared down at the floor, seemingly embarrassed by the show of affection and gratitude. Or perhaps he was pissed at losing, Tess thought.

Tucker Fauquier embraces his lawyer, Michael Abramowitz, moments after an Anne Arundel County jury returned a death sentence for the murder of Joey Little. It is expected Fauquier will now enter guilty pleas in the other murders of which he is suspected.

Tucker Fauquier. Tess remembered him. Anyone who had been alive in Maryland that year remembered him. Born in the western Maryland town of Friendsville, he had decided one day to work his way across the state by killing and sexually molesting a boy in each county. He was twenty-two when he began, venturing out to distant counties—Worcester, Cecil, Dorchester—where he would kidnap a boy, kill him, then bury him. At first he was careful, spacing out his visits, and law officials made no connection, not publicly. Baltimore, Prince George's, Calvert. But after six cautious years, Fauquier became bolder. He kidnapped a boy from his home county of Garrett, then went to Allegany where he procured another boy to witness the first boy's murder. Then from Allegany to Washington County, where a Hagerstown boy watched him kill the Allegany boy. And so on. He was halfway to his goal—twelve victims out of Maryland's twenty-four jurisdictions—when an Anne Arundel County boy, the latest witness and soon-to-be victim, leaped from the car as Fauquier slowed to pay the toll on the Bay Bridge.

Tess studied his picture. She had been in college at the height of Fauquier's spree and knew his name far better than his face. A slight man, with bad skin and straggly blond hair. He could have been anyone at the edge of one's life—a gas station attendant, convenience store clerk, pants presser at the dry cleaner's. Just one of those vague, blurry faces on which one never quite focuses. He had been lucky to have Abramowitz for his lawyer. His execution may not be the state's first in the modern era, but it would be the most eagerly anticipated.

Abramowitz's other losses in death penalty cases were less interesting. A robber, a rapist, another robber. *Rich man, poor man, beggar man, thief,* Tess thought to herself as she wrote down another group of names. The cases against them were notable only for the futility of presenting a defense at all.

As she moved forward through each year of clippings, Abramowitz seemed to disappear. Fauquier was his last big case. The murder trials on page one gave way to briefs, five-paragraph stories about sexual assault trials and what were known as misdemeanor murders—one lowlife killing another lowlife. Once Abramowitz left the public defender's office, his practice had been the kind of DWI/slip and fall/birth defects office that seldom draws any publicity, except for occasional editorials and columns decrying ambulance chasing and lawyer advertising. This second phase of his life had produced only one full-length clipping, a feature story about a rap song inspired by his instant camp commercials. "I'm highly flattered," Abramowitz had told the reporter.

At least half the file contained photographs of him at society events, most taken in the past year, perhaps part of a desperate attempt to make himself respectable. Abramowitz at the symphony, Abramowitz at a concert to benefit a local AIDS foundation, Abramowitz at the March of Dimes ball, Abramowitz at the United Way kickoff. He never seemed to have a date or a smile, and he was never photographed with anyone who really mattered, except for two pictures with his employer, the senior "O" at Triple O, Seamon P. O'Neal. In both of those, taken at fund-raisers for the foundation named for O'Neal's famous father-in-law, developer William Tree, Abramowitz's arm was slung around O'Neal's neck while O'Neal stared deeply into his cocktail glass, only the part in his hair visible. Abramowitz smiled broadly in these photos, obviously proud to be seen with someone considered the model of integrity and class. He had made it.

Other than these photos, the last phase of Abramowitz's life had garnered little attention. There was a short, one-graph item about his decision to close his own practice and join the Triple O, published in the fall of 1992. And, in June of this year, there was a column item, a "brite," albeit one written by someone without much feel for the form.

DISGRUNTLED PLAINTIFF GOES TO BAT

A Baltimore man who was awarded $850,000 in one of the last nonconsolidated asbestos trials showed up at the law offices of O'Neal, O'Connor and O'Neill carrying a Louisville Slugger and demanding justice.

The elderly but spry man chased lawyer Michael Abramowitz around his desk with the bat, demanding, "Where's my money? Where's my money?" He continued to chase Mr. Abramowitz until police arrived and subdued him. The firm represents Sims-Kever, one of the asbestos manufacturers now in bankruptcy.

Ironically Mr. Abramowitz, once known for his "Sweet Sue" commercials, was not with the firm when the case was decided, but has since taken over the asbestos defense. The firm declined to press charges against the man, but noted his energy and vitality raise doubts about how badly he suffers from asbestosis.

Typical, Tess thought. The columnist uses irony to denote anything interesting or strange. Common liability in newspaper writing.

Finally there was a feature article about local support groups. Survivors of incest, cancer, traffic accidents, even a chlorine leak on the Southwest Side. At first Tess couldn't see its connection to the dead lawyer. Then she found a mention of Victims of Male Aggression (VOMA), a group for rape "survivors." Its founder, a woman who had been attacked in her apartment, recalled with great bitterness how Abramowitz had done everything to get his client off.

"He couldn't ask me about my sexual history—it wasn't that long ago," the woman, identified only as "Mary," told the reporter. "But he still managed to twist everything around, make it look as if the man who broke into my apartment was some neighborhood guy I had been having fantasies about. A lot of the women in our group faced lawyers like him. We call them the real rapists." VOMA, according to the two-year-old story, met every Monday night. It offered support, psychological referrals, and instruction in the martial arts.

Tess looked at her little piles. Not much of a life. Still, it was more of a paper trail than most citizens would leave, especially those whose only distinction was being loved by their families and going to work every day.

Should she go to the Monday night VOMA meeting? It was her only lead. Tyner had told her explicitly to wait for his instructions, not to do anything without checking with him first. Whitney had called her a coward and a wimp. Whitney was right. Tess had become tentative and timid, and not just in the past three days. Ever since the *Star* folded, her life had been on hold. She wasn't much different than her father, with his patronage job as a city liquor inspector, or her mother, reporting to her glorified secretarial job at the National Security Agency every day for almost thirty years now. Except Tess didn't have a do-nothing job to go to, or a pension to look forward to. According to the severance papers she had received when the *Star* shut down, she could look forward to about $4,200 from the pension fund in thirty-five years or so.

As she sat there, imagining the tiny pile her own life would make, the phone rang. She let the machine pick it up.

"Tess, it's Tyner." His voice rattled teacups in her cupboard. For one paranoid moment she imagined he had read her thoughts and was calling to rebuke her. "We need your expertise tomorrow. Damage control. I'm going before a judge to get permission for Rock to row in out-of-town races, and we want to keep the local jackals at bay. We need you, Tess. Call me."

She let the machine record it all. After Tyner hung up she played the message over. "We need you, Tess." She re-wound, played it again. "We need you." It seemed such a long time since anyone—a boss, a lover, a friend—had said those words to her. "We need you."

She pulled a page out of her notebook and began, from memory, diagramming the Clarence Mitchell Courthouse. Stairs, elevators, entrances, and exits. Getting in was easy. Getting out undetected would be the challenge.

Chapter 11

Like most midsize cities at the millennium's edge, Baltimore had one newspaper, four television stations with evening newscasts, and an Associated Press bureau. Two radio stations also did some original reporting, rather than going the rip-and-read route with the AP broadcast wire, but most of the news came from the *Beacon-Light* by way of the AP. In fact news was one of Baltimore's most successful recycling projects. The *Beacon-Light* reported the story and sent a copy, an electronic carbon, to the AP. Unless the paper asked for special credit—"the *Beacon-Light* is reporting in today's editions"—AP could rewrite it and put it out on the broadcast wire, which allowed some sonorous-voiced anchor to intone: "Channel 9 has just learned . . ."

"And it's not a lie," Tess said as she explained all this to Tyner at lunch the next day. "Chances are, the folks at Channel 9 have just learned it at exactly the moment the story moved on the wire."

It was noon, a hot, blue-sky day in Baltimore. In honor of Dies y Seis, Mexican Independence Day, the Hasty-Tasty, a downtown diner that worked hard to earn its reputation as a greasy spoon, was offering an enchilada plate special. Two frozen tortillas stuffed with shredded chicken, rice and canned beans on the side, and a pale green substance billed as guacamole.

Rock, the only one who had dared order it, was now

sculpting tiny figures with the large avocado mound left over at meal's end, uninterested in Tess's impromptu seminar on the local media.

Tyner, however, was intent on every word. His small practice had not brought him into contact with the media, and he prided himself on never reading the local paper. Still, he was savvy enough to know he wanted to avoid the ''perp walk''—the parading of a suspect through a gauntlet of cameras. And he was astute enough to know that ruining the picture could ruin the story for the local television stations; he just had no idea how to do it. This was Tess's job.

Tess warmed to her topic. ''TV reporters, no matter how dumb, excel at the chase. They love nothing better than to follow a moving target, whether it's through the courthouse, outside police headquarters, in front of some row house. It doesn't matter if they yell inane questions and get no answers in reply—it's good video, and good video leads the news and gets more time. They will lead the newscast with footage of a fireman rescuing a kitten from a tree if they have good pictures. But bad video, or no video, and the story gets less time.''

''Is it possible the television reporters will skip the hearing, since the state of Maryland doesn't allow cameras in the courtroom?''

''Doubtful. In fact you can bet someone in the state's attorney's office or the police department will remind them to come. It's an unusual move, petitioning the court to allow a murder defendant to leave the state so he can compete in head races. If we're not careful Rock could look very unsympathetic, worrying more about his rowing than his murder trial.''

Rock looked up from his guacamole sculpture. ''I wish you wouldn't talk about me as if I weren't here. I don't care what the paper says, or the television stations. I'm innocent, and I know Tyner will be able to prove it. Why do we worry about this trivia?''

''The less publicity, the better,'' Tyner said. ''That's our rule. Somewhere out there a potential juror may be watching television tonight. I'd prefer not to have an image of you, face averted as you run through the courthouse, planted sub-liminally in his brain.''

Rock ran the back of his spoon along the banana-shaped line of his guacamole, then stuck two toothpicks on either side perpendicular to it. He finished by placing a single pinto bean in the center of the avocado, between the toothpicks. *A scull,* Tess marveled. *He just built a racing shell out of his lunch, and he's the pinto bean.*

''You are either extremely calm or on the verge of crack-ing up,'' she told her friend.

''Can't you be both?'' he asked.

They were scheduled to go before Judge R. Robert Nich-olson at 2 P.M. Avoiding the media hordes on the way into the courthouse was quite simple: They showed up an hour early and asked the clerk to let them sit in the empty court-room. Once they were inside the cameras could not follow them. About 1:55, the TV reporters realized Rock had slipped past their stakeout along the broad steps at the court-house's main entrance, and they began drifting in, leaving their cameras in the hall.

The courtroom was a grand, imposing space, with the touches of seediness endemic to public places in Baltimore. The wooden benches didn't match and were running to splin-ters in the grooves worn by generations of behinds. Delicate tulip-shaped sconces lined the walls, but three held burned-out bulbs. The gilt paint on the elaborately patterned heating vents had started flaking off. Still, the room was double height, with limestone walls leading to Palladian windows, five on each side—affording a view of blue sky and gray pigeons.

The oddest decoration in the room was a golden bas-relief eagle, perched on a verdigris half globe jutting about five feet above the judge's red leather chair. It looked like a crown in flight, but it was impossible to tell if the eagle, gripping the crown in its talons, had just absconded with it or was about to drop it on the judge's head.

Rock, who had taken the afternoon off from his job, wore

his work garb of khakis, a plaid shirt, and a navy blue blazer. Tess had dressed much the same, although she had on jeans. Tyner had given her a curt look, as if to say: "You'll do." *At least my hair is up*, Tess thought, *and my black Weejuns are as shiny as Rock's.*

"All rise," the clerk said. By now all the reporters were here—Tess recognized Feeney, the *Beacon-Light*'s overworked court reporter, looking bored and irritable as he joined three women in the front row. The women had heavy, almost theatrical makeup and vacant, stunned looks. TV reporters. They seemed to shut down when their cameras weren't around, Tess noticed, as if recharging their own batteries.

"All rise."

In profile, Judge Nicholson looked like the eagle flying over his head. Slight, with a huge nose, he held his head to the side as if daring one to try and look at anything else in the room. Given that he was so far above the courtroom, it was difficult not to stare *into* his nose. Tess was so entranced by his nostrils she forgot to sit down once the judge had taken his seat. Tyner had to yank her down by her blazer.

"Luckily he hated Abramowitz," Tyner hissed, then rolled forward to present his case.

Judge Nicholson's face was unreadable as he listened to Tyner argue that Rock, who had paid a bail bondsman ten percent in cash for his $100,000 bail, was not likely to flee if allowed to go to Pittsburgh, Boston, Virginia, and Philadelphia over the next eight weeks. He pointed out Rock's work history, his ties to the community, his eagerness to be acquitted by a jury of his peers in this matter.

"Your Honor, we absolutely object to allowing the defendant to leave the state," said the state's attorney, a thin young woman whose shrill voice bounced painfully off the limestone walls. She wore a cheap suit with a nylon blouse, the kind with a bow at the neck. Her shoes were scuffed and run-down at the heels. Tess, who knew how poorly prosecutors were paid, almost felt sorry for her. She looked quite mousy next to Tyner, splendid in a pale blue shirt, red bow tie, and navy suit.

The judge's eyes narrowed like a bird closing in on a particularly fat worm.

"Does Mr. Paxton have any prior arrests?"

"No, Your Honor."

"Does he have any prior convictions?"

"No, but the crime was quite violent and impulsive. Pre-Trial Services recommended he not be allowed to leave Maryland under the circumstances. The state believes he is at risk for flight."

Tyner whispered to Tess: "The state believes it had better look as tough as it can on this case, so no one accuses the state's attorney's office of being soft on a white defendant."

The judge glanced at Rock. Seated, his overmuscled torso hidden by his blazer, his legs concealed beneath the table, he looked like a stocky nerd. The judge turned his stare back to Tyner.

"Mr. Gray, would you be willing to accompany your client out of town and to guarantee his return?"

"It had not been my plan, Your Honor, but it could be arranged." Tyner tried to conceal his delight. Things were working out better than he had planned, Tess realized. The judge had just made it possible for him to deduct, as a business expense, his usual fall trips to the head races.

"Then it is the opinion of this court he can go." The judge stood and left so rapidly that he was gone before the clerk barked out, "All rise." As Tyner had predicted, the hearing had been easy. Now came the hard part: leaving.

At Tess's signal the three put their heads together. "Let's just pretend to confer urgently," she said in the huddle. "That will keep the reporters at arm's length."

"The judge looked familiar," Rock whispered.

"He's on the board of the Baltimore Rowing Club," Tyner said. "Lightweight four, Princeton."

The *Beacon-Light*'s Feeney, who probably would write no more than a brief on this routine court action, sauntered out.

The television women had bolted for their cameramen and were outside, white lights blazing.

"Here's my plan," Tess said once the courtroom was cleared. Rock knew part of it already. She had prepared him that morning at the boat house. Tyner listened, grasping it immediately.

Minutes later they burst out of the courtroom at full speed, and the camera crews trotted through the hallways in orgasmic delight, recording the fleeing Mr. Paxton with jacket over his head and attorney rolling alongside. The elevator arrived quickly, but that didn't stop the reporters and their crews. Some crowded on, while others ran down three flights of stairs and met the elevator on the courthouse's first floor.

"Why is it so important for you to row, Mr. Paxton?" "Did you kill Michael Abramowitz?" "How do you feel about being allowed to leave the state?" The questions came, fast, furious, and dumb. Tyner just kept rolling. He still had a lot of upper body strength and could move quickly along the smooth floors. The TV crews followed him through the hallways of the first floor, picking up speed. But Tyner appeared to be outpacing them until they split into two groups, then cornered him in a long hallway on the building's west side.

Here, benches along both walls were crowded with young men just starting out in the criminal world, parents accused of abuse and neglect, children caught up in nasty custody cases between their parents and the state. There were a lot of tired-looking women, surly teenagers, and screaming children, but no men. No fathers. Tired and bored, they welcomed Tyner's little sideshow.

Sure he had everyone's attention, Tyner nudged his jacketed client. Tess whipped Rock's blazer off her head and smiled broadly at the cameras. Given her height and Rock's huge jacket, which hung well below her hips when draped over her piled-up hair, no one had noticed they were following blue-jeaned legs instead of khaki ones.

"Ladies and gentlemen of the press," Tess said, bowing. "Darryl Paxton has left the building."

"As you can see," Tyner said, "this is not Mr. Paxton. And if you show videotape tonight suggesting this was Mr. Paxton running through the courthouse, you can expect a lawsuit by tomorrow morning. Of course, you are free to report you chased Tess Monaghan through the courthouse, as long as you report she is my assistant, and is accused of no crime. Thank you."

The teenage boys in the hallway, many of whom could look forward to a day when they would make their own desperate runs past television cameras, began whistling and stamping their feet. They didn't know what was going on, but they knew someone had been humiliated, and they liked it. The weary mothers began laughing; the children clapped their hands and shouted. Bailiffs came running from nearby courtrooms, demanding silence, but the laughter and shouts only escalated. Tess's trick seemed to free something in that sad place, and she and Tyner began giggling as well. Only the television reporters were unamused, their lipstick-thick mouths thinning into severe lines.

Rock, of course, was long gone. He had slipped out a side exit, one used primarily for the incarcerated men brought to the courthouse from city jail. His bike had been in the trunk of Tess's Toyota, parked a few blocks away. He had taken it out with Tess's spare key, leaving her blazer in its place. He would be crossing North Avenue by now, Tess calculated. Almost home, if not home free.

Chapter 12

Friday night. The Shabbat candles burned brightly on the mantel, creating a redundant halo effect for the cheap watercolor of Jesus hanging above them. Tess pushed her pot roast around on one of her mother's "meat" plates, hoping to create the illusion of eating. At the end of the table, her father was eating a cold cut sub on a paper plate and drinking a Pabst from the can.

Her mother, a striking woman despite the deep frown lines cut deep along her mouth and forehead, ate daintily from her steaming plate, wiping sweat from her face between bites. She wore a toast-colored dress of polished cotton, flattering to her dark eyes and hair, her tanned face and arms. Although her legs were also deeply tanned, she had sheathed them with panty hose, one shade lighter than her dress. Her suede pumps were also toast colored. Bite, chew, wipe. The weather had turned warm again, but Judith Weinstein Monaghan did not believe in air-conditioning or cold suppers after Labor Day any more than she believed Jesus Christ was the son of God.

"What's the matter?" she asked, not fooled by Tess's childhood habit of pretending to eat. "It's pot roast. You love pot roast."

"Not when it's ninety. I can't believe you cooked on a day like today. Cold cuts for everyone would have been fine."

Her father, whose bright red hair and clear skin made him look fifty instead of sixty, belched.

"Nice," her mother said. Her voice was mean, but the look she gave her husband was sultry. "Very nice."

"A man's home," her father said, belching again, "is his castle."

They all fell to eating and not eating again, and silence filled the room. It had always been a quiet house, a house deprived of the children Patrick Monaghan, the oldest of seven, and Judy Weinstein, the youngest of five, had assumed were their due. Tess, born less than a year after their wedding day, had been an only child. "I wasn't planned," she liked to say, somewhat inaccurately, "but the others were, the ones who were never born."

Her mother had insisted on putting Weinstein on her birth certificate, claiming: "They do it in Mexico."

"Oh, Mother," Tess had said when she was older. "The only thing you know about Mexico is that Uncle Jules got the trots in Cancún from having ice in his gin and tonic."

As a child Theresa Esther Weinstein Monaghan had called herself Tesser. Her doting aunts and uncles called her that, too. They changed it to Testy when she showed her temper, which, contrary to stereotype, came down from the Weinstein side of the family.

As a teenager Tesser became Tess, who complained endlessly about her name.

"It's a compromise," her mother said.

"A compromise means picking an alternative course, not choosing everything. You and Dad just force your incompatible choices to live side by side, much as you do."

Her parents were united on one subject: the shame of her vocational limbo.

"You found a job yet?" her father asked her now, after coming back from the kitchen with another can of Pabst. Her mother was drinking hot coffee, while Tess had a Coca-Cola in front of her. It had never occurred to her parents to offer her beer, wine, or a good stiff drink.

"Not exactly. I'm doing a little work for a lawyer—"

"As a paralegal?" Her mother's voice was pathetically hopeful. "They make very good money."

"Nothing permanent, nothing like that. A little freelance."

"And how does a little freelance pay these days?" Her mother sawed through her meat, trying for a casual, uninterested tone she had never mastered. Tess could tell she was driving her crazy.

"A little pays a little."

"There's no need to take that tone with me, Theresa Esther." Tess took a bite of her pot roast, hoping the several minutes necessary to chew the meat would give her, and her mother, a chance to cool down.

"Well, why not think about being a paralegal," she wheedled. She had a way of making Tess feel like a ragged cuticle on her perfect hands. "It's a perfectly good job, and it would pay the bills."

"I'm paying my bills."

"With what Kitty and Donald pay you."

"It counts. It's work; they give me money, not Green Stamps."

"Sure, if you don't mind Donald stripping his nest egg bare."

"What's *that* supposed to mean?"

Patrick Monaghan glared at his wife and belched again, perhaps to distract her, or Tess. But Patrick Monaghan had been given to gas all his life, and it had been a long time since a well-timed belch could distract either woman.

"Do you really think Donald has state money to pay an assistant? And if he did, he would be allowed to hire you? Donald pays you out of his own pocket because he feels sorry for you. He even has you fill out those time sheets so it looks legitimate. He never expected it would go on this long. No one did."

Tess replied almost automatically: "Hey, if Uncle Donald wants to give me money, he can just write a check every month. I'm not proud."

Strange, the words were true before she said them, but once out she could hear how false and hollow they were. It was bad enough to be someone who would do anything for money. It was worse to be someone who would do nothing for money. But that was her arrangement with Uncle Donald and, in her heart, she had always suspected it.

"Gotta go," she said, rising, the dutiful daughter, heading toward the kitchen sink with her plate and glass.

"Oh, Tesser," her mother said. "Don't go off in a huff."

"I'm not, I'm not," she assured her. "I just realized I have to be somewhere."

No, it wasn't a huff. More of a funk, as dark as the moonless night.

Her mood did not improve when she finally got to Fells Point, only to find no free parking spaces within eight blocks of Kitty's place. It was almost nine, and Fells Point's nightlife was coming to life. She circled the bookstore several times, then crawled up Broadway, looking for a spot. No luck. She ended up parking in the pay lot at the foot of Bond. She had only recently spent the better part of a day at city hall getting a permit so the two-hour restrictions throughout the neighborhood didn't apply to her. The permit was a hollow badge of honor when there were no places to be had.

On this particular night the crowd at the bookstore ran heavily to embroidered dresses and fiesta skirts. *Oh shit,* Tess remembered. Frida Kahlo night. Kitty was offering a twenty dollar gift certificate to the couple who most resembled the Mexican artist and her husband, Diego Rivera. The more serious contestants had penciled in heavy mustaches and forced their dates to stuff their shirt fronts, the better to resemble Diego's girth. But the winner had really stacked the deck: She not only had a rotund Diego, but another man dressed as Trotsky, who was believed to be Frida's lover.

"*Todos vuelven,*" Ruben Blades sang seductively from the stereo system. Kitty had translated the song for her once. Everyone returns. But first you had to go somewhere.

The contest over, most of the couples were now drinking sangria and snatching up books. Kitty held court in one of those slit-skirt Mandarin dresses requiring a perfect body.

She didn't let the dress down. Officer Friendly was at her side, wearing a poncho and looking vaguely lost without his gun and bicycle but absolutely devoted.

"These theme nights seem to be working out," Kitty said to Tess. "What should I do next? A 'George' night, with Eliot and Sand? Rita Mae Brown? Or suppressed Catholic girls night, with McCarthy's memoirs? We could put little girl mannequins in the windows, in Catholic girl uniforms and those shiny shoes."

"Do people still read McCarthy?"

"Good point," Kitty turned to her Zapata-ed beau. "Thaddeus, do you know who McCarthy is?"

Officer Friendly looked panicky, and Tess found herself rooting for him. This obviously had not been on the civil service exam.

"Normally I would say the witch hunt guy from the fifties," he said. "But I guess you're talking about some woman writer I never heard of."

Good answer. Thaddeus was a tad brighter than he seemed, smart enough not to bullshit, a rare quality in a man. Kitty almost cooed with pleasure at her protégé.

"There's nothing wrong in saying you don't know something, Tad. We'll read some McCarthy together later tonight."

She gave him a large, wet kiss on his left ear. Tess looked at them and all the happy couples around her—boy-girl, boy-boy, and girl-girl alike—and had an overwhelming need to be alone. No one was stopping her. She went to Kitty's kitchen, hijacked a bottle of Riesling, and climbed the stairs to her apartment.

The piles she had made of Abramowitz's life just two nights earlier still sat on the floor. She had a sudden desire to kick them into the air, or shred them into confetti and toss them from the roof. Instead she sat down and reviewed what she had written so far. Lists and lists of names. Rock's chronology of the night of Abramowitz's murder, side by side with Joey Dumbarton's account, and Mr. Miles's. Something was missing. *Someone* was missing.

Ava. Rock had never mentioned if Ava was at his apartment when he returned. Where had she been when the police arrived and arrested him? If she had still been sleeping there, they would have taken her in, too, for questioning. But the police didn't find Ava until later, which is why Jonathan had known so little about her when he came by two nights after the murder.

"I guess I do have a job to do," Tess said aloud. Really two jobs—her official chores for Tyner and these unofficial chores she kept assigning herself. If she had not earned Rock's money before, as Tyner had suggested, perhaps she could now.

Chapter 13

Ava may have sinned, but she had not been forced out of Eden. Late Saturday afternoon, Tess stood across President Street from the luxurious apartment building, trying to think of how she could slip past the uniformed doorman who guarded the entrance to Eden's Landing. At least she assumed it was a uniform and not his clothing of choice: Bermuda shorts, hiking shoes, a pith helmet. She walked around the corner to the underground garage entrance on Pratt Street. No sentry here. She slipped inside and checked to see if Ava's silver Miata was there. It was, a guarantee Ava was home. Except for work, Tess hadn't seen Ava walk anywhere. And Ava didn't strike her as the kind of person who went to work on weekends unless she was trying to impress the boss. If the boss was dead, what was the point?

The parking garage had an elevator leading to the apartments, but one needed a key to summon it. Tess patted her pockets frantically, as if looking for a key ring, until she saw an older woman, loaded down with shopping bags and a bakery box, heading to the elevators. Tess ran toward her, pretending a fit of gracious concern.

"Let me help you," she practically sang to the woman, taking the box by its red and white string. The woman looked a little nervous, as if Tess might be a mugger who prowled Baltimore parking garages for baked goods, but she didn't protest. When they reached the elevator Tess again made a show of trying to find her keys, but her hands were full of cake.

"Let me," the woman said quickly. She keyed the elevator, got on, and pushed four. Tess pressed the top button, but insisted on walking the woman to her door. In their three minutes of acquaintance, she told the woman she was new in the building, living in a studio apartment, and studying at the Peabody Conservatory.

"What instrument do you play?" the woman asked politely in the bored tone of someone who couldn't care less.

"I'm a vocalist," Tess said. "Soprano, but I have an enormous range. I'll be appearing with the Baltimore Opera this fall."

Unfortunately this piqued the woman's interest. "Really? What role? My husband and I are subscribers."

Tess thought for a moment. She had never been to the opera and, although she knew a few titles, she couldn't describe any plots or name any characters. But there was one opera the local company seemed to produce year after year. She tried to recall the ads she had heard on the radio.

"*La Bohème*?"

The woman did not notice she had answered in the form of a question. "Are you singing Mimi? Musetta? Or are you in the chorus?"

They had reached the woman's door. As long as she was committed to lying, Tess decided, she might as well lie big. "Mimi. I'm playing Mimi. If I don't go to New York first. The Met has a standing offer for me to sing Mimi there."

The woman, now thrilled, put her packages on a small table inside the door, but she made no move to take the cake box from Tess. Instead she handed her a pen.

"I know it's silly, but could I have your autograph?"

Tess signed the box with a flourish. *Teresita L. Mentiroso.* If she remembered her high school Spanish correctly, that translated to little Theresa, the liar.

Her opera career behind her, she ran up the stairs to Ava's apartment on the sixth floor. Feeling smug and devious, she rang the doorbell. But when Ava opened the door, her face quickly deflated Tess. She registered no surprise, no interest. For a moment it wasn't clear if she even recognized Tess. *What did Rock see in this incurious, self-absorbed woman?*

"Well, come in then," Ava said at last, gesturing with a half-empty glass of white wine.

She led Tess through the apartment toward the terrace without even a perfunctory show of hospitality. Unlike Joey Dumbarton or Frank Miles, Ava did not mistake this visit for a social call.

Her apartment faced the harbor and downtown, which added at least $30,000 to the price, Tess estimated. Whatever the extra cost had been, it appeared to be a stretch Ava could ill afford, even on a lawyer's salary. The one-bedroom apartment had a sparse, undernourished look, and it wasn't because Ava liked minimalism. The apartment simply didn't have enough furniture. And what was there looked shabby and worn. Ava was living paycheck to paycheck.

Once on the terrace, there was only one place to sit, a cheap director's chair with a torn orange seat. Ava took the chair and let Tess have the concrete floor. There was a crystal wine cooler by the chair, a nice one, possibly from Tiffany. But when Ava pulled the bottle out to top off her glass, Tess recognized the label, a Romanian Chardonnay available for less than six dollars, even at package stores, which gouged you. Tess had tried it. Once.

"What do you want now?" Ava said. She sat with her back to the harbor, indifferent to the view. Or perhaps she considered the sunset, a brilliant red orange heightened by the smog, something of a rival. Its warm hues did little for her pale, cool beauty.

"I'm working for Rock's—for Darryl's—lawyer. It's pretty routine stuff, just gathering as many facts as we can about the night of the murder."

Unlike Joey the security guard, lawyer Ava did not remind her that murder was a legal term. She simply continued to stare at Tess, waiting. Some people, smart people, learn early the power of saying nothing. It forces the other person to gush and stutter. Ava had mastered this. Tess had not. Her mouth, as always, rushed into the breach.

"You were asleep when he left that night, so you can't help us much there. But do you remember what time you got over there and what time you feel asleep?"

"I got there about nine. I was pretty upset, thanks to you. He made me some tea, he held my hand, and I fell asleep. It could have been fifteen minutes later, or forty-five minutes, or an hour. I lost track of time."

"Good." Tess ignored the little barb directed at her. "Now, did you wake up when he came back? Did you notice what time it was? Or did you not wake up until the police came?"

"I can't see why that matters."

"It sets parameters. The earlier he gets home, the easier it is to prove there was time for someone else to kill Abramowitz."

Ava smiled, showing dimples but no teeth. "You can't possibly believe that, can you?"

"It's my job to believe it. What do you believe?"

She leaned forward, as if taking Tess into her confidence. "Just between us—who else could have done it? Mind you, I don't care. I think it's terribly romantic and, with a good defense, he has an excellent chance of being acquitted. But what are the odds that someone happened to kill Michael the same night Darryl confronted him? It's terribly unlikely, isn't it?"

"Rock told me he's innocent, and that's all I need to know," Tess said, uneasy to hear Ava ask the question she had asked just six days ago. "I would expect at least as much from his fiancée."

"He hasn't told me he's innocent," Ava said.

"He's been instructed not to speak to you at all, for the time being. What about when the cops came and dragged him out of bed? Didn't you talk then?"

Ava's eyes slid away from hers, and she took a large gulp of wine. "Well, there wouldn't have been time for confidences then. Right?"

Her tone gave her away. She was testing a theory, seeing if Tess would buy it. If she didn't, presumably another would be offered.

"Not right, Ava. Not even close. You left before he came home, didn't you? You faked falling asleep, then sneaked out as soon as he had gone to do your dirty work for you."

Ava said nothing.

"Taking the fifth?"

She clenched her jaw muscles so hard they twitched, making a second set of dimples, but she still didn't speak.

"Maybe *you* killed Abramowitz," Tess suggested, not because she believed it, but because she wanted to goad Ava into saying something, anything. "You followed Rock to the office, worried Abramowitz's version of your relationship might not agree with yours. You hid in your own little office, then came out and finished what Rock had started. Or maybe you did it in front of Rock, and he's covering for you."

"Right. I strangled and beat a man about twice my size." Ava laughed, a high-pitched girl's laugh learned in grade school and sharpened by years of ridiculing others. "But, please—go with that theory. I'm sure Darryl would love a defense based on implicating his fiancée."

"Then tell me why you left his apartment. Were you worried what he might have done? Did you think he might come back and tell you all, making you an accessory? Or did he go down there because you asked him to, because the only way you can prove your sexual harassment story is if Abramowitz isn't alive to give his side?"

Ava started to speak, then sipped her wine again, cooling herself down. "If I didn't know better I would assume you were a failed novelist, not a failed journalist. You were a journalist, right? I mean, when you still had a job."

"I may have left the newspaper business, but at least it wasn't because I kept failing some test. You know, Abramowitz told Rock you were sleeping with him because you kept failing the bar. He also said he couldn't do a damn thing for you, but he slept with you anyway. Now that he's dead, are you going to start sleeping with another partner, hoping

for a reprieve from the firm's 'three-strikes-and-you're-out'
rule?''

Ava's jaw muscles flickered like neon and her eyes narrowed. If she had been a dog, her ears would have flattened
back, too. Tess could tell she longed to bite her, or at least
throw her wineglass. Instead she took a sip of wine, then
another. When she spoke her voice was calm, but only
through great effort.

''If Abramowitz said that, he's lying. At any rate I can't
believe Rock wants a defense based on humiliating me in
court, but I'll mention it to him when he calls. He calls me
all the time, you know. I just don't pick up the phone. That's
why we haven't talked, not because of any instructions he
received. But I may pick up the next time he calls. And
perhaps I'll offer my services to his lawyer. I'm sure I could
do better than an unlicensed amateur.''

''Well, you're definitely not an amateur. The services you
provided Abramowitz lifted you out of that category. I won't
pretend to compete with you there.''

She did throw her wineglass, then, but her aim was poor.
The glass sailed past Tess's shoulder, flying out to the sidewalk. There was a tiny crash, and a woman, probably a tourist, cried out: ''Harry, did you see that?''

''Sorry you couldn't help me with Rock's alibi, Ava,''
Tess said. ''Maybe you better work on your own.''

She felt pleased with herself, a little cocky, but the mood
quickly vanished when she left Ava's apartment. For outside
Eden's Landing, she saw Rock on his bicycle, riding up and
down President Street like the nerdiest kid in school cruising
past the head cheerleader's house, lovesick and forlorn.

''You're not supposed to be doing this,'' Tess admonished
him. ''Tyner told you to stay away and not to talk to her.''

''I don't remember him telling you to talk to her, either,''
Rock said. ''How did she look? How's she holding up?''

''OK, I guess.'' Tess thought of Ava in her empty apartment. ''Tell me something, Rock. Where does her money
go?''

''Well, she has a big mortgage and loans from law school.

Maintenance is high, and she can't even deduct it from her taxes. But she had to have it. She figured it wouldn't be so bad once we got married and were splitting the monthly payments.''

''Were you going to live there together?''

''She thought so.'' Rock looked embarrassed. ''I let her think so. But it is so small and so expensive. I was going to wait until we got married, then try to talk her into a little house down in Anne Arundel County, on the Severn. A place with a dock.''

''That wouldn't come cheap, either.''

''No, but I have some money put aside. And it would have been worth it to have a place on a river where I could practice. Now it looks like I'll be using my savings for attorney's fees.''

''Did Ava know you had a lot squirreled away?''

''Sure. She couldn't understand why I lived the way I did—driving my car only when I had to, living in such a cheap apartment. So I booted up my computer one day and showed her my investments. She was pretty impressed.''

I bet—impressed enough to accept an engagement ring.

''Look, Rock, I'm not going to tell you what to do, because you never listen to anyone. But try not to do anything really stupid, OK? Stay away from Ava. Trust Tyner and trust me. We have your best interests at heart.''

''Are you saying Ava doesn't?''

''I'm sure she does, too—as long as they don't conflict with hers.''

Rock stared wistfully up at Eden's Landing one more time, then pedaled away, waving good-bye to Tess over his shoulder.

Although worried about Rock and effectively shut out by Ava, Tess still felt upbeat and lighthearted. She had made a start, and she had so many other leads to follow. That support group. Tracking down the mystery man with the Louisville Slugger. She had earned a reward, she decided. French fries, perhaps, or a hot dog from the Nice N Easy.

She walked over to the convenience store on Broadway and asked for a kosher dog.

"It'll take a minute," the sullen girl behind the counter told her.

"Luckily I've got a minute. Hand me that paper, will you?"

The *Beacon-Light* she shoved at Tess was not the Saturday paper, but the early Sunday edition, the bulldog. Filled with fake news and feature stories, the paper was of little use, except to those who wanted a jump on real estate ads or the Super Deals at the Giant. Tess, lacking the space to store toilet paper purchased in bulk and the funds to buy property, usually had little interest in the bulldog. Then she saw Jonathan Ross's byline on page one, under a catchy headline:

THE LAWYER, THE ROWER, THE LADY:
UNLIKELY TRIANGLE LEADS TO TRAGEDY

Friends called Darryl Paxton "Rock." The nickname was a testament to his discipline as a sculler, a demanding sport that requires an almost absolute fanaticism if one is to be successful.

But "Rock" also referred to his daunting physique, the heavily muscled arms, back, and legs that had carried him to so many victories, time and time again.

Sunday night, police say, Paxton used that strength to crush his latest opponent—famed lawyer Michael Abramowitz, believed to be a rival for Paxton's fiancée, Ava Hill, a young associate who had been working with Abramowitz. Four days later Paxton went before a judge: not to show remorse, or enter a plea, but to request that his murder trial not interfere with his sculling schedule.

In an exclusive interview the woman at the center of this unlikely triangle told the *Beacon-Light* that Paxton was insanely jealous of anyone close to her. His mind poisoned by misinformation, Ms. Hill said, he had even come to believe that Abramowitz was sexually harassing her.

"I tried to tell him he had it all wrong," said a tearful Hill, recounting the night of the murder. "But once Darryl had an idea in his head, nothing could dissuade him."

Paxton appears calm and cool to those who know him best, but he is no stranger to violence. In college in Pittsburgh, he once beat a man in a local bar, injuring him so badly he required medical attention. The man, however, declined to press charges. Contacted today, ten years after the incident, he says he still fears Paxton too much to go on the record against him.

Meanwhile, childhood friends of Paxton describe cold, uncaring parents, interested only in his rowing accomplishments. His father, in particular, is described as a brutal taskmaster who would berate a young Paxton whenever he failed—whether at rowing or his studies. His father wanted him to be a doctor, according to one family friend, but Paxton preferred the less stressful life of a researcher.

Neighbors in Baltimore described Paxton as a quiet man who kept to himself. "He always seems a little preoccupied when I see him down at the mailbox," said Tillie Van Horne, who lives in his building. "Polite, but not real interested in other people. When his girlfriend was with him, he couldn't see anyone else in the world."

It was all there. Rock, faithful to at least one of Tyner's instructions, had not spoken to Jonathan, so Ava's account was allowed to float out over Baltimore, unchallenged and untested. In spite of herself Tess was impressed by Ava's ability to weave lie within lie. Caught in a compromising position, she had made up the story of sexual harassment to defang Tess. When it had backfired she claimed the story was a figment of Rock's overheated imagination. Abramowitz was dead, so no one could corroborate Rock's hearsay account that Ava had initiated the affair.

By the end of the overblown piece, which Tess read still standing in the Nice N Easy, her hot dog growing cold, the average reader would be convinced of two things: Rock's guilt and Ava's innocence. Every detail of their lives had been offered up to serve that purpose. Rock emerged as the brooding, obsessive Heathcliff of the Patapsco. Jonathan even called him a "loner," newspaper code for deranged. Ava was a golden girl, the straight-A student from Pikesville High School whose only false step was her involvement with this lunatic. Oddly Abramowitz hardly figured into his own murder story. A single man with no living relatives, he had no one to speak for him and no life to re-create outside the law. Old associates at the public defender's office recalled him only as a prickly workaholic. His current partners had declined to be interviewed for the story, saying the tragedy was too fresh.

But Tess didn't care about Abramowitz. And she wasn't particularly concerned about the article's effect on the case. Ava could lie to a newspaper reporter. She could even lie to Rock, convince him she was quoted out of context, or that she granted the interview only to help his case. In court she'd have to tell the truth, or at least settle on one, noncontradictory version of the truth.

No, Tess saw the article as a gauntlet, flung down by Jonathan to prove he could always get what he wanted, even without her cooperation. He had ferreted out details of Rock's life not even Tess knew—she had always assumed his parents were dead—and gotten the interview with Ava before it occurred to Tess to talk to her. Jonathan was a far more vicious opponent than Rock, who ultimately rowed against himself and his own records.

Jonathan couldn't win unless someone else lost.

Tess read the story again. Abramowitz was barely a person, just a MacGuffin, setting the story into play. What did anyone really know about him? Tess thought again about the little man with the baseball bat who had chased Abramowitz around and around the desk. She remembered the bitter woman, the one who had joined a support group just to forget her experience against him in court. Certainly they could help flesh out what was known about Abramowitz.

Of course, if Jonathan had read the *Beacon-Light*'s files, he knew about these people, too. But he hadn't tracked them down. He had gone for the easy story, the one visible from the surface. Let him have the lady and the rower. She was going in search of the lawyer.

Chapter 14

Tess rehearsed her cover story on her way to meet the women of VOMA. She had concocted an elaborate tale of date rape, in which she was defiled by a star football player who had taken her out for coffee after studying for a test on the 19th-century novel. As Tess climbed the broad stone steps of the old school administration building, she was wondering if she could summon up tears on cue.

The gray stone building, an elegant Victorian, had been defiled during a 1960s stab at modernization. Egg yolk yellow, Sunkist orange, shiny contact paper in a floral pattern—inside it was mod with a vengeance. Time had not dulled the yellow linoleum, and the heavy wooden doors were still imprisoned in layers of shiny orange paint, chipped in places and coated with a thin film of grime.

The city school district owned the old school, but it was not foolish enough to use it, preferring to spend millions to renovate a nearby high school for its own headquarters. The old administration building now functioned as a kind of community center, although there was no community to speak of in the blighted area. And if nature did not abhor a vacuum, then support groups must. More than a dozen had rushed in to fill the cavernous space, and each classroom that night was filled with people at various stages along the twelve steps.

Tess walked past hand-lettered signs for AA, NA, Adult

Survivors of Incest, Al-Anon, Shoppers Anonymous, and, cryptically, Bings of Baltimore, which she thought might be for people who couldn't stop watching *White Christmas*. Then she saw the women inside, hands wrapped tightly around cups of black coffee, hushed voices speaking rhapsodically about the merits of various doughnut shops.

"Oh, no, honey," one emaciated woman said, leaning forward to touch the bony knee of another. "Those krispy kremes at the Super Fresh aren't made there. You have to eat them hot, right out of the oil, to have the real krispy kreme experience. The nearest store is down in Virginia, in Fairfax County."

Oh, *Bingers* of Baltimore. *Maybe someone ate the other letters.*

VOMA was in the last classroom on the left. After glimpses at the sullen or tearful faces in the other classrooms, Tess had expected VOMA to be even more downbeat, if possible. Instead a party was in full swing. A portable stereo played bluesy music, and a couple of women were dancing, moving with a loose and sexy grace. Others gathered around a card table with bowls of M&M's, a plate of brownies, a tin of frosted cupcakes, and a cut glass bowl of bright red punch. Only one woman, a tall redhead, stood apart disapprovingly, her arms crossed and her mouth severe. Tess had a strong sense of *déjà vu*. Third grade, the class Valentine's Day party. But instead of candy hearts with *Hep Cat* and *U Drive Me Crazy*, there was a bourbon bottle on the table.

The women seemed embarrassed when they finally noticed her in the doorway. Someone snapped off the stereo and the others fled to their metal folding chairs as if Tess were an inspector from the national office of VOMA. They folded their hands in their laps and looked down, taking the posture Tess had expected to find. Only the redhead, an Amazon who had a good three inches over Tess, remained standing. Unused to looking up into a woman's face, Tess disliked her instantly. She reminded her of every class secretary she had ever voted against. Confident, with a hint of head nurse about her, always ready to give one an enema.

"Are you looking for the bingers?" Big Red asked. "They're in 211. We're 221. A lot of their people come here by mistake."

Her sense of mission protected Tess from obsessing over the insult, real or imagined.

"No, I'm looking for Victims of Male Aggression." The women stared back blankly. "This is it, right? VOMA?"

"Oh." The redhead considered Tess carefully. The other women kept their eyes downcast and hands folded, as if embarrassed by the card table of childish sweets. Or perhaps the bourbon was outlawed, given that half the people on the floor could lose all twelve steps if they knew a fifth was in room 221.

"I'm Pru," the redhead said brightly, sticking out her hand. "And if we seem caught off guard, it's because you've caught us in a rather . . . out-of-the-ordinary meeting. One of our members, little Cece, is getting married, and we wanted to throw a wedding shower for her."

"Does that mean your next regular meeting won't be until next week? Should I come back then?"

"Well, it depends. Do you have a referral?"

"A referral? No, I saw the group's listing in the *City Paper*'s calendar and thought it might help me. You see, I've just come to accept that I was the victim of an acquaintance rape in college—"

"Date rape!" Pru interrupted. She seemed relieved. "Your therapist needs to put you in touch with another group. You do have a therapist? Because VOMA is only for women who have been through the criminal system, the double-raped as we call them. Did you press charges? Can you still take him to court, or has the statute of limitations passed?"

"Well, no, but—"

"Then we're just not for you," Pru said, shaking her head adamantly. "You need the DAR."

"The Daughters of the American Revolution?"

"No, DAR, Anonymous. Date-acquaintance rape. I think they meet at one of the local elementary schools."

"Union Memorial has a space for them," offered a petite woman with brunette hair cropped so close that Tess wondered if she had recently undergone chemotherapy. "They meet the first Wednesday of the month. The hospital switchboard should have the phone number."

"Thanks, Cece." Pru turned back to Tess, who had the distinct impression the woman wanted to put her hands up to her chest and give her a gentle shove. *I guess I've outstayed my welcome.* Then again, Tess had the sense she had never been welcome here at all. Pru had wanted her to leave from the moment she saw her.

She looked around the room one more time, taking in every detail. Fifteen women, all white. Typical of segregated Baltimore. Statistically black women were the more likely victims, but white women formed the groups. Tess swept her eyes over all the faces; without names she would never keep them straight. She'd remember Pru, of course; she may even have a few nightmares about her. And the little one, Cece, whose impending marriage they were celebrating. She had a strange look on her face, sort of terrified and determined at the same time, but Tess assumed most brides-to-be looked the same. And a rape victim going through chemo would probably have more fears than average.

She waved good-bye, wishing she could fake a few tears. Of course, trying to fake one's way into a support group was arguably much worse than running an exclusive one, but Tess was still inexplicably angry at VOMA for rejecting her. Groups for rape victims should welcome everyone.

"I guess I'll go check out the Bingers," she said as she left. "But they'll probably kick me out because my devotion is to Goldenberg Peanut Chews instead of doughnuts."

Tess ran down the hall, enjoying the loud, smacking noise her shoes made on the old linoleum. Once outside she got in her car and pulled up to the corner, then turned off the engine and waited for the meeting to break up. She still wanted to find the woman quoted in the clipping. Pru, of course, would not help, although she wouldn't be surprised to find out the woman *was* Pru. Mousy, distracted Cece—that was another story.

All the support groups left at 9 P.M., but it was easy to spot the women from VOMA. They carried flashlights and cans of mace, held stiffly in front of them like bayonets, then linked arms, walking the member who was parked farthest away to her car, working back toward the old school. Cece drove off in an old Mustang. Tess quickly jotted down the tag numbers, which would get her the address from the MVA in case she lost her tonight. Then she pulled out behind her.

Cece headed downtown, stopping at a coffee bar. Although Baltimore was generally known as a place where trends came to die, the city had anticipated the national mania for coffee. Tess watched from the street as Cece ordered a cappuccino from the counter and took her steaming cup to a shadowy corner, wedging herself in as if she didn't like to have her back to anyone. She pulled some papers from her purse and studied them. Tess waited two minutes, then sailed in and ordered a decaf latte, ignoring Cece. *If she sees me first,* Tess reasoned, *it will seem more like a coincidence.* She sat at the counter with her profile turned toward the young woman, staring intently into space, but Cece never lifted her eyes from her work. It wasn't part of Tess's plan to dunk her biscotti, miss the glass, and spill the whole operation, but it worked. Cece's eyes met hers. She then looked away, skittish and uncomfortable, gathering up the papers spread out in front of her.

"You're the one getting married, right? Cece?" Tess said, walking up to her table.

"Cecilia. Cecilia Cesnik. Cece's a nickname I'm trying to outgrow, only no one will let me." She blushed and looked down at the table.

If Tess hadn't met her through VOMA, she would have assumed Cecilia was one of those people who had never overcome the adolescent habit of finding everything about themselves embarrassing. There was a lot going on behind the delicate face—edginess, fear, irritation at having her solitary moment disturbed. In Cece's case—*Cecilia*'s case—it was probably her history as a rape victim that made her want to disappear.

"I'm sorry if Pru seemed kind of rude," Cecilia said. "But VOMA really is very specific. It's not for everyone."

"I felt as if I had walked in on one of those girls' clubs that were always forming in grade school."

"It's in your best interest. I mean, it would be even worse to get into a group and find out it couldn't help you. You're not the first person Pru has turned away. Sometimes even men have tried to join." She lowered her voice when she said "men," as if the word itself were an obscenity. "We couldn't have that."

"Why would men want to join?"

"They have daughters or wives who have been raped, and they're looking for a way to make sense of it. But VOMA isn't for them, either."

"How long have you been a member?"

"Six years, from the beginning," she said with a small sigh. "Pru recruited me. The group was her idea, and she spent time at the courthouse, going through files and looking for victims whose rapists walked. I was raped almost seven years ago."

"And now you're getting married. I bet there was a time when that seemed remote."

"Yes. Very remote." She laughed. "I can't quite believe it myself."

They sat in awkward silence. Tess wondered if her face betrayed her conflicting emotions. The idea of anyone hurting this tiny girl made her sick. She was glad, now, that she hadn't told her rehearsed story. They would have known she was making it up. This was a kind of pain one couldn't fake. Then again, VOMA, with its celebration of victimhood, gave her the creeps. She just wanted to find the woman quoted in the piece and find out if she still was harboring a grudge against Abramowitz.

She slid one of her business cards across the table. Luckily it gave nothing away. "Well, if VOMA ever changes its policies, give me a call." She was hoping her overture would prompt Cece to offer her number, but she just pocketed Tess's card. Then she reached toward her head to play with the hair that was no longer there. Her hand dropped abruptly back into her lap.

"You know, you actually look pretty good with such short hair," Tess said. "Not many women would."

"Yeah, I had a pretty bad case."

"Um, cancer?"

Cecilia laughed again, a full-bodied laugh this time. "No, although you're not the first to think that. I had Highland-town hair—dyed, permed, with the little side bangs in the front and the rest hanging down to my shoulders."

Highlandtown was an East Side working-class neighbor-hood, home to the city's tallest beehives and thickest accents. Tess had never heard of Highlandtown hair, but she understood instantly what Cecilia meant.

"Why did you cut it off? The neighborhood must be shocked."

"Not as shocked as they were when I quit my secretarial job and got a scholarship to the University of Baltimore's law school. Or when I stopped pronouncing the second 'r' in 'warter' and 'Warshington D.C.' People told my pop I was getting uppity." Cece—Cecilia—was suddenly sitting up straighter, and she had lost the shy, shambling style. "They were right. I am."

"What prompted all the changes?"

"VOMA. It brought me together with a lot of women I might not have met otherwise. Rich women, from Roland Park and Guilford. Accomplished women. Pru really en-couraged me. But she thinks I'm uppity, too."

"Why?"

Cecilia shrugged. "It happens. Someone's your mentor, then suddenly you don't need a mentor anymore. Hey—what was yours like?"

"My mentor?"

"No, your rape."

Tess stared into her glass, mumbling: "Oh, typical date

rape. I was helping a guy study, and we went up to his room."

"Mine was a burglar. I asked him to . . . pull out. I was scared of, I don't know, pregnancy, or AIDS. I think I had this idea it would be more tolerable if he didn't come inside me. Of course he found the whole thing hilarious."

"How did he get off?"

"His lawyer used the thing about pulling out. He said I was so calm, so thoughtful, it must have been consensual. That it was my form of birth control. But that's not the reason he got acquitted. Someone, the lab or the cops or the prosecutors, lost the physical evidence, the swab. The case fell apart without that."

"How does VOMA help?"

"Oh, self-defense classes. Lectures. We even looked into some kind of civil suit."

"Against the lab, for losing your results?"

"Something like that. VOMA worked pretty well."

"Worked, past tense? Are you quitting because you're getting married, or because of law school?"

"Right. Exactly. Because I'm getting married." Cecilia jumped to her feet, gathering up her purse and the sheaf of papers on the table. In her haste she knocked everything to the floor. When Tess tried to help her pick the fluttering papers up, she panicked.

"Don't touch anything! Just let me put it back in order!" she shouted, her voice as shrill as a police whistle. It was a commanding sound, coming from such a tiny body. But Cecilia's voice merely startled Tess into holding the papers even tighter, crumpling the sheets in her fist.

Cecilia dropped into a practiced crouch, fingers curved as if to gouge someone's eyes or stab a larynx, but her self-defense training was of little use unless someone came at her. Tess merely stood there, staring at her, along with everyone else in the coffee bar, except for two chess players who were using a timer for their game. Cecilia knew how to defend, but not how to attack. Tess knew how to attack, but she had no intention of doing so. After a few moments of this standoff, Cecilia improvised, throwing her body against Tess's knees in a blatantly illegal tackle and bringing her crashing to the floor.

As Tess fell she reached out blindly with both hands, dropping the crumpled sheets. Cecilia grabbed them and bolted, leaving Tess in a puddle of steamed milk and crockery.

"Just another coffeehouse brawl," Tess told the manager when he rushed over to examine the damage, not to her but to the heavy cups and saucers. "Caffeine makes some people very aggressive."

It hurt, being dumped on one's butt on a concrete floor. Of course, Tess thought, a coffeehouse couldn't have anything warm or soft underfoot. As she pulled to her feet, she saw a coffee-splattered piece of paper under the table. Greasy and gray, it appeared to be a page from some company's articles of incorporation. Tess remembered seeing such documents when she was a reporter. This was the last page of the charter, bearing two signatures: Prudence Henderson, president and treasurer of VOMA, and the lawyer who had filed the charter for her: Michael Abramowitz.

Chapter 15

The president of the United States came between Tess and her bagels the next morning, and it wasn't in one of her strange dreams.

Nor was it the first time. Like most Baltimoreans, Tess had more experience than she wanted with visiting presidents, First Ladies, cabinet secretaries, and their ilk. Just forty-five miles up the parkway from Washington, Baltimore had become the destination of choice during the last decade, an easy photo op for those who wanted to surround themselves with local misery or color. Real folks. Even the queen of England had felt obliged to put in an appearance at an Orioles game. But whether it was a monarch or a president, a Democrat or a Republican, it all meant the same thing for the local populace—traffic jams and security checks, breathless reports on television for a week before and after, a disruption of life in general.

Cranky at being deprived of her breakfast routine, Tess splurged on a chocolate-filled croissant and a cup of hazelnut coffee from one of the stalls inside the old Broadway market. She had planned to savor the high-calorie treat and gourmet coffee, but she ended up bolting both when she saw the bus crossing Broadway. One reason her Toyota had survived this long was because she used public transportation when possible, as long as she didn't have to transfer. Baltimore's bus system didn't make it easy. Today she ended up six long blocks from her destination, the complex of state office buildings at Preston and Martin Luther King Boulevard.

The bland gray towers here housed hundreds of state employees from several divisions. Tess took the elevator to room 808, home to all corporate charters filed in the state of Maryland, for businesses and nonprofits alike. Cecilia's smeared copies must have come from here, from the old microfilm files, a technology now almost as quaint as telegraphs and Morse codes.

It was a dusty, overheated room, always crowded and tense. When Tess was a reporter, jazzed up on caffeine and deadlines, just being here had pushed her to the edge of teeth grinding irritation. The too-small room seemed to affect everyone's reflexes, until employees and visitors alike moved as if suspended in honey. There was always a crowd at the banks of filing cabinets, always a line at the front desk, never enough clerks to help out. Strange little gnomes, male and female, hogged the microfilm machines and tables. Tess had never known, or cared, who these people were or what they were doing.

Now she was one of them. A free spirit, liberated from the forty-hour-a-week grind. Tess waited to surrender to the same lethargy the others had, to shuffle to the front desk, where she would get the folio number for the file she wanted, then to the cabinets where the files were kept, and to the machine where she could scan to the page number she needed. But the only feeling she had was her usual urgent desire to get out as quickly as possible. It took a mere five minutes to get the reel of microfilm, but the microfilm readers were already taken by people with piles and piles of film stacked at their sides. A bad sign, Tess decided, a very bad sign. She would have to rely on her more devious instincts, becoming sharper by the day, to jump ahead in line.

"Anybody parked on Howard Street?" she asked brightly. "Because they're ticketing."

Immediately three people rushed for the doors. One left a microfilm reader vacant and Tess usurped it, ignoring the glares of those who had not moved quite so quickly. She scanned on fast, which made her head ache as the pages rushed by in a blur. The machine gave off a noxious smell, a combination of ink and dust, laced with a burning odor from the old motor. VOMA's charter began on page 1,334, fairly deep into the file. She slowed the scan to a crawl, but she had already passed it by and had to reverse direction for several hundred pages before she could zero in.

She was looking for more names to add to her growing list. Tess knew from writing about charities that a nonprofit typically had officers and a board. A lawyer filed the incorporation papers, but the lawyer usually didn't have any further dealings with the group. Still, it seemed an unlikely coincidence that Abramowitz filed the papers for a group that had at least one member who hated his guts. The original filing for VOMA, the Victims of Male Aggression, listed only Prudence Henderson as president-treasurer, and the "agent," lawyer Michael Abramowitz—the same names she had found on Cecilia's fragment in the coffeehouse. No board, and nothing unusual in the bylaws, basically a statement of purpose ("a nonprofit that seeks to educate about sexual assault") and a promise not to support or oppose individual political candidates. That was boilerplate, a federal law any tax-exempt group had to follow.

Tess scanned idly through the other charters in the file, curious to see if Michael Abramowitz often helped out with filings. His name did not come up again. But there were hundreds of thousands of corporations on file here. Abramowitz could have filed for any number, or helped out on just this one. Searching for his name this way was useless. She scanned back to the VOMA charter and pushed the "print" button. The greasy, smudged copies were free, and Tess believed one should always take advantage of government freebies. *Your tax dollars at work.*

Before she left, she asked at the front desk to see the group's latest filing, an annual update known as the pink sheet, because of its color. If a board had been installed since the original filing, or if new officers had been named, VOMA would provide the list with its annual statement, another source of names and leads. When Tess was a reporter, a clerk would bring out the entire file, standing guard to ensure one looked only at the top pink sheet, which was public. The rest of the file was confidential. It had been a simple and painless process. Too simple and painless apparently: The legislature had changed it. The clerk told Tess she now needed twenty-six dollars, check or cash, to get the pink sheet today, nothing if she could wait for them to mail it, which could take up to two weeks. Tess wondered if she could bill it to Tyner without explaining to Tyner what she was doing. Nope. Better to go the cheaper route. Why gamble twenty-six dollars on a long shot?

She left the building, heading south to the greatest library in the free world.

Well, not anymore. Probably not ever. But the central branch of the Enoch Pratt Free Library still was a place of wonders to Tess, even if the book budget had been slashed and the hours cut. Her parents had made a lot of mistakes, a fact Tess compulsively shared on first dates, but she gave them credit for doing one thing right: Starting when she was eight, they gave her a library card and dropped her off at the downtown Pratt every Saturday while they shopped. Twenty-one years later, Tess still entered through the children's entrance on the side, pausing to toss a penny in the algae-coated fish pond, then climbing the stairs to the grand main hall. If she could be married here, she would.

She found a seat in the business and technology section, between two homeless men researching the Voting Rights Act, and pulled out a small, spiral-backed notebook and her sheaf of lists, all the names she had been able to link to Abramowitz. She started with the current phone book and worked backward, using the old directories on microfilm to find numbers and addresses for those not in the most recent book. It was boring detail work, the kind of thing she had always done well. Too well. Tess had a talent for the small stuff. It was the big picture that often eluded her. In another time, another place, she would have been bent over a large quilt, sewing away at her one tiny block of fabric, the pattern so close to her eyes it had blurred.

But there were few rewards today. Most of the names on her list were not there, or too common to track. People had left Baltimore, disappeared, or died.

Except for Prudence Henderson, on University Parkway in the current directory. Tess was familiar with the area, a place of old apartments and co-ops, with a few rambling brick houses thrown into the mix. Of course, she could have found the same information by just looking it up in her phone book at home, but the discovery still pleased her. Heartened, she checked for a Cecilia Cesnik in Highlandtown, only to find too many Cesniks with East Baltimore exchanges. Did Cecilia say she still lived with her father? He could have been anyone from Anthony to Zachary.

She looked through her lists again. Who was missing? Oh, the mystery man, the disgruntled plaintiff with the Louisville Slugger. No one at the library could help with that, but she had an idea about someone who could. She gathered up her papers and went to one of the old pay phones, shutting the folding glass door and dialing a number to an office only blocks away.

"Feeney," a bored voice answered. It was a low, gruff voice, a voice that choked off all pleasantries. Kevin V. Feeney, the courthouse reporter for the *Beacon-Light*, worked out of a small pressroom in the courthouse, the better to escape his editors.

"Hey, Feeney, it's Tess Monaghan. Saw you in court the other day, but I didn't see your byline on Sunday's story. I bet you did a lot of legwork for Jonathan's story."

He grunted. "Yeah, I did all the scut work. As usual. But you know Jonathan. At least, that's what they say."

Tess let the last remark go. Feeney needed to get his shots in.

"OK, I'll admit it, I'm calling for a favor. Did one judge handle most of the asbestos cases before consolidation? I'm trying to track down a plaintiff, but all I know is how much he was awarded and that he's still pretty feisty for someone who's dying.''

"Those cases go from judge to judge. It's a real dog assignment. And I can't see any plaintiff standing out from the crowd. They're just a bunch of sick old men.''

"That's the thing: This old man was healthy enough to chase someone around with a Louisville Slugger not long ago.''

Feeney laughed. "Well, unless he chased the judge, he's not going to have made much of an impression. But drop by some day—not today, because I have a hearing in fifteen minutes—and we'll play with the *Beacon-Light*'s library, see what it can kick out for us.''

"Thanks, KVF.''

"See ya, Tess.''

She hung up and left the library the way she had come in, and headed to Tyner's office, ready for a day of photocopying and answering phones. Tyner had started sneaking all sorts of work on her plate, things that had nothing to do with Rock's case. The secret tasks, the ones she assigned herself, made those dull jobs tolerable. In fact she loved sitting in Tyner's office, knowing she had done an end run around him.

At dinner that night, Tess had Kitty to herself, a rare thing. She adored Kitty, but even thirty years after junior high her aunt still threw herself into her affairlets with a single-minded vigor that left everyone else behind. Tess missed Kitty when she was in love, and she was almost always in love.

Kitty topped off their wineglasses. "You've got the Monaghan constitution, Tesser, despite that unhealthy obsession with exercise. I'm not sure it's such a blessing, though. For one thing, it costs more to get a buzz on.''

"I don't know. I think my high tolerance for all things comes from both sides. The Weinsteins probably were all addicts, back when they had the drugstore. I bet Poppa had pharmaceutical cocaine and the Weinstein women scarfed down speed to keep their weight down.''

"Cocaine wasn't Poppa Weinstein's vice," Kitty said, then clapped her hand over her mouth as if she had given something away.

"What? What? What are you talking about?"

Kitty shook her head, her hand still cupped over her mouth, her green eyes wide, little tears of laughter at the corners.

"Tell me. We never have secrets." It was a lie, for Tess had always hoarded a few, but the lie worked. Kitty left the room and came back with a wooden box stamped TUXEDO SHOE POLISH.

"As you know this place was the Weinstein Drugs flagship. Well, I found this in the third-story storage room, the one that became your apartment, when I bought the place," she said, flipping up the lid and revealing a blinding flash of cleavage. The box was filled with skin magazines. Blondes, brunettes, redheads, in nightgowns and bathing suits and nothing at all. But the overwhelming impression was of breasts, in hues ranging from creamy white to coffee brown.

On closer inspection, which Kitty and Tess were glad to make, the twenty-year-old magazines seemed almost wholesome by today's standards. No S and M, no single-theme issues dedicated to big rear ends or freakish chests. Just lots and lots of naked women. *Oh, Poppa Weinstein,* Tess thought, *and we assumed all you cared about was real estate and competing with Rite Aid.*

"Are you sure they were his?"

Kitty shrugged. "It was pretty well hidden near an old safe. I don't think they belonged to Rachel." That would be Momma Weinstein, whose only known passion was for her beloved springer spaniels. If Tess had been married to Rachel Weinstein, she might have had a similar stash.

"Why did you keep them?"

"I thought I could use them for a censorship display one day, or one on pornography. They're so retro it's almost innocent. No AIDS, no condoms, and the pill was still a godsend. I was in my twenties when these magazines came out. I could have *been* in one of these magazines."

Kitty and Tess drifted into their discrete musings. Kitty appeared to be thinking about her glory days, which Tess doubted were one-tenth as glorious as her current life as Fells Point's resident goddess-merchant. Tess was mulling over Poppa Weinstein, her dirty old grandpa. At first she felt the way one does after making the connection between one's conception and one's parents. But after the initial queasiness subsided, Tess decided it was sweet. Well, not sweet, but OK. *At least he wasn't luring little girls behind the soda fountain, just curling up with the very magazines he refused to sell.*

She hoped.

The phone rang in Kitty's office, a narrow room between the kitchen and the bookstore proper. "That should be Thaddeus." She floated to the phone, ever the teenage girl, but was back in a few seconds.

"The thrill is gone?" Tess asked.

"No, it's for you. Since when do you give the store number out?"

"Tyner put it on my 'business' cards because he knows I don't always answer upstairs. Sorry—it didn't occur to me anyone was going to use it."

In the office Tess picked up the sleek, modern phone on Kitty's desk. A deep voice, hesitant and sweet, spoke softly into her right ear. "Miss Monaghan? It's Frank Miles, the custodian from the Lambrecht Building."

"Mr. Miles." She imagined him, girth squeezed into his easy chair, scarfing down a whole bag of Hydroxes. A black Santa Claus on his throne. No beard, though. "What can I do for you?"

"I was thinking—I have so much time to myself, to sit here and think—and I remembered something. There was a man, Miss Monaghan. An angry man."

"Where, Mr. Miles? At the office?"

"Yes. He came to see Mr. Abramowitz a few months ago and said horrible things, ugly things. It was after hours, so I heard them. He wanted money. He said he would kill Mr. Abramowitz if he didn't get his money."

"Was it a man with a baseball bat? The man written up in the paper? Do you remember what month this was?"

"No—maybe spring, maybe summer."

"With a baseball bat?"

"A baseball bat? I think there was. Or maybe I just heard about it later."

"Did you catch his name, Mr. Miles? Did you see him?"

A long, sad sigh. "No. No. I'm sorry." He sounded hurt and defensive, as if he regretted disappointing her.

Tess wanted to sigh, too, with frustration. He hadn't told her anything she didn't know. But he had kept her card. He had called. Maybe he would remember something worthwhile.

"I *am* going to check into it, Mr. Miles," she reassured him. "It's a good tip, a really good tip. I bet there's something there."

That cheered him up. "He was an angry man, Miss Monaghan. Angry over money. Isn't that a shame? He was mad because they hadn't paid him for dying, the way they promised. Who needs money for dying?"

"It's a good tip," Tess repeated. "And I think I know who it was." *I just don't know his name*.

"You're good at your job, Miss Monaghan. You're very conscientious, a good, hard worker. I noticed that right off. Good night, Miss Monaghan."

Conscientious. Good at her job. When had Tess heard that last? She couldn't remember. The words almost made her want to weep, to thank Mr. Miles profusely, to make her parents proud of her, to get an MBA or go to law school.

But all she said was, "Good night, Mr. Miles."

Chapter 16

Tess woke up the next morning with an unfamiliar pleasant feeling. She sat up in bed, trying to figure out what it was, this fluttery sensation deep in her stomach. She was eager to begin the day, the real day beyond her workout, before she had to show up at Tyner's office. Of course. This was what it felt like to have something to do, a job to which one wanted to go. After her conversation with Mr. Miles last night, she was more sure than ever it was essential to find the man with the baseball bat. She couldn't wait to go see Feeney at the courthouse.

But Tyner had other plans. He was waiting when Tess docked at 7:30.

"I need some help around the office today. What's your schedule like?"

"I owe Kitty a few hours this morning. And I had some stuff I wanted to do on my own this afternoon."

"Work for your uncle?"

"Not exactly."

Still in her shell, Tess bent over her shoes and untied them slowly, with great concentration, more than the task required. When she looked up again Tyner was giving her the hard glare usually reserved for a novice who was dogging it, or an experienced rower who caught a crab—rower jargon for putting one's oar in at a wrong angle, so the entire shell lurched. A single crab could lose a race or overturn a four.

"I hope you're not playing detective, Tess. You come to my office this afternoon. You haven't even earned back all that money Rock paid you. Maybe you can do some typing for me."

"On Rock's case? Or some of your other cases?"

"Whatever I tell you to do, you'll do, when I tell you to do it. That's our arrangement." And he rolled away while Tess sat in her shell, nonplussed.

Feeling mildly defiant, she did not dress up for her afternoon at the law office, prompting a stern look from Tyner when she arrived at 2 P.M., an hour late, in black jeans and a white T-shirt. She bet the jeans bothered Tyner more than her tardiness. Tyner was something of a dandy, obsessed with clothes.

Today, at least, he didn't insult Tess by making her perform tasks that had nothing to do with Rock's case. That was the adoring Alison's job when she wasn't finding endless excuses to leave the anteroom and bustle into the office.

"She has a crush on you," Tess said after the third interruption.

"Not at all," said Tyner. "She just loves her job. I don't really need her, but her father owns the building, and if I have a bad month, he'll let me deduct her salary from the rent I pay."

"Whatever you say, Tyner. I'm sure a girl whose father owns a Mount Vernon town house has nothing better to do than answer your phone and fetch you coffee."

She was reviewing the statements collected to date, including police reports and a preliminary autopsy, and noting any contradictions. Using Tyner's color-coded system, she marked every mention of time, separating out "good" and "bad" testimony—i.e., what favored their version of things (red), and what could undermine Rock's case (blue).

"How's the autopsy look for us?" Tess asked.

"Well, it doesn't jibe with Rock's story. Abramowitz *was* choked, and Rock's fingerprints are all over his office. But he also has a skull fracture, and the medical examiner ruled the cause of death was blunt force trauma—a repeated beating against the corner of his desk. It wasn't pretty, Tess. Whoever killed him was in a rage. Half his skull was on that desk. They were picking the rest of it out of the carpet for days, I bet.''

No wonder Frank Miles had been so worried about cleaning up. ''What about Rock's clothing? Did they find any of Abramowitz's blood on his stuff?''

''Now that's one of our few breaks. Rock's clothes appear to be missing.''

''Missing?''

''Rock was wearing a fresh T-shirt and a pair of jeans when the cops picked him up. They went through his laundry basket and found no shortage of soiled shirts, but not a single one with blood on it.''

''So Rock *didn't* do it.''

''Or he thought quickly enough to get rid of a piece of incriminating evidence. He could have pulled off his shirt and stuffed it into a trash bin on Howard Street. But that's for the prosecutors to wonder about, and prove.''

Tess bent back over her work, uncomfortable with Tyner's train of thought.

Her notes now. Joey Dumbarton—a ''good'' witness, for Tyner could confuse him easily, especially after a few more interviews. Frank Miles—he would testify for the state, but Tess made a note of last night's conversation. It wouldn't hurt for Tyner to ask him about the mystery man, to plant in the jury's mind the idea of an angry man, furious at being denied his money, enraged enough to kill for it.

Of course, killing Abramowitz wouldn't have accelerated the payment, quite the opposite. Who, besides Rock, had a motive for Abramowitz's slaying? Tess stared out the window at the tiny park in the shade of the Washington Monument. Ava might. Her sexual harassment claim, which couldn't be refuted now, may have boosted her bargaining power with the firm. She could have held them up for money, or for unlimited chances at the bar exam. Then again, she had recanted her story awfully fast. Perhaps she had been counting on Abramowitz to pay her off to keep her from telling the other partners? His private practice was thought to have been a lucrative one, and his estate should be entitled to some of the profits the Triple O made this year, up until his death.

"Hey, did he leave a will?"

"Abramowitz? No, surprisingly. Or perhaps not so surprisingly. Some doctors don't get physicals; some lawyers put off writing their wills. He left a sizable estate—almost one million dollars in investments and real estate—but he has no living relatives. It's in probate at orphan's court, where all estates go when there are no wills."

"Is that what orphan's court is for? It always sounded to me like something out of Dickens, a place where orphans were auctioned off to pay their parents' debt. Perhaps I should feel sorry for Abramowitz, the poor little orphan with no one to leave his millions."

"When we get through with Abramowitz in court, the one thing I can guarantee you is that no one will feel sorry for him."

"What do you mean?"

"It's simple. We're going to try the victim. An ugly strategy, but an effective one. If you can convince a jury someone deserved to die, the jury might acquit. It's not supposed to work that way, yet it does."

Tess lowered her eyes, and the reports in front of her blurred and shimmied. She wasn't naive; she knew a legal defense had little to do with innocence. It was a game. The state had to prove its case, and if it failed then one was "not guilty." Not too long ago, a man on Death Row had been released when DNA testing proved he had not raped a little girl who was murdered. "He's not guilty," the prosecutor said, "but I'm not ready to say he's innocent." Tyner was accustomed to those semantic realities. Tess wanted to be able to declare, with all her heart, that Rock was innocent. For only Rock's innocence could establish her own.

They worked in silence until Alison hurried in again, full of her own importance as she announced a phone call from Seamon P. O'Neal.

"Of O'Neal, O'Connor and O'Neill," she added as Tyner picked up the phone. Tess tried to eavesdrop, but Alison wanted to chat.

"I didn't make the connection at first," she said, wrinkling her perfect, perky nose. "He pronounces his name 'Shaymun.' Isn't that funny? I thought it was Seamen."

"It's Irish. And Shaymun is preferable to Seamen, don't you think? Consider the homophones." Alison blushed and practically ran from the room. Tess couldn't be sure if it was the oblique reference to semen, or the word "homophone," that Alison thought obscene. She turned her attention back to Tyner, but the call was already over.

"He wants to see us—to see *me*," Tyner said, hanging up the phone. "He says it's about Rock's case."

"Are you meeting him at his office?"

"No, at his house. 'Sixish, for cocktails,' he said. But I have a feeling he expects us at six sharp and drinks will be an afterthought. Successful lawyers usually do not arrive home by six, ready for cocktails. Not even founding partners with wealthy wives."

"Expects *us*. You said, 'Expects us.' "

Tyner sighed. "It will probably be a boring little fencing session in which Seamon tries to figure out what we know and the implications for the firm. That's all he cares about, his law firm's reputation."

"And I'm the one who knows where and when the star associate spent her lunch hours with the newest partner."

Tyner threw up his hands. "You want to go, you can go, as long as you drive and stay quiet. I'd like to think you have something better to do with your evenings."

They left the office at 5:30, usually more than enough time for the three-mile trip to Guilford, one of the wealthiest neighborhoods within the city limits. But the O'Neals lived on Cross Place, a hidden cul de sac unknown to Tess and Tyner, both Baltimore natives. After several wrong turns they finally found their way to the street, a leafy enclave set off by a stone archway thick with ivy. A small sign advised them it was a private block, which may have explained why it was missing from the city map they had studied futilely. NO TRESPASSING, it warned in black, curving letters.

"Cross Place. Of course," Tyner said. "William Tree, Seamon's father-in-law, married Amelia Cross and bought this property for her. It was a huge estate at one point, almost two hundred acres. But Tree, always a developer at heart, couldn't resist subdividing his own land over time."

"I thought the philosophy was to hold on to land, because they're not making it anymore."

"That's fine if you don't need any cash flow. Tree had expensive tastes. The center house was his, and the houses on either side were for his two children, William Jr. and Luisa Julia—Ellie Jay. William Jr. died young in an influenza epidemic. The O'Neals took over the center house when her parents died. The O'Neals have a son and a daughter, too, but they apparently gave up on living here in harmony. The other houses were sold a few years back, almost as soon as William Tree, Sr., was in his grave."

Rambling, redbrick mansions, the houses were identical in almost every aspect. But the middle house had a subtle grandeur its mates could not match. Its lot was a little larger, its lawn crosshatched like the field at Camden Yards. Ancient crepe myrtles wrapped around the house, their blooms just past. A few tiny blossoms, in hues ranging from pale pink to almost purple, littered the grounds, faded confetti after a parade.

As soon as Tess pulled into the driveway, a maid came running to meet them, a pale blue and white banner in her hand. She tied it to the antenna of Tyner's van.

"The neighborhood watch group gives these out," she explained matter-of-factly. "It means you're invited. When people see strange cars these days, they get jumpy."

This nervousness was new, Tess realized. Once, Guilford had been a safe neighborhood, its grand homes untouched by crime and larceny as if by some secret arrangement. This summer, people in the poor sections to the south and east had started making forays into Guilford. An armed robbery here, a break-in there, at least one rape—the sort of things the rest of Baltimore had lived with for years. But Guilford's residents were outraged. A covenant had been broken. The homeowners, many of whom were paying as much as $15,000 a year in property taxes alone, lobbied city hall for the right to hire their own security force. Grudgingly the city had allowed them to pay for the services it could not provide.

The concern for security did not stop at the curb. Waiting in the O'Neal foyer, Tess peeked into the closet and saw the green and red lights of a complicated alarm system. It even had a "lock down" designation, a term Tess had heard only in connection with prisons.

"Why do we have to wait?" Tess whispered. "They told us to be here at six and it's past that."

"We wait for the same reason one always waits in these situations. Shay O'Neal has to remind us he's more important than we are and his time more precious."

Exactly nine minutes later the maid took them into the sun room at the rear of the house. This was the O'Neals' version of a den or family room, although Tess knew the furniture cost more than the living room set her mother kept encased in plastic slipcovers. But she was less interested in the room's plush furnishings than she was in the view, something one never suspected from the house's staid, formal front.

"Look, Tyner," she said, walking to the bank of louvered windows. "They did save part of the estate after all. It's like the rest of Baltimore doesn't even exist back here."

It was no backyard, but a wooded hill where leafy paths wove in and out. The trees were just beginning to turn, so glints of red and gold shone among the green. One could barely see the houses on the hill's far side, their windows winking through the trees.

"It's a woodland garden," a woman's voice began before it was quickly overwhelmed, then smothered by a man's booming voice.

"We *both* enjoy our garden. We've certainly paid enough to get it to look as random as it does."

Tess turned and faced two of Baltimore's most famous

citizens, expecting to know them instantly—and realized she had never seen them before. Their faces were at once familiar and strange. Just as she had thought Abramowitz was an old friend because he had been on television, she had imagined she knew the O'Neals because their names were everywhere. On museum wings and soup kitchens, on fat checks to charities. On programs at the symphony and every year's list of big United Way contributors. Seamon P. O'Neal and Luisa J. O'Neal, on behalf of the William Tree Foundation. It was always worded this way, presumably because Shay did not wish his dead father-in-law to reap all the credit for the fortune he had made and Shay had enlarged.

Still, they looked as Tess might have predicted. Shay was a dead ringer for the generic man featured in the background of catalogs from Talbot's and J. Crew, always slightly out of focus. A white-haired man with rosy skin and bright blue eyes, he looked as if he feasted on rare roast beef, washed down with robust burgundies or cabernets, followed by a good dose of port. He looked the way Tess had always thought a vampire *should* look after a good meal—not pale, but suffused with blood, red and vivid.

In contrast the woman at his side could have been a vampire's victim. Pale Luisa J. O'Neal had a bruised look around her eyes and she was thin, almost too thin. Tess knew instantly she was one of those loathsome people who can never keep weight on, who regularly misplace five pounds as if they were car keys. Luisa O'Neal looked as if she lived on weak tea and water biscuits, with an occasional cup of beef broth to liven things up. No wonder her childhood nickname, Ellie Jay, was still in use: She had a birdlike, fragile air. She wore an ankle-length flowery skirt with Fortuny pleats, pearls, and a Chanel-style jacket of deep green, a perfect match for the skirt's background. *Not Chanel-style,* Tess corrected herself. *This would have to be the real thing.*

Still, she was far less intimidating than her husband, and Tess found it easier to answer her. "If this were my house, I guess I'd be looking out the window all the time."

"I do spend most of my time here," she answered in the

accentless voice common to Baltimore's best families. "The view changes constantly. And because it faces west, there are lovely sunsets over the hill. I also like it because the stream at the bottom—you can barely see it this time of year, the trees are still so thick—is named for my father and my mother. Cross-Tree Creek."

"Cross-Tree Creek!" Mr. O'Neal interrupted with a snorting laugh. "Only the Trees ever called it that. It's Little Wyman Falls on any city map I've ever seen. The city renamed it thirty years ago, after William sold off that parcel. Of course, now it's worth a hundred times what he sold it for."

Tess was used to such sniping in her own family, but it made her uncomfortable here. Unsure of what she should say, if anything, she stared at Mr. O'Neal's teeth through her eyelashes. They were long and ocher colored, very refined in her opinion. Perhaps they were dentures, made to look so unappealing no one would guess they were fake.

Husband and wife took their seats in matching wing chairs as Mrs. O'Neal launched into a droning litany of hospitality. Coffee, tea, wine, beer, whiskey, a cocktail, water, Coke, ginger ale, juice? Tea, Tyner and Tess agreed, although Tess secretly longed for one of those mellow amber whiskeys she saw in crystal decanters on a butler's bar. But even tea, it appeared, was not a simple choice. "Hot or iced?" Mrs. O'Neal asked. Hot, they agreed. Herbal? Sure. Lemon. Of course. Or cream? No, lemon. One lump or two? Two, they guessed. By the time she finished quizzing them, the maid had arrived pushing a rolling cart with a teapot in its cozy and plates of petit fours, cheese straws, and crustless sandwiches. The cozy was dingy looking, covered with an unskilled cross-stitch. Probably the handiwork of a Tree ancestor and already promised to whatever museum had agreed to put up the requisite plaque: Donated by Seamon P. and Luisa J. O'Neal, on behalf of the William Tree Foundation.

Tess was so overwhelmed by the tea's production values

that she almost forgot she and Tyner had been summoned here.

After a few observations about the weather and the Orioles, O'Neal segued neatly from a humorous anecdote about his latest case to the matter at hand. "Now, you're representing that Paxton boy, is that right, Tyner?"

Tyner nodded.

"Yes. Tragic situation. And a very ... public one. We wonder—at the firm, the partners—if it might be the sort of thing best suited to a plea bargain. We might even be able to help the young man if that was the case, call on some of our contacts in the state's attorney's office. Although I've never done any criminal defense work, I do have some ties there."

"Plea bargains work best for guilty people," Tyner said.

"Of course. Yes." Mr. O'Neal added another two lumps of sugar to his tea and stirred it energetically. "My understanding is your client might fit that, uh, profile. The evidence is, I understand, quite damning."

"Circumstantial."

"Yes. Well." O'Neal whipped his tea madly again, then put it aside. Tess sensed he had put his manners aside, too, that the conversation had shifted suddenly. "We think it would be better for everyone if it didn't go to trial. Perhaps Abramowitz was a pig, but what's the use of going over that in a courtroom? A lot of people's lives could be upset, and the conclusion probably will be the same, albeit with more jail time for your client. A trial would just be an exercise in vanity—your vanity, Tyner. I have it on good authority the prosecutors will settle for manslaughter and a sentence of ten years. He could be out in five. That's nothing."

Tess tried to imagine Rock in prison for five years. He would never last. Oh, he could protect himself against the most vicious inmates, but weight lifting and basketball could never replace his rowing routine. And nothing would compensate for the crush of people. He would hate that most of all.

Tyner regarded O'Neal quizzically. "When you represented Nance Chemical, did you advise the CEO of that company to pay the fine and be done with it? Did you ever tell the folks at Sims-Kever to forget about a trial, just go ahead and pay those pesky asbestos victims?''

''That was different.''

''Exactly. Your clients were guilty. Mine isn't.''

The two men stared at each other across the expanse of a kilim rug that Tess estimated to be worth her take-home pay for the year. O'Neal's face had flushed a deeper shade of red, but he seemed calm, almost jovial. She *had* seen that face before, she decided. The photo in the newspaper file? No, in that one, he had been looking down, so all one saw was the part in his hair. She had seen him laughing and smiling, enjoying himself immensely. Pleasant and harmless, the way he had seemed when their tea party began. A benign grandfather, showing a favorite grandson his back swing. Not, not back swing—a backhand. And not a grandson. A girl. A woman.

''You look different with your clothes on,'' she blurted.

If O'Neal had been sipping his tea, he might have executed a perfect spit-take. Instead he stammered and blustered while his wife fastened her bruised eyes on him. Mrs. O'Neal did not seemed altogether surprised, but she was certainly interested.

''I saw you at the Sweat Shop talking to Ava Hill the other night,'' Tess said. ''You weren't *not* dressed—I mean, you weren't naked—but you had on workout clothes. Or squash clothes, I guess. That's what I meant.''

''Of course.'' He turned to his wife. ''Ava stopped me at the club, worried to death about the implications of her fiancé's arrest.''

''Now that's interesting,'' Tess said, knowing she should stop, yet incapable of shutting up. ''Because this was more than a week before Abramowitz died. Did you talk to her before *and* after the murder? Or were you lying just now?''

She was glad then for the length of the room and its high ceilings, for a smaller room could not have held the ensuing silence. O'Neal was now the color of a plum tomato. Mrs.

O'Neal's face was impassive, staring off into the hills as if the matter was of no interest to her. Every inch a lady, Tess noted. Tyner looked furious—probably with her because she had spoken, and because she had not shared an important fact earlier. He didn't like surprises. But she hadn't realized what she knew until she watched O'Neal speak, seen the same bobbing gestures he had used when Ava had stalked him at the Sweat Shop. She was often the last person to realize what she knew.

"Oh, the sun is going down!" Mrs. O'Neal cried, clasping her hands together. It was the bland, borderline insipid remark of a woman trained to defuse tricky social situations, a woman who never had trouble setting a table, no matter how many sworn enemies were invited to the same dinner party. It worked, for her husband suddenly found his tongue, as smooth as ever.

"I talk to Ava all the time. She is an associate at our firm, with a promising future," O'Neal said. A vein throbbed at his temple, but he was otherwise composed. "Her fiancé's murder trial could damage that future. Clients don't like lawyers who have been too close to felonies and felons. Or law firms where people are murdered. O'Neal, O'Connor and O'Neill doesn't deserve this. We've always avoided publicity, good or bad."

"You brought Abramowitz in as a partner," Tyner said. "You must have known publicity would come with him."

"It didn't, not at first. He was happy to go to charity balls and have his picture taken. And, to be fair, it's really not Abramowitz's fault he became front page news by becoming a corpse. Your client gets the credit for that."

In the space of ten minutes Tess had reassessed her opinion of Seamon P. O'Neal almost ten times. He had seemed silly and harmless, then harmful. He had lied; she was sure of that. An associate who had failed the bar twice didn't have a promising future. But he wasn't a stupid man, merely someone with a radically different viewpoint. He had spent his career protecting large corporations from the complaints of individuals. It was consistent he should hold to this view when it struck close to home.

"My firm means the world to me," he said. "Its reputation is priceless. If you insist on going to court with this case and trying to build a defense on whatever your client *thinks* was going on between Mr. Abramowitz and Ms. Hill, I can promise you we will be of no help. The tiniest thing you want from us—a file, information about the girl's employment history, interviews with employees—will have to go through a judge. You'll need a court order to call me on the phone. And I don't think you'll get any cooperation from Ms. Hill, either. Wouldn't it be better if we were all on the same side?"

"Only for you." Tyner said. "And I could give a fuck about the Triple O. I would consider it a bonus if this trial damaged the undeserved reputation of O'Neal, O'Connor and O'Neill."

O'Neal's eyes flicked across Tyner's wheels. With his red face and beaky profile, he reminded Tess of a copperhead snake.

"I'd forgotten what a bitter bastard you are," he said. "I suppose I would be, too, if I were a cripple with only one accomplishment of note, and it was more than forty years behind me."

Mrs. O'Neal picked this moment to ask: "More hot water, Tyner?"

But her good manners could not save the tea party twice. "Don't worry about it, Seamon," Tyner said, his voice oddly jovial. "You've got a few years. With some luck you might have something to be proud of, something better than a law firm and your father-in-law's millions."

Tyner's line cried out for a grand departure, but the O'Neals' home, for all its graciousness, did not provide him with the unfettered passage needed to roll out dramatically. Tess helped him navigate the kilim rug and the slippery runner in the hallway, a thin rug that bunched up under his wheels. At the front door she had to help him back away from the door before she could wrench it open. When she finally threw it open, a screeching noise filled the air, a horrible sound that echoed endlessly up and down Cross Place. She had set off the O'Neals' alarm system, apparently programmed for automatic, as if they expected Tyner and Tess to bolt.

Tyner made his way down the driveway and swung himself into the van's passenger seat. The days were growing shorter, and the fading light barely penetrated through the trees along Cross Place. In the doorways of the houses to the left and right, Tess saw silhouettes of men drawn by the still-shrieking alarm. As her eyes grew used to the dusk, she saw one had a lacrosse stick and another held what appeared to be an antique revolver. Slowly the men started moving toward the van. Tess threw the wheelchair in the back, not taking time to fold it. The Wasp avengers had reached the end of their curving walkways and were still approaching, silent and sure of themselves. Tess leapt into the driver's seat and floored the engine, backing out of the driveway and burning rubber as she accelerated off Cross Place, the alarm screaming in their ears, the neighbors almost on them. She was on St. Paul, heading back to the city, before she realized the blue and white flag still flew from the antenna.

"I think I'll save that," she told Tyner, pointing at the wind-whipped flag. "After all, we might be invited back for tea sometime soon."

Chapter 17

After dropping Tyner and his van off at his office, Tess walked up to the Brass Elephant and ordered a Scotch and water at the restaurant's upstairs bar. The long, narrow bar deserved to be famous, if only for its martinis. Its regulars, however, were jealous and, as if by unspoken agreement, brought few new customers. Tess had some unresolved feelings about vermouth, but she drank martinis here because she believed in supporting artists at work, and Victor the bartender was nothing if not an artist.

Tonight, however, she was still thinking about all those golden liquids lined up in crystal decanters at the O'Neals. She was convinced their liquor was finer than anything she would ever taste, finer than anything she could buy, no matter how much money she had in her pocket. Then again, perhaps the O'Neals were cheap, the sort of rich people who bought inexpensive brands of Scotch and bourbon and cognac and put them in decanters so no one knew their pedigree. Scotch and water wasn't what she really wanted. Gloomy and out of sorts, she left her drink unfinished on the bar and went home.

Kitty and Officer Friendly were in their bathrobes, wolfing down one of those postcoital picnics peculiar to a relationship's beginning, when sex brings other appetites to life. Tonight they were working on a hunk of summer sausage, Italian bread slathered with olive oil, sliced apples, and Camembert. They invited Tess to stay, but her memory of O'Neal's blood red face robbed her of the usual pleasures she found in cholesterol.

"Not even some bread?" Thaddeus asked. "Olive oil is a relatively benign monosaturate." She wondered if Kitty had taught him that, or if he had unplumbed depths. Shaking her head no, Tess grabbed an apple, sawed off two thick slices of bread, poured a healthy slug of white wine, and carried it all to her rooftop. She would rather have her own solitary picnic than be an unwanted guest at someone else's.

Her dinner finished, Tess felt so cozy in her wallow of self-pity that she decided to smoke a joint. She didn't pay much attention to the harmonica tune wafting up from the alley below. Fells Point had no shortage of panhandlers who tried to pass themselves off as musicians. And this was a particularly overachieving busker who seemed to fancy himself the Jimi Hendrix of the harmonica, segueing raggedly from "The Star-Spangled Banner" to a blues song. *Oh say can you see . . . that my woman done left me.* No, this was a song about a *good* woman, someone who washes out a man's knife wound and doesn't mind when he leaves in the morning, having drunk all her whiskey and left nothing but a bloodstain behind in her bed.

"Oh, shit." She knew this song. It was Jonathan Ross's mating call.

That should have been number five on this fall's list, Tess thought. *Stop seeing Jonathan.* She could, she knew she could. It was her choice to let him in. She flicked the last bit of joint off the roof, crawled back inside, and pressed the buzzer that let him in the side door.

Jonathan took the stairs two at a time and began kicking the door lustily, his harmonica still wheezing in his teeth. She knew by the sound of his cowboy boots on the door that he had come to crow. Tess experienced Jonathan only at his extremes—cocky and in need of affirmation, or depressed and in need of affirmation. Once, in conversation with Whitney, she had compared her Jonathan encounters to eating Oreos without any filling.

"Well, that's what you sign up for when you keep company with men who are virtually engaged to other people," Whitney had said in her blunt way. "Licked-clean Oreos."

Tonight the plain chocolate cookie in question had brought, along with the harmonica, a bottle of mescal, a Big Mac, and a large order of fries. He pressed the warm, grease-stained bag into Tess's middle as he hugged her, giving her a wet kiss tasting faintly of salt and Hohner Marine Band steel.

"Oh, you shouldn't have," Tess trilled in falsetto, cradling the brown paper bag. "Let me get a vase for these fries."

He grabbed the bag back from her, growling deep in his throat, and began to cram French fries in his mouth by the fistful. When obsessed at work Jonathan sometimes forgot to eat until his need for food became so acute he almost fainted. Once he did find sustenance he guarded it as jealously as a dog. Tess knew what a hunger like this meant.

"Big story?"

"Huge," he said around a mouthful of fries. "Enormous. Gargantuan. Pulitzer material. Do they give the Nobel in journalism? I'll win that, too."

Tess felt her stomach lurch. Feeney, damn Feeney. If he had told Jonathan about her call, Jonathan might be following the same lead now. He would find the mystery man with the Louisville Slugger first. He would solve the murder. He would win.

"Abramowitz?"

Jonathan held up his hand as if he were a traffic cop, motioning her to wait while he worked his way through the last handful of fries. "Better. Much better than any dead lawyer."

He offered Tess the mescal bottle, but she shook her head. With a glass of wine at her side and a half-joint still in her system, she had enough substances going. Jonathan took three swallows, then began pacing back and forth, bent over in an unconscious parody of Groucho Marx.

"Tell me," Tess wheedled, unconvinced Abramowitz was not part of it. "You know you're dying to tell someone."

"No. Not yet. I don't have it on the record yet, but I will. I will!" Jonathan dumped a shot of mescal on the Big Mac, then consumed the burger and his own special sauce in three bites. Like Kitty and Thaddeus gulping summer sausage, Jonathan's appetite had little to do with his stomach.

"Give me a hint. Tell me something. Tell me how big it is."

Jonathan stopped pacing, if not chewing, and considered her question. "It will change . . . everything. It will be like a coup, by journalism. Killers will roam the streets of Baltimore. Institutions will be suspect."

"And the president will resign, right? You don't have to hype your story to *me*, I'm not the page one editor. And I'm not buying it."

"You'll buy it eventually. You'll take your fifty cents down to the newspaper box and you'll buy it along with 300,000 other people. No, make that a dollar fifty and 500,000 people. This is a Sunday story, all the way. *The New York Times* and the *Washington Post* will woo me. Movie producers will want the rights. Actors—the dark, brooding, romantic kind—will vie to play me." He grabbed her hands and pulled her to him. "Reporters will want to interview *you*, because you knew me."

"My dream come true." Tess pulled away. Jonathan oversold all his stories, so it was hard to know if this one was truly special. But something told her the little boy who cried wolf—this little boy who called, "Extra, extra, read all about the wolf!"—was going to come through this time. He had unearthed a journalistic treasure. And she was the first to know, the unnamed native servant, following the great white hunter into the forbidden temple and watching in pagan terror as he contemplated a sacred object she had never dared to touch. Once he lifted this golden artifact from its perch, nothing would be the same. The earth would move, the temple would rumble, and Jonathan's future would be made in the brief moment when he decided to run with his treasure. And he would run with it. Of that she had no doubt.

Still, she could not give him the satisfaction of seeming

impressed. "I'll believe it when I see it. As you said, you don't even have anything on the record."

"But I will. You know I will," he said, pulling Tess down on top of him, a new hunger in him.

The imminence of fame and success was an aphrodisiac to Jonathan. He was tender and insatiable, as if Tess embodied the dreams hovering close. They made love once, twice, three times, drinking mescal shots between bouts of lovemaking, talking of everything but the source of Jonathan's excitement. They still had not slept when Tess's alarm went off at 5:30 A.M., summoning her to the boat house.

"Skip your workout for once," Jonathan murmured wetly into her neck. For once Tess did, although she had a slight twinge of guilt about Rock. He worried when she missed practice, assuming she must be gravely ill.

She made a pot of coffee and they climbed to the roof to watch the sun rise. The temperature had dropped thirty degrees overnight as a cool front moved through, and Baltimore looked glorious. No polluted haze over the harbor, just a clear, almost white sky, the kind that would deepen to cerulean blue as the day wore on. A bright red tug moved slowly across the harbor. The bay was green gray. Even the seagulls looked fresh and clean. Tess felt closer to Jonathan than she had in years, as if they were the couple they had been in their *Star* days. She tried not to think about his girlfriend, waking up alone somewhere outside D.C. At least she assumed the girlfriend woke up alone. Maybe their relationship was more complicated than she knew.

"Great view," Jonathan said admiringly. "Some people pay two thousand dollars a month for this view, and you get it for almost nothing."

"Yes, I lead such a charmed life."

"Well, you do, you know. I've always envied you."

"My fabulous career? My riches?" Tess tried for a light tone, but Jonathan's praise felt like pity to her.

"Your family, your sense of place here. In some ways I'm still this schmuck from the suburbs. I don't know the city the way you do. I don't have your credentials."

"You have talent, which is better."

"But I feel like such a fake sometimes." This was familiar territory, the other side of the Oreo, Jonathan ebbing, surrendering to every neurotic doubt, expecting her to prop him up.

"I still remember my first day at work, when I didn't know the city at all but pretended I did. 'Oh, yeah, I went to Hopkins, man, Russell Baker's alma mater. I know this place cold.' They sent me to a fire, and I couldn't find it. I fucking missed a five-alarm. I had the address, I had my little grid map. I could see the smoke, I could hear the trucks, but I couldn't find the fucking fire. It was in one of those odd little wedges off Frederick Road, you know?"

Tess knew. Southwest Baltimore was a series of such wedges, where streets disappeared only to begin again several blocks later. A lot of her father's people had lived there when it was still semirespectable.

"Nick, the rewrite man, got more by phone than I did by going out," Jonathan continued. "He had everything just from working the crisscross, calling neighbors. And when I came back to the office with absolutely nothing, he looked at me and said: 'Nice job, Sparky.' Everyone laughed. He called me 'Sparky' for two years. Right up to the point when the *Star* folded. Then he went off to the unemployment line, and I went to the *Beacon-Light*."

"I kind of remember that. But I always thought it was sweet. You know, well-intentioned hazing."

"Trust me. It wasn't sweet. There's not a day I go to work and don't think about Sparky and Nick." He struggled to his feet. "In fact, I need to confront the beast right now, after a quick shower and some aspirin. It will probably be the first time in a decade someone has shown up with a hangover at the *Beacon-Light*. Half the people there are in AA. The other half have families and can't stay out all night drinking."

"Hey, face it. *The Front Page* is history. Most journalists aren't much different from the pencil pushing bureaucrats they cover."

"Watch that kind of talk, or I might have to take a piss

off the roof and pretend the alley is the Chicago River, just to show you the old tabloid spirit lives.''

Jonathan punched her shoulder. Why did every man she know give her these comradely pokes?

''Jimmy's is open,'' she said, trying not to sound wistful. ''Want to grab breakfast?''

''No time to eat. I'm not even hungry.''

They climbed back into her apartment. Jonathan pocketed his harmonica and ran down the stairs at top speed. He whistled as he ran, tunelessly but happily. She watched him go, feeling pretty shitty herself, in need of ibuprofen and sleep. He should be crawling into bed, hung over and miserable, Tess thought. *He should feel as bad as I do.*

She did feel bad. Her stomach hurt and her head ached, and there was a bad taste in her mouth. Mescal and lack of sleep probably explained the first two symptoms. Eating the worm may have caused the third. She had a vague memory of doing just that at 3 A.M. That had been her idea; she had no one else to blame. And she had no one else to blame for the way she hated Jonathan, at least a little bit, as he rushed headlong toward his brilliant career.

Chapter 18

It was almost noon before Tess could face being vertical. She sat on the floor of the shower and let hot water pound on her, trying to decide if this made her feel better or worse. It was a draw. Finally she slicked her hair back into a tight, damp ponytail—the tension from the elastic band seemed to help her headache—and set out for the courthouse press-room.

"Feeney's law," a sign on the door warned. "The second-worst editor is a failed reporter. The worst editors were all successful reporters."

She pushed open the door and found the *Beacon-Light* courthouse reporter leaning back in his ergonomic chair, his feet on the antique rolltop he had salvaged with the help of a friendly custodian. He had the phone cradled in his ear, a computer keyboard in his lap, and an entire bag of Utz potato chips in his mouth. Sour cream and onion. She could smell them from across the room.

"I don't care what you told 'em at the eleven o'clock budget meeting," he drawled, crunching between words. "You see, unfortunately, it didn't happen that way. The judge just didn't understand your need for simplicity, for—what do you call it?—a hard, clean narrative line. Maybe by the time you go to the three o'clock budget meeting you can get it right. If not, try for the four o'clock meeting. Hey, but it's not your fault. You're an editor. You're a moron."

He placed the phone carefully back in its cradle. If Feeney had slammed down phones or raised his voice, he might have been fired long ago for insubordination. That or the death threats he made against editors every other day. But he was so calm, almost jovial in the way he verbally abused his bosses, that they assumed his attitude was a joke. They never guessed, or at least never admitted, that Feeney's contempt for them was genuine.

Feeney was everything his office sanctuary was not—untidy, with hair forever straggling over his collar and his shirttail always slipping out of baggy khakis. He ate only those foods that could be purchased within fifty yards of the courthouse, a self-imposed restriction guaranteeing a steady diet of hot dogs, which had added a slight paunch to his lanky frame now that he was in his forties. Once a month he shaved, usually on the day he went in to file his expense account. He had been at the newspaper for almost three years, and most of his coworkers were not sure what he looked like. He preferred it that way.

"Darlin' Tess—what can I do for you? Are you going to run around again with a man's coat over your head? I didn't get a chance to see that, but it's the talk of the courthouse."

"Next time I'll tip you off. Today I just want to figure out how to track down an individual asbestos plaintiff."

"What do you know about him?"

"He's an elderly man."

"You've really narrowed it down. Next I guess you're going to tell me he worked at the shipyards."

Accustomed to Feeney's sarcasm, Tess pulled out the clipping and consulted it. "He was awarded $850,000 in one of the last nonconsolidated trials, whatever that means. And Sims-Kever was the only defendant, at least in his case."

"That's a start." The keyboard still in his lap, Feeney tapped in the command for the *Beacon-Light*'s library system. "Luckily I got a hard drive. A lot of the bureaus don't have the library hookup, but I told 'em I did too much deadline work not to have access."

"It keeps you out of the building, right?"

"You got it. Now I'm trying to convince them to give me my own Lexis/Nexis account. But they keep bitching about the invoice I put in for a microwave. Damn, the system's slow today." He punched the keys viciously and, eventually, a form appeared on the screen, requesting information for a search. Feeney typed: "Sims-Kever" and "asbestos."

"I'm gonna put in a time line," he explained to Tess as he jabbed at the keys with two fingers. "They consolidated all the asbestos cases into one big trial a few years back, trying to free up the courts, but before that there were dozens every year. I'm going to tell the computer to search before consolidation."

He pushed a button. *Ninety-seven items found,* the computer replied.

"Jesus, ninety-seven stories. That's way too much to go through. We gotta narrow it down. Hand me that clip." He skimmed it. "Whatta piece of shit. Why'd they give this guy a column, anyway? Wait, here's another little detail." He typed in "Eight hundred and fifty thousand dollars."

Three items found, the computer replied.

"That tells me there are three stories in the system in our time frame that mentioned Sims-Kever, asbestos, and $850,000." Tess looked over his shoulder, enthralled. Electronic data bases were new to her. The ailing *Star* had never been on-line. In fact the morgue at the *Star* was famous primarily for being about five years behind at any given moment. And for filing photos of Mickey Mouse under "Rodents, famous."

Feeney called up each story, the words rolling so fast beneath his fingers that Tess could barely skim them. "You've lucked out. Here are three plaintiffs who got $850,000 from Sims-Kever, two in the same trial, both in the same court, Judge West. If I were you, I'd take these names over to his clerk, see if any ring a bell. But I wouldn't count on it."

"I also could just call 'em up, if they're still alive."

"Yeah, but what are you going to say? 'Hey, are you the old dude who chased that lawyer with the bat?' Or are you going to pretend to be doing a telephone survey on baseball bat ownership?''

"Good point. You're better at this than I am.''

"What exactly is 'this'? You a private eye now? Or are you planning on law school?''

"I'm not sure, Feeney. But if there's a story here, I promise to tell you before anyone.''

"Even Jonathan?''

"He'll be the last to know. Hey—you didn't tell him that I called the other day, did you?''

Feeney shook his head. "I didn't know I had anything to tell. Even now that I've seen the clip and know where you're headed, it seems like a long shot, Tess. What are you trying to prove, that some little old man did the lawyer? It's a big leap from running around with a baseball bat and banging someone's head to a pulp.''

The phone rang. He let it ring five times, then picked it up as if he had all the time in the world. His voice was sweet and mellow, even if his words were not.

"Feeney here. What? Well, that's the stupidest fuckin' idea I ever heard. How'd you get this job anyway? You sleeping with somebody over there?'' Tess could hear the editor's nervous laughter on the other end. She pantomimed good-bye and slipped out. An old political reporter on the *Star* had once given her three rules for success in journalism: Be a star. Be a columnist. Report from a different city than the one in which your newspaper is based. Feeney had found his own city, just six blocks from the *Blight*'s offices.

It was still lunchtime, but she thought she might find Judge West's clerk at her desk, wolfing down a sack lunch. Courthouse employees didn't make enough to dine out regularly at any place finer than Taco Bell. Sure enough, a round-faced young woman was hunched over her desk, a can of Coke, a bag of chips, and an egg salad sandwich on a napkin in front of her.

"Hey, I'm Tess Monaghan. I used to work at the *Star*. I think we met a couple of times, Ms. . . . Collington.'' She had never seen the woman before in her life, but the clerk was considerate enough to have a nameplate on her desk: D. COLLINGTON.

"Donna. Donna Collington." She was a black woman with a reddish undercast to her skin, no more than twenty-eight or twenty-nine, with a sweet baby face and fingernails long enough to rip someone's heart out. Plump, she strained the seams of a tight purple dress, but in a way most men would find attractive.

"I work for a local law firm now, and we've got this messy criminal case. I mean, it's crazy." *So far, all true.* "My boss wants me to find this guy who might be able to testify for our client, but all we know is he was one of two plaintiffs in this court two years ago, in an asbestos case. I have the names, but I can't figure out which one he is."

"Why not call both?"

Good question. "That's what I thought. But my boss told me specifically not to call them. And when I asked why, he told me it was none of my business, just do it his way."

Donna Collington laughed as if she understood.

"Been there, done *that.* But I still don't know how I can help you. Those asbestos cases are all a blur. Just one long line of old men spitting into handkerchiefs and dragging their oxygen tanks around."

"Well, this gentleman would have been one of the last ones, before consolidation. He also appears to have been rather rambunctious."

"Rambunctious?"

"Feisty. Bad tempered. Prone to outbursts. Maybe he made threats, or acted up."

Donna laughed again. "You mean like somebody who might have tipped the judge's water pitcher on a lawyer's head?"

"Yes, for example."

"Not 'for example.' For real. He was this little guy, looked like an elf, cute as could be. He didn't even seem that sick, compared to the others. But he got so upset when some of the others got more money that he grabbed the judge's pitcher—splash, all over the lawyer's head. His lawyer. I'd hate to see what he'd have done to the lawyer for the other side if the bailiff hadn't cuffed him.''

Yes, you would, thought Tess, who had seen the photographs in the autopsy report. ''Do you remember his name?''

''Only his first name. Because his wife was screaming it out over and over, trying to calm him down. *'Oh, Abner. Oh, Abner. For the love of God, Abner.'* I almost wet my pants. And the judge was trying so hard not to laugh, he *split* his. Li'l Abner, we called him.''

Tess checked the printout Feeney had given her. Abner. Abner Macauley. A match.

''Thanks, Donna.''

''No problem. You go make your boss happy, now.'' She smiled sweetly, wagging a long red nail at her. ''Tyner Gray should be real happy with you today. But next time don't come in here telling me lies, girlfriend. I knew who you were working for all along. Everybody in the courthouse knows about that long-haired girl who ran the fifty-yard dash through here last week.''

Tess blushed. She had forgotten what a small world the courthouse was, how little was secret here. All along, Donna Collington, with her innocent baby face, had known who she was and what her ''messy case'' was about. Humbled, she headed back to Fells Point and her shift at the bookstore, for which she was already late.

Kitty gave her a baleful stare when she showed up at the register on a run from the bus stop. She was rearranging the children's section, setting up for a *House at Pooh Corner* party for the weekend. After reading a magazine article about the increasingly competitive nature of children's birthday parties, Kitty had decided to go head-to-head with Chuck E. Cheese, luring Baltimore's more bookish parents into the store for theme parties—Pooh, *Alice in Wonderland, The Wind in the Willows.* All the children received five dollar gift certificates to the store. A shrewd investment, as their parents inevitably dropped at least fifty dollars more when they came to pick the kids up.

''Kitty!'' Tess said, going on the offensive. ''You're actually wearing clothes! Is Officer Friendly out making Baltimore safe for democracy?''

Instead of her usual kimono Kitty wore black linen pedal pushers with tiny bows at the cuffs and a black cotton sweater several sizes too large for her small frame. It kept sliding back and forth, exposing first one shoulder, then the other. Crow, perched on a ladder in the women's fiction section, was almost dizzy from watching the sweater swoosh back and forth.

''At least I made it to my yoga class this morning,'' she said. ''I don't let men disrupt my life. I disrupt theirs.''

So Jonathan's visit had not gone unnoticed. Kitty didn't disapprove of casual sex, just of Jonathan. She thought Tess could do better. Tess knew she could do worse.

''Look—some of us aren't goddesses. We have to settle.''

''Even goddesses don't always settle.'' That was Crow, from his perch. ''Athena never wanted a man. The nymph Laurel turned into a tree rather than end up with Apollo. And he *was* a god.''

Tess ignored him, lowering her voice so only Kitty could hear. ''Jonathan's not so bad. When he's excited about something, about work, he needs someone who understands. His current girlfriend doesn't.''

''Doesn't understand that he needs to sleep with someone else? No, I suppose she doesn't.''

Crow was staring at them so intently that Tess was sure he was going to fall off the library ladder. She whispered, ''It's not really about sex. The sex is secondary, almost . . . perfunctory.''

''All the more reason not to have it,'' Kitty said smugly.

Tired and irritable, Tess was on the verge of saying something wounding to her aunt, something she might regret, when she noticed a wan, tiny figure approaching the register. Head down, the woman moved resolutely, a posture the store's employees usually identified with someone intent on finding the Kama-sutra or a book with orgasm in the title.

But it was Cecilia, the little Kung Fu–fightin' bride-to-be from VOMA. Tess wondered what book she wanted. Kitty had an entire section about rape, including several books about trying to have a normal sex life again.

"Your card didn't say it was a bookstore," Cecilia said. Her voice sounded faintly accusing but also confused.

"I guess it didn't." Tess groped desperately for whatever persona she had presented the other night. What had she told her? Who had she been?

"We're partners," Kitty said, a smooth and accomplished liar. It dated from her early days in the business when she was juggling bills and creditors.

"Oh." Cecilia rocked on her heels in front of the counter, her eyes on the wide wooden planks beneath her feet. "I called on the phone to get directions, but I've never been here before. I guess I wasn't sure what it was."

Tess gave Kitty a look and she evaporated, gesturing to Crow as she retreated to her office that he should take over the cash register. Tess led Cecilia to one of the old library tables.

"At first I felt bad about the other night," Cecilia began, her eyes studying the grain in the oak table. "We shouldn't be in the directory—almost no one who shows up meets the criteria—and we always end up turning people away. For some of them there's not always another place to go."

"Well, no harm done," Tess said brightly. *Apology accepted. That's that. Please leave, as I have no memory of what I told you about myself the other night.* "I'm not holding a grudge."

"I said 'at first.' " Suddenly Cecilia had no trouble making eye contact. Her transformation was swift and sure, much faster than it had been Monday night, when she had metamorphosed more gradually from little Cece to Cecilia. "But then I realized you weren't really interested in joining the group. You were there to spy on us."

"What makes you say that?" *Other than the fact that it's true.*

"You went to all this trouble to find VOMA and made a big stink when you couldn't join, presumably because you needed to talk about what happened to you. But in the coffee bar, when I asked you about your rape, you didn't want to talk at all. I could tell from the questions you asked me that you didn't know what it was like. You were too tentative, too polite.''

Tess said nothing.

"I want you to tell me why you were there."

"You tell me something first. Is there a woman named Mary in your group? A woman whose rapist was represented by Michael Abramowitz?''

Cecilia smiled oddly. "No, no Marys. But we have lots of women who know Abramowitz's work.''

"How many?"

"You haven't answered my question."

"I'm not sure I'm going to." Tess felt an odd power. She wasn't sure why, but she sensed Cecilia feared her. It was a novel experience, and an exhilarating one. "How many, Cecilia?''

Cecilia looked to the ceiling and ticked the names off her fingers, as if calling roll. "Well, there's Pru, Meredith, and Maria—but not Mary. Joan and Melody. Cynthia. Stephanie. Susan. Nancy and Hannah. Leslie, Jane, Ellen, and Lisa. Me—is that everyone? That's the nucleus. A few others come and go, but those fourteen are always there.''

"I guess that's not a coincidence," Tess said. "That others come and go. You seem intent on keeping it private."

"It makes more sense if you know the real name." Cecilia leaned across the table, as if to take Tess into her confidence. Her mood seemed lighter, more carefree. Whatever brief power Tess enjoyed had now vanished. "Victims of Michael Abramowitz. Monday, of course, was our final meeting, our own little wake for the late, great lawyer.''

"Nice try. But I saw the group's charter, remember? You left it behind at the coffeebar. Its official name is Victims of Male Aggression, and Abramowitz filed the papers. Why would he help set up a group of women who hated him?''

Cecilia gave her an appraising look. "Good question. It's the one I asked Pru three weeks ago, when I looked up the charter. She told me it was her own little joke. She asked

Abramowitz to file the charter when he was in private practice, playing on the do-gooding instincts he carried over from the public defender's office, where he made a career out of putting rapists back on the streets.''

"So Pru put the group together and keeps everyone else out?''

"You got it. It's not enough to be a rape victim. You have to have had the singularly unpleasant experience of watching your tax dollars at work, as Public Defender Abramowitz got your rapist acquitted.''

"But that was his job,'' Tess objected. "What would you rather have—public defenders who just throw their clients on the rocks, or people who really try? He wasn't trying to hurt you. He was trying to help poor young men. It wasn't personal. Besides, he left the public defender's office years ago. Isn't it time—''

"To get on with our lives? Actually, for a while, I was getting on with my life. Then his face started showing up everywhere, and his voice. I saw him on television, heard him on the radio. I drove by his billboards on my way to work. That's when the group started—when all these women saw that face again, heard his voice. It brought it all back.''

"Wouldn't it have been healthier to stop watching those UHF channels? Switch to NPR? Find a new route to work?''

Cecilia slumped in her chair, as if worn out by the conversation. "You're just proving Pru's point. Other people don't understand. I never thought I'd have to say this to another woman, but you just don't get it.''

No, she got it. She understood their anger and frustration. But she was uncomfortable around people who based their identities on being victims—even if she herself had done it from time to time. It was counterproductive. Instead of healing, these women ended up tearing off their scabs every week. Their idea of rebellion was to serve cupcakes at a wake, celebrating the fact that someone else had carried out their pathetic revenge fantasies.

Assuming it was someone else.

"So did VOMA ever talk about killing its raison d'être?''

Cecilia rolled her eyes. "We're victims of violence, not perpetrators. Most of these women are scared to go out alone after dark."

"Well, let me ask you this: Did the group discuss the murder? Do you know where everyone was that night?"

"I know Pru was at the ball game, with two dozen kids on crutches and some other people from the accounting firm where she works. The other women were probably doing what they do most nights. Sitting up in bed, with all the lights on, afraid to go to sleep."

"What about you?"

"Home alone. The classic alibi, right? My rapist planned to use it if the case hadn't been thrown out of court. That's the beautiful thing about a defense—it doesn't have to be consistent. 'I wasn't there.' 'I was there, but I didn't do it.' 'I was there, but she wanted it.' "

"How consistent is *your* story?"

Cecilia recited back in a bored monotone, "I was home alone. I was there, but I didn't do anything. I was there, but he wanted it."

Tess remembered—her bruised rear end remembered—how Cecilia had taken her on in the coffee bar. Abramowitz was shorter than she was, and he probably didn't spend two hours a day rowing and lifting. Yet life was unfair. A short, fat, out-of-shape man was still stronger than she was. Cecilia wouldn't have had a chance—would she?

"So what's the point of this visit, Cecilia? All you've done is convince me VOMA's members should be deposed in Abramowitz's murder case."

"I thought you knew something. I thought you wanted something. Now I'm not so sure."

"About Abramowitz?"

"No. Actually it couldn't have less to do with him." She got up to leave. "I don't expect you to understand this, but we're not really happy he's dead. At least I'm not."

"Maybe you can set up a support group for him. VO-MAINSOMA: Victims of Michael Abramowitz in Support of Michael Abramowitz."

For a second little Cece, scared and vulnerable, appeared in Cecilia's eyes. She raised her hand, and Tess was glad she had a heavy oak table as a buffer between them. But Cecilia was reaching for her missing hair, looking for a strand to wrap around her finger as she thought.

"It must be nice to be so strong and to think it's because you're good, that you live right and eat right, so you deserve your health and happiness," she said, almost as if she was working this out for herself for the first time. "But there is such a thing as luck, and there's more bad luck than good in this world."

With that she walked out of the store. She was tinier than Tess remembered. Prettier, too, especially when anger swept over her features and she found the courage to make eye contact. A man looking at her might be a little slower than usual off his reflexes, especially if someone had just finished banging him around. By the time he saw that little foot heading for his ear, it would be too late.

Chapter 19

Cecilia's visit bothered Tess—and not only because there had been some truth in her parting words. It made no sense for Cecilia to seek Tess out, only to tell her more about VOMA than she had ever known, and then insist it had nothing to do with Abramowitz's death. Then again Cecilia obviously had taken to heart the maxim that the best defense was a good offense. She might have miscalculated, thinking a preemptive strike would end curiosity rather than inspire it.

Still, Tess couldn't see a killer in that group. Whatever VOMA stood for, being a victim was the one constant. These women had built their lives around passivity and inaction.

She could feed the story to Jonathan—support group formed around slain lawyer celebrates his death with Hawaiian Punch and homemade cupcakes—and see what happened. Although leaks and balloons were the common metaphors, Tess had always thought placing a well-timed newspaper story was like testing a griddle: Toss a few drops of water on it and see if they pop. But she didn't want Jonathan to turn his attention back to the Abramowitz story. Besides, he wouldn't be interested now that he was happily frying bigger fish. Perhaps she could feed this morsel to Feeney or one of the lesser mortals at the *Blight*.

"She doesn't know what you're doing." Crow, interjecting again. She had forgotten he was there.

"What do you mean?"

"She doesn't know you work for Rock, or that you're interested in the murder. She knows you're not a cop, so she's not worried about anything criminal. She thought you were checking her out for something else."

"How do you know so much? How do *you* know I'm working for Rock?" He was right, though. Cecilia had never mentioned Rock or Tyner. Tess had steered the discussion toward Abramowitz's death, but anyone who read a newspaper might have done that. Cecilia only knew Tess wasn't the victim she pretended to be. She hadn't figured out who she was, or what she wanted.

"I listen a lot. It helps when you forget I'm here—the way you did just now. The way you do all the time."

He smiled, pissing Tess off. It seemed as if everyone was a step ahead of her today—Feeney with his computer, Donna Collington with her long red nails, Kitty with her not-so-secret reservations about Jonathan, Cecilia with her mysterious mission. Now Crow had joined the gang. It didn't help that he was right.

It also irritated her to notice how fair Crow's complexion was. His skin was blue white, like milk, which made the dreadlocks framing his face seem even darker. The skin of someone who stayed out at night, prowling.

"Do they call you Crow after that robot on 'Mystery Science Theater,' or because you look like that singer from Counting Crows?" Actually he was better looking, with good cheekbones and a broad forehead. If he stopped slouching he would have six inches on Tess.

"I was Crow long before either came along. Back in my native Virginia. If you're nice to me I'll tell you the story some day."

"Sorry, that's too high a price to pay." But he had gotten her to smile.

Tess finished her shift, then spent the rest of the evening trying to call Abner Macauley's number, a Dundalk exchange. Each time she dialed, a woman answered and refused to put Mr. Macauley on the phone unless Tess identified herself. Each time Tess refused.

The impasse continued through the evening and into the next morning, after she had returned from rowing. Rock had been at the boat house, looking confused and distracted. The Head of the Ohio was in two days, and Tess knew from looking at him that he wasn't even close to being ready. He didn't look as if he could even complete the course.

"How are you holding up?" she asked.

"I'm not sure I am. Ava still won't talk to me." He looked guilty. "I know, I know—I'm not supposed to talk to her. But I don't understand why her story changed. She tells me—tells you—one thing. Then she tells some newspaper reporter it's all a figment of my overheated imagination. Why would she do that?"

Because she's a louse. "I have a hunch she had to choose between you and the law firm. Given her credit card situation, she had to go with the law firm or risk losing her job."

"Maybe. All I know is I'm not going to row well until this is cleared up. Tyner says I'll be lucky to go to trial by January."

Rock looked so low, so discouraged, she wanted to hold out some hope. "Look, this is kind of premature, but I'm working a lead. I think I might find the guy who really killed Abramowitz, or at least someone with a good motive."

"Tyner didn't say anything about that."

"He doesn't know yet. Let's keep it this way for now, OK? Just between us, I have a feeling I'm on to something."

"Just between us." She tensed, waiting for the inevitable punch, another black-and-blue mark to add to the collection of marks Rock's affection left on her. To her surprise he kissed her brow instead.

By Friday morning Tess had still not been able to get past the hound of hell guarding Macauley's telephone. She had to be on the right track. Then she remembered she was an investigator, not a reporter. Time to lie again. She put on a thick Baltimore accent and dialed the number, which she now knew by heart.

"Excuse me, ma'am, could I speak to one Abner J. Macauley?"

Her long Os and nasal tones worked like a mating call on the woman, presumably Mrs. Macauley, whose Bawlmer accent Tess could have been parodying.

"He's here, hon, but can I ask who's calling and why? He don't get around that well, you know." No, just occasional forays downtown armed with baseball bats.

"Oh sure," she said. "I'm from O'Neal, O'Connor and O'Neill, and we wanted to talk to him about his settlement."

The woman squealed with excitement. "Oh hon, he's taking a nap, but I know he wants to hear about that. Can you call back in a half hour?"

"Actually we'd like to send one of our people out to talk to him in person. Could he see someone in an hour?"

"Well, that's during the noon news, but I guess it would be OK. You tell him just to come on out. You know the way? We're off Holabird Avenue, past Squires, the Italian restaurant?"

If Tess had not lived in Baltimore all her life, she would not have had a clue what the woman was saying. "Holabird" came out "hahlaburd," while Squires was "squi-yers." Italian, of course, was pronounced with a long "I."

"Sure," she replied, almost slipping into her normal voice. "By the way, it's a girl who's coming out, not a gentleman. But she's OK."

"OK, hon. See ya!"

Despite Tyner's repeated exhortations to dress like a grown-up, Tess sensed the Macauleys would be more comfortable with someone who looked as if she had gone to Catholic school with their daughter or dated their son. She paired a plaid skirt with a white blouse, then added a man's navy vest. *To do the Catholic girl bit properly,* she thought, *I should put on knee socks and roll my waistband up until the skirt barely covers my ass.* That had been the parochial school look of her era. Instead she slipped penny loafers onto bare, tanned feet and braided her hair. Fetching, she decided, sort of like a field hockey player on her way to church.

In her Toyota she headed east past Canton, past the quaint row houses of Greektown and Highlandtown, leaving the city limits and heading into Dundalk. On a map East Baltimore County looked promising. It sat on what should have been prime real estate, the meandering coastline of the Chesapeake Bay, with tiny points and inlets. And perhaps it was gorgeous, once upon a time, a time before Bethlehem Steel. But there was no Dundalk before Beth Steel, which had built the community in 1916 to house its workers. In the 1950s, when steel production was at its height, red dust from the mills had fallen steadily over the community, sifting over everything. Cars, clothing on lines, the rooftops and windowsills. They called it ''gold dust'' and were grateful for it, because it meant the shipyards were busy and jobs plentiful.

There was still gold in Dundalk, but not so much for those who lived there as for the men who represented them in court. Few households had been spared asbestosis or one of the other degenerative diseases associated with the onetime wonder fiber. One lawyer alone had built an empire on asbestos, earning more than $250 million in a single class action suit. Now he owned the Orioles. Some of the widows of Dundalk were doing pretty well, too, but none had a sports franchise, not yet.

But, as Mr. Miles had, Tess wondered why Mr. Macauley was so focused on money. Technically he was one of the lucky ones. There were thousands of men throughout Baltimore who had been diagnosed with asbestosis, or the related cancer, mesothelioma. Asbestosis—white lung—was said to be a particularly horrible way to die. The lungs collapsed slowly, until you felt as if you were suffocating. And it wasn't enough to prove asbestos had done it. You had to know which brand of asbestos was poisoning you if you wanted to collect.

Yet Abner Macauley had won in court, one of eleven plaintiffs in the last of the preconsolidation trials. He was due $850,000, and he had won it before he died. The other rewards ranged from $900,000 to $2.1 million, according to the clip Feeney had found, for a total of $15 million. How had the jury decided the costs of eleven men's lives? Macauley had worked a relatively short amount of time—a mere eight months during World War II—and had been able to show he was never exposed again. Someone who could enjoy the money should get more, Tess decided, not less. The scale of suffering seemed inverted to her.

The Macauley house, off Holabird Avenue as promised, was a hideous 1950s-era ranch, a sprawling structure of brick and sea green trim that looked as if it had crawled out of the bay and died on this lot.

Small yappy dogs threw themselves at the Macauleys' storm door when Tess rang the bell. They didn't seem particularly vicious, but she wouldn't have turned her back on them. After almost two minutes, which seemed longer with dogs panting and snarling, a short, chubby woman came to the door. She wore cherry red pants, a red and white striped jersey, and toilet paper rolls in her tinted strawberry blond hair. Tess knew the look. It was one of the favorite local methods for preserving a salon-made beehive.

"You must be the girl!" the woman said cheerfully. "Just let me get this last bit of paper off my hair. One of those mornings, I guess you know."

"Sure," Tess said, feeling agreeable now that she was on the threshold of an important discovery. On the drive over she had convinced herself Macauley had to be involved in Abramowitz's death. She hadn't figured out the details, but her intuition was practically buzzing.

Inside, the house was early Graceland, decorated with ceramic monkeys and kittens. Mrs. Macauley led her to the family room at the end of a long dark corridor. Here, two recliners sat side by side, facing an old-fashioned console television whose color had taken on a distinct lime tint. TV trays stood in front of both chairs, and two hot microwave dinners waited next to sweating cans of National Bohemian. It was how the O'Neals might have lived if their fortune had been a hundredfold less.

"We always eat lunch in here," said the woman, presumably Mrs. Macauley, although she had never introduced herself. "Abner loves his programs."

"Where *is* Mr. Macauley?"

"He'll be out directly," Mrs. Macauley said, eyes fixed on the television screen. Her beehive, now unwrapped, was remarkable, a towering structure whipped from hair normally as thin and runny as egg whites. It wasn't a look to which Tess aspired, but she admired its defiance of nature and gravity.

She stared at a door at the end of the corridor, eager to lock eyes with Macauley. In her imagination everything would be revealed in a glance. Her only fear was that her earnest face would inspire an inadmissible confession on the spot.

Finally a door swung open and Macauley stepped out, dragging a reluctant animal on a thin, pale yellow leash. She saw him give the leash a yank, swearing under his breath. A *sadist*, she thought with some satisfaction as he started down the hall, practically dragging the poor animal.

He moved deliberately, with the measured tread of someone quite sure of himself, a hideous yellowish smile frozen on his face. As Tess's eyes began to adjust to the dim light, she realized he didn't have a pet with him, but something on wheels. Squinting into the dark hallway, she saw the yellow leash was a tube, leading to some contraption at his feet.

"Sweet Jesus Christ," she said under her breath.

What she had taken for a grotesque smile was a breathing tube stretched across his face. The "pet" was his portable oxygen tank. Macauley came down the corridor as slowly as a debutante bride moving across rose petals at the cathedral. And when he finally arrived in the family room, Tess was the one ready to burst into tears, equal parts frustration and pity.

"I've only been on the tank a month or so," he said by way of introduction. "Takes some getting used to."

"Certainly," Tess said, bobbing her head in inane affirmation. She was still trying to reconcile this frail old man with the wrathful monster she had imagined.

"Vonnie says you have news of my check." Each syllable was breathy and measured, a sibilant wheeze. "I was glad to hear of it. I had begun to think I might not live long enough to see my money."

"Yes, the check." She was mesmerized by his face and the tube, staring like a little kid who didn't know any better. "Of course. I'm afraid . . . it's not good news. You see, Michael Abramowitz's death has only complicated things."

Mr. Macauley flushed, but it was an anemic, blue-tinted rush of blood to his face, so he looked more as if he were choking. In his disappointment he couldn't form any words at all, only a faint hiss.

"Abner! Abner!" Mrs. Macauley cried, looking up from the television, and Tess remembered how Donna Collington and the judge had laughed over her cries in the courtroom. "Control your breaths! Remember, the doctor says you have to control your breaths."

He waved his hand in front of his face, miming he was fine. It was several seconds before he spoke again.

"I don't understand. I read in the paper how some of the others, the ones in the consolidated trial, got their settlements, and they came *after* me."

"It's a different case. The consolidated trial isn't being appealed, I guess. Truthfully it's all a little over my head. I'm basically an . . . errand girl for the firm."

"We won two years ago. At first I said, I just want my check before I have to use an inhaler between sentences." He paused for a breath. "And then I said, well, as long as I get it before I have to cart my oxygen tank, that's OK, too. We could go somewhere, I thought, take a little trip. Now—" He paused, waiting for his breath to replenish itself. "Now all I can say is maybe before I'm bedridden. Maybe before I die."

"It's a bum deal," Tess blurted out. "I'm sorry."

"What's $850,000 anyway? Money that big isn't even real. We don't have any children. The lawyer takes his cut, and it's $600,000. It's so much money, more than we ever had, and it doesn't mean nothing. Just a number someone put on me.'' He paused for breath again. ''They plugged it into a formula, you know. It's nice to be worth $850,000, on paper. But until I see the check, I won't believe it. They think they can keep from paying me, you see, because they think I'm not important.''

''Is that why you went to the office with the Louisville Slugger? Because you saw other asbestos victims were getting their checks?''

He smiled shyly, proud of himself. ''The newspaper got that wrong. It got a lot wrong. For one thing it was an Adirondack, a black bat. I got it right here.'' Sure enough, there was a black bat leaning against his recliner. ''And the other thing the newspaper didn't get was the part about my gun.''

''You had a gun?''

''Sure did. Nice little Colt, .38 caliber. Kept it for protection. I put that gun in my pocket and made Vonnie drive me downtown—she hemmed and hawed, but she finally did it—and I told that punk security guard to let me up without announcing me.''

''And he did it?''

''After I gave him twenty dollars, he did.''

''Blond kid? Lots of wrist watches?''

''Yep.'' Interesting detail about Joey—it didn't cost so much for him to forget he ever met Miltie and his Minutemen. She'd have to remember to tell Tyner.

''So I went up. I had never seen this Abramowitz—he wasn't with the firm during my trial. Even after they hired him and put him in charge of the asbestos cases, I could never get him on the phone. I just got some youngster.''

''Ava Hill?''

''No, Larry Chambers, same guy who handled the case in court. Smooth. Butter wouldn't melt in his mouth.''

''So you go upstairs,'' she prompted, trying to get him back on track.

''So I go upstairs. The lawyer, he's sitting at his big desk, looking out the window at the water. No work in front of him, nothing going on. Just staring out the window, hands folded, like a kid waiting to be dismissed from school. I pointed my gun at him, told him someone should kill him for what he had done.''

''Was he scared?''

''No. He smiled, I mean really smiled, like I was his buddy. Then he said: 'How right you are.' A real smart ass, which pissed me off. So I went for him. But I couldn't catch my breath, and he—well, he kinda hugged me, held on to me like a little boy. Then he took my gun away and called the police.''

''So he just made up everything else—the Louisville Slugger, you running around the desk?''

''And he kept my gun. He said it was for my own good, it being illegal to carry a revolver, even if it was registered. Which was true—I'd have been in a lot more trouble if they'd known about that. Him dropping the charges wouldn't have made any difference.''

''I didn't have the impression Michael Abramowitz was someone who did things to be nice.''

''Maybe he wanted my gun for a reason. Maybe he knew that young fella was coming for him.''

Tess didn't bother to defend Rock to Mr. Macauley. He thought she worked for the Triple O. It might have been unseemly if she made excuses for the man accused of killing her putative boss.

But she was tantalized by the thought of that gun. Did Abramowitz fear someone else? Did he suspect it was only a matter of time before that person came for him? If he had hidden it well, the gun might still be there, and its existence could be used to prove Abramowitz had felt threatened long before Rock could be considered a suspect.

''So when do you think I'll get my check, young lady?'' Mr. Macauley asked. His wife looked up hopefully.

Tess weighed her options. She could lie, tell them what they wanted to hear, only to have them weather another disappointment eventually. She could come clean and admit she had nothing to do with the check. Or she could choose a middle path—telling them it was unlikely while not confessing her own masquerade.

"Soon," she said emphatically. "I have a good feeling about it." And she got up to leave, hoping she had given them just one afternoon in which they didn't need to think about $850,000 and the days clicking by faster than the tenth-of-a-mile marks on a taxi meter. If Mr. Macauley had a year to live, each day was worth at least $1,700, she calculated, even after attorney's fees. It was the most expensive gift she had ever given someone.

Mrs. Macauley walked her to the door.

"Miss?"

"Monaghan. Tess Monaghan."

"If they find Abner's gun, will they send it back to us?"

"They might." *After the trial.*

"Maybe that's not such a good idea."

"Why not?"

"Because, hon, if we still had that gun, I'd probably use it on Abner one night, then do myself and the dogs. Abner wants the money because he needs proof he won. It's a trophy to him. But they can't pay me enough to sit here and watch my husband die."

Chapter 20

By the time Tess returned to Women and Children First, she knew she had to find out if Abner Macauley's gun was still in Abramowitz's office. It wasn't much, but it could give Tyner something else to play with. They needed every toy they could find at this point.

She waited until 4:55 to call the Triple O. Seamon P. O'Neal was true to his word: The request to visit Abramowitz's office was rejected—through an intermediary, of course. Fine. Tess considered the refusal an invitation to get what she wanted by any means, fair or foul. Not that she had told them why she wanted to look around. It had been risky to call at all: O'Neal might order a sweep of the office and dispose of anything out of the ordinary. That's why she had called just before 5 P.M. on a Friday. It gave her the entire weekend. To do what, however?

Kitty refused to brainstorm with her. "It gets complicated," she said, "dating a cop." But Crow was all too willing a coconspirator.

"Disguise yourself as a janitor," he suggested. "No—a courier. Put on bike shorts, a helmet, the whole uniform. Maybe the guard will be confused enough to let you up."

"The guard knows me, unfortunately. Even if he didn't, a courier wouldn't necessarily get upstairs," she said, thinking about Joey Dumbarton, the earnest security guard who never let anyone by him unless the person signed the sheet or slipped him a twenty dollar bill. Then again Joey might regard her as a quasi-official, deserving of certain privileges. If she played it right he would wave her up. Then, the gun found, she would leave it in its hiding place and call Tyner, who could get a court order to search the office. Or something—she was a little fuzzy on the legal issues here. The hardest part would be explaining her scheme to Tyner after the fact.

"You need backup," Crow announced. "I should come with you."

"It's a borderline felony, and Tyner's not going to bail your ass out of jail if we get caught. I'll be lucky if he bails *me* out."

"You need a lookout, someone to keep watch while you're rifling through things," he said with the conviction of someone who had watched too many detective shows. "Be bold. It's the only way."

In some circumstances this might have seemed a straightforward if slightly stilted statement. But something in Crow's tone—an arch, self-mocking tone—caught Tess's ear.

"Say that again."

He grinned. This time his treatment was even campier. "Be bold. It's the only way."

"*Double Indemnity.* Insurance salesman Walter Neff says that to Phyllis Nirdlinger when they're planning to kill her husband—"

"She wants to do it in a bathtub, but he tells her it's a bum idea. He tells her everyone thinks the bathtub is the way to go—since some insurance adjuster put out a newsletter saying most accidents happen there. Which is funny because . . ."

"A bathtub accident was the plan Cora and Tom first hatched in *The Postman Always Rings Twice.*"

"Exactly. I never thought anyone else noticed that."

She stared at Crow. A James M. Cain fan. And not just any Cain fan, one who could quote him.

"Have you read all his books? What's your favorite?"

"*Double Indemnity.*"

"I have a soft spot for *Mildred Pierce*. The working girl trying to make something out of herself."

" 'In Glenwood, California, a man was trimming trees,' " Crow recited.

"What did you do, learn it all by heart?"

"I have a photographic memory of sorts. After I read something twenty or thirty times, I remember it. So can I go? No one in a Cain novel ever tried to pull something by themselves."

"No one in a Cain novel ever got away with anything, either," she reminded him sourly. "But I guess you know what you're getting into. Meet me back here about ten to-morrow night. We'll just have to hope even the most ambitious young lawyers take Saturday night off."

The truth was, if Crow hadn't been so impossibly gung ho, she would have been tempted to blow it off. Perhaps it was better to do what Tyner told her to do, and nothing more. Well, this would be her last burst of initiative.

On Saturday night Tess donned her version of work clothes: Blazer, jeans, plain white shirt, loafers. Crow, how-ever, seemed to think he was in a spy film. He had on a black turtleneck, black jeans, a black cap pulled down over his black and green hair, even black gloves. Everything but coal smudged on his face. He carried a large flashlight and looked enormously pleased with himself.

"I've been thinking," he said. "This is kind of like our first date."

"Are you settling for me since Kitty is taken? I should mention I'm not partial to green highlights."

"It wouldn't be settling," Crow said. "And I can make my hair whatever color you like."

"Great, we'll get some Lady Clairol later. Let's get going and get this over with."

They took Crow's car, which Tess had assumed, with some dread, would be on a par with his art school hair and personality. Original. Dangerous. Slightly annoying.

Instead it was a Volvo station wagon, a late model with

private school decals and a state-of-the-art stereo system that almost blasted her into the back seat when he turned the key in the ignition.

"Demo tape," Crow explained. "I have my own band. Po' White Trash."

"I guess I should have seen that coming." *Then again, my perceptive powers haven't been 100 percent lately.*

"I suppose you listen to opera," Crow said. "Cain did."

"Crow, I like reading Cain. I don't want to *be* him. I'm a word person. I like old songwriters—Rodgers and Hart, Cole Porter, Jerome Kern—because of the lyrics. I like Bob Dylan and those folksy, waifish bands on 'HFS. Stephen Sondheim is as close as I get to opera."

"He writes for gay men," Crow said matter-of-factly.

"I thought colleges today gave demerits for remarks like that. Who cares if musical theater appeals to gay men? They have the best taste of anyone; that part of the stereotype is true. And don't gay men like opera, too?"

"I have a theory about this. Gay men like things in code, and maybe that's justified, given they historically have been forced to live in hiding. They like musicals because they're camp. They like Sondheim because so much is hidden in his lyrics. So a Sondheim musical is for people who like hidden meanings and thick layers."

"What's your point?"

"In opera, if you don't know the language, you have to listen to the music. You have to leave words and cleverness behind. Cleverness is the last refuge for smart people. That's your problem, Tess. You're too clever. You're listening to the words instead of the music."

"Is there something wrong with cleverness?" Tess asked sharply, uncomfortable with Crow's attitude. He was suppose to be her Sancho, servile and worshipful, not a hectoring Henry Higgins. "We're about to embark on a potential felony in which cleverness will be our only protection."

"If you say so."

They parked on a side street to the west of the Lambrecht Building. There was no home game tonight and, once one got past the Inner Harbor, downtown had its usual ghost town feel. There are a lot of things one can do to make a city look good, and Baltimore had done it all. But they couldn't put its heart back. Downtown was hollow at night.

Joey Dumbarton was at the guard station, beating on the desk to whatever head banger tune ran through his headphones, played at a volume loud enough to make normal ears bleed. At night, under fluorescent light, he was exceptionally pale, like one of those white catfish living deep in an Arkansas cavern. Evolution and history had passed him by. A generation ago he might have been a steelworker, making good wages with his high school education, set for life. Now he was a minimum wage rent-a-cop. At least he didn't have to worry about asbestos or environmental hazards. If he was lucky he'd get shot in the leg before he was thirty and retire on workman's comp.

Tess whipped out her driver's license, flashing it past him as if it were a badge. "Remember me, Joey? I need to go upstairs, check out Abramowitz's office. You can let me in, right?"

"That's against regulations."

"Honestly, Joey. You know I'm a private investigator working for a lawyer. What's the big deal? We're only looking for something the cops might have overlooked."

"I could get in trouble," he said, a dent appearing above his nose, a sign of deep thought.

"Hey, I'm going to sign in. So is my buddy here." Crow gave Joey his most dazzling grin. "And we're going to sign out. What I'm *not* going to do is give you a twenty dollar bill, the way some visitors do."

Joey may have been dim, but he knew a threat when he heard one.

"I only did that a few times. And I didn't do it the night you're worried about, I can tell you that."

She didn't say anything, just kept staring at him.

"OK, OK. I'll let you up."

To her surprise Joey left the front desk empty as he took them up to the Triple O offices. Certainly this was not in the

Minutemen manual, either. Something else to tell Tyner.

The Triple O offices were dark and empty, as Tess had hoped. Joey let them in, then lingered, as if he intended to supervise.

"If we pull the door to when we leave, will it lock?" Tess asked.

"Oh, sure. Yeah. Just pull the door to." And Joey headed back to his desk and his Walkman.

Once he was gone Crow took his post by the receptionist's desk and Tess let herself into Abramowitz's office. The police tape was long gone, as were any stains left behind by his demise. But no one had rushed to claim the office, despite its panoramic view and lush appointments. Apparently lawyers were a superstitious lot.

She went to the obvious places first. In Tess's experience people weren't creative when it came to hiding things. Certainly she wasn't. If the cops ever raided her apartment, it wouldn't take more than five minutes to find the box of marijuana under the bed. Burglars would need less time to find the coffee can in the freezer, where she kept a few pieces of good jewelry and loose bills. She pulled open desk drawers, searched behind the legal books. Nothing. If the police had found the gun, it should be on an evidence list. If the Triple O had done its own sweep, for whatever reason, there would be no gun. Or could Abramowitz have taken it home?

She was trying to jimmy open a file drawer with a Swiss Army knife, without much success, when she heard Crow's voice in the hallway. "Hello there, sir. May I help you, sir? Sir? Sir?" She crouched under the desk and listened to footsteps drawing closer.

"Can I help you, sir?" Crow's voice, insistent and panicked.

"I don't think so, young man," a familiar voice said. "I don't think you're supposed to be here at all."

Tess peered around the desk. Crow was in the doorway, trying to keep the custodian, Frank Miles, from entering the office. The weekend custodian. Their visit coincided perfectly with his shift. Sighing, Tess crawled out.

"Hey, Mr. Miles. I'm just looking for some things that might be relevant to the case."

He looked at her knowingly. Not suspiciously or meanly. Just knowingly. "Then why do you have to come sneaking around at night?"

"Mr. O'Neal isn't kindly disposed to my boss or his client these days."

Mr. Miles continued to take her measure, sober and thoughtful. It was the kind of face you saw when you tried to sneak in past curfew, Tess thought—wise, beyond bullshit. He may never have been a father, but his years as a custodian in the school system apparently had taught him everything he needed to know about a young person's cunning. Tess knew he wasn't fooled, that he was deciding whether to throw them out or call the cops.

"We won't be long," she promised. "It's not our fault we had to sneak in. Frankly Mr. O'Neal's being a prick, if you'll pardon the expression."

He smiled at that. "Have it your way. But I don't know what you expect to find. I cleaned that carpet myself after the police were through. I guess you just had to see for yourself. You really are conscientious, Miss Monaghan."

He pushed his cart down the long hall to an office in the southwest corner. Tess realized he was making a point of trusting them, of not watching them too closely.

"Cool guy," Crow breathed. "I love his voice."

Now that Mr. Miles had given his tacit consent, Crow helped Tess go over the room one more time. It was an impersonal room, without a trace of Abramowitz in it. She had expected he would be the type to put his clippings on display, matted and framed. Or, failing that, some silly, in-your-face piece of art, a raucous poster or obscene sculpture. There was nothing to suggest Abramowitz had ever been here. Even the calendar on his desk was snowy white, devoid of appointments. She noticed it was still on April, almost six months behind. She ran her hands over the paper, marveling at its virgin state. There were no indentations, no sign that the previous months had been any less pure. But something at the center felt odd. Puzzled, she pressed down again. It wasn't her imagination; there was a thin, square shape in the middle. Flipping the calendar over, she found a computer disk taped to the inside of the cardboard backing.

"Got something," she said to Crow. "What kind of computer does he have here?"

"Macintosh, a really powerful one."

"Good, it's compatible with mine, as long as he uses the same word processing software." She pocketed it. "I guess this is it."

"The files?" Crow asked.

"Locked. I was trying to get into them when you and Mr. Miles showed up. I don't have much experience at breaking locks."

Crow looked at the filing cabinet with great concentration. Then he kicked it as hard as he could. Nothing happened, except that he fell over backward in pain, holding his foot.

"Did you check his desk drawer for a key?" he asked after several seconds, when he started breathing normally again.

Tess slid out the center drawer and immediately saw a key glinting among the pens. They unlocked the first bank of files. This was tricky territory. Lawyers' files are private, and random pawing could affect cases. But Abramowitz's files were as empty as his calendar. Legal-size folders sat, waiting for labels and files. Nothing more. The other drawers didn't even have folders in them. Finally, in the bottom drawer, they found a few mouse droppings.

"I guess the floppy is going to be our only souvenir from this trip," Tess said, patting her pocket.

"What about the gun?" Crow asked.

"If it's here, it's too well hidden. Or maybe it's in his house. Still, we'll always have Macauley's deposition about what happened. That might help."

"Won't he testify when the time comes?"

"When the time comes Macauley may not be alive."

Mr. Miles watched them leave. "Did you get what you came for, Miss Monaghan?"

"Not exactly," she said. "We found something, but it wasn't what we were looking for. I'm not sure what we found."

In the car, as Crow's voice assaulted her in stereo, she expected to feel depressed. They had failed. They had not found the gun. The legal status of the diskette in her pocket was dubious at best, its utility unknown.

But they had gotten in. She felt a buzz of pleasure from that fact alone.

"C'mon," Tess said. "I'll buy you a drink, as long as you order something that doesn't embarrass me. No girlie drinks."

"Sexist. What's a girlie drink?"

"Anything made in a blender, except a frozen margarita."

She directed him to one of her favorite bars, Frigo's, a neighborhood place that could not, despite the best efforts of five subsequent owners, be stripped of everything that made it pleasant and interesting. After five renovations, which included the addition of a Formstone exterior and a rickety deck, Frigo's, on the boundary between Fells Point and Little Italy, still had a tin-pressed ceiling, gleaming wood floors, and a mahogany bar.

More importantly it had one dollar drafts and a metal rack of Utz potato chips, which provided Crow and Tess with a three-course supper: barbecue, sour cream and onion, and, for dessert, crab flavored. The meal went surprisingly well with bourbon and water, Tess's drink of choice that night and, inevitably, Crow's. She suspected if she chose to dive into the harbor fully clothed, or announced a little bank job as their next assignment, Crow would have followed her without batting a thick black eyelash.

It was as if he had slipped his heart into her purse while she wasn't looking, so complete was the transference of his affection. Now Tess had the peripatetic, panicky feeling you have when guarding something special to someone else but of no particular value to you. She assumed she was safeguarding it only temporarily. Any day, any moment, he would want it back, undamaged, to hand to someone else.

"Do you think you'll find anything on the diskette?"

Crow asked. "Should we go back to your place and read it now?"

"I don't expect to find anything. And, no, I don't need you to implicate yourself in this crime as well. There's a chance some privileged stuff might be on there. I did appreciate your help tonight, though."

Crow gave her a lovesick smile. His silly all-black garb was oddly flattering. In the dim light of the bar, his green highlights temporarily hidden, he looked halfway normal and almost attractive. He also looked very young.

Flustered, she took on the pedantic, lecturing tone of teacher to pupil, feeling a need to create some distance between them. She was, after all, at least six years older. Maybe seven.

"Tell me how you started to read James M. Cain."

"I saw *Postman*—the original one, with Lana Turner and John Garfield. I loved it, but I knew something was missing. It was like watching a movie on TV, knowing they've cut out the dirty parts. But, in this case, I figured the dirty parts were in the book. I was right."

"Yes. Cain once lamented he had a flaw that made it impossible for him to write something that wasn't censurable." She knew her voice sounded obnoxious and prim, but she couldn't stop herself. "I'm not sure how he would fare today, when anything goes. I think he'd be dismayed by a world in which nothing is censurable."

"I don't know; he lived until 1977," Crow said. "I bet he kept up. And there are plenty of things still censurable in this world. I don't care how cynical you are, the world will always find a way to shock and surprise you."

Miffed, Tess took a gulp of bourbon, washing the blend of chip flavors out of her mouth. When she was in the throes of a doomed crush, she had the good sense to be agreeable, to nod her head happily, surrendering to every silly thought voiced by the object of her affections. Crow managed to hold on to himself, even when he fell. He was younger than she: Didn't he understand he was supposed to be more stupid as well, less experienced in all things?

Chapter 21

Tess asked Crow to drop her on Bond Street outside the darkened store. He would have preferred walking her to the private side entrance in the alley, but she wanted to avoid any datelike resonance. Fog had rolled in, and even though the air was warm and humid, the night was too romantic for her taste. She was worried Crow might try to kiss her. She was worried she might enjoy it.

Walking down the alley, she had an uneasy feeling. The fog obliterated the stars and the streetlights, so it seemed darker than usual. There was no moon. Maybe shooing Crow away hadn't been one of her best ideas. She stopped halfway down, thought about doubling back to the front doors, then thought better of it. The store had closed for the night, and she didn't want to cut through Kitty's private quarters, not when she was busy with Officer Friendly.

I'm being silly, she told herself. *All this cloak-and-dagger nonsense at the law offices has gone to my head.*

She started walking again, the soles of her loafers making a loud, flapping sound against the pavement. Her footsteps seemed to echo. Or was there another set of footsteps, shadowing hers?

Her keys were out, stuck between her fingers in the improvised brass knuckle technique her father had taught her before she went off to college. She had reached the heavy metal door that led to her staircase. But as she put the key in the lock, a man darted out of a recessed doorway on the other side of the alley and grabbed her right wrist.

Too startled to scream, she turned toward the street, ready to run, but her attacker held her firmly. She lashed out with her left arm and, although her aim was wild, it was a good, solid blow, striking hard against the man's cheekbone and nose.

"Goddammit, Tess." Jonathan Ross dropped her arm, putting his hands up to his face. "When did you get so skittish?"

"As a crime reporter you should know some of us city residents are a little nervous these days. A murder a day, almost."

"I think I'm bleeding."

"Don't be a baby." She unlocked the door. Her hands were shaking; in fact she was quivering all over as if she had been drinking cappuccino instead of bourbon. She pulled Jonathan inside and examined him under the light at the bottom of her stairs.

She was impressed by her handiwork. The corner of his right eye was discolored and beginning to swell. Her nails, although short, had scratched two parallel lines from cheekbone to forehead. Blood beaded in the narrow grooves—actual blood.

"I think I broke your nose," she said solemnly.

"My nose? You broke my fuckin' nose?" Jonathan had a nice straight nose, one that his father, a plastic surgeon in the Washington suburbs, liked to tell patients he had sculpted. In fact it was a gift of nature and one of Jonathan's greatest vanities.

"Just kidding. Come on upstairs. I'll give you a washrag and some brandy. You can use them in whatever way you see fit."

In her apartment, as Jonathan examined his face in the bedroom mirror, Tess took off her blazer, slipping the diskette out of the pocket and trying to slide it unobtrusively onto the bedside table.

"What's that?"

"My work for Uncle Donald."

"I thought you turned in hard copy. I thought your Mac wasn't compatible with the state IBM clones."

"There's some program that translates it. The system manager does it." Typical. Jonathan had never shown the least bit of curiosity about her work for Uncle Donald before this.

"I've never heard of anything like that," he persisted. "The state can't even computerize its own welfare cases, but their system manager can do stuff like that?"

"Did you come by to scare me to death or quiz me on my part-time employment?" She yanked her shirt out of the waistband of her jeans. She hated clothes that made contact with her body, that pressed in at the waist. Ideally she would have liked to wear a caftan all the time, but she didn't want to look even larger than she was. Slowly, deliberately, she began unbuttoning her shirt.

"Still got that body?"

"Why don't you come over here and find out?" Tess sat on the edge of the bed and began to take off her jeans.

His face damp and warm from the washrag he had been pressing against it, Jonathan knelt between her legs and finished the task for her. She placed the back of her left hand on his forehead, as if testing for a fever. Her right index finger traced the lines she had drawn across his face.

"If you had been a mugger," she said tenderly, "I would have kicked your ass."

"Really?" He pushed her back on the bed, holding her down by the shoulders, squeezing the tight muscles that bunched up there whenever she was under stress. "You row. You run. You lift weights. Me, I play basketball once a week if I'm lucky. Try to get up."

She didn't try, for she knew she would fail, knew how hard it was for a woman to be as strong as a man. Strangely she heard Cecilia's voice in her head. *It must be nice to be so strong.* She hated being weak, hated knowing Jonathan could do just that if he wanted to.

"In the alley I wasn't on my back."

"You might have been if you hadn't let me inside."

The heightened adrenal rush of their earlier encounter, the bourbon buzz from Frigo's, the memory of Crow's worshipful stares, the very nature of this politically incorrect conversation—it all combined to make Tess feel wanton and powerful. Jonathan's equal. In the past year, when he had come back into her life, it had been under his terms. He came when he wanted to, he slept with her, he owed her nothing except an orgasm or a good-faith attempt at one. She had pretended—to others, to herself—this was all she wanted, too. But she had known, and Jonathan had known, it was all she could get. She had been settling.

He had straddled her. She raised her right leg slowly, her foot caressing his leg until she could press her knee against the underside of his groin.

"If I wanted to get up, all I would have to do is push this knee up a little more with all the force I can muster, and your balls would be up around your liver. Luckily for you I don't want to get up."

"Isn't that convenient?" *Yes. It was the way she had always been, pretending what she had was what she wanted.*

She snaked her legs outside his, first the right and then the left, and wrapped them around his waist. He was right. No matter how much she lifted, how fast she ran, how hard she rowed, she could never match him in upper body strength, not without a good dose of steroids or human growth hormones. Below the waist, however, it was a different story. She squeezed her thighs together, thinking about the 200 pounds she pressed when doing her adductor work. Jonathan weighed 175, 180 tops. Unlike a weight machine, he could exert force of his own.

"I've still got you pinned," he gloated, enjoying her python act.

Tess, as much to her amazement as his, bit him on the wrist, breaking the skin. Shocked, he pulled his right hand away, which gave her the chance to roll on top of him.

"Still got that body?" she asked.

He nodded, liking this new game, the danger in it, the right amount of danger. She pulled his jeans down and lowered herself on him. She was in the position he had held a few minutes before—her legs straddling him, her hands pressing his shoulders into the bed. She held him there, making love to him, interested only in her pleasure. If Kitty was listening that night, she heard Tess's cries long before Jonathan's.

When they finished, Tess sent Jonathan to the kitchen to scavenge for provisions. As soon as he was gone, she hid the diskette in her desk, which locked. She supposed it was a bad sign be so skeptical of someone who had just left her bed. Then again, she knew him awfully well.

"All I found was white burgundy and Swiss chocolate," he said upon his return.

"What more do you want?"

They munched distractedly, wrapped in private thoughts. Tess was longing to read Abramowitz's disk and hoped Jonathan would leave after he finished eating. But Jonathan, now that sex was past, seemed gloomy and depressed. She steeled herself for a late night, in which she would be expected to make lots of supportive, murmuring noises. To her surprise she had run out of them.

He sighed elaborately, her cue to start. "OK, what's wrong?"

"I'm having more problems than I thought with that story. I haven't been able to fit all the pieces together."

"What's it about, anyway? You wouldn't tell me anything last time—except that it was going to shake Baltimore to its foundations." She laughed a little cruelly.

"It wasn't an exaggeration. This story's huge. But my source is getting cold feet. He's a real twisted fucker, Tess."

"Nice way to talk about a source."

"Hey, it's not just me. Everyone calls him that. It's practically his nickname. But he had a great story to tell. Now he wants money for telling it, and the *Beacon-Light* doesn't make those kind of deals. He's threatening to go to the television stations. Of course, they don't pay either. But the tabloid shows do."

"How credible is he?"

"He's on Death Row for a crime he admits he committed,

so he doesn't have much to gain. Except a little flurry of attention before he dies. Remember I told you I thought Thanos's execution changed the dynamic on Death Row? Well, it's not quite the way I imagined it. A lot of these guys don't want to play Avis to Thanos's Hertz. Nobody remembers number two. So this guy comes forward with a story about a crime someone else committed but got away with because he was rich and connected."

"Someone local? How rich, how connected?"

"He won't tell me. He gave me all these tantalizing hints, but when I went to see him yesterday, he suddenly pops up with this request for $25,000."

"What's a guy on Death Row going to do with $25,000?"

"I don't know. Give it to his mom, maybe, except he hates his mom. He just likes playing with people. The money is about leverage." He sighed again. "He is one twisted fucker."

"Death Row, huh? But it doesn't have anything to do with Abramowitz? I guess that's possible—only three of the thirteen guys there were his clients."

Jonathan grinned. "OK, I misled you a little bit last time. Actually, though, it doesn't have anything to do with who killed Abramowitz. But this guy got in touch with me because he saw my stories on that case. I'm afraid, Tess, you're going to have to come to terms with the fact your buddy probably did it."

"I think Tyner's going to have a lot to work with."

"Tyner could recover the use of his legs during the trial, tell the jury it's because the defendant is really Jesus Christ, and it still might not be enough to get Paxton off. The only thing you've got going for you is the innate hostility Baltimore juries harbor for the state's attorney's office." He grabbed her wrist, his voice suddenly husky. "Then again, maybe you could slap the jury around a little bit. You've got a future as a dominatrix."

But Tess, exhausted and drained, just lay back and let Jonathan lead the way. *I'm going to stop doing this,* she promised herself. She closed her eyes, then opened them again when she realized Crow's face had slipped into her mind.

Afterward, as Jonathan started to doze off, Tess whispered in his ear: "You're not keeping me from the boat house tomorrow. The alarm goes off at five-thirty. You can leave with me or stay here."

"Sick, very sick, this compulsion of yours," he murmured. "But I guess I'll go with you. Make sure I get up, OK? If I'm home by seven I can make bed check. Daphne likes to call early in the morning." In seconds he was snoring, as Tess lay awake, realizing she had never heard his girlfriend's name before.

In late September, when the city was still under daylight saving time, mornings were quite dark. Traces of last night's fog lingered as Jonathan and Tess left through the back door and walked down the alley toward Bond Street and their cars.

The air was heavy and humid, like a wet fur blanket. Jonathan, in a fit of politeness, tried to hold Tess's hand. But she couldn't bear to feel someone else's flesh on such a damp morning, and she shook her hand loose from his grip.

They were almost to the street when, behind them, a car's engine came to life, racing madly. Tess turned to look for headlights, but there weren't any, just the sound of an engine revving. In silhouette it looked like one of those humpbacked old taxis, a Checker or a Marathon, but its motor sounded ferocious and souped-up. For a split second the car seemed to hesitate, like a bull readying its charge, then came straight at them.

Jonathan and Tess also hesitated. *Like deer in the headlights,* Tess thought, *except there are no headlights. Why are there no headlights?* Their reflexes slowed, their depth perception thrown off by the darkness and the early hour, they did not move for several seconds, assuming the car would veer to one side. Even the car, for all its furious noise and speed, seemed slowed by the humidity. But it was still coming straight toward them.

Jonathan reacted first, bursting into action like someone

breaking through the surface of a pool after a long swim underwater. He pushed Tess, hard, to the south side of the alley, stumbling to one knee as he did. His shove sent her a good ten feet, and Tess rolled into the bookstore's rough brick wall, skinning her knees and bruising her shoulder, scraping flesh from her palms. She flattened herself against the wall, covering her head with her arms as if it were an air raid drill. Then she struggled back to her feet, trying to get her bearings. *Where was the car? Where was Jonathan?*

She saw Jonathan first. His jeans were ripped from where he had fallen, but he was up and running. He made it to Bond Street and was a few feet from a row of parked cars when the old taxi hit him. It seemed to rear back and take aim before it struck, catching him at hip level.

Like most reporters Tess had seen only the aftermath of accidents. In movies, people who get hit by cars fly effortlessly, lightly, like rag dolls. If they're heroes, they get up again. Jonathan was a more leaden target. Instead of flying through the air in a graceful arc, he looked like a sack of potatoes being thrown off a truck. He landed hard on the hood of some doctor's BMW, denting it. Tess waited for him to get up, assumed he would get up. He was a hero, he had saved her life.

The humpbacked car sped away, heading north on Bond Street. Tess stood in the alley, her back still flat against Kitty's store, her fingers trying to find a handhold on the brick. Her palms were skinned and bleeding, but she kept digging at the brick. A car alarm wailed, probably the BMW on which Jonathan rested. Lights came on, and people began running outside, pulling bathrobes around their skimpy, hot-weather sleeping outfits. Every house on the block seemed to empty. The car alarm wailed. People kept coming.

Tess couldn't understand all the people. A car alarm was a common sound in Fells Point, especially on a Sunday morning, when the last drunks brushed against the parked cars on their way home.

Then Kitty was there, her silk robe barely covering her, shouting in Tess's face. It was only when she heard Kitty's voice that she realized the alarm's piercing drone had been drowned out by her own voice, shrill and keening. She had never heard herself scream before, so she stopped to listen. Then there was nothing to hear, a fact she found hilarious. Tess began laughing as Kitty held her in her arms and rocked her like a baby.

"I shut up to hear myself! I stopped screaming so I could hear myself scream!" She laughed at her own idiocy, then cried. Finally she ran out of noises to make, appropriate and otherwise. She listened for ambulance sirens, but the morning was still new. The car alarm had been shut off. Tess saw a man, probably the BMW's owner, bend over Jonathan and shake his head. Now she knew why there were no sirens, why everyone was moving so slowly, as if there was no reason to rush. There was nothing anyone could do.

Chapter 22

"No one murders reporters."

Tess sat at the big pine table in Kitty's kitchen, surrounded by what looked to be the most unorthodox of families. Kitty, in a slip dress that covered less than most negligees, was Mom. Dad would have to be Thaddeus. Torn between the immodesty of appearing in his bathrobe, or the indiscretion of wearing his bicycle patrol uniform, he had chosen the latter. Rounding out the group was Gramps—Tyner, in a pale rose polo and matching sweats, cantankerous as always. At the emergency room Kitty had called him after Tess begged her not to call her parents. Now Tess almost regretted her injunction. Her parents, more respectable than this crew, might have given her some much needed credibility with the two traffic detectives she faced.

"No one murders reporters," detective number one repeated. Or was it the other one, echoing his partner's sentiments? The two men looked so alike—medium height, sallow complexions, brown hair and eyes—that Tess worried her fall had made her see double. Only their names were markedly different: Ferlinghetti and Rainer.

"Like the poets?" Kitty had asked Ferlinghetti, squinting at his ID.

"If you say so," he had said. "Can we talk to Miss Monaghan?"

While Tess had been in the emergency room and Jonathan

in the morgue, the detectives had spent the morning interviewing neighbors, pacing off the distance between the point of impact and where Jonathan's body had landed, drawing little diagrams of the accident. The day was unseasonably warm, and both men now had half-moons of sweat under the arms of their short-sleeved dress shirts. They were hot and irritated, and their mood was not improved by Kitty's hot, bitter coffee or Tess's insistence the old cab had been lying in wait for her, for Jonathan, for both of them, for someone.

"It looks like he was killed on impact," one of the detectives said, as if this should be cheering news. Tess kept replaying the scene: Jonathan running toward open ground, trying to take refuge behind the parked cars on the other side of the street, the car bearing down on him, his graceless flight. He may have died instantly, but he had a lifetime to think about it. If she knew Jonathan he was composing his own obit just before the car caught up to him.

"It *looked* intentional," she ventured. Each time they asked her, she became a little less sure.

"What do reporters know?" Ferlinghetti asked, for once desiring no answer. "What can reporters do? They're just typewriters. You don't throw a typewriter out the window when it gives you bad news. You don't kick the floor because the roof leaks on it. You fix the roof. Am I right?"

"You're right," Rainer assured him.

The two detectives then looked sternly at Tess, waiting for her to echo her agreement. She wanted to, wanted desperately to be cooperative, if only so they would leave her alone with her scraped palms and splitting headache. But the events of the morning kept running through her head on an endless loop she could not control, or stifle.

"That car was *aiming* for us," she insisted.

"Hey, don't get me wrong. I'm not saying it couldn't have been on purpose. I'm saying it's not a workman's comp case. Someone wanted to kill Mr. Ross, it probably had more to do with his hobbies. Does he have a wife? A girlfriend?"

Tess shook her head "no" to the first question, nodded miserably to the second.

"Maybe someone had the wrong idea." Ferlinghetti took a sip of Kitty's coffee and winced. "Maybe someone had the right idea."

He was repeating himself, or repeating what his partner had said. They had already discussed most of the particulars that led up to Jonathan being with her at 6 A.M., down to the scratches she had left on his face, the bruise on his cheekbone—but not the bite on his wrist. She had recited, like an inventory, every glass of wine they had drunk the night before, every bite of Swiss chocolate eaten. She had admitted they had an off-again, on-again sexual relationship. But she insisted it was off again, at least on this night. Jonathan had dropped by to sleep off a hard night of drinking. She didn't care what the detectives thought of her, but she did want to blunt the pain for Jonathan's girlfriend. Bad enough he was dead; did he have to be a cad, too?

"His girlfriend—Daphne—didn't like to see him drunk. At least that's what he said."

"And when you found him at your door, where were you coming from?"

"A date." Crow would have liked hearing that.

"Your date got a name?"

Tess, realizing she had no idea what Crow's real name was, looked blankly to Kitty for help, who swiftly provided the answer: "E. A. Ransome. He works for me. I can get his number if you want."

"It wasn't a *date* date, exactly," Tess confessed.

"What was it?" Rainer asked.

Oh, breaking and entering at the city's biggest law firm, a few drinks at a neighborhood bar. "He's a friend. We went to a bar and talked about books we liked. He's six or seven years younger than I am, for God's sake."

Kitty hid a smile behind her palm. Thaddeus nodded soberly, as if Tess had made an excellent point. He had long forgotten Kitty's chronological age.

"So he was a friend and Jonathan Ross was a friend. You have a lot of friends."

Tyner raised his right hand slightly, a signal to say nothing. Tess ignored him.

"I just want you to understand this isn't about Crow being jealous of Jonathan, or his girlfriend, Daphne, being jealous of me. Jonathan and I were old friends. There was nothing for anyone to be jealous of."

"You'd be surprised what makes people jealous. Sleeping with a woman's boyfriend, for example. A lot of women don't like that."

"Well, if she was the one, wouldn't she have run *me* down? It would have solved everything."

"Hey, women drivers." Ferlinghetti looked at his notes. "All I'm saying is, if you want to talk murder, don't tell me it was because Jonathan Ross was some big shot investigative reporter. Who do you think it was? An editor, the cops he covered? He wasn't *that* good a reporter."

Rainer snickered at that. "Not *that* good a reporter," he repeated. Tess remembered not all police officers had loved Jonathan. While he had ingratiated himself with homicide detectives, portraying them as hero-warriors on an urban battlefield, he had ignored the more prosaic cops. Traffic investigators, for example, many of whom yearned for assignments to homicide.

"What about me, then?" Tess asked. "Is it possible someone was trying to kill me, and Jonathan got in the way? Someone other than Daphne?"

"You piss a lot of people off as a bookstore clerk? What do you do—shortchange people? Refuse to gift wrap?"

She looked at Tyner, who again raised two fingers on his right hand, waggling them slightly. *Don't tell them anything they don't know.* Classic defense attorney, she thought. She yearned to brag to these unimpressed, smug detectives, and to Tyner as well. To tell them about her one-woman investigation into Michael Abramowitz's death, or her night raid on the Lambrecht Building. Then they might understand why she thought someone other than Jonathan was waiting for her in the alley last night. But why? What did *she* know? If someone thought she had discovered something, anything, they were sadly mistaken. She opened her mouth, ready to confess, eager to boast, then closed it again.

"No reason," she said. Tyner nodded his head slightly, happy she had taken his advice for once.

Tyner knew best. That's why Kitty had called him while Tess was in the emergency room, where the resident on duty stuck a tongue depressor in Tess's mouth, peered into her ears and eyes with the little light, and tried to convince her to have a series of X rays. Unsure if her HMO would pay for them, she refused and he gave her a faded pamphlet: *What to do in case of concussion.* When she asked for salve for her cuts, or a prescription for painkillers, or just some lovely tranquilizers to help her sleep, he shrugged and said: "Any over-the-counter antiseptic cream will work on the abrasions, and ibuprofen will take care of the aches. As for sleeping—try a shot of brandy in your coffee." She planned to do that as soon as the detectives left.

"I still think the car was trying to hit us," she said, but it came out as a question this time. She wasn't sure what she thought any more.

"Any other day of the week, I might agree with you," Rainer said. "But on a Sunday morning? In Fells Point? Hey, in this neighborhood it could have been some college kid who drank all night, then scored a little flake and was still flying. We see hit-and-runs around here a lot on the weekends—not usually fatal, I'll admit. Look, it's a hit-and-run, which is bad, and if we catch the person he or she faces some tough penalties. But it's *not* a homicide."

"Of course it's not, officers. Would you like some more coffee? Another pastry?" That was Kitty, in her silkiest tones, a smooth contralto a full octave below her normal speaking voice. Only Tess, and maybe Thaddeus, knew her well enough to realize how angry she must be. Impeccable manners were a danger sign with Kitty. She had been icily polite right before she bounced the rutabaga off that disgruntled parent's head. Apparently she was tiring of serving up pots of coffee and plates of kolaches to the good officers. Time to go, boys.

The detectives looked down into their mugs of coffee, too bitter to finish, and their kolaches, too hard to eat, and decided their stomachs could not afford any more of Kitty's hospitality. They left, promising to be in touch. As they walked out through the store, Ferlinghetti could be heard to say to Rainer, or vice versa: "This won't go in the pool."

"Fuck no. This is staying in traffic where it belongs. Which suits me fine, I got stuck with a low number—three fifteen."

"We'll hit that by Halloween. I drew three sixty-six—a murder a day and one to grow on."

Kitty looked at Thaddeus: "What's that all about?"

He ducked his head, embarrassed. "Some of the guys have a pool on the number of homicides this year. But they drew numbers out of a hat, because there're only thirty numbers anyone really wants, three thirty-five to three sixty-five."

"Are you in it?"

"Of course not," he said, frowning. Honesty compelled him to add, "You had to put in a dollar to draw for one of the slots, then five dollars if you got the right to make a pick."

"Assholes," Kitty said, taking the good coffee beans out of the freezer. She had been serving Ferlinghetti and Rainer four-year-old canned decaf from the back of the refrigerator and stale kolaches someone had brought her after the Polish Festival in June. She tossed the pastry into the metal trash can, where it thumped loudly, then put Thaddeus to work making *huevos rancheros* for everyone. Tess was so disoriented from the events of the day, she didn't know if she was famished or nauseous. A little of both, she decided.

"Do you really think the driver was after one of you?" Tyner asked a little later as she sopped up her eggs with wholewheat tortillas.

She hesitated and watched again as Jonathan flew herky-jerky through the air. "I keep a pretty regular schedule, you know. Someone would only have to watch me for a day or two to know when I leave for the boat house."

"I hate to agree with detectives Ferlinghetti and Rainer,

but why would anyone want to kill you, besides Mr. Ross's girlfriend?''

"I don't know, unless it's because I know something I don't know I know. I don't know if I mentioned it, but I've, um, been doing a little work on Rock's case on my own time."

Tyner gripped his coffee cup so hard, Tess thought it might shatter in his hand. She knew he was yearning to scream at her, as if she were some undisciplined novice, but felt he had to restrain his temper in front of Kitty and Tad.

"How did you have time to do things on your own when I made you come to my office every afternoon?"

"There are twenty-four hours in a day, Tyner. I knew I'd have to tell you eventually what I was up to, but I thought . . . I thought I'd have found out who killed Abramowitz, and then you couldn't be too mad at me."

"And did you find out?"

"No," Tess admitted, frowning. "I found out a lot—but none of it seems to have anything to do with Abramowitz's murder."

Her story tumbled out, a disjointed narrative that shot forward and back in time. The trip to VOMA, the strange visit from Cecilia. Her talk with Ava. Rock's refusal to stay away from Ava, even though she wouldn't return his phone calls or see him. Tracking down Abner Macauley. Trying to find Macauley's gun.

"Jesus, Tess—what were you thinking?"

"I don't know. I thought it would show he was worried about his safety. It seems pretty lame now, I admit."

"Did you find anything at all?"

"A floppy disk taped to his calendar. I was going to read it last night, but Jonathan showed up. . . ." They all knew how that had ended. "It's probably not anything. The weird thing is, all his files were empty. Does that mean anything? Could there have been something incriminating there?"

"I'm sure moving his files to other offices would have been routine under any circumstances. Death can't interfere with the business of law, not when one's hours are billed at six hundred dollars per," Tyner said. "That floppy you found is useless. No matter what's on it, the prosecutor would have it barred from the trial. There's no way to prove whose it is, or where it came from. It's too easy to tamper with those things."

"I hadn't thought about that."

Thaddeus slipped out, but Kitty stayed, sponging down counters that were already clean. Tess sat miserably, the complete failure.

"So it was a simple hit-and-run," Tyner said. "Some drunk at the wheel. Maybe he thought it was funny, chasing you two down the alley, then he panicked when he hit Jonathan. As the song says, it could happen to you. After all, it happened to me."

Kitty had taken all of this in, uncharacteristically quiet. Now, as she poured fresh coffee, she asked: "What about the possibility the car was after Jonathan, had followed him here? Maybe they waited all night for him."

Tess shook her head. "No, Ferlinghetti was right about that. You don't kill the reporter, you kill the source."

Tyner chewed his eggs. "I think you're a little paranoid. That's what happens when you skulk around, poking through other people's drawers, literally and figuratively. If you had followed my instructions, you might not be in conspiracy mode right now."

This was no fake gruffness. Tyner was angry. Then again, Tyner was always angry.

"Can I ask you something, Tyner? Something personal?"

"I did not kill Michael Abramowitz, Detective Monaghan."

"No, seriously. Were you always so mean, or did getting . . . hurt make you bitter, the way O'Neal said? The only time you're nice is when you're coaching. Even then you're always yelling."

"No, Tess, getting hit by a car didn't make me bitter. In fact I'm actually nicer than I used to be—but that's about age, not about circumstances, about realizing that winning a silver medal in the Olympics isn't something you can coast on forever, which I might have done if I had been able to keep rowing. Believe it or not, I don't live my life in a perpetual state of before and after. The accident changed my life, but it didn't define it. I've just got a lousy personality. And you seem to bring out the worst in me, Tess.''

''Me? Why?'' She had assumed Tyner's constant fury was general, not specific.

''Because you're so goddamn lazy!'' He banged his mug down on the table, so hard the silverware jumped. ''You could be one of the best female rowers in Baltimore, but you won't work at it. You could be a good-looking woman, but you run around in baggy clothes with that stupid braid hanging out of your head. You're smart enough to find a new career, but you'd rather moon over your lost reporting job.

''So I finally accepted you as you are. I told you: Don't extend yourself, don't take any initiative, do only what you're told—and you do the exact opposite. You expend all your energy on foolish causes. You're a mule, Tess. A stubborn, cantankerous young woman wrapped up in herself. I could kick you, if I could kick at all.''

Tess felt a strange, almost masochistic thrill at Tyner's harsh words. It was at once awful and fascinating to hear her flaws enumerated so well.

''Does this means I'm fired?''

''It means you've fulfilled your contractual obligation to Rock.'' Tyner's voice was almost sad. ''I don't think I'll need you anymore, Tess.''

''Don't worry. I'll find a way to fill my days.'' Tess pushed away from the table and ran upstairs. His words hadn't hurt her—her own parents had said much worse many times—but they had hit home in a way her parents' criticism never could.

Before-and-after mode. That's how she had been living for two years, since the paper folded. No, not quite. She had been stuck on the fence, longing for ''before,'' refusing to let ''after'' begin.

She sat on her bed, looking in the mirror over the bureau, the same mirror in which Jonathan had examined his face last night, so worried about his nose. The memory did not sting as much as she thought it would. She was still a little numb. Eventually, she knew, she would have a thousand memories to confront, tucked away in every corner of her small apartment. It would hurt more before it hurt less.

She unlocked her desk drawer, fished out Abramowitz's disk, and loaded it into her computer. Her Mac, an older model, almost seemed to shudder as the floppy went in. ABRAMOWITZ: A LIFE, was the floppy's label, but it contained only one document. It had last been changed on September 12, the day Abramowitz died. Eagerly she called it up, noting the number of characters in the lower lefthand corner. It was a huge file, perhaps 1,000 pages, she calculated.

Yet the screen she faced was nothing more than electronic wallpaper in a narrow font, single spaced. Nada. Nada, nada, nada. Nada, nada, nada—it filled the first page, and the second, and the third, and the fourth. She told the computer to jump to the end of the file. Still solid nada. Upper case, lower case. Sometimes separated by commas, sometimes set off by semicolons, sometimes underlined, but all nada, always nada. And it wasn't a program, she was sure of that. Michael Abramowitz had sat at his desk, drawing a partner's salary at the city's biggest law firm, and written "nada" word by word, over and over again, playing with formats and fonts and point size. It was strange, it was crazy. It made perfect sense, for she felt like doing it herself right now.

Nada, nada, nada.

Chapter 23

Tess had known Jonathan was Jewish. But it was only when he was dead, and she was staring at heads covered with yarmulkes, that she really believed it. Sitting in the back of a suburban Washington funeral home, trying to be inconspicuous among the journalists who had gravitated toward the final rows of white folding chairs, she found herself wondering if his parents had left the diamond earring in his left ear, or trimmed his unruly hair. She had met them a couple of times, back when she and Jonathan really dated, and they had wasted little time letting her know they disapproved of journalists, Baltimore, and the lowlifes Jonathan chronicled for the newspaper. Oddly they had approved of her, although Tess suspected it was because of Weinstein Drugs and their mistaken belief she would come into money one day.

Obit-wise, the *Blight* had done well by Jonathan, assigning one of its best writers and placing the story at the bottom of the front page, all editions. Most accidental deaths don't merit p-i, newsroom jargon for the front page, but Jonathan's stories had always gone there, so his death did, too. ''Sheer force of habit,'' Feeney observed. Tess knew it was also one of the unacknowledged fringe benefits of working for a newspaper: One's death is treated very seriously.

Of course, the *Blight* hadn't taken Jonathan's death seriously enough to go beyond the police report. No one had called Tess to ask for her eyewitness account. Too bad; she could have told the writer how Jonathan saved her life, breathing some much-needed action into a story almost as moribund as its subject. The prose had been too flowery and portentous for her taste, more suitable to the treatment *The New York Times* gave some onetime ambassador or an inventor of something one had never heard of. Then again, giving interviews would have necessitated confronting once more the tricky questions about why she was with Jonathan at 6 A.M. Tess had never realized how suggestive a time of day could be, but now she saw there was a large space of time, from midnight to almost nine, in which there was no decency.

"I never thought I'd grow up to be Megan Marshak," she whispered to Whitney, who smiled, one of the few people who would instantly recognize the name of the woman with Nelson Rockefeller at the time of his untimely death.

Even without the hero angle, Jonathan would have loved his obit. Good play, a serious, hushed tone, a few good anecdotes. He had outlived one of his oldest fears. When he started in the business, before coming to the *Star*, he had put in a year on a medium-size newspaper in Peoria, Illinois. Jonathan spent every day he was there—467 in all, he once told her—writing about labor problems at Caterpillar and trying to get out. He had worried he would be linked to the town for posterity, that he would be on a plane when it crashed outside of Chicago, the only local angle on board. He saw the headline—*Peoria Man Dies in Crash*—and he knew he had to leave before he became Peoria Man.

And he had, had escaped it altogether. In his obituary there was no mention of his humble beginnings, just his Baltimore résumé, and the prizes won, and the belief shared by everyone that great things waited for him. Jonathan did not die as Peoria Man, or City Man, or Local Man, or under any of those generic rubrics newspapers are so quick to bestow. He was, in the headline, for posterity, a "*Beacon-Light* reporter, prizewinner, dead at twenty-eight." Tess had never thought about the fact he was younger than she.

Whitney was on her left and Feeney on her right, *goyishe*

spies in the temple. Many of those attending had never been at a Jewish service before, but Whitney, shiksa incarnate, was the one who drew the most skeptical looks. Jonathan's relatives seemed to regard her presence as a kind of sacrilege. Perhaps they, privy to details the newspaper had not printed, thought she was the mystery woman of the morning. Dignified and stern looking, Whitney paid no attention. At one point she handed Tess a handkerchief smelling of Shalimar. Taken with the fact she knew someone who carried a perfume-scented handkerchief, Tess stopped crying immediately.

Bruised and dazed, feeling more Jewish than usual, she saw a certain wisdom in the custom of burying the dead as quickly as possible. As a child she had always thought the practice was dictated by a practical fear of germs, much like the ancient bans on pork and shellfish. To be Jewish, she learned from her mother's family, was to embark on a never-ending campaign against germs and bacteria. But it was nice, she realized, to still be numb. It seemed a little surreal. Jonathan would be long buried before she really felt his absence.

He had saved her life. Or had he? More importantly had he intended to save her life? Less than thirty-six hours later, all she could remember was dropping his hand in the damp, sultry morning, unwilling to have any contact. The last touch of his she had to remember was a hard shove. Because of it she was alive and Jonathan was not.

She suspected he had intended to live. If he had sensed it was an either-or situation, he might have handled it differently. His heroism had been reflexive, his desire to survive instinctive. He was avid to live, sure of the accolades and successes so close at hand. Greedy Jonathan, he had assumed he could save Tess and himself, much as he had assumed he could have his girlfriend and Tess.

The rabbi, a young man who had actually known Jonathan, was trying gamely to bring him back to life. But the hot spell had not broken, the funeral home's central air-conditioning was inadequate, and the sweaty mourners were impatient. Tess glimpsed the woman she assumed was Daphne, between

Jonathan's parents down front. The name had always evoked for her someone sultry and petite, not unlike Ava Hill. But Daphne was a friendly-looking redhead whose natural demeanor was probably warm and cheerful. She looked like Tess, although a little shorter and a little rounder. She even had an overbite.

"Jonathan was a deeply spiritual person," the rabbi was saying.

Feeney whispered: "Yeah, he used to pray every day he would win the Pulitzer."

"And when I was thinking today what would be appropriate to his death, I thought of a poem, a poem a lot of us studied in school. . . ."

The journalists and ex-journalists throughout the small, muggy room shifted nervously in their seats, worried they might laugh. Many were professional funeralgoers who had sat through too many memorial services in which they had nothing at stake. They could sense a cliché rushing toward them.

The rabbi cleared his throat once, then twice, and began in an earnest, adolescent voice that seemed on the verge of cracking: "The time you won your town the race/We chaired you through the marketplace . . ."

Whitney passed a note to Feeney, which Tess read over his shoulder: "You owe me one drink. Told you it was going to be Housman's 'To an Athlete Dying Young.' "

"Who knew?" Feeney scribbled back. "Thought Catholic church owned the rights and would lend it out to other denominations only when deceased was varsity football player who had run his Trans Am up a tree."

For all its adolescent timbre, the rabbi's voice was compelling, bringing emotion to the time-worn lines. "Smart lad, to slip betimes away/From fields where glory does not stay/And early though the laurel grows/It withers quicker than the rose."

A few rows ahead, Tess saw Nick, the old rewrite man who had made Jonathan's life at the *Star* so miserable. Not even fifty, he looked old and bent. His job in public relations at a local hospital had aged him fast. She saw a few other *Star* folks, but far more *Beacon-Light* staffers. Jonathan was theirs. Police officers also were scattered through the crowd, even the chief. The mayor had sent a representative. The city council president, who wanted the mayor's job, was there in person. Tess wasn't sure if she believed in an afterlife, but she hoped it provided the bittersweet pleasure of watching one's funeral. Only if it was cheering, as Jonathan's would be to him. If you drew a small or indifferent crowd, you should be spared seeing it.

"Now you will not swell the rout/Of lads that wore their honors out,/Runners whom renown outran/And the name died before the man." The rabbi bowed his head.

"Good choice, ending there," Feeney whispered. "This bunch wouldn't know what to make of 'the garland briefer than a girl's' that is on the athlete's head in the last stanza. They'd think it had something to do with Jonathan's earring. I'm buying *everyone* a drink when this is over."

Everyone proved to be Whitney and Tess. The other reporters and ex-reporters hurried back to their jobs, while Feeney turned his beeper off and Whitney phoned the office to say her engine had thrown a rod.

"I'll tell you one thing," Feeney said to Tess when they were well into their third pitcher of Rolling Rock. Whitney was at the bar, trying to convince Spike's cook to make her a sandwich that didn't require frying or grilling. "He read the wrong Housman poem. You couldn't have dragged Jonathan kicking and screaming from these fields, no matter how short-lived the glory."

"What would you have read?"

"Terence, this is stupid stuff."

"Hey, I'm not a Housman scholar. No reason to get rude."

"That's the name, 'Terence, This Is Stupid Stuff.' It was going to be part of a volume called *The Poems of Terence Hearsay*. It's about a guy who drinks and eats until he's stupefied."

"That doesn't sound like Jonathan. He ate and drank, but only to fuel some inner machine. He didn't want to dull his senses."

"How's this? 'Luck's a chance, but trouble's sure,/I'd face it as a wise man would/And train for ill and not for good.' "

"Better, but I'm not sold."

Feeney took this as an invitation to perform. He stood up, placing one foot on the booth's cracked vinyl seat, his right arm across his chest. He looked like Washington crossing the Delaware. But when he spoke, his voice stripped of its gruffness, everyone in the bar turned to listen. The words took on an Irish lilt, the kind Tess's father developed midway through a six-pack of Carling Black Label.

> "... *And down in lovely muck I've lain,*
> *Happy till I woke again.*
> *Then I saw the morning sky:*
> *Heigh-ho, the tale was all a lie;*
> *The world, it was the old world yet,*
> *I was I, my things were wet,*
> *And nothing now remained to do*
> *But begin the game anew."*

He gave a little bow and took his seat. It was a side of Feeney Tess had never seen. The editors he terrorized would tear him limb from limb if they had ever sensed the melancholy poet beneath the crust.

"How do you know so much Housman by heart?"

"Mad Ireland hurt me into poetry."

"That's Auden, writing about the death of Yeats."

"She shoots, she scores!" Feeney gave her a high five.

Whitney approached with a huge sandwich, overflowing with cold cuts, cheese, lettuce, and hots. "Oh, great, the English majors' convention is in town. How would you like it if I started jabbering in Japanese, *my* major?"

She took the top slice off her sandwich, picking at the

contents with her long fingers, licking mayonnaise from her French-manicured nails.

"Whitney, that's gross," Feeney said.

"Am I offending somewhere here at Spike's? This is the only way to eat a sandwich. Bread is just a buffer, something that gets in the way of you and the meat. It's like the preface and the footnotes. You don't really need it. It's nothing. It's nada."

"Nothing," Tess repeated. "Nada."

"Nada, nada, nada," Feeney droned, then laughed. "An old man is a nasty thing." He was quite drunk, Tess realized.

"Hemingway," Whitney said. "*A Clean, Well-Lighted Place.* I can play, too."

Tess stood up abruptly, grabbing Feeney's car keys from the table and tossing them to Spike. "Have someone drive them home when they're done, OK?" She turned back to her startled companions. "You're both too drunk to drive. Just tell Spike when you're done, and he'll have someone take you home. And tell him to put everything on my tab." Which was another way of saying it was on the house. Spike had never taken a dime from Tess.

"What about you?" Whitney asked. "Are you in any shape to drive?"

"Unfortunately, yes. I've never been more sober."

In the Toyota she raced along the curves of Franklintown Road, running every yellow light and a few red ones. She took the stairs to her apartment two at a time and thought of Jonathan doing the same thing not even a week ago, when he was on the verge of a discovery. Now she knew what he had felt.

She turned her computer on. Abramowitz's disk was still in the drive. There it was again, the nada wallpaper at beginning and end. But she had never looked at the middle of the long manuscript. That was the problem with shortcuts. She instructed her computer to look for the one word she knew was in everyone's copy, the word one could not write without.

"Find 'the,' " she told her Mac. The computer complied.

Twenty pages into the file, she found the meat in the sandwich.

"*Monday, Monday,*" it began. "*I actually like the beginning of the week now. I can trust this day. I come in, thinking, 'This time will be different. I will find work to do. I will force them to give me work to do. I will take a criminal case pro bono.' But it's no good. Having forced myself in here, I can't remember what I hoped to gain. I can't bear to practice law, in any form, yet I can't leave here. So I come in each day and draw my percentage as a partner and I count paper clips and I make bets with myself about the seagulls I see outside the window. I can't wait for spring. I wish there were more day games at Camden Yards. With the radio on and a pair of good binoculars, it's better than a sky box.*"

The writer—Abramowitz, it must be Abramowitz—had then written in the words to "Take Me Out to the Ball Game." This was followed by several lines of poetry, many of which meant nothing to her. But she recognized Milton toward the end: "*When I consider how my light is spent.*" This line was repeated for three pages, until it changed subtly: "*When I consider how my life was spent.*" And then, for two more pages, increasing in type size as if he were screaming: "*My life!*" "*My life!*" "*MY LIFE!*"

It was like a little boy writing on the blackboard after school, but this little boy had devised his own punishment. It was like *Finnegans Wake*, if Joyce had been a pudgy Baltimore lawyer without much feel for language. It was like a frog dissecting himself. Fascinated, she continued to work her way through the dense, difficult prose.

He wrote about Northwest Baltimore in the 1950s, going to synagogue in the old Park Heights neighborhood, where many of his mother's people still lived. His family apparently was Orthodox, and he was obsessed with *trayf*.

"*I am nine,*" he wrote. "*I must eat something nonkosher. I have thought about my betrayal at great length. My sin must be a large sin. I walk miles, so I am far from the neighborhood, so I am somewhere no one I know has ever been. Or so I think. I order a cheeseburger and a milk shake. It is amazing how much significance I place on these two foods. I am certain that the world will change when I take a bite from that cheeseburger. And I'm right. I still remember that first bite, juice coming out of the burger like venom, cheese running down its side. I have high expectations for sin, and all of them are met. Sin is wonderful. I will be drawn to it all my life.''*

The Proust of Park Heights, she thought. What an odd little guy. Then, just as the narrative seemed to be leading somewhere, he spent ten pages writing the Bill of Rights over and over again, italicizing different words in each version. Was he having a nervous breakdown, or just trying to fill his days, days that were mysteriously empty? A little of both, she suspected.

The Bill of Rights gave way to a discussion of the death penalty, filled with legal cites. Now he appeared to be working on a brief, aimed at releasing everyone from Maryland's Death Row. But the legal argument gave way abruptly.

''Because I didn't want to face the difficult decisions posed by my personal life, I chose a professional life. Now that I've lost my professional life, I have no personal life to go back to. After being asexual for much of my life, how do I start being sexual, much less homosexual, at age forty-two? I don't have a clue.''

Homosexual? Tess did a double-take, reading the sentence again. Michael Abramowitz was gay. No, he must be bisexual; he had made a pass at Ava, after all. The circumstances of their affair may have been in doubt, but she had seen them together, and Abramowitz had admitted the relationship to Rock.

Or had he? She went to her desk, where she kept copies of the transcripts she had prepared for Tyner. What had Rock said?

''And he said, 'But she really is beautiful.' So I hit him.'' Rock had treated this as a confession, much as Mr. Macauley had assumed Abramowitz was a smart ass when he agreed someone should kill him. Macauley had tried to pummel Abramowitz, and Abramowitz had held him in his arms and protected him from arrest. Rock and Macauley had expected a villain, and so they found one. But what if Abramowitz had been sincere? Then, "But she really is beautiful" became a compliment from someone trying to be polite. And "Maybe you're right," the rejoinder to Macauley's assertion that someone should kill Abramowitz, was simple agreement.

She scrolled through the memoirs, looking for some other reference to his personal life. She was barely fifty pages into the 1,000-plus pages and Abramowitz had returned to his brief, slogging his way through case law again. Then she found these words.

"Burned all your bridges. I know the term, of course, but I always saw it as linear. You burned a bridge and moved on. There was always another road ahead, a place to go. I burned a bridge at the public defender's office, got out. I burned another bridge, came here. Now I see I am a little island and I have burned every bridge that led to me. I am alone now, isolated, and no one can help me. I put myself above the law and, by doing so, lost it. I have nothing now but time."

"Wrong again, Abramowitz," Tess said to her computer screen. "You didn't even have that. C'mon, give me a clue. Who wanted you dead?"

She instructed the computer to search for Macauley's name. Nothing. What about O'Neal? The computer came up empty again. Ava? No, no names were mentioned. A lawyer to the end, Abramowitz had violated no one's confidentiality but his own.

"How do I start being sexual, much less homosexual, at age forty-two?" Good question. She knew one person who could help her answer it.

Chapter 24

The next evening, when Ava Hill opened her door at Eden's Landing, Tess could see immediately that there had been significant changes in Ava's life, or at least her bank account, since Tess's last visit. The cheap-looking leather sofa had been replaced with a longer, better-made version, this time in a rich shade of dark green. The same color snaked through the navy rug, brushed the legs of a low coffee table, then disappeared only to reappear at the throat of a vase on the glass-topped table. Even Ava's new briefcase, resting on an antique hall tree in the foyer, was the exact shade of dark green. Tess remembered this, the Coach bag Ava had stroked so lovingly before hurrying to the Renaissance Harborplace Hotel and Michael Abramowitz. It was a new decorating trend, Tess supposed, using an expensive handbag as a theme for an entire room.

"Your circumstances seemed to have changed," Tess told Ava, whose dress, a burgundy coatdress, provided the perfect contrast against the sofa. Tess was seated in the old director's chair, the one from the terrace, with the torn orange cover. Apparently the apartment was a work in progress, with some improvements left to be made. Tess would have liked to urge some restraint. From her perch she could see the once-empty dining room. Now the room was too full, overwhelmed by a glass-topped table and six sleek chairs of blond wood, upholstered with peach damask. Expensive, but impractical to

Tess's eye. The seats would be destroyed by one stray buttered pea, or a sesame noodle slipping from its chopstick.

"Yes. I came into some money."

"An inheritance from a dead relative?"

"No, no such luck." She smiled at the expression on Tess's face. "Oh, lighten up. I'm only trying to live down to your expectations of me. I assume, from your urgent phone call this morning, you have more accusations to hurl at me. You've always thought the worst of me. I'd hate to start disappointing you now."

"I was wrong, wasn't I?"

Ava looked at her suspiciously, not persuaded by Tess's conciliatory tone. "Wrong about what? It's such a long list. As I recall you accused me of having an affair with my boss, then of setting up my fiancé to kill my boss. You even suggested I'd killed my boss. Is that everything?"

"Until now. I do have a couple of new ones, though."

"This should be fun." Ava cradled a glass of wine the color of her dress, warming the globe with her cupped palms. She had not offered Tess any. Her circumstances had improved, but not her manners.

Tess took a deep breath, trying to remember everything she must say, how to say it, the order in which it had to be said. She would have liked to use notes, but Kitty had thought it would make her look tentative and unsure of herself, and Officer Friendly had agreed.

After mulling over the one real revelation in Abramowitz's diary, Tess had dragged the happy couple from bed the night before, almost literally, and begged for their help. Seated around the kitchen table, each with a legal pad, they had tried to fit together the pieces. Thaddeus wrote down what was known, irrefutable, absolute. *Fact,* he had written in bold, black letters. *Ava could not pass the bar. Fact: Ava was in a hotel with Michael Abramowitz.* Tess wrote down what she suspected. Kitty kept track of the theories linking the two lists. To Tess's surprise Thaddeus had shown a real flair for fitting a puzzle together. Disinterested, with no knowledge of the personalities at hand, he had no agenda.

He was going to be a good detective one day. It was Officer Friendly who had found the place to start, who picked up on a discrepancy Tess should have noticed long ago.

"Remember the night I met you at The Point, when you didn't know who my client was at first?"

"Of course. That's the beginning, isn't it? Do you ever wonder how things might be different if you hadn't made those reckless accusations, forcing me to go to Rock before you could poison his mind against me? Do you ever think about that?" Ava sipped her wine, pleased with herself.

Every night, you bitch, every night. But she couldn't afford to play this little game of gotcha, what kids in Baltimore schools had called giving a tight face. "You seemed relieved when you heard it was Rock. I realize now you thought someone else might have had you followed, someone you couldn't manipulate. Someone who could cause problems for you."

Ava was still smiling over the rim of her glass, but only with the lower part of her face. Her eyes were narrow and there was a pinched look around her temples.

"You thought Luisa O'Neal had hired me."

"Are you going to accuse me of sleeping with Mr. O'Neal now?" Ava's indignant reaction was convincing. If Tess hadn't seen her play the same part before, she might have been more easily persuaded. "You have an awfully one-track mind. You're as preoccupied with sex as a spinster." Tess was surprised she didn't pinch her cheek between thumb and forefinger, as they would have done in junior high after such an insult. *Tiiiiight.*

"I do have a one-track mind. But I don't make the same mistakes twice. You aren't sleeping with O'Neal—not yet. You will, if it means keeping your job. That had been the plan with Abramowitz, right? You had all these bills, and if you didn't pass the bar this winter, you were going to be out of a job with no way to pay them."

"I thought you were going to cover some new ground today. This sounds suspiciously like what started all the trouble in the first place. I wasn't sleeping with Abramowitz.

And he wasn't sexually harassing me. I lied to you because I didn't think you'd believe the truth, not when you had a sordid alternative.''

"What is the truth?''

"You'll find out in court.'' Ava smiled, then repeated happily, "I wasn't sleeping with him.''

"Oh, I know that. And I knew you couldn't testify to that in court. You weren't Abramowitz's type. Michael Abramowitz was gay. Or would have been, if he had any sex life at all.''

Ava's face seemed to light up for a moment, then just as quickly shut down. Tess would bet anything she had agonized over Abramowitz's indifference, worried she was losing her charm. But whatever personal vindication she found in Tess's information, she wasn't ready to change her story.

"How could you know that? I never heard—I mean, people in law offices gossip. It's true, he never had girlfriends, but he wasn't very attractive.'' She laughed at herself. "That's a euphemism. He was ugly. He may not have had girlfriends, but he didn't have boyfriends, either.''

"As I said, I don't make the same mistakes twice. This time I really do have proof, a long letter Abramowitz wrote at his computer when he was supposed to be working. A letter I'm prepared to give to a reporter I know, along with my own theory about what really happened between the two of you.''

"So? I told the police and the press that Darryl fantasized this whole thing. Revealing Abramowitz was gay is only going to make my story more credible. My statement,'' she amended quickly. "It will make my statement more credible.''

"True. But what if there are other things in Abramowitz's diary? He wrote more than a thousand pages, plenty of room to include your problems with the bar and his embarrassment at your attempted seduction.'' Tess had leapt from Officer Friendly's world of facts to her own list of suppositions, but Ava couldn't know this. "If you didn't sleep with Abramowitz, it wasn't for lack of trying. The Renaissance Harborplace Hotel was a nice touch. Your idea, I assume?''

"It's probably not admissible in court, that journal of his. Mr. O'Neal will keep it out of court."

"Good, very good, Miss Hill. You get an A in criminal law this semester. But it is admissible in a newspaper."

Ava busied herself with the skirt of her dress, smoothing it under her, then adjusting the hem. Tess waited. She was learning how to be silent.

"Look, what do you want?" Ava asked at last. "You can make my life miserable, but it won't help Darryl. I didn't kill Abramowitz. His death actually jeopardized my job at the firm. They assigned me to him after I flunked the bar the second time, because they didn't expect me to last out the year. When he died they could have fired me."

"But they didn't, and I need to know why. I also want you to fill in some blanks for me. You were as close to Abramowitz as anyone was before he died. You may actually know something without realizing what you know. You help me, and I won't release his diary. Deal?"

Ava nodded warily.

"OK, here's what I know. A year ago you joined the Triple O with a lot of debt hanging over you. You took the bar in February. You flunked. You took it again in July, flunked again. Now you've got even more debts, because you can't stop buying clothes—and because your skills as a shoplifter are limited to the lighter stuff, underwear and jewelry."

"I don't know why you keep talking about shoplifting, I have *never*—"

"Save it, Ava. Let's stay on point. You were desperate. You decided your best chance of staying on the payroll was seducing Abramowitz. I don't know what interim approaches you tried, but eventually you convinced him to meet you regularly at a local hotel. I guess you thought he'd have to succumb to your charms in such a setting. How'd you do that, by the way?"

Sulky now, almost pouting. "He was helping me study for the bar. I told him it was one place we were assured of not being interrupted. He actually bought it."

"Impressive. So you figure it's just a matter of time before this guy is all over you. But he never touches you. In fact he really tries to help you with the bar, which isn't exactly what you want. He even makes you cancel your vacation with Rock so you can study harder. He says he can whip you into shape."

"I can't pass the bar. I have this anxiety about it. It's, like, a syndrome. It's not my fault. I went to see a doctor and—"

"Of course it's not your fault. You're a victim. Everybody's a victim. But Abramowitz, who didn't have anything else to do, didn't buy it. He loved the law and he wanted you to love it, too. In fact I bet he was driving you nuts, making you work too hard. So you started working on a contingency plan—Seamon P. O'Neal. If you're sleeping with the big boss, who needs the little one? And, who knows? You might pass the bar after all. You were studying with one of the best lawyers in the state.

"But you're so busy with Plan A and Plan B, you start neglecting Plan C—your fiancé, a nice guy who happens to have a nice big nest egg. A big enough nest egg to pay off all your student loans and most of your credit card debt, if it comes to that."

Ava looked toward the lights of downtown and the harbor. "Darryl wasn't a plan," she said in a soft, almost regretful voice. "He was strong. I liked that. I thought he could protect me. He couldn't help me with this, though. I needed my job if we were going to have any life at all together. He makes less than $50,000 a year. How can two people live on that?"

It wasn't a bad speech, possibly even a sincere one. But Tess was unmoved.

"You might have to cut back on a few leather sofas, but it's possible."

"It wasn't just money. Darryl didn't want me to work at all. We fought about that a lot. I was so tired of arguing, I didn't even mind when Abramowitz told me I should use my vacation week to study. I was glad for an excuse to get away from him.''

She and Rock had fought? Funny, he had forgotten to mention that small detail. But she had to concentrate. This was the tricky part, the part where she had to admit how clever Ava was, how stupid she was.

"So, one day, some not-too-bright woman pops up." She mocked her own voice, trilling in a falsetto. "'Hi, I'm a private detective and I know you're having an affair.' Of course it's not true. But you're fast on your feet. You see instantly the circumstantial evidence that convinced me—the hotel, the covert meetings—are enough to convince other people, too. Especially the increasingly sympathetic O'Neal. In fact this could solve all your problems. Maybe you'll get a nice fat settlement. Maybe Abramowitz will get fired and you'll get another chance. It was a good plan. With Abramowitz dead, it was an even better plan.''

"How do you figure that?'' Ava's voice was sharp again, stripped of the velvety tone she had used when talking about Rock.

"If Abramowitz is dead no one can contradict you, right? And I assume a firm that hates publicity would prefer to pay you off, as long as you agree to tell the press a more genteel version of events.''

Tess gestured at the new furnishings around them.

Ava sighed. "You're right, more or less, but what's the point? None of this changes the case against Darryl. He thought Abramowitz had forced me to go to bed with him. He went down there and he killed him. Don't get me wrong, I hope he gets acquitted, or manslaughter, but I still think he did it. Frankly it's a little frightening to think I came so close to marrying a man with that strong a violent streak.''

For the first time she seemed absolutely without guile. There was no indication that Ava remembered her own pivotal role in this, that her lies had sent Rock to Abramowitz's office, that none of this would have happened if she hadn't been such a schemer. They had both been so clever. But Tess couldn't afford to think about this now.

"There are still some missing pieces. Why didn't Abramowitz have any work to do? Did people in the firm know he wasn't doing anything? Did he have something on O'Neal?"

"I asked Shay about that once." *Shay,* Tess noted. "Of course, I didn't ask it quite as rudely as you did. He told me Abramowitz had screwed something up, an important case. He didn't really have a lot of experience in this kind of practice, you know. He knew the law, but he didn't have the style the firm's clients expected. He upset an important client. So they stopped giving him work, hoping he would leave. That's how they do things at O'Neal, O'Connor and O'Neill. But Abramowitz wasn't gracious enough to cut his losses. He was greedy."

Tess could hear the too-hearty voice of Seamon P. O'Neal—no, *Shay*—reeling off those last few sentences. Ava was a quick study, at least at some things.

"Did everyone know he was being frozen out?"

"No, no one was suppose to know. Not even me—I. They just wanted him to leave; they didn't want to destroy his reputation. But after three months of creating busywork, he began running out of things for me to do. At first I thought he didn't trust me because of my problems with the bar. Then I saw his files were empty, and one day . . . well, one day I opened his briefcase. All he had in it were a law journal and a ham sandwich."

So Abramowitz had never lost his taste for trayf. Tess liked that.

"He never got mail. Almost no one called, never any clients. The Sims-Kever people were always meeting with Larry Chambers, a young partner at the other end of the office, while I was moving death certificates around in my files."

"No mail or phone calls at all? What about personal stuff?"

"He did get letters from inmates—I saw the Department of Corrections numbers on the envelopes. He said a lot of his clients from his public defender days stayed in touch. He was proud of that, which was odd. Those were the cases he lost.''

"Maybe he was proud the men liked him, even though they lost.''

"Maybe. One sure didn't, though. He used to call and harangue him, which always upset Michael.''

"Did he ever say anything about those calls, who they came from? Maybe a client with a grudge had been released from prison recently.''

Ava shook her head. "He'd just get all red in the face and say, 'I hate that—' Well, I'd prefer not to repeat what he would say.''

"Give me a break, Ava. We've established you're not exactly Emily Post. Tell me what he said.''

"He'd say . . . 'I hate that twisted fucker.' ''

"Twisted fucker? He called him a twisted fucker?''

"Yes, and it was odd, because he never used words like that, not around me. When I complained he told me everyone called him that.''

And when Tess had told Jonathan not to refer to his source by that name, he had said the same thing. "It's not just me. It's practically his nickname.'' The twisted fucker.

"Ava, this is important. This guy could have been released from prison, he could have come after Abramowitz.''

"No way. Not this guy.''

"Why?''

"Because this man is on Death Row, I know that much. The only way he's leaving prison is on a gurney.''

Death Row. Jonathan's source had been on Death Row, too. It had to be the same man. He had contacted him after he wrote about Abramowitz. The night before he died, Jonathan admitted the source was connected to the lawyer, but not to the lawyer's death. But Jonathan could have been wrong.

Tess stood up to leave. "You've actually been a big help, Ava, although I can't tell you how.''

"You're not going to give that letter to the newspaper, right? That was our understanding.''

"The letter? Oh, you mean Abramowitz's diary, with all that stuff about you in it? Well, I should tell you two things, Ava. First of all the newspaper could give a fuck about your story. It's not news and only an egomaniac would think it was. The second thing is—I made it all up. Oh, Abramowitz *was* gay, but he never mentioned you, or your attempted seduction, although he did work out some practice questions for you. I lied to get you to talk to me, Ava. I owed you that much, don't you think?"

Ava dropped the glass of wine in her lap, spilling the dark red burgundy. Tess had been wrong: The wine and the dress were not the same color. The wine made a satisfyingly dark stain across the skirt of her dress, then ran down the sofa to the rug. Yes, that color did look nice next to the green.

"You know, my mom always uses plastic slipcovers on the good furniture," Tess told Ava. "You might want to try that, given your problems holding on to wineglasses."

Chapter 25

Tess did not have to dig far through her file of Abramowitz clippings to guess the identity of the twisted fucker. The "nickname" was a play on the man's real name—Tucker Fauquier. During his trial his name had become a spoonerism of sorts, with would-be wits calling him "that fuckin' queer." Times had changed. "Fucker" was more acceptable, "queer" less so. Fauquier had, wittingly perhaps, provided the alternative. In one of the clips from the newspaper file, he called himself "one twisted fucker." Actually, Tess saw, he had called himself "one twisted f-----," but even a child could have solved that puzzle.

"I was lucky to have a lawyer like Michael Abramowitz," he had told the reporter. That was *after* his conviction for the one killing with a witness, after he had pleaded guilty to the other murders, receiving so many sequential life sentences he would have to top Methuselah's 900 years before he would qualify for release.

Why had his gratitude metamorphosed into rancor? Tess slumped back in her chair and tried to find an answer. Was it simply because death seemed more likely now than it had ten years ago, when it appeared Maryland would never again execute someone? Was it the result of time alone, time to think up new grievances? She studied the old photo of Fauquier, his arm slung around his lawyer's neck. It was Abramowitz who looked unhappy, staring down at his feet.

Abramowitz, the man who was glad to receive mail from his other clients in prison, could not bear to be with Tucker Fauquier. Was it because he had lost the case? Or because, as a man grappling with his own sexuality, he could not bear the touch of someone who raped boys, then killed them so no one would ever know?

Fauquier had been Jonathan's source. Fauquier had been Abramowitz's client. Both men were dead. Did she dare go see him, too? She felt she had no choice. It was as if she were in a boat, a boat rushing forward of its own momentum along an unfamiliar route, with no coxswain to steer or warn her about obstacles in her path. Of course she could always stop, give up, go to the police or Tyner, tell them everything she knew. Or she could keep going.

She dialed her uncle Donald's number at work. He answered on the third ring, as he always did, hoping to seem busy.

"Tesser! Where were you last week? I had to write those damn things myself. How could you let me down like that?"

"I couldn't come back after Mom told me who was really paying my 'salary.' I never wanted a handout, Uncle D. I don't need money that badly."

"Neither do I. And after doing this job on my own, I'm ready to double the price. Anything. Just come back to me." He sang the last line, adding: "*On A Clear Day You Can See Forever.* It was on cable the other night. If I sing like Yves Montand, will you take your job back?"

"No deal. I need a big favor from you. In all your state jobs, did you ever pass through the Department of Corrections? I have to get in to see a condemned inmate as quickly as possible."

"I did a DOC rotation a few years back. Deputy director of prisoner relations. You write a letter, the inmate has to give his consent, and the lawyer has to agree. It can take a long time, though. Tell you what: You write the letter and fax it to their office first thing tomorrow morning. I'll call someone I know over there and tell 'em—what will I tell 'em? Wait, there's a Monahan in Maryland who gives the governor a lot of money. Spelled without the 'g,' but who'll notice? I'll call a guy I know, whisper in his ear you're Monahan's granddaughter, doing a sociology thesis. They'll have you in by tomorrow afternoon.''

''Will that work?''

''Tesser, if they believe you're Ed Monahan's granddaughter, they'll probably let the guy leave the prison with you on a one-day pass. Ed Monahan is the daddy of a thousand redheaded Eskimos. Half the laws on the state books were written exclusively to benefit his seafood company. The governor would do anything for him.''

''You're the best, Uncle D. I'd do anything for you.''

''They can't take my pension away from me for spreading bad gossip. The worse they can do is transfer me again. You know, the only department they haven't stowed me in yet is Employment and Economic Development. Which is too bad, because I definitely have expertise on how to stay employed. And our arrangement showed a real flair for economic development.''

Tess thought of her uncle's bare office, the clean desk, the legal pad with his mock bets scribbled on it. He had never married, never had any interests outside politics and the track. Since the fall of his onetime employer, he had been living in a kind of exile, his talents wasted.

''Is it hard, Uncle Donald, doing nothing?''

''Hey, it's a *gift*.''

''No, seriously. I know you're grateful for the check and the pension you're going to get. But isn't it hard, filling your days?''

His answer did not come quickly. Tess knew he was not thinking about her question, only how to say out loud the truth he had hidden so long from everyone, even himself.

''It's the hardest thing I've ever done, Tess. If I had been younger maybe I could have found a different job, not a job I loved as much, but one that used a few brain cells.'' He sighed. ''Oh, hell, I was lucky I wasn't indicted, too. Of course, if I had been indicted maybe I could've become a lobbyist. If you get indicted and beat the rap, it gives you a lot of credibility.''

"True. But the best lobbyists are the ones under constant threat of indictment. They have an edge the others lack.''

Donald laughed appreciatively. "You're a smart one, Tess. Maybe you should go into politics. Don't be like me. Don't let losing your first love keep you from finding a second.''

She hung up, stunned he had assumed her questions had been prompted by her own situation. She had been thinking only of Abramowitz. Hadn't she?

The next morning Tess typed the letter as Donald had instructed, sending it to the Department of Corrections over Kitty's fax machine as soon as the state offices opened at 8:30. She simply stated her request, letting Donald tell his lies behind the scenes. Later, if someone found out she wasn't the right kind of Monaghan, Donald would simply say: "Who knew? I guess the grapevine had it wrong.'' The approval of her visit was faxed back within forty-five minutes. Theresa E. Monaghan could see Tucker Fauquier that afternoon.

Crow arrived for his shift, bearing pastries, fancy ones in a box. Napoleons, éclairs, turnovers, quite a splurge on his meager salary. In the past few days he had begun showering on Tess the attentions he had bestowed on Kitty. He gave Tess the looks she had once coveted, brought her gifts of food, tried to talk about James M. Cain, and composed little songs. But she was tired of discussing Cain and too numb to feel anything more than a dull, sisterly affection toward Crow.

Today, in addition to the pastries, he also brought her a glass of fresh lemonade from the Broadway Market. Tart, with lemon slices. She sat on the old soda fountain and drank it slowly, savoring it. Neither of them spoke, but it was a companionable silence. As Crow had once said, the light here was lovely in the morning, fresh and clean. Kitty, in cowboy boots and a fringed skirt, dreamily rubbed lemon-scented furniture polish into the library table. The Everly Brothers sang about devotion over the store's speakers. Crow took out his guitar and played along, looking at Tess when he thought she couldn't see.

A sharp rap on the glass door interrupted his song just as Tess was becoming uncomfortable with his steady gaze.

"Go away," Kitty called cheerfully. "We open at ten."

But Tess recognized the tiny figure at the door. It was Cecilia, holding a sheaf of papers to her chest.

"I need your help," she said when Tess let her in. She was getting better and better at jumping into her assertive mode, with fewer stammers and downcast glances with each encounter. "I thought I could do it by myself, but I can't. I need to know what you know."

So many possibilities flooded Tess's mind, she couldn't begin to sort through them. What special knowledge did she have? To what was Cecilia confessing: Abramowitz's death? Jonathan's hit-and-run? Why had she come back to Tess, whom she had dismissed as of no use just last week?

"What kind of help do you need from me, Cecilia?"

"Documents." She shoved her armful of papers at Tess. "It took me six weeks to figure out how to find the charter for VOMA. You told me you went and looked it up after our meeting. So you know how these things work, and I don't. I want you to help me. I'm tired of wasting time on wild goose chases."

Tess took a step back. Cecilia's energy, concentrated as it was in such a small person, was a little frightening, uncontrollable. She wanted to be safely out of arm's—or foot's—reach.

"Who do you think I am, Cecilia?"

"Well, at first I thought you worked for the Internal Revenue Service."

Everyone laughed at that, but no one harder than Tess. She laughed so hard her legs became weak and she had to sit on the floor, still laughing. She laughed until she remembered how long it had been since she had laughed—not since Saturday night.

"Cecilia, I've been called a lot of things, but no one ever thought I was the tax man. What put such an idea in your head?"

"You know how when something's on your mind, you forget it's not on everyone else's mind?" *All too well,* Tess thought. "Well, when you tried to sneak into our meeting, it never occurred to me you were interested in Abramowitz's death. I mean, he got killed, they arrested the guy who did it, end of story. To me, there's no mystery, no reason anyone should care. Even after I realized that's what you were after, it didn't bother me. I knew no one in our group did it."

"But what would an IRS agent want with you, Cecilia? Did you forget to report a scholarship? Claim a few extra dependents on your tax form?"

Cecilia shook her head impatiently. She was speeding along and wanted Tess to catch up. She was almost vibrating with tension. Too many coffee bars for this young woman, Tess thought.

"Not me. VOMA."

"What about VOMA? I assume it's a nonprofit."

"A nonprofit that asks its members to kick in a lot of money. We pay fifty dollars a year in dues and we're always holding fund-raisers. Bake sales, silent auctions, walkathons. Pru is always dreaming up another one. Then we turn in our money and we never see it again, and we never get anything for it. No one else seemed to care, but when I asked Pru, she got hinky about it. Said we were funneling a lot of money to NARAL and NOW, and we had to pay rent for the room."

"So you got suspicious and went to find the charter."

Cecilia nodded her head in the affirmative this time, shaking it so hard she looked like a toy dog in the back of someone's old Chevy. "Yes, after six weeks of calling virtually everybody in state government, in between school, studying, and working at my pop's bar. They don't make it easy for regular citizens, let me tell you. I got to the right person about once out of every ten calls, and then that person was usually on break. But I finally found the charter. When I asked for tax forms, the incorporations office sent me to the attorney general's office. But they didn't have any record of VOMA under either name. Dead end.''

"More like a wrong turn," Tess said, but Cecilia was too caught up in her breakneck recitation to hear her.

"Then you showed up. I knew after I talked to you the second time that you weren't an IRS person, you were too clueless—"

"Thanks."

"But you did mention you had looked up the charter. And this was just two days later! It took me six weeks! Can you find the tax forms that fast? Our annual meeting is next month, and I want to see where the money went before we elect Pru to another year."

Tess could tell it had never occurred to Cecilia that she might not help her. For her, the only issue was how fast Tess could solve her problem. Free of charge, of course. She didn't understand the code of the full-time freelancer, who never traded time without receiving money. Still, it was an easy enough job, and one that wouldn't result in anyone getting killed.

"You were on the right track, but in the wrong office. The attorney general's office is for *foundations,* the folks who give away the money. If you want to see the files on charities, which raise money, you need the secretary of state's office in Annapolis."

"OK, let's go." Cecilia actually grabbed Tess's arm and started hustling her toward the door. She was not only quick but strong.

"Hold on a minute." Tess shook her arm loose with some effort. "I'm not exactly in a position to head off to Annapolis right now. I have an appointment later. But I may be able to help you out with a quick phone call."

Covering the United Way had finally paid off. Tess found an old friend at the secretary of state's office who agreed to fax VOMA's latest tax statement. Within minutes the 990 forms were peeling off Kitty's fax machine. Cecilia grabbed each one as it arrived, staring at them uncomprehendingly.

"Here, let me show you what to look for," Tess said, taking the facsimiles from her. "In its last tax year, 1992, VOMA received almost $35,000. Most of it, about $30,000, appears to be from a grant. The rest is presumably from your fund-raisers."

"But why are we having fund-raisers if we get $25,000 a year? Pru acts as if we're always broke. She didn't even want to have that party last week. Everyone had to kick in, and the chips came from Price Club."

"Got me." Tess flipped through the pages. "Strike that. Got Pru."

She held out the page on which all compensated officers had to be listed. Prudence Henderson, according to the form, was receiving $30,000 a year for her services as president-treasurer.

"Is that legal?"

"As long as the board agrees, and Pru is the board. Under state and federal law all VOMA has to do is file these papers. It's outrageous, paying most of a charity's proceeds to one person's salary, but VOMA is a one-woman show. Besides, anyone can look up what we just looked up. Pru is betting they won't. After all, the salary doesn't look exorbitant— unless you know she pulls down another full-time paycheck. She does, doesn't she?"

Cecilia nodded. "At an accounting firm."

"Which means she can do VOMA's tax disclosures herself, saving a few more dollars—for herself. It's sleazy as hell, but I think she stayed within the law. If you took it to the newspaper, someone might write about it. But if I were you I'd just tell the other members what you know. I'm sure, as a group, you can reach a consensus about what to do with Pru."

Cecilia didn't seem to be paying attention. She beat Kitty's desk with her tiny fists, making the fax machine and phone jump alarmingly. "Dammit. Goddammit to hell."

"Don't be so hard on yourself. This is arcane stuff. Not many people know how it works."

"You don't understand. I wish Abramowitz were still

alive so I could ask him. He filed the charter, he may have known something. I went to see him—''

"You went to see Abramowitz? What did he say?''

"Not much. He was dead.''

In her astonishment Tess unwittingly did a very good imitation of Joey Dumbarton. "But you weren't on the sheet. No one goes up without signing the sheet.'' *Or bribing the guard.*

"Look, when I want answers I want them *now*. I tracked Abramowitz down at his office, and he said I could come see him, although 'client privilege' might keep him from telling me anything. The guard let me up in exchange for my phone number. Not a real one, of course. But when I got up there, Abramowitz was on the floor, with blood everywhere, so I left. When I got home I called 911, but they had already been notified. If the police hadn't caught the guy the next day, I might have told someone what I saw. But they had him, so I figured it wasn't important. And I didn't want to explain to anyone why I was there. I never want to testify in court again. And I wanted to keep VOMA out of it. Even if Pru is a crook, it's a private matter. I don't want to hurt the group.''

Tess pinched the bridge of her nose. She had a feeling she was about to get a tension headache. "Do you remember the time you went up to his office? I mean, more or less.''

"Ten-twenty, ten twenty-five.''

Great, they had lost fifteen minutes. Rock said he had been outside by 10:10, according to the Bromo Seltzer tower. Frank Miles had called the guard at 10:35. That had given them twenty-five minutes. Cecilia's visit meant someone else had to enter the office, kill Abramowitz, and leave in less than fifteen minutes. Maybe ten.

"You know I work for the . . . suspect. He's a friend of mine.''

"I figured that out. Give him my thanks.''

She got up to leave, gathering the fax papers together.

"Are you going to confront Pru? Or tell the rest of the group what was going on?''

"I think I'll give Pru a chance to explain herself first. She was a good friend to me once. She did run the group; maybe she deserved a little money for it. Besides, being greedy's not the worst thing in the world. Not even close."

As Cecilia strode through the store, Tess saw Crow's eyes following her appreciatively. She sensed a new crush forming and immediately wished he were staring at her again. She hadn't expected much from Crow, but she had expected his adoration, from a comfortable distance, to warm her a little while longer.

The bookstore's door, as if bewitched by Cecilia's over-abundance of energy, slammed shut behind her with a heavy thud. Tess jumped at the unexpected noise, then turned to Crow.

"The sound you just heard," she told him, "was the sound of Rock's case going straight to hell."

Chapter 26

Tess had been to the state prison just once, under unusual circumstances. Were there usual circumstances for a fourteen-year-old girl to visit the Maryland Penitentiary for Men? In Tess's case, it all began when she decided to dance. Her determination was born of a desire not to be a dancer, merely to look like one: to be small, one of those tiny, curveless adolescents, all ribs, eyes, and pelvic bones. Tess realized most dancers began small and starved their bodies to keep them in perpetual preadolescence, but she thought she might be able to work backward.

After 12 weeks of classes, even though she still had a convex stomach, the teacher insisted Tess join her dance troupe, which performed throughout the community. Flattered, Tess jumped at the opportunity, assuming the instructor had glimpsed something not even Tess could see. She had—a pair of promising biceps. Tess was recruited to dance only one part, a Comet can in the instructor's own modern-day version of *The Sorcerer's Apprentice*. "It's a big part," the instructor promised. This was literally true. The Comet costume, more than six feet at full extension, was made of heavy painted canvas, strung on three Hula Hoops, so Tess could collapse and expand throughout the twelve-minute dance. For long stretches of time she had to hold her arms straight over her head, elbows locked, to give the Comet can

238

its full shape. Only a strapping girl with a lot of upper body strength could have survived in that costume.

Their first performance was at the jail. The smaller girls, the real dancers, got to be 409 bottles and Brillo pads and Lemon Joy, pointing their painted Capezios and twirling lightly across the dingy linoleum. Tess rose and fell, rose and fell, creeping across the floor in bare feet, which were black afterward. Still, it was not the dirty floor, jealousy of the daintier girls, fear of the prison, or even the anonymity of her costume that convinced her to give up dancing after one performance. It was the sudden catcalls of the inmates, when she emerged from her Comet can, a lush Botticelli among the less sturdy dancers, the sweat on her leotard an obscene blueprint of the erogenous zones of her precocious body. The futility of her plan clear, fourteen-year-old Tess hung up her Comet can.

All this came back to her as she circled the complex of prisons and jails east of downtown, trying to find the right entrance. By the time she reached Super Max, home to the state's most dangerous prisoners, she was sweating heavily.

"Death Row?" she asked the guard, as she had asked at two other entrances, only to be turned away wordlessly.

"Ain't no Death Row in Maryland, miss. Some of the guys are here, some over at the state penitentiary. Who you here to see? What's your name?"

He checked his clipboard and sent her to yet another door, where a state officially waited eagerly to escort her to Tucker Fauquier.

"The guard at the other gate told me there was no Death Row," Tess said, perplexed.

"No, there isn't. Not like in other states," the official agreed. "The guys are scattered around. If they're a danger to themselves or—more likely—in danger from the other inmates, they go to Super Max. Otherwise they're here in A-block. Tucker used to be over in Super Max in the beginning. But he's a model prisoner now. Besides, so few of the others remember why he's here. In prison time it was a generation ago."

The official—Garfield Lardner, according to the photo ID clipped to his polyester jacket—was a breathless, pink-cheeked little man with a shiny bald head on which Tess could almost see her reflection. He searched her purse, apologizing for the intrusion, and barely passed the metal detector wand over her, apologizing again as he did so. She was touched by his concern and solicitous attention—until she remembered it was meant for someone else, the granddaughter of a politically connected seafood king.

The concern for security seemed to end once they passed through the various checkpoints and a series of anterooms. Lardner led her to a room with a long conference table surrounded by leather chairs. No bulletproof glass, no phone—nothing she would have expected from the prison movies she had seen. Just an ordinary, if slightly shabby, meeting room.

"The parole board usually meets here," Lardner said. "On the first and third Wednesdays. No one should disturb you today. But Tucker can't see you for much more than forty-five minutes. He has a meeting."

"A meeting? With someone else from outside?"

"Oh no, it's the leadership counsel. Just an in-house thing. He's the secretary. Let me go get Tucker."

As he scurried out, Tess called to him: "Will the guard be in here with us? Or will you post him at the door?"

Lardner stopped, as if this had not occurred to him. "We don't usually have a guard at all. Do you want someone, though? I'm sure I could arrange it."

"No, no, that's fine." *At least no one will be around to eavesdrop on my "sociology project."*

She sat in the chair at the head of the table, then decided this would seem faintly authoritarian. She moved to the far side, to a chair in the middle. Should she stand when he entered? Offer her hand? Engrossed in the etiquette of the moment, Tess did not realize it had already passed her by. Tucker Fauquier was in the doorway, waiting for her to acknowledge him.

He was a small man, clean shaven, his hair slicked back with water. Tess had carried in her mind a picture of a younger man, the man in the photograph with Abramowitz. Even scrubbed and cleaned up for the trial, that man, with his longer hair and bad skin, had lived up to expectations of a serial killer–pervert. This man had the pale, blue-veined look of someone who had not seen the sun for a long time. Yet it wasn't creepy or unhealthy looking. In fact his skin was lovely, almost creamy, an advertisement for sunscreen and broad-brimmed hats. He had to be almost forty now, yet looked younger. Involuntarily, Tess brushed a hand against her own sun-coarsened cheek.

He smiled, and she tried but failed to find anything especially chilling in his face. The canine teeth, while unusually sharp, giving him a feral look, were straight and white. A dozen years ago news accounts had made much of this smile, suggesting it had been the reason he could so easily entice his victims. It was a pleasant smile, Tess decided, but not hypnotic. You couldn't charm a bird out of a tree with it, or a young boy into a car. In fact Tess didn't think anyone would ever notice Tucker Fauquier, not under normal circumstances. Perhaps that had been the problem.

"Mr. Fauquier, I'm Tess Monaghan."

"Yes, they told me you were coming. They said you're working on a school project." His voice was soft and whispery, which only magnified the slight lisp Fauquier was trying to downplay.

"There must have been some confusion, Mr. Fauquier. I'm not sure why they told you that." *Aside from Uncle Donald's gossip along the phone lines.* "I'm working for a lawyer who thinks you may know something about Michael Abramowitz. Could you answer some questions for me?"

"About his murder." It wasn't a question. He seemed amused—by her manners, or by her deceit, which he seemed to grasp instantly.

"Something that might shed light on his murder, actually. Although, if you'd like to confess to arranging the whole thing, it would make my job easier, I admit."

Fauquier smiled again. "I think I've made enough confessions in my day. They'll have to solve this one on their own.''

He was in the chair across from her, almost preternaturally poised, rocking slightly. He had drawn one foot under him, which seemed an odd, uncomfortable way to sit, but it also had the effect of making him look taller. Tess could tell he was enjoying himself, enjoying the attention.

''I thought there was something you wanted to talk about, Mr. Fauquier. Something you promised to tell Jonathan Ross. Only you reneged.''

She had surprised him. Fauquier leaned back in his chair, pressing the heels of his hands against the table, showing off his forearms. They were slender, but the veins stood out against them, bright blue bas-relief. A weight lifter, Tess judged, one who lifted for strength and tone, not bulk.

''Well, then Jonathan reneged, too, didn't he? He told me our interviews were off-the-record. Then he turned around and told you what I said. That's a lot worse, what he did.''

He reminded her of a little boy, rationalizing away a petty infraction by blaming his older brother for a larger one.

''Not exactly, Mr. Fauquier. Jonathan told me he had been meeting with someone condemned to die, someone 'twisted,' who got in touch with him after Abramowitz died. That gave me a one-in-thirteen chance to guess. Someone else, a woman who worked with Michael Abramowitz, said he complained about one of his clients, also a 'twisted' gentleman convicted of a capital crime. The odds fell to one in three. Both men called you a twisted fucker. You liked to call yourself a twisted fucker. Mr. Ross and Mr. Abramowitz are dead. Is it all a coincidence?''

''Stranger things have happened.'' He grinned. ''I happened, didn't I?''

''Tell me the story you were going to tell Jonathan, the one you wanted to tell before *you* die. It's no good if you're dead, is it? You need the story to be told while you're alive. You want something, attention or time. Maybe both. I can give you one of those things.''

"I don't care that much about attention, and I'm not worrying too much about dying right now."

"You should. Maryland is losing patience. People want to see you guys executed—especially you. Ever since Thanos went, there's been a lot more momentum. You could be dead by next summer."

"Fuckin' Thanos," Fauquier said, as if commenting on the weather or the Orioles' season. "Fuckin' crazy Greek motherfucker. Just because he wants to die doesn't mean the rest of us have to."

She tried a different tack. Perhaps if she mixed up her questions, flitting from subject to subject, she could surprise Fauquier into telling her something, anything.

"Why were you angry with Abramowitz?"

"Hey, he did a shitty job. I'm here, aren't I? Then he dropped me, foisted me off on some other public defender to handle my appeals. He fucked me. I'm not sorry he's dead, but I can't kill anyone from here. Even if I could I don't think Abramowitz would be my first choice."

"Really? Who would you kill?"

"Ben." The name of the boy who had watched him kill, the only one who had escaped. "I loved him, and he ratted me out."

"Really? I thought you were going to kill him, too."

"Oh, I was. But I was going to love him first. I loved all of my boys, but Ben was the handsomest. You know, Jonathan looked liked my Ben. I almost thought he was Ben, the first time I saw him. Of course, they tell me Ben's in a mental hospital somewhere, but they won't tell me where, which is a shame. I'd love to write him a letter sometime."

Fauquier smiled, waiting for Tess's reaction. She tried not to show how sickened she was, which she assumed was the point of his dreamy recitation. In a copse of trees almost within sight of Governor Ritchie Highway, Fauquier had strangled his last victim with a piece of red and white bunting from a roadside produce stand, then dismembered the body and buried it. Tess suddenly remembered a strange, stray detail from the trial. Ben had testified that Fauquier sang as he shoveled. Cole Porter's "You'd Be So Nice to Come Home To."

She shook off the ugly memory. This was her only chance. Someone was going to figure out that Ed Monahan, seafood king, did not have a granddaughter. "There was a time when you thought Abramowitz was your best buddy. You told reporters you were lucky to have him. What changed?"

Fauquier, his arms still braced against the table, looked at his fingernails. He had a French manicure, Tess noticed, and there were no nicotine stains on his fingers.

"Suppose you did something?" he asked, his voice still dreamy. "Something wonderful. Your life's work. And no one appreciated it, no one knew?"

She stifled a sigh. "Do you really think what you did was wonderful?"

"It was ingenious." He leaned across the table toward her, eyes glowing happily. "A lot of people thought I started because of John Wayne Gacy, but I started way before that. I had killed my first one before anyone ever heard of that clown. I was careful. I was going to kill a boy in every county. Then I realized I needed verification, or how would anyone know? I was going to make Ben watch, then sign a little paper about what he had seen. Repeat, county after county, from the mountains to the sea. In the amber waves of grain. God bless America."

" 'America the Beautiful' is the one with the amber waves and the purple mountains' majesties above the fruited plain. You're mixing the two songs up."

His eyes flickered. "What do you mean, 'fruited'? You saying I'm queer?"

"Of course not."

" 'Cuz I'm not, you know. I was an artist. I shoulda been in Guinness, that's what I was aiming for. You gotta have proof to get into Guinness."

"I don't think Guinness keeps tabs on serial killers. Besides, you topped out at, what, twelve or thirteen? You're not even a contender any more."

"Well, I certainly expected some movie producers to

come around, or someone who wanted to write a book. But no ever did. At least that's what my Jew lawyer told me during the trial. I wonder now. You know, your lawyer controls who gets in to see you. My new lawyer, he doesn't interfere. He doesn't do shit. But Abramowitz could have kept all those people away from me, and I never would have known.''

A decade ago no one had wanted to read the details of his story. Of course, today there would have been two paperbacks on the shelves within weeks of Fauquier's arrest, a television movie, and a horde of tabloid television reporters, ready to pay anyone for the tiniest piece of his story. Maybe Tucker Fauquier's frustration was justified. He had been ahead of his time.

"What would you do with money anyway, assuming state laws allowed you to keep it? You're never leaving here." Even as she spoke she heard Jonathan's voice, answering her question, prodding her. *"The money is leverage."*

"How do you know what something's worth if no one ever pays you for it? I told Abramowitz to find a buyer for my story. The best he could do was find someone to pay me $50,000 a year *not* to talk."

"Why would someone pay you to shut up?"

"They paid me to talk, but only once. Then they paid me, every year, not to talk about something I didn't do. Not bad, huh? It's like a double negative. If I don't talk about what I didn't do, I must've done it."

"So this guy comes forward with a story about a crime someone else committed but got away with because he was rich and connected." Jonathan again, coaching her, coaxing her through. Rich enough to pay someone to confess to a crime he didn't commit? What was another murder to someone sentenced to die, a sheaf of confessions in his file?

"But you did talk. You talked to Jonathan. You're not very good at keeping promises, are you?"

"Promises!" He spat the word back at her. "Ask Abramowitz about promises. That kike set up the deal, then took all my money. A year ago I asked to see my bank statement.

I knew the money had to go through him—the people who were paying me didn't want me to know who they were. He told me he invested it. But when I asked to see the statements, to see *my* nest egg, he hems and haws, then tells me: 'Oh, I gave it away to some good causes.' Can you believe that shit? He didn't give it away. He *stole* it. How do you think he started that private practice of his? *He* was the good cause. He took my money. My money!''

When he was agitated Fauquier's voice did not get louder but raspier, and his lisp became more pronounced. He was hissing wetly now, spit flying from his mouth with each liquid word. It took all Tess's resolve not to recoil or duck.

''You told Jonathan all this.''

''Eventually. I drew it out more. I liked talking to Jonathan. He was pretty.'' Fauquier looked at her slyly. ''Didn't you think he was pretty?''

''Did you tell him which was the fake confession?''

''I was going to, if he paid me. But he said he wouldn't pay me. And you know what happened to him.''

Yes, I was there, you schmuck.

''Do you think Jonathan was killed because of what you told him?''

''I don't know and I don't care. They can't get *me*. That's the funny thing. The hardest person to kill in Maryland is someone who's condemned to die. I'm just holding out for the best offer. How much money do you have?''

Fauquier leaned closer, until his face was only inches away. Tess rolled her chair back, trying to keep her distance. There was something wrong with Fauquier's story. Something was missing. Even if Jonathan had been able to pick out the false confession, he would have to know who had been shielded. That was the sexy part. Somewhere out there the parents of a young boy had the scant comfort of thinking his killer was in prison and scheduled to die, even if it was for another boy's death. You wouldn't want to take that away from them unless you could advance the story, tell them who really did it and why. Fauquier lied, so what? He was still a killer. Who benefited?

"I wouldn't pay you anything," she told Fauquier. "You don't know the most important part. You don't know who you took the fall for. Without that your story's just a fairy tale."

The pun had been unintentional, but it enraged Fauquier. "Who're you calling a fairy, you cow? You *whore*. You think you're so smart. Well, you try to figure out which one I didn't do, much less who really did it. Jonathan thought he could. Maybe that's why he's dead right now. I hope it is."

He was standing now, his voice a hoarse scream, spit flying at her. Tess stood up, too, glad to see she was at least five inches taller.

"I'm going to call for Mr. Lardner now. I want you to stay on your side of the table."

It was eerie how quickly Fauquier calmed down. He wasn't scared of the prison official, Tess realized, or of her. He wanted to be in control. The "model prisoner" probably tried to hide his rage as much as possible. By the time Lardner arrived he looked angelic.

"Did you have a nice visit?" he asked Tess and Fauquier.

"We sure did," Fauquier said, beaming. "She's pretty, don't you think, Mr. Lardner? I'd sure like to take her out on a date."

The official nodded as if this seemed reasonable.

"I'm not exactly your type," Tess said. "And not just because I'm a woman. You see, Mr. Fauquier, I don't think you could be attracted to anyone you couldn't kill or hurt. And unlike your little boys, I could definitely kick your ass. You are one twisted fucker."

Fauquier glowered. Garfield Lardner stood openmouthed, shocked that the granddaughter of Ed Monahan, the seafood king, would be so crude.

Chapter 27

Home again, Tess tried to think like a newspaper editor, like Jonathan's boss. She sat in front of her computer and transformed herself into someone pedantic and nit-picking, someone who could lecture for hours on "infer" and "imply," unaware a five-alarm fire burned across the street.

What hoops would an editor have asked Jonathan to jump through in order to get his story in the paper? First of all he would have had to figure out, without Fauquier, which was the wrong confession. There could be any number of ways to do that. Interviews with homicide detectives from the time. Examining the police reports and court papers.

But that wouldn't be enough. With Abramowitz dead and Fauquier condemned to die, about as disreputable as a source could be, Jonathan needed to find the money, where it came from, and where it went. Like a bird building its nest, he would have ferreted out every available material. Twig, string, paper. Mainly paper.

Follow the money, Deep Throat had whispered in a Washington parking garage. Or had he? It didn't matter. Journalists of Jonathan's generation and ambition had been intoning those instructions ever since, their professional mantra. Follow the money. Michael Abramowitz had left an estate of almost one million dollars. That was one place to start. But a shortcut through Jonathan's brain would be nice. His brain being unavailable, Tess would have to settle for the next best thing.

Tess reached for the phone and called Whitney at her office.

"Have they cleaned out Jonathan's desk yet?"

"Not yet, but I'm sure they will soon. They don't have enough desks around here for prolonged periods of mourning. And Jonathan's desk was by a window, so a lot of people want it."

"What about his computer files? Are they still in the system?"

"Hmmmm—actually, the head computer geek is at some conference learning how to make the system even more complicated and cumbersome to use, so he hasn't been here to reclaim all that storage space for his precious mainframe. But you couldn't get in without Jonathan's password, and only the geek would know that."

"I'd never get permission to go into the *Blight*'s computer, anyway. Even if Tyner went to court, the paper would have to claim it's privileged, on principle. And if the judge decided in Rock's favor, the computer geek would 'accidentally' kill everything."

Whitney laughed. "You have it all figured out, don't you? I bet you even have an alternative plan."

"I will, after you explain the *Blight*'s computer system to me. But Whitney—I want to do this tonight."

Several hours later Tess and Whitney set out from Fells Point in Whitney's Jeep Cherokee. Like Crow, Whitney seemed to find this a great adventure, but she was better dressed, in black leggings and an open-weave black sweater over a white T-shirt. She had accessorized with clunky black boots with white socks, and gold earrings set with onyx and seed pearls.

"No white gloves?" Tess asked facetiously, only to have Whitney thrust a pair at her, probably left over from dancing school.

"I can afford to leave fingerprints in the building. You can't, my dear."

"White gloves with blue jeans after September first? OK, but I think this is a major fashion faux pas."

Technically an all-day newspaper, the *Beacon-Light* liked to boast it had reporters on duty twenty-four hours. From midnight until 4 A.M., however, the staff consisted of a solitary police reporter. Young and scared, he sat by a scanner, petrified he might have to leave the building. He seldom did, but Tess and Whitney could avoid him altogether just by using the back stairs. The electronic traps were a little harder to elude.

First they had to get in the building without leaving any trace. Whitney had a key card, which unlocked the doors along the way, but she didn't want the security system to have a record of her entering at 1 A.M., a record that could come back to haunt her if someone discovered the computer had been breached. Whitney had solved that problem easily. After Tess's call she had waited until the editorial writer in the cubicle next to hers had gone to the men's room, then she'd slipped his card out of his jacket pocket and left hers in its place.

"I'll swap back tomorrow," she told Tess, sliding the card through the lock at the building's side entrance. "Ted will never notice he spent twenty-four hours being 1375 instead of 926. And, if someone ever asks him what he was doing here in the middle of the night, he should be very convincing in his protestations of innocence."

After taking the back stairs to the fourth floor, Whitney led Tess to the editorial department's writing room. The editorial writers had their own cubicles, but they were forced to use a communal room when it was time to put their punditry on the computer screen.

"They thought we needed to develop camaraderie," Whitney said. "Instead all the editorial writers have developed crushes on different computers, claiming there are significant differences. They pitch fits if they can't get their favorites."

Whitney signed on. "I'm not using my real handle, but the all-purpose one they give the interns," she explained. "OK, look—reporters create stories in all-access baskets, but they can store them in confidential baskets only the system manager can access. Jonathan was more paranoid than most and always used his private basket. But there's a chance he ran out of storage space and had to depend on one of the obscure all-access baskets for backup. There are hundreds of baskets hidden in the computer no one knows about."

She typed in "Ross," instructing the computer to pull up any file created by that user. It gave her only two, which Whitney quickly scanned.

"A FOIA request from last winter to the chronically corrupt housing department. Nothing odd there—we file one of those every week. And a copy of a wire story about the Chicago foundation that gives out those 'genius' grants. It has the address, out in Chicago. I guess Jonathan was trying to figure out how to apply for one." Whitney turned to Tess. "End of the line. If you want to find any more, you have to get in as Jonathan."

To log on as Jonathan, all Tess had to do was stroke the command button, type in "Ross," then fill in his password. The computer would give her three chances to get the password right. If she failed to guess correctly, the terminal would freeze and send a message to the internal security system, warning it someone had tried to break in, a message that would probably go ignored until late tomorrow morning when someone reviewed the tapes. No one could tie Whitney to the infraction—thanks to the stolen key card and the intern user handle, it couldn't be proven she had been here—and it could escape notice, just another line in the thousands of messages recorded every day. But it would still be recorded somewhere.

"So, do you know his password?" Whitney asked Tess.

"No, but I think I know Jonathan well enough to guess. And I've got fifteen tries, right? Three per terminal."

"Uh-uh. Too dangerous. Trying to use someone else's password is grounds for firing. One weird little incident might not ring any bells. But if someone strikes out fifteen times, at one A.M., on all five editorial terminals, they'll start looking hard. I can't risk that. It's one machine or nothing, Tess.''

With fifteen, Tess had felt cocky. Ten—a cinch. Even five would have seemed a sporting chance. Three was narrow and arbitrary, straight out of the Brothers Grimm. Being clever wouldn't be enough. She would have to be lucky.

She hunched over the screen, feeling like a reporter again. She was on deadline and all she needed was the first word, her lede. Once she had it, all the other words would follow.

"P-u-l-i-t-z-e-r," she typed, thinking of Jonathan's unabashed ambition.

Strike one! the computer replied.

"Try his girlfriend's name," Whitney whispered in her ear. "Or his middle name. A lot of people use middle names."

"I had thought he might use one of his journalism idols," she said, but typed in D-a-p-h-n-e, anyway.

Strike two! the computer said, a bit smugly, Tess thought. One more shot.

Tess closed her eyes. She knew Jonathan. She had him under her fingernails. She just had to dig out the right piece, the incriminating hair or fiber. Their last night together—but he hadn't given up anything then. He had lied to her that night, told her Abramowitz was inconsequential in the story he was pursuing. While she was hiding the floppy disk in her drawer, he had been hiding far more.

That wasn't the night she wanted to remember. It was the time before, the time he didn't die. Even then, Tess knew now, he had been feeling a little smug and superior—he already knew Abramowitz was Fauquier's lawyer, and he knew the connection was not incidental. Why would he withhold such information when it might have helped Tyner? Because, whatever he knew, he remained convinced Rock had killed Abramowitz.

Still, he had been so nice that night, as nice as he had ever been. Perhaps as nice as he could be. They had watched the sun rise. What had they talked about up on the roof? How he had envied her for being from the city, when he was just a suburban mall rat. Her family, her roots here. Their days at the *Star*. A story about a fire, a fire he couldn't find. The way the rewrite man had ridiculed Jonathan for the rest of his days at the *Star*, calling him Sparky. The way Jonathan had gloried in getting a job while the rewrite man went into PR.

"Trust me," he had said. "There's not a day I go to work and I don't think about Sparky and Nick."

Not a day. She had two choices here, but only one chance. She typed in the old nickname, taking special care. The computer blinked, went blank, then, seemingly a million years later, blinked again. *Sign-on successful, just a moment please*. Tess was now Jonathan Ross.

Even in his personal basket, paranoid Jonathan had taken steps to keep prying eyes from his notes and stories. He had slugged his stories by the dullest names possible in order to deter browsers. *Tax bill. City ordinances. Utility rates. Mayor's speech. Insurance rates. Sewers*. Tess tried the last one, finding a list of prison sources and their numbers.

Zoning—city. Here was Jonathan's first interview with Fauquier, transcribed, apparently, from a tape recording. *Zoning—county*. More Fauquier. But nothing Fauquier hadn't told her, in fewer words and less time.

"Check the keyword," Whitney advised. "He might have assigned the same keyword to all his notes on this."

Access issues. Whitney showed Tess how to request the computer to sort the stories with that heading. Within seconds they had a list of eleven files.

"No printouts," Whitney hissed. "They make records, too." Tess nodded and began reading through the various entries, retracing Jonathan's steps chronologically.

Apparently he had first met Fauquier in July while doing research for his series on how the first execution would affect life on Death Row. But Fauquier was not to be the focus of the piece. Jonathan was concentrating on another inmate, a cop killer who seemed positively benign alongside Fauquier. He had interviewed Fauquier merely for his assessment of his colleague. Miffed, Fauquier had tried too hard to be outrageous, claiming repeatedly he should be the star of Jonathan's series, for he was so much more "accomplished."

"*F: He kills one little cop while he's high, and you want to write about him? Why, because he says he's a Christer now and writes letters to the guy's family? I killed more people than anyone here. If you want to write about us, you have to write about me! That other guy, he's a nigger, anyway. It's easy for a nigger to get condemned. But a white man has to be really bad. If I killed some cop while I was on dope, I wouldn't even be here. It's just like everywhere else—affirmative action. The standards are so much lower.*

"*JR: Well, my purpose is to get readers to understand the humanity of the people here. Focusing on you wouldn't achieve that. It would be more like* Frankenstein—*the villagers would storm the jail, torches in hand, ready to execute you.*"

Nice comeback, Jonathan. Much better than my threat to kick his ass.

The interviews began again after Abramowitz's death. Fauquier had lured Jonathan back to him with his boast about the fake confession and the cover-up. Then he had teased him languidly, enjoying the attention and, perhaps, a slight sexual charge from boyish Jonathan.

"*Too bad I can't go see Abramowitz,*" Jonathan had typed at the end of one file, a summary of Fauquier's legal history. "*Tess's friend didn't do me any favors by killing him.*" Tess smiled. That egocentric touch was pure Jonathan, like hearing his voice again.

The other files were series of facts from Fauquier's confessions, broken down into categories. Dates. Nothing seemed out of place there. Methods of dispatch. All of Fauquier's victims had been strangled or their skulls crushed, then buried in well-concealed graves. Victims' names. Victims' addresses. Names of the investigators in each case. Where the bodies were found.

"He left his bodies in some nice places," Whitney observed, peering over Tess's shoulder. "State parks and wildlife refuges out in the country, little wilderness areas hidden in the city. Look—Damon Jackson died in a much nicer place than he ever lived. I guess in murder, it's the same as real estate. Location, location, location.''

"Location, location, location,'' Tess repeated. She turned off the computer.

"Did you find what you wanted?"

"I found something. Whether I want it, or can use it, remains to be seen."

It was not yet two when she arrived home. Whitney, charged up by their midnight mission, had wanted to go to a bar or an all-night diner, but Tess's body was still indifferent to alcohol and food. All she wanted was her bed, solitude and, maybe, a joint.

Kitty had shoved some mail under her door. Just as Tess's phone calls sometimes went to the bookstore, her mail inevitably was mixed up, too, going to the front entrance instead of the side. It was seldom anything to mourn. No love letters had been mislaid, or million-dollar checks from Publishers Clearinghouse. Tonight's offerings were typical. A "Dear Occupant" brochure from a local dating service, Great Expectations. She wondered if Miss Havisham was a satisfied customer. A Victoria's Secret catalog—she had bought four pairs of underwear from the company three years ago and they continued to send her a catalog every two weeks. A form letter from the state, never good news. Was it already time to get a new driver's license?

A thin photocopy fluttered out. Her copy of VOMA's pink sheet. She had forgotten requesting it and, knowing state government as she did, had never expected to see it in less than the two weeks promised. And then Cecilia had convinced her, more or less, that VOMA was a dead end.

She studied the blurry copy. Yes, two board members had been added to VOMA the last time the nonprofit renewed its charter, just this spring. Seamon P. and Luisa J. O'Neal. Abramowitz was still listed as the agent and had attached this addendum to the annual tax statement. Hadn't Pru told Cecilia his involvement was incidental, a onetime irony? Tess felt Abramowitz tugging on her sleeve, trying to point

the way, much the way Jonathan had seemed to be guiding
her today through the interview with Fauquier and his own
computer files.

They were both leading her in the same direction, to the
same place.

Location, location, location. According to Jonathan's files,
one of Fauquier's early victims, Damon Jackson, had been
discovered behind the O'Neals' house, along Cross-Tree
Creek. That's what Fauquier had called it in his confession,
although the police report listed it as Little Wyman Falls.
Cross-Tree Creek. Little Wyman Falls. If it had not been for
the O'Neals' silly bickering over the name, Tess never would
have remembered it.

Chapter 28

Tess wanted nothing more than to sleep. If she could have forced herself, she would have squeezed four or five hours of oblivion out of the night's remains, then gone to the boat house for a good, punishing workout. She would have gone to Jimmy's and eaten her bagels, glad again that the cook threw them on the griddle the minute she walked in the door. She would have done all her routine things, the things that made her feel strong and capable. She wanted her rut back.

Instead she stayed up all night, watching the clock, making lists and waiting, for the second time in two days, for state offices to open. At 8:30, a mug of strong coffee in hand, she set herself up in Kitty's office, working the fax, the phone, and old sources at the secretary of state's office and the attorney general. It took some coaxing, but by 10 A.M. she had the documents she wanted spread out in front of her. Then, her hand shaking slightly, she called the O'Neals.

The maid answered, as Tess had expected. She was prepared to play the bully. To her surprise Luisa O'Neal came on the line when she heard who was calling.

"Oh, dear," she said, gracious as ever. "I know Shay has a very full schedule today. And we're leaving for the beach after work. We're taking a long weekend at our little place in Bethany."

A little place on the beach with six bedrooms, five decks,

and two Jacuzzis. Tess had seen photos in the *Blight*'s Sunday magazine last year.

"Actually, Mrs. O'Neal, I wanted to talk to you."

"Oh, dear," she said again, as though she had longed to visit with Tess. "I have tennis this morning. But I could meet at one-thirty. The girls always like to have lunch after."

"I'll see you then."

At 1:15, sure of her destination this time, Tess headed north. There was a chill in the air, as if fall had decided it had to make a fainthearted stab at showing up just in time for the last day of September. This was Baltimore at its best—clear blue sky, a steady breeze, warm in the sun and cool in the shadows. As she did every year at this moment in time—and it sometimes seemed no more than a moment—Tess forgave the city its wretched summer and forgot winter would return. Constant clemency and a talent for amnesia. Both were key to life here.

She turned off Charles Street onto Cross Place. PRIVATE PROPERTY, a sign reminded her. TRESPASSING FORBIDDEN. Luckily the blue and white banner she had saved after the last visit flew from her antenna. In the weeks since Tyner and Tess had fled the street, autumn had taken hold here, too. The trees along the cul-de-sac were scarlet and gold. Blood and money, Tess thought.

No maid met her at the curbside, not today. And when Tess knocked it was Mrs. O'Neal who let her in and led her to the sun room.

"Tea?" she began, but Tess held up a hand.

"I don't really need any refreshments," she said. "This isn't exactly a social call."

Without her husband in the room, Mrs. O'Neill did not seem so washed-out and fragile. Her face was still strikingly pale—she must wear a cap on the tennis court, Tess thought—but her limbs, left bare by an all-white tennis dress and the cardigan across her shoulders, were deeply tanned. The bones of her shins were long and sharp, her wrists knobby. Tess had not realized how tall Mrs. O'Neal was, almost six feet, or how muscular.

"Yes, I understand that. I am surprised, Miss Monaghan, you didn't want my husband here. We have no secrets, you know. We are partners in everything."

I didn't want to be double-teamed. I'm not ready for two-on-one. "Everyone has secrets, Mrs. O'Neal. If I remember correctly you didn't know about your husband's interest in Ava Hill until my last visit."

"I should say we don't have secrets about important things." She walked over to the window and looked out, sighing and hugging her arms. The leaves behind the house were already thinning out. Baltimore's cruel, brief autumn. It did improve the view, however. One could see all the way to the creek bed, to the meadow beyond. The houses on the far hill were almost visible, instead of just windows winking through the trees.

"You have such a nice view," Tess said.

"We owned all of this once, you know. Up until ten years ago we still owned the houses on either side and all the land to the creek."

"Did something happen ten years ago?" Tess's voice wavered a little, despite her best efforts.

"You tell me, Miss Monaghan."

She walked back to her wing chair, crossing her legs at the ankle and folding her hands in her lap. Tess, feeling like Scheherazade, took a deep breath. After weeks of telling lies and bluffing, with uneven results, it felt odd to speak the truth, to say only what she knew and nothing more. It also felt dangerous. If she was right about Mrs. O'Neal, the woman would do anything to protect her family.

"Ten years ago Tucker Fauquier's killing spree ended. He had been raping and killing little boys off and on since the late 1970s, since he was eighteen. But when he was arrested they could charge him with only one murder, because only one was witnessed. It was a capital crime and he got the death penalty. But because Fauquier buried his victims in carefully concealed places, only confessions could resolve the other murders. Encouraged by his lawyer because he was already condemned to die, he eagerly told police all the details. Bodies were found all over the state—twelve in all. One of them was unearthed at the foot of your property, along Little Wyman Falls. An eleven-year-old named Damon Jackson. He lived near the old stadium, off Greenmount Avenue, and had disappeared early in Fauquier's career, as he prefers to call it.''

''Yes, I know all this. I was at home the day the police came. I watched from here as they unearthed the body. Actually we didn't sell the property until after that, so I guess it was less than ten years ago.''

''Did you have to wait to sell the property until the body was found?''

Mrs. O'Neal gave Tess an appraising look. Tess glanced down the long hallway to the front door, ready to bolt.

''What is it you think you know, Miss Monaghan? Why don't you just tell me that?''

''You and your husband paid Tucker Fauquier a lot of money—well, not a lot of money to you—to confess to that murder. The details were passed through Abramowitz. What the boy looked like, where he was buried. Fauquier was a little vague about where he found this particular boy, but it was a long time ago and Fauquier didn't know Baltimore that well. Yet he remembered he had buried the body near Cross-Tree Creek, according to his confession. As your husband once said, nobody calls it that. Except your family.''

Tess looked up nervously, as if Mrs. O'Neal were a stern professor, giving her an oral examination. But she merely nodded, a sign for Tess to continue.

''So if you paid Fauquier, where's the money?'' At this point Tess almost forgot about Mrs. O'Neal. She was figuring this part out as she went. ''He said Abramowitz stole it, and Abramowitz did leave a sizable estate. But Abramowitz was a good lawyer; he might have earned much of that while in his own practice. Or maybe he got paid, too. After all, he was obstructing justice, suborning perjury—disbarment was the least of what he was facing if caught. Of course, he was too clever and you were too careful to write out personal checks. You had to pass it through something innocuous. Luckily for you, the William Tree Foundation, which your family controls, gives out more than five million dollars a year. What was another $50,000?''

Tess pulled out the faxes she had collected this morning, clutching the papers so hard that only the sweat on her palms kept them from tearing. ''Today I asked a friend at the attorney general's office to send me the William Tree Foundation's allocations list for the past three years. Year after year, only two grants, which happen to total $50,000, are made in perpetuity—to VOMA and the Maryland Coalition for Survivors, both chartered by Michael Abramowitz. They're also the only two crime-related groups on your list. Everything else goes to the arts, the poor, the mentally ill, or religious-based charities.''

''Catholic, Protestant, and Jewish,'' Mrs. O'Neal said. ''My father set it up that way.''

Tess didn't even hear her. ''I'm guessing now. I'll admit that. The foundation made the allocations to the two groups Abramowitz had set up. But instead of passing the money on to Fauquier, he let the charities keep it. In the case of VOMA, which gets $30,000 a year, he was ripped off by a greedy accountant, but that's another story. He thought he was doing a good deed. As for the Maryland Coalition for Survivors, it receives only a $20,000 grant, so it has no tax disclosure forms. It does, however, have a mailing address in Friendsville, Maryland: Care of Delores F. Compson. Tucker's mom. She remarried.''

Mrs. O'Neal pulled her white cardigan over her shoulders, as if she had caught a sudden chill. When she spoke, her voice was cool, too.

''Mr. Abramowitz emerges as a somewhat heroic figure in your theoretical account. The money goes to a support group for rape victims and the poor mother of his notorious client. Of course, he does violate several laws and enrich himself in the process. Otherwise an admirable man.''

''I think he was trying, in his own confused way, to do what was right. Some people are good and bad.''

''Yes. Well, in that case, Mr. Abramowitz and I have

much in common." Mrs. O'Neal stood up, and Tess almost flinched. Did she really think Luisa O'Neal would hurt her? No, she'd pay someone to hurt her. Mrs. O'Neal walked back to the window, looking down the hill.

"My parents had two children, a son and a daughter. It was my father's wish we should grow up here, on either side of him. But my brother died in a flu outbreak when we were young. My parents died less than a year after my marriage. Shay and I moved into this house. We had a son and a daughter. Mary Julia and William Tree O'Neal. I thought, as my father had, that my children would live on either side of me. But Mary Julia married a Chicago boy. She lives in Lake Bluff."

"And William?"

"William lives out of state. He has for years."

"Since he killed Damon Jackson? Did you see that, too, from your window? Or did you just watch him bury the body?"

Luisa O'Neal did not answer. Her eyes, deep gray in the shadowy light, stared down the hill. Whatever she had seen, she was seeing again. Tess almost felt sorry for her, but she had come too far to stop asking questions just because the memories might be hurtful to someone.

"Why did you ask Fauquier to confess? Damon Jackson's body probably never would have been found. It had been there almost five years by the time Fauquier was caught. It was on your property. Even if the body had been discovered, you were the only eyewitness."

"One can be too neat," she said, still staring outside. "The people who make fortunes, men like my father, are reckless and bold. The people who inherit them, or marry them, tend to be more timid. Shay doesn't like loose ends. I didn't like the idea of a woman forever wondering where her son was. Besides, we could never develop the property as long as the body was there. As it turned out Ms. Jackson was a prostitute junkie who had seldom known where her son was when he was alive. But I didn't know that when Shay came up with his plan. I thought it was a good idea."

"So you approached Abramowitz."

"Shay did, yes. He said he was representing a friend, but Mr. Abramowitz didn't believe him. It didn't matter. Mr. Abramowitz was burned out. And so very poor. He was paid the same as Fauquier, in the same way as Fauquier. You did a good job, Miss Monaghan, but there were three other 'dummy' groups on that list: the Park Heights Soup Kitchen, the Hank Greenberg Scholarship Fund for Young Boys, and the Ladies Auxiliary of the Temple Beth-El Gonif. All tax-exempt. Mr. Abramowitz made sure of that. Another law broken, of course."

"You made checks out to the Temple Beth-El Gonif? Don't you know it means 'thief'? The Hank Greenberg Scholarship Fund? Even I know he played for Detroit, not the Orioles. Abramowitz was hiding clues everywhere. He even put you and Mr. O'Neal on the VOMA board last year. He wanted someone to figure this out."

"I wouldn't know about the temple. I don't know Hebrew. But you're right about Abramowitz's longing to be caught. He felt guilty and he wanted everyone else to feel guilty, too. That's why he insisted on joining the firm, so Shay would have to see him and—these were his words—'think about it every day, as I do.' The only thing Seamon thinks about every day is whether his bran has done its work and where his next affair will come from, the associates or the secretaries."

Tess liked the image of red-faced Shay on the toilet, daydreaming of secretaries. But she couldn't afford to be distracted.

"So Abramowitz blackmails his way into the firm, and they give him a nice office with a harbor view and no work. It was brilliant. The best way to drive a workaholic crazy. That was the point, right? To drive him crazy? To make him quit, or commit suicide?"

Mrs. O'Neal's eyes seemed to darken. "No," she said, "I wouldn't wish insanity on anyone."

"Your son is insane, isn't he? That's why you give so much money to mental illness causes."

"We earmark about half our donations for the mentally ill." Very careful, Tess noticed. If she had been recording the conversation, Mrs. O'Neal would be able to argue she never admitted to doing anything. She wasn't taping it, however. For some strange reason she had thought she would be safer if she didn't.

"Does your philanthropy make up for your son killing someone?"

This time Mrs. O'Neal met her eyes. "Yes, Miss Monaghan, it does. In fact it more than compensates."

"How do you figure?"

"If William had been arrested he never would have been judged competent to stand trial. He would have been committed to some state asylum, at the state's expense, until he was. Instead he is in a nice place in Connecticut, which costs me $80,000 a year—about four times what prison costs in Maryland, by the way. And my family is still here, contributing to the community. If my son's crime had been publicly exposed, we would have left, taking the foundation with us. There's no stipulation the grants be made in Maryland. The city would have lost out, not us."

"I see—it was in the best interest of the taxpayers. What if the taxpayers preferred not to pervert our legal system?"

"Lawyers pervert the system," she replied. "The jurors pervert it. We sidestepped it."

"And Jonathan Ross?"

"The reporter? What about him?"

"He was murdered."

"Really? I read his death was ruled a hit-and-run, an accident."

"He was going to figure this out. He was starting to research foundations. He had talked to Fauquier. He would have put it together as I did, eventually."

Mrs. O'Neal just smiled.

"Am I going to be in a police report, Mrs. O'Neal? Am I going to be an accident?"

"Seamon tends to . . . panic. You've seen how red he becomes, how his voice starts squeaking. Another sign of the compulsively tidy. But when he has time to think—time to listen to advice—he is quite rational.''

"Fauquier will write more letters to other reporters. He wants to tell his story. He wants attention.''

"Yes, he does. You visited him yesterday, I understand. Your name was on the sheet. We've been taking note of his visitors since Mr. Abramowitz's death. Today—'' She glanced at her watch, the kind of gold simplicity that costs dearly. ''It's already happened. Shay held a press conference at one-thirty and announced the firm was going to take over Mr. Fauquier's appeals as a memorial to their slain colleague, Mr. Abramowitz. Larry Chambers, a quite capable young man, will handle the case. And if Mr. Fauquier tries to tell him any stories about fake confessions, Larry's going to assure him it will only hurt his appeal. He's also going to inform prison officials that you are not to visit Mr. Fauquier again, nor will any reporter. You need the lawyer's permission, you know.''

"I know.''

Now it was Tess who did not want to meet Mrs. O'Neal's eyes. If Luisa saw the past through her window, Tess saw the future. Fauquier's appeals would run out. His lawyer would whisper to him: ''Don't say anything about that fake confession yet. We have a plan. We're going to announce it just before they give you the injection. You'll get more publicity than any condemned prisoner in the country.'' And so Fauquier would go obediently, quietly, sitting in the chamber and waiting for the door to be flung open, waiting for his lawyer to rescue him. The pellets would drop, and Fauquier would die. The last living witness.

"There's only one thing I don't understand, Mrs. O'Neal. Why did you have Abramowitz killed? Was he so miserable that he was going to confess?''

"I'm afraid, dear, you can't blame us for that. We have no idea who killed Abramowitz, although we probably owe whoever it was a debt. It has worked out nicely for us. He was becoming quite a nuisance.''

"Aren't you worried I'll tell?''

"No. I think, on some level, you see my side of things, Miss Monaghan. Justice was done. A boy was killed, a man confessed. My son is in a hospital for the rest of his life, which is longer than he would have stayed in jail. What more would you ask?"

"I don't see your side. I could never think the way you do." Tess was almost yelling, frantic in her hope that she was telling the truth.

"Well, then, I'll tell you the second reason I'm not worried. You're no one, and no one will ever believe you. But if you'd like a little money, a reward for being so clever, it could be arranged."

"Actually," Tess said, surprising even herself, "I might."

Chapter 29

Tess left the O'Neals' and drove to a copy store out in the suburbs, a bright, lively place with an espresso bar and throngs of people. Despite Mrs. O'Neal's kind assurances that she was too inconsequential to kill, she felt safer in public. She paid for computer time and typed up the story she had told Mrs. O'Neal, fleshed out now with Mrs. O'Neal's details. At the end she listed all her resources, a bibliography of sorts. She smoothed out and photocopied the crumpled, damp faxes, paid for the disk on which she had worked, and put everything in a manila envelope, which she then sent by certified mail to Kitty. She wrote on the back flap, "*To be opened only in the event of my death.*" Kitty was one of the few people who would unquestioningly follow those instructions. She wouldn't even find it particularly odd. Tyner, while the more logical choice in some ways, would have opened it immediately.

Strangely Tess almost believed Mrs. O'Neal when she said they had not arranged Abramowitz's death. More importantly she believed she couldn't prove it if they had. All this work, all this effort, and she had ended up solving the wrong case—Jonathan's death and the death of a little boy whose name she had not even known two days ago.

That's why I hated being a reporter. You were always getting the wrong answers to your questions.

The thought darted across her mind like a cockroach running from the kitchen light, trying to disappear into a dark crevice. But Tess caught it before it vanished. Hated being a reporter? No, she had loved it. She had worked hard at it. It was the only career she had ever known. She had been a reporter because . . . because.

Because Whitney wanted to be a reporter, and you could never stop competing with Whitney. Because Jonathan was a great reporter, and you loved him once and wanted him to love you. Because James M. Cain was a reporter who went to Washington College, then had gone on to write wonderful books and have an interesting life. You wanted to be a writer with a regular paycheck. That didn't make you a reporter. Or a writer. It made you a coward and a fake. An imitation.

Her package mailed, she drove home and flopped on her bed. She had not exercised for five days, since Jonathan's death, and she'd eaten little. Her body felt puny and weak, her stomach flat, the kind of flat that comes from the atrophy of muscle. *A workout's effects are lost in seventy-two hours,* Tess chided herself, then tried to remember the last time she had gone three days without running or rowing. About five years ago, when she had sprained her ankle. Even then she had done bicep curls with cans of Progresso plum tomatoes and tried chin-ups from her door frame.

She stood up, determined to run, but her legs felt too rubbery. Instead she left her apartment and began walking. First north, then east. The neighborhoods through which she walked were the cornerstone of the Baltimore myth, the places enshrined in the travel pieces written by every slumming journalist who had ever swung a crab mallet at Obrycki's. Here were the marble stoops, the celebrated ethnic mix, the vast green spaces of Patterson Park. It looked good, from a distance. But Tess knew teenagers were smoking PCP and crack in the alleys, and that no one walked in Patterson Park because of the crime. She knew fewer and fewer women scrubbed their marble stoops every day. Even the Elvis mural had been defaced, so it had to be painted over. And when Baltimoreans started turning on Elvis, times were bad.

She walked past the old Francis Scott Key Hospital and through Greektown. The air was full of grape leaves, roasted lamb, potato pancakes, and, near the Brazilian restaurant, a scorched pork scent her nose recognized as the "national dish of Brazil." She passed Cesnik's Tavern. It could be Cecilia's father's place. She walked all the way to Dundalk, down Holabird Avenue, to the small hideous rancher owned by Abner Macauley.

Mrs. Macauley, her hair a few inches higher since Tess's last visit, opened the door.

"Oh, hi, hon," she said. "He's not well enough to talk."

"He doesn't have to." Almost rudely she pushed past the woman and into the living room.

Mr. Macauley looked worse, if that was possible. Grayer, thinner, frailer, a husk of a man. Tess thought his arm might collapse when she touched it, dry as dust beneath her fingers.

"Mr. Macauley?"

He was dozing and woke with a start, not recognizing her at first. He looked around her, found his wife, and relaxed. He was not dead, then, facing down an Amazonian angel at heaven's gate.

"You're going to get your money, Mr. Macauley. All of it. I talked to someone from the law firm and they promised. By next week."

He smiled. Gently Tess picked up one of his hands. The palms were still rough, all these years later, but the backs of his hands were paper thin. She stroked his hand and listened to his breathing through the plastic tube, the squeak of his recliner. An old Perry Mason show was on television. Tess had forgotten Raymond Burr once had a dark, frightening grace. She also had forgotten what a weenie Hamilton Burger was.

"I've seen 'em all," Mr. Macauley rasped. "I never remember who did it."

They watched the show together, silently. As a little girl Tess had watched it with Poppa Weinstein and he, much like Mr. Macauley, had seen every episode. She had thought this was how it worked—that everyone sat in the courtroom together, that attorneys were frequently surprised by the answers they heard, that the case was always solved as a witness dissolved in tears or shouts. In the back of her mind she had thought it would be like this for Rock.

"Jew bastard," Mr. Macauley said suddenly.

"Perry Mason?" Raymond Burr? Hamilton Burger?

"Abramowitz," he said. "Jew bastard." He fell back asleep. She continued to hold his hand. Everyone thought she was on their side, that she was one of them.

"You should go," Mrs. Macauley whispered a little nervously. Did she worry her husband would wake up again, or was she simply frightened by this odd woman in her living room, holding her husband's hand in front of an old Emerson?

"Sure." She walked to the door, Mrs. Macauley trailing her. "I meant to tell him. You won't get the money all at once. You'll get quarterly payments over the next few years. And the checks will be from a local foundation, one associated with the law firm. That way you can get it faster." The idea had come to her so quickly. If the William Tree Foundation was so generous with its funds, why shouldn't Abner Macauley get his cut? Mrs. O'Neal had been amused but happy to help. Tess would be quiet as long as Macauley got his checks.

"What will you do?" she asked Mrs. Macauley. "With the money?"

"Oh—nothing." She shrugged, as if $850,000 was no more than hitting a Pick 3. "He's so far gone. We thought Florida, once. Or one of those places with a golf course right next to your house. Now I'd just like to see he has as little pain as possible."

Tess hiked up to Eastern Avenue and caught a westbound bus home.

"Sweet Jesus Christ," she announced to Crow as she banged through the front door of the shop, empty except for him. "We ought to get stipends for being part of the local color. Someone just took a picture of me carrying my groceries home, like I was a Parisian with a string bag. Welcome to Charm City.''

"How's the case?" Crow asked, looking up from his book and giving her a full-force smile, obviously trying to cheer her up. "Have you found out anything new?"

"There is no case," she said harshly. Hurt, Crow went back to his reading.

"I'm sorry. I'm not having a great day." No answer from Crow, his eyes still fixed on his book. *Possession*, by A. S. Byatt. Interesting choice, she thought. A literary mystery in which a man and a woman team up to solve a puzzle and fall in love. "Look, I owed you an apology and I gave it to you. Now you owe me an explanation."

"For what?" Eyes still downcast. He had a talent for sulking.

"You never told me where you got your nickname."

He looked up then. "My nickname? Well, you've had a few clues. First of all, there's my hometown, Charlottesville, Virginia."

"Is the crow the UVA mascot?"

"Second hint: the name of my band."

"Po' White Trash. So?"

"Third hint: my initials."

She had to think about that one. She had only heard them once, when Kitty told Ferlinghetti his full name. "E. A.?"

"Right. My dad couldn't resist naming his only son Edgar Allan, after Virginia's great writer."

"Excuse me, but Edgar Allan Poe is a Baltimore writer."

"He was born in Virginia. He died in Baltimore. You can argue about which place has the greater claim. Anyway, my dad started reading Poe to me when I was a little kid—the poems, not the really dark stuff. And when he read 'The Raven,' I didn't know what he was talking about. My dad explained it was a big black bird. And I, with the wisdom of a six-year-old, said, 'Why not call a crow a crow?' It's been my name ever since. It's better than Edgar or Ed." He closed his book. "There—you've finally solved a mystery."

"So your band is really *Poe* White Trash?"

"You got it. It's a great name, cuts across class lines. The rednecks from Hampden and Remington come because they think it's a redneck industrial band. But the literary college students like it, too."

"Not very politically correct, is it?" she said in that strange schoolteacher voice Crow inspired in her. "If you think about it, white trash is a term with overtones of racial superiority."

"Shit, you don't need to find Michael Abramowitz's killer. You need to find your sense of humor."

Tess, who felt she had come legitimately by her newfound dourness, shocked herself by bursting into tears at Crow's gentle rebuke. Holding her groceries, she cried and cried, unglamorous, racking sobs that shook her body. Her nose ran, her eyes began to swell, but she held her ground and she held her groceries. She wept for Jonathan, she wept for Abramowitz. She wept for Damon Jackson. She wept because she had spent the past two weeks tightening the noose around a good friend's neck, systematically eliminating every other possible suspect. She barely noticed when Crow put his arms around her, hugging her tight until her tears ran out.

Crow was not the kind of person who would have a handkerchief or even a crumpled Kleenex. Inelegantly she wiped her nose on her own sleeve.

"Well, that was pretty," she said. "I'm sorry."

"You don't have to apologize."

"Yes, I do. I'm tired and worn-out. One of my friends is dead and another is probably a killer. I don't even care. To tell you the truth, alongside some of the people I've met recently, Rock seems absolutely wholesome. He got mad, he did it himself—temporary insanity. He probably doesn't even remember. Maybe Tyner ought to go that route. Get enough men on the jury, put Ava on the stand, and they'd buy it. She is the kind of woman men would kill for."

"That's a compliment, I guess. But if there's one thing you know about a man who would kill *for* you, it's that he might kill you, too."

"You're pretty smart for—how old are you, anyway?"

"Twenty-three. A mere six years younger than you." He took the grocery sack out of her arms and sat it on the counter behind him, then drew her to him. Tess lifted her face to his, then changed her mind and dropped her chin, so his kiss caromed off her forehead. She was trying to find the resolve to deflect any other attempts when Kitty walked into the store, her high heels like castanets on the wood floors. Odd, for Kitty usually made no noise when she walked, no matter what she wore.

"Sorry to interrupt," she said, waving a slip of paper. "But I wanted to make sure Tess got this message that came in on the office phone this afternoon. Your rowing buddy called and said he needs to talk to you. Said to meet him early at the boat house tomorrow, before anyone else gets there."

"How early?"

Kitty peered at her own handwriting. "Five-fifteen."

"Typical Rock. He wants to see me, but he doesn't want to sacrifice a second of morning light for his row. He's so efficient he'll probably do push-ups and sit-ups while we talk."

She grabbed her groceries and headed to the back stairs. But she couldn't resist looking back over her shoulder at Crow. He was smiling, as if he knew he would have made contact on his second attempt. It had been a strange week. Make that a strange month.

Technically the difference between getting up at 5 A.M. instead of 5:15 is fifteen minutes. But for Tess the earlier hour was much more difficult, especially after a week of not rowing at all. She contemplated staying in bed, pretending she had never gotten Rock's message. But that was why people called the store. They knew Kitty was more reliable than Tess's answering machine.

She detoured through the bookstore, careful to lock it. She still didn't trust the alley, not in the dark. She drove through downtown in silence, not awake enough to stomach the radio, or any sound at all.

The boat house was dark, with no cars in the parking lot and no sign of Rock's bicycle. Of course he knew she had a key—it was a copy of the one he had pilfered. She locked her purse in the trunk, unlocked the door, threw her key ring in an empty locker, and stretched out on a mat in the small workout room between the two locker rooms. A bar with about forty pounds on it lay nearby. Mindlessly she picked it up and began doing bench presses. It only weighed fifty pounds, much too light for her. What had happened to her 100-pound goal and the seven-minute mile? What had happened to all her goals for the fall? They had been subsumed by what she once thought would be the easiest job she ever had.

She heard footsteps in the men's locker room and glanced over, expecting Rock's sturdy calves to come through the swinging door. Instead she saw the lower half of a crabber, a bushel basket in gloved hands, heavy black rubber boots on his feet. Sneaking a bathroom break and taking a shortcut through the building—not permitted, but what did she care? She continued to pump the bar, indifferent, until her eyes traveled up and she noticed something odd. The crabber was wearing a ski mask.

''Look—'' she began as the crabber fumbled in his bushel basket, then took out a revolver.

''I'm sorry,'' he said, and took aim.

Tess threw the bar at his head. It caught him in the chest, knocking him down with a hard thump, the handgun flying from his hand. Only fifty pounds, but the bar had done its job. But when she tried to rush past him toward the locker rooms, he grabbed her ankle, pulling her to the floor. Now he was crawling toward the gun and trying to hold on to her ankle at the same time. Tess kicked free, got up, and fled down the circular staircase, sprinting to the storeroom where the boats were kept.

It was dark there, and she could only hope he wouldn't know the location of the light switches, hidden behind a small closet door at the foot of the stairs. If he stopped to look for them, she might have time to go out the dock doors.

Behind her she heard his heavy tread on the metal stairs. Scared to stand upright, she crawled across the floor, ducking under the rows of hanging boats. *Oh say can you see...* Why was "The Star-Spangled Banner" playing in her head?

The concrete floor was cool on her palms and knees. *By the dawn's early light...* Of course, she was worried about the dawn. Finding the logical connection almost made her smile. Soon the pale morning sun would start streaming through the oblong windows on the dock doors. But if she raised the doors, she would be backlit, the perfect target.

She pictured the boat house's layout in her mind. The doors to the dock were about sixty feet away, three of them, one at the end of each long narrow aisle. A gunshot could destroy one of the Baltimore Rowing Club's beautiful shells. Silly, but she'd hate to have that debt follow her through eternity.

Tess kept crawling until she ran out of room, wedging herself into the southeast corner. Perhaps she could hide until the other rowers started arriving. She glanced at her watch 5:20. No, ten minutes was too long to play this game of hide-and-seek, assuming anyone even showed up that early. Most of the rowers didn't arrive until six. The light would start coming in, his eyes would adjust to the darkness, he would find her. She could hear one of his rubber boots squeaking as he walked back and forth, sighing patiently. He was keeping sentry along the west wall, waiting for her to rush the stairs.

Would she make the paper? Given the hour, she had a good chance at the front page. The street final of the evening paper was always looking for a cheap, late-breaking crime to create the illusion there was news in the later editions. She tried to write the story in her head. *A twenty-nine-year-old city woman was found dead today...* City Woman was quite famous, almost as famous as City Man. She died, she fell, she was rescued. But what would be the phrase, stuck between two commas, that would summarize Tess's life for posterity? The appositive, it was called. Baltimore native? Former reporter? Bookstore clerk? Lanky brunette with overbite? She imagined the rewrite man bent over his keys, happy with the details of her death, the tiny, knowable mystery of it all. Rich, but not too rich, easily captured in 400 words and fifteen minutes. A death dispatched in one edition, then reduced to a brief.

The twenty-nine-year-old native, who police described as an unemployed woman playing at detective . . . Yes, that would be it, except it should be whom. Whom police described.

The boot was squeaking, coming closer now. Only one squeaked. Up one aisle, down the next. Dawn was filtering into the boat house, sneaking in around the edges of the heavy metal doors. And now that Tess thought about it, wasn't "dawn's early light" redundant? What else could the dawn's light be? The boot seemed to chirp an off-key accompaniment to the song in her head. *And the rockets' red glare/The bombs bursting in air.* God, she hated that song.

She tried to shrink into the corner and had to stifle an involuntary cry when a splintery piece of wood pressed into her back. A broken oar. At first she cursed the lazy rower who had left it there. Then she grabbed it, squeezing it tight as she listened to his boots. Otherwise he was silent, unnervingly so. He wasn't stupid, the kind of person who felt he must explain why he was killing someone. Had he killed Abramowitz? Or Jonathan? Either way, it didn't matter to him if Tess went to her grave knowing the full details. It was only important she go to her grave.

She heard the squeaking boot again, heading up the final aisle. Her aisle. Squeak, squeak, squeak. Straight toward Tess's hiding place. *Oh say does that star-spangled banner yet wave?*

She considered her options. She could stay hidden, assuming she was hidden. She could beg, stalling for time. Both were cowardly, prone to failure, and not entirely out of character for her. She waited, listening to his footsteps, watching his feet approach in the dim light. If she could see his feet, it was only a matter of moments before he could see her. She thought about how a race started, a sprint, the kind of race decided with the first few strokes. "*Êtes-vous prêt? Partez!*" Are you ready? Go! And then the gun would go off.

No penalties for a false start here. She was so low to the ground, oar in hand, her cheek brushed the cement floor. His rubber boots were about eighteen inches from her nose. A Hail Mary ran through her mind, followed by the one ragged piece of Hebrew she knew from Passover. *Why is this morning different from all others?* Because someone is about to kill you.

She stared at his boots and thought about her unfinished life, wondered if she would get an obituary proper along with a news story. Maybe not. It pissed her off, thinking about how her death would be treated. Another little death, not even good enough to make what the obit writers called the *mort du jour.* She deserved better. But if she wanted better she'd have to live a little longer and die a little differently.

Still low, she took aim and cracked the oar across the man's shins as hard as she could, just above the rubber boots, then rose with a terrible noise, unlike any sound she had ever made or would ever make again. With her second swing, the flat end of the oar caught him smack in the face, throwing her forward with its motion. Talk about a power piece. Talk about a burst. If she had been able to muster this much adrenaline in a race, Washington College would have had the best women's eight in the country. She swung again, knocking him backward. This time he held on to the gun with both hands as he fell. Good—he didn't have a hand free to grab her.

She leapt over him and headed for the door straight ahead, yanking its cord just enough to raise it twelve inches, allowing her to roll under it. Her attacker was broader; if he wanted to follow, he'd have to stop and raise it farther. Now outside, she looked up the hill to Waterview Avenue, empty at this time of day. Her car keys were back in the locker room. The garage door groaned as it opened wider, its cord tugged by rough, impatient hands. How fast could he run? How well could he shoot? How far could a bullet go?

The phrase "between the devil and the deep blue sea"

popped into Tess's head and she looked toward the not-so-deep, not-so-blue Patapsco. Her worse nightmare, once upon a time. It had just been supplanted. She ran at top speed across the pavement, down the ramp and across the splintery dock, flinging herself into the dreaded water. Mouth shut tight, she swam beneath the surface until her skin was burning and her lungs bursting.

She came up about thirty yards from the dock. Was it far enough? She knew nothing of guns or how they worked. She heard two shots and submerged again, turning west, toward the marina and the glass factory, gliding under the water, then coming up for air every twenty yards. Two more shots sounded, but she was almost to the marina now. She stopped at the first boat, a Boston whaler, and grabbed its side. Peering around it, she looked back to the boat house, coughing up the filthy water.

The man was standing on the pier, looking around him. Behind him the boat house was coming to life. Lights were on in the storage room, cars pulling into the lot. A solitary sculler walked toward the water with his oars. The man looked back to the boat house and out to the water one more time, raised the gun to his head, and fired. Even as he pulled the trigger, the sculler had dropped his oars and was running toward him, shouting as if to stop him.

Tess continued to hold on to the Boston whaler. It had a name painted on the stern, one of those whimsical names so many boat owners prefer. *Paddy's Wagon,* it proclaimed in merry green letters. She was holding on to the boat and still staring at those letters when someone from the shore finally spotted her and sent out a launch. It was Rock. Without saying a word he pried her fingers from the Boston whaler, lifted her into the small motorboat, and took her back.

He tried to lead her away from the body, but Tess wanted to look. It was a surprisingly neat suicide. There was a small black hole at his right temple and a little blood pooling beneath his head. She could smell burned wool where the powder had made contact with the ski mask. Ignoring Rock, shaking off his arm as if he were some frail old man, Tess dropped to her knees by the body and pulled the mask up.

The mouth was slightly open, exposing perfect white teeth. The cheeks were cherubically round, the belly full beneath the windbreaker. It was, even in death, even after attempted murder, still an appealing face. The body still had the jolly girth that made one think of a beardless Santa Claus.

"You are conscientious, Miss Monaghan," Frank Miles had told her more than once. She had thought he meant it as a compliment.

Chapter 30

After a tetanus shot and a visit from two homicide cops who wanted to review the morning's events, Tess took to bed—actually, Kitty's bed—with a bad case of paranoia. Twice she bolted to Kitty's turquoise tiled bathroom to vomit up small portions of the Patapsco. Her muscles and joints were stiff and sore, the way they can be with a fever. Exhausted, she tried to sleep. But whenever she started to doze off, she jerked awake, terrified.

Frank Miles was O'Neal's hit man. She had not told the police that; she had not told them anything but the morning's barest facts, for fear she would be transported to Spring Grove and wake up in a ward full of poor William O'Neals whose mothers could not afford alternative justice systems. Miles had killed Abramowitz and probably killed Jonathan. Unquestionably he had wanted to kill her. She would bet anything it was Macauley's gun he was brandishing this morning, stolen from Abramowitz's office. Perhaps he had originally planned to implicate the old man, then Rock had given him a better opportunity.

No, it didn't wash, not even in her weary, confused mind. A professional wouldn't have been lurking in the Lambrecht Building as a custodian, biding his time. He wouldn't have to steal someone's gun. And he certainly wouldn't kill himself when trapped. Of all the deaths and near-deaths, only Jonathan's had been competently handled. Miles had been an amateur. Like her. His only link to Seamon O'Neal was his compulsive neatness. A generous man, he had credited her with solving Abramowitz's murder when she had never been further away. There were probably reams of physical evidence to link him to Abramowitz's murder, but no one had paid attention. After all, he was the custodian, the man who had found the body, the man who scrubbed the blood-stains from the carpet.

Finally she slept, her body surrendering to sleep as it had surrendered to the river. She didn't want to go, but she had to. It was almost six when she woke, and the room was dim. Through the filmy curtains that shrouded Kitty's four-poster, she saw someone waiting for her.

"Kitty?" Her voice came out thick and rusty. She had already taken two showers today, but there were parts of her that would not come clean. The river seemed to coat the insides of her ears, her mouth, and her throat. It clung to her hair, thick and stiff. "Crow?"

Little Cecilia approached the bed, a rolled-up newspaper under one arm, looking impatient as always. She pushed the curtains aside.

"Your aunt said I could wait here for you to wake up, but she'd toss a dictionary at my head if I didn't let you sleep. I've been here almost an hour."

Tess slid down under the covers, pulling them up to her chin. "I'm sorry, Cecilia, I'm not in the mood to help you investigate anything today. Can't you come back later?"

"Who said I need your help? Didn't it ever occur to you I could help you?"

Cecilia unfolded the newspaper. It was the final evening edition, but Tess had not made the front page. In fact she was on the back of the state section, next to the weather map. Maybe if she had died she would have gotten better play.

"A sixty-two-year-old former middle school vice principal shot himself outside the Baltimore Water Resource Center after attacking a woman there," Cecilia read slowly.

A vice principal? She thought Miles was a custodian with the city schools. But that had been her assumption because of his current job. Miles had said only: "I used to be with the school system."

Cecilia continued, picking up speed, a random Baltimore "O" occasionally creeping into her speech. Otherwise her voice was almost accentless, a trick of transformation that had taken far greater effort than cutting her hair and letting it return to its natural color. "Police are now investigating whether Frank Miles may be linked to the recent hit-and-run death of Jonathan Ross, witnessed by the same woman, Theresa Esther Monaghan of Bond Street. Mr. Miles met Ms. Monaghan, who works for lawyer Tyner Gray, when she conducted a routine interview in connection with the Michael Abramowitz murder case." She tossed the paper on the bed.

"Except for the fact that's one of the worst-written stories I've ever heard, I'm not sure why you decided to come over and read it to me this evening. But thanks for sharing."

"It's not the story. It's the photograph."

Tess picked up the paper and looked at Frank Miles, smiling his gentle smile in a staff photo that must have been at least fifteen years old. Nice of the school system to provide it to the paper, she thought. Would they have been so cooperative if he was still employed by them?

"Typical head and shoulders shot. Probably every principal and vice principal in the city has one on file. What's so interesting?"

"Because if it wasn't for the photo, I wouldn't have remembered him by name. I know Frank Miles. He tried to join VOMA. Abramowitz had defended two men who raped his daughter."

"Did he know the group's real name, or was it just a happy coincidence that a real VOMA happened into VOMA?"

"We'll never know." Cecilia sat on the bed. "Pru turned him away, of course, the way she always did. I see now she recruited the original members with an eye to finding women who wouldn't look too closely at the group's finances. She wanted weak people, passive people. She didn't want anyone she couldn't control."

"Did he get angry when you turned him away?"

"No. He was very sweet and understanding. He had brought brownies to the meeting, so Pru let him stay, just that once. His daughter was raped back and front by two neighborhood boys, classmates of hers. They said she was a whore who had done everyone in the neighborhood. She killed herself a month after they were acquitted. Pru told Mr. Miles he should find a group for people who had lost children to suicide."

Tess remembered his shadowy living room, the dusty photographs on the wall. "I don't have any children," he had told her. "Just nieces and nephews." But there had been a beautiful girl in a graduation gown.

"Can you prove this? Will the others remember?"

"I'm a few steps ahead of you—again." Cecilia smiled. "He filled out a membership form so he could get on our mailing list. Not that Pru ever mailed anything but fundraising solicitations. I got her to give it to me after I saw the paper this afternoon. She raised a stink, but I reminded her she's not in a position to call the shots anymore."

She unfolded the old sheet of paper. Frank Miles's handwriting was neat and plain. Tess recognized his West Baltimore address.

"Are you going to the cops with this?"

"That's my next stop. Not because I care about your friend, although I guess no one should do time for a crime he didn't do. I want people to know a sweet, gentle man was driven crazy by what happened to his daughter. If Abramowitz had driven me to my death, I'd like to think my pop would have killed him, too."

Tess reached out and put her hand on Cecilia's arm. "I know you hate Abramowitz, but he did have a conscience. He agonized over the choices he made in his life and he paid for most of them. I read parts of a diary he left. He was very . . . self-aware. I grew to like him, reading it."

The corners of Cecilia's mouth moved in an odd way that, technically, would qualify as a smile. The ends turned up, a shadow of a dimple showed in her right cheek, but it was the saddest face Tess had ever seen. "Did he ever mention the rape cases in his diary?"

"Well, I didn't read it all," Tess said. It sounded weak, even to her. She saw Cecilia's point. Michael Abramowitz may have been tortured by his capital murder cases, his estrangement from the law, his futile campaign against Seamon O'Neal. But the rape cases weren't important to him.

"Yeah. That's what I thought. Ever read *Don Quixote*?"

"No, I keep meaning to read it, but—I did see *Man of La Mancha* at Painters Mill when I was a kid."

"The nuns make you read it in honors. I keep thinking of this one line. 'What thanks does a knight-errant deserve for going out of his head when he has good cause?' Frank Miles had good cause, Tess. His family played by the rules and was destroyed by them."

"He didn't have good cause, not against Abramowitz. If he wanted to avenge his daughter's death, he should have killed the rapists."

Cecilia shrugged. "For all we know, he did. I can do research, too. The two guys who raped his daughter were killed in a drive-by last year. Together, just the two of them. Maybe it's just a coincidence."

With that she walked to the door, then turned back. "I am sorry Frank Miles tried to kill you. I guess that was uncalled for."

In spite of herself Tess had to laugh. Cecilia had a talent for making her laugh at the oddest things, when she thought nothing in the world would ever seem funny again. She was still giggling when she fell back asleep, a restful sleep this time. When she woke again it was Saturday morning and Kitty was kneeling by the bed, shaking her awake and telling her Tyner was on the phone. The police had agreed to review the physical evidence from the case. Cecilia was not the only new witness who had come forward. Ava Hill, accompanied by lawyer and mentor Seamon O'Neal, suddenly remembered all sorts of suspicious behavior on the part of Frank Miles.

The charges against Darryl "Rock" Paxton were dropped by mid-October, a week before the Charm City Classic.

Epilogue

Tess, Whitney, Crow, and Cecilia stood on the west side of the Hanover Street Bridge, leaning over the railing and waiting for Rock's race to start.

"You're supposed to call it the Vietnam Veterans Memorial Bridge now," Whitney informed the others. "But no one does. The Vietnam veterans want us to write an editorial on it next month for Veterans Day."

"Great, another group of victims, showing up to demand their due," Tess said, then looked at Cecilia. "Sorry. I didn't mean—"

Cecilia shrugged. "No offense," said VOMA's newest director, who in just three weeks had opened the group to all sexual assault victims as well as their relatives and spouses. She had also become ubiquitous in the media. Surprisingly she could be tactful and thoughtful in front of television cameras, decrying Frank Miles's violence, but maintaining he had been driven to it.

They heard the crowd's roar: The 2,000-meter race had finally started. Crow and Cecilia, not even sure which one of the five scullers was Rock, yelled and clapped indiscriminately. Whitney, watching through field glasses, shook her head and passed them to Tess. Rock was out in front, but his timing was off, his form ragged. Tess could tell he wasn't holding anything back, he was going to collapse toward the finish. Shorter races, head-to-head with other boats, had always been tougher for him than the longer races, run against the clock and himself.

The five boats passed under the bridge and shot out the other side before Tess could dodge the traffic on Hanover Street and position herself to see the finish. Rock was still in the lead, but his energy was flagging. The closest boat was gaining on him inch by inch. Tess pressed her feet against the sidewalk, as if she could give Rock an extra boost. He held on, slipping across the finish line in front of his late challenger, but well off his best time.

"I guess being accused of murder and breaking off your engagement doesn't do wonders for a training regimen," Tess said.

"Not pretty," Whitney agreed, "but it will do."

They left the bridge and headed to the docks so they could carry up Rock's scull in a show of fealty. Along the banks of the Patapsco, it looked as if Whitney's extended family was staging a reunion. Lots of sockless men in plaid pants and V-neck sweaters, women in kelly green, so much blond hair it created a glare.

As they neared the boat house Tess found herself trying to keep her distance. Soon she would have to go back, especially when she had her own Alden hanging inside, a partial payment from Rock and Tyner. They had wanted to give her something sleeker, a Vespoli or a Pocock, but Tess had been firm. The Alden was durable, well-suited to her rowing regime, and less likely to tip. She didn't plan on going back into the Patapsco any time soon.

Tyner was waiting for them near the dock, squinting unhappily. Even from this vantage point, far from the finish line, he knew how badly Rock how rowed. But when Rock appeared, subdued and drenched with sweat, Tyner smiled and handed him a banana for potassium depletion. The lecture could wait. Whitney draped a stadium blanket around Rock's shoulders, while Tess showed Crow how to hoist the scull and set it on sawhorses to be washed before it was put away. In the midst of all this activity, Cecilia hung back, overwhelmed by Rock's bulk.

Suddenly Tess was as happy as she had been in months. It was a beautiful fall day, she was alive, Rock was rowing again and would be in top form in time for the Frostbite Regatta in Philadelphia, the last race of the season. She was surrounded by friends, old and new. And she was going to have a job soon: Tyner had promised to apprentice her to a lawyer he knew, someone who needed a full-time investigator. A forty-hour workweek loomed, complete with benefits. It was almost enough to make her wistful for her carefree life.

Snip, snip, snip. Everywhere loose ends were being trimmed. She heard this sound in her dreams, she read it between the lines of the short items in the *Beacon-Light*. First there had been a story that the murder charges against Rock had been dropped when police became convinced Miles had killed Abramowitz and Jonathan. A few days later, an item about an old Checker cab abandoned out in the country, with some of Jonathan's blood on its fenders. Stolen, of course, before the hit-and-run. By Miles, police said now, who assumed this had been the first attempt to kill Tess. *How strange no one found the car until after Miles was dead,* Tess thought. *How fortuitous for the Triple O there would be no trial of Abramowitz's murder, no investigation into Jonathan's death.* Tess wondered if Jonathan's hit-and-run could go in the homicide pool now. *Snip, snip, snip.*

Another brief, in the business section. Ava Hill was leaving the law firm to work with the William Tree Foundation. An in-house audit's discovery of "financial irregularities" had prompted the board to bring in new people. Tess, thinking of Ava's shoplifting hobby, had a hunch the financial irregularities were only beginning. But passing the bar would no longer be a problem for Ava Hill. And Ava Hill would no longer be a problem for Luisa J. O'Neal, not if she was paying Ava's salary.

Tess had pieced it together. Shay O'Neal, panicked by Jonathan's visits to Fauquier, had arranged for someone to kill him, a nice anonymous someone in a Checker cab who was still roaming Baltimore, no doubt, at O'Neal's disposal.

When Frank Miles made himself handy as a suspect, O'Neal had used him with Ava's help. Only Tess knew, or could guess this, and she could never prove it, which is why she had settled on the payout to Abner Macauley. Her deal with Mrs. O'Neal, along with the sealed envelope Kitty kept in the store safe, should protect her. This was business, another ad hoc arrangement in Luisa O'Neal's eyes, no different than the one she had put together for her son. Tess would be fine. As long as Seamon O'Neal didn't panic again.

And then there was Frank Miles, another person out to create his own justice. A patient man, unlike O'Neal, willing to bide his time. He had waited for his opportunity to kill Michael Abramowitz. And he had tried to send Tess down blind alleys, hoping he wouldn't have to kill her. Poor man. In the end he was the one person in this whole mess who had believed in her.

Lovely muck, as Feeney's poem would have it. *The world, it was the old world yet. I was I, my things were wet.*

Whitney and Rock had gone off in search of more food, with or without potassium. Cecilia, her shyness overcome, was arguing animatedly with Tyner about something she had learned in law school. The sudden appearance of a bagpipe band, wheezing through "Maryland, My Maryland," drowned them both out.

Was it Carroll's sacred trust and Howard's warlike thrust, or vice versa? No one ever remembered, and few sang along. The state song finished, the skirted band began the national anthem, accompanied this time by the quavering voices of the dutiful crowd. Baltimoreans seldom complained about the song, given its local origins, but they sang it as poorly as anyone.

"You sing it wrong, you know." That was Crow, at Tess's elbow.

"I never sing it at all."

"People, I mean. Marylanders. Everybody. We sing the first verse, which is all questions. Francis Scott Key was asking *if* the flag still waved, if the United States had been victorious over the British. We should sing the last verse, when he knows they've won and is exultant.''

"I never knew that." *Nor particularly cared.*

"I'll tell you something else you don't know. Cecilia doesn't really have a fiancé. That was just another of Pru's lies, when you crashed the VOMA tribute to Abramowitz's death. Whitney says I ought to ask her out.''

"Will you?" She found herself caring about the answer more than she wanted to.

"Naw, because Whitney missed a salient detail: Cecilia's gay. Besides, I like tall women. Muscular women.'' He squeezed her bicep.

Tess looked away but didn't take his hand off her arm. "Crow, you don't know what you want. A few weeks ago you were delirious over Kitty, and she's not exactly tall.''

"Everyone falls in love with Kitty. It's a rite of passage. Then you move on. I like you, Tess. I really like you.''

If he had said he loved her, or couldn't live without her, she would have been unmoved. If he had quoted poetry or put his arms around her, she would have pushed him away. Crow's understated declaration was harder to ignore. He *liked* her.

"Do you have a fiancée? Or a wife?''

In reply Crow kissed her—a simple, outdoors kiss, a kiss promising much, but not too much. He wasn't saying forever. He wasn't even saying next week. Just now, this afternoon. She kissed him back, then pulled away, aware they were in a crowd. People were watching.

The Patapsco looked almost blue today, shiny in spots. Oil, Tess thought, shuddering a little. Toxins. *Lovely muck.* She turned her back on the river and faced the boat house. A handsome building, she decided, a perfectly innocuous place. *A place couldn't hurt you.*

On the veranda, along the second level, officials and VIPs crowded the rail, where they paid more attention to one another than to the races below. Light skipped and bounced along shiny surfaces—tiny prisms created by diamond rings, gold earrings, silver flasks. Tess saw a rainbow trapped in a crystal glass half filled with amber liquid, a large hand holding tight to the glass. The hand belonged to Seamon O'Neal, laughing, even redder than usual, Ava on one side, Luisa on the other. Tess had never noticed the similarities between the two women—the dark hair, the heart-shaped faces, the good bones. Only, Ava looked like a cheaper version, the fine lines blurred in translation, like a knockoff of a designer dress.

Tess stared at the trio steadily. Neither Seamon nor Ava looked down, but Luisa's wounded eyes caught hers, held them for a moment, then closed as she raised her glass to her mouth.

You see my side of things, Miss Monaghan. Justice was done. . . . You're no one, and no one will ever believe you.

She had not told—not Tyner, not Kitty, not Whitney—especially not Whitney, whose loyalties would have been sharply tested. Her mother substituted in Luisa's tennis foursome.

Tess turned back to Crow. "Do you really like James Cain?"

"Jesus, Tess." He rolled his eyes. "I have better things to do with my time than study up on your literary preferences, hoping to impress you. I counted on my charm to win you over. James Cain was a lucky accident."

"Last line of *Mildred Pierce*. What does Mildred say to Bert?"

"Bert says it to Mildred first: 'Let's get stinko.' "

"Let's get stinko, Crow. And then—then I'm going to tell you a story."

The bagpipe band, terrifyingly hearty, swung into the anthem's final lines. It had started as a poem, and a bad poem at that. Tess didn't need Crow to tell her that much. She also knew it was set to a drinking song, ugly and clumsy, from Great Britain. But the anthem belonged to Baltimore.